Recalculating Truth

Paul H. Raymer

Salty Air Publishing

Falmouth, Massachusetts

Cover Photograph: Paul H. Raymer
Publisher: Salty Air Publishing
Author's Website: www.PaulHRaymer.com

Publisher's Note: This is a work of fiction. Names, characters, places, and incidents are a product of the author's imagination. Locales and public names are sometimes used for atmospheric purposes. Any resemblance to actual people, living or dead, or to businesses, companies, events, institutions, or locales is completely coincidental.

Book Layout © 2014 BookDesignTemplates.com
Cover Design: www.ebookcoverdesigns.com

Recalculating Truth/Paul H. Raymer. -- 1st ed.
ISBN 978-0-9906781-1-3

DEDICATION

For James O. Brown who kept me writing

And

James O. Brown Jr. - a friend indeed

If you add to the truth, you subtract from it.

—THE TALMUD

Acknowledgements

Here's the thing: books don't just happen. At least not to me. Stories and characters do like to take on a life of their own and push their own destinies around, but getting the words and all the other mechanics straight takes input from a bunch of people. I am grateful to my family and friends who gave me back some invaluable input starting with my amazingly, patient wife, Kate Raymer. David Goehring was exceptionally encouraging, particularly with his well grounded publishing knowledge. Jim Brown to whom this book is dedicated and Lenny Battipaglia, best man at both my weddings, are the kind and tolerant friends any writer should have. Mike Duffy is a writer that everyone should read. His technical input was invaluable. John Dolen (the Deacon) is not only the best neighbor anyone could have, but also a valuable source of psychological information and how people work. Ed and Kathy Furtek are the teachers that we all wish we had, and it was an honor to have their input.

Steve Aubrey never got to read this book, but I'm sure he would have, and I'm sure that he would have told me what he thought about it, perhaps after some good, single malt, Scotch. We shared a love of reading and particularly sea stories. One way or another he will always be a part of my words.

CHAPTER ONE

April 2000

The time was late even for a corporate law firm. Boston was darkening. The lights in the surrounding towers were gradually dimming. The other lawyers and associates had finally surrendered the day. But Diamon Jakes was still there and so was her associate, Boyd Willis. If Boyd could have stepped back and contemplated his surroundings, if he could have wondered at the view of the city outside growing quiet, if he could have listened to the silence of the empty Tittle and Baines offices, if he could have appreciated the colorful glow painted in the darkened shadows by the drifting screen savers on the monitors, maybe he could have enjoyed the moment. But he was not enjoying the moment. He was not enjoying being alone with Diamon Jakes.

When he had been hired by Tittle and Baines out of Harvard Law, she had awed him. She was an intense lawyer, a fast rising African-American woman, top of her class at Yale Law, who won cases and wrote opinions that the legal community listened to. And she was beautiful. She was shorter than he was, and she held herself like an aristocrat – shoulders back, head up, hands at the ready. She had scary, piercing brown eyes. Boyd could only maintain an exchanged gaze with her for a few moments. He also felt that she was taking apart every word that he said, looking for the lie, even in benign statements about the weather.

She had a natural way of adjusting her facial expressions to control how she intended the situation at hand to go. She could sharpen or harden the flair of her nostrils or the lines around her eyes and mouth, arch her eyebrows in surprise or narrow them to fiery slits. Boyd wished that he could study her face more carefully to learn how she did it, to learn how she could manipulate a roomful of powerful white men to do exactly what she wanted them to do without a word.

And when she turned on her voice, she completed the control. She knew how to play the sound of her voice like a Stradivarius. She could raise the pitch or the volume, change the pacing, or pause. Nobody used silence the way Diamon Jakes used silence. She had an incredible knack for getting people to perform any task for her and making it feel like an honor to have been asked!

Her personality had made Boyd nervous when he first started working as her associate and the other associates were not helpful in mitigating those fears. They informed him that she expected perfection. It didn't matter to her that his degree was from Harvard Law and hers was from Yale. Credentials meant nothing to her. Boyd had been hired by Tittle and Baines; he must therefore be qualified to perform whatever tasks were put in front of him, and she expected no less than instant perfection.

He considered himself an average blue eyed, white male. He liked to keep his blond hair short, almost in a crew cut, but he had never thought of himself as what he had heard women call "a beefcake". He didn't quite clear the six-foot mark at the exit doors of banks, and he had carpenter's hands with short fingers. Diamon Jakes was six years older than he was, and she was his boss, but her recent behavior made him exceptionally nervous.

Now he was standing next to her, behind her desk to see what she was indicating on her computer screen. He could feel the heat of her body, distracting him, causing him to lose the focus of what she was saying. She was so expressive with her face and words and thoughts that his brain scrambled to try to sort out what she was trying to tell him with her body language. Was it perhaps something that would be totally unprofessional and out of character? He stepped back and shook his head. Maybe he was just tired. But this wasn't the first time she had sent him what seemed like psychic physical messages. A few days before she had passed him in the hallway, paused for a moment causing him to stop in his tracks, and said, "I like your tie" which had nearly caused him to drop the stack of papers he was carrying. He mumbled, "Thanks!" and continued on, wondering where that had come from.

He was peering into the vending machines in the break room a day later, and he felt her come up behind him. He stood up and turned to her, expecting some sort of verbal slap for "wasting" time, and he found her gaze particularly uncomfortable. "I'll have the brief for you momentarily, Ms Jakes," he apologized.

"Good," she replied, and smiled at him.

Expecting something more he asked, "Is everything okay?"

She didn't reply, giving him one last appraising look and then turning away.

He suddenly thought that maybe she liked him, but he quickly threw that thought out. He was under the impression that she didn't like anyone. He must be misinterpreting her behavior. Maybe this was some sort of lesson or test. Whatever it was, he found it distractingly out-of-character.

Now they were alone in her office and she was looking up at him where he had stepped back toward the glass wall that separated the office from a 30-story drop to the street below. It was a personal look. She was probing his personal thoughts, but she asked, "Did you see that?" Nothing more.

"Yes," he mumbled. What else could he say? He started to explain, "Yes, but I . . . . "

"Here. Sit down and look at this. This is their weak spot!"

"I'm sure you're right, but how . . . ?"

"Sit," she said. "You need to learn."

So he sat. He tried to concentrate on the screen, but he felt her come up behind him. He leaned forward. He felt her lean with him. He felt her hands on his shoulders. Her touch almost seared through the shoulders of his shirt. Then he thought he felt her breasts on his back. He felt her breath in his ear. He could smell her perfume. He could smell her hair that brushed against his cheek as she leaned in toward the flickering text illuminating their faces. She tapped the heavy glass screen of the monitor with her long, red pointed fingernail. "Tink, tink, tink!"

Under other circumstances, if Ms Jakes had not been who she was, if this had been a casual, personal encounter, Boyd would have been pretty turned on by the situation. And the fact was that he felt himself getting physically turned on despite what all the professional circuits in his brain were telling him he should be doing. At the same time, he was scrambling for the next move.

Moments of crisis seem to slow time. Instincts, training, passions, emotions all get compressed into tiny bits, tiny bits that can alter the course of a life. There isn't time to sort through them all, put them into logical order, weigh the pros and cons, choose the best alternative, selecting from a variety of outcomes. There is in fact only time to react.

Boyd spun in the chair, breaking the physical connection and jumped to his feet. "Yes," he said, almost shouting. "Yes, I see what you were talking about. I'll get a draft together in the morning."

Ms Jakes had staggered back a foot from his abrupt ejection from the chair. She looked at him in the darkening room. After a pause she said, "Yes. You're right. This can wait until morning. It's late."

Boyd was relieved that there was no explosion, no comments, no acknowledgement of anything beyond the time.

Then she said, "Let's go have a drink."

Boyd hadn't even known that Ms Jakes drank. Although with all the socializing she was forced to do in her job and her rapid climb to her position, it was hard to believe that she didn't have to do at least social drinking. But he was glad to be leaving her office. A bar is a public place.

He grabbed his jacket. She pulled her dress into shape with a nonchalant twist of the fabric, ran her hand up for a quick adjustment of her curls, grabbed her bag, clicked off the computer monitor, and strode across the thick carpet of her office, flicking off the light at the door, leaving him trailing behind in almost complete darkness.

As they waited for the elevator he said, "It's a perfect site for the project." They both stared at the elevator doors. "I can't see why they wouldn't get the okay from the city to proceed."

"It's not a case of logic," she replied. "It never is. The issue comes in compelling all the parties to agree on the financial returns and tip-toeing through the environmental implications."

"What they are proposing should fit into the Department of Environmental Protection guidelines," Boyd said. She had moved uncomfortably close to him, as though they were going to have to step into a crowded elevator. There were no crowds. There were no other people.

"Ah," she said, looking at him with a smile, leaning toward his face to make her point, "as the guidelines are now!" She stepped back, still looking at him. "That, my young friend, is the very point I was trying to make."

He couldn't help noticing the fire in her eyes. She was in hot pursuit of an idea, a thought, an angle. He just didn't want it to be him.

They were silent as they rode down in the elevator and exited the building, walking down the brick steps to the street. She set the pace as they strode along the brick sidewalk past the bronze Hungarian statue in the middle of Fisherman's square portraying something about a woman and fish that he didn't understand and didn't want to think about, slipping past the darkened shops and alleys and glass fronted spaces for lease, to the glow of what served the business neighborhood as the local bar.

There were times when the place was packed, squeezed up to its glass storefront with people. This was not one of those times. The high-top tables were empty. A handful of patrons sat at the long, copper topped bar. A couple of black-shirted barmaids with towels over their shoulders leaned back amongst the bottles and the beer taps. They were greeted by the smells of spilled bar food, fried fish, and stale beer lingering in the air.

Ms Jakes angled for a table in the back. The building was old and the bar had been remodeled in industrial chic. The heating ducts spanned the ceiling and up there in the darkness were pipes and wires and sprinkler systems. But no one looked up there except building inspectors. The lights directed their glare down toward the wooden floor, warped and squeaky from the years of spilled beer and spiked heels.

The brick of the wainscoting complimented the sidewalks outside. The walls were sparsely decorated with black and white images of the city outside from days past. The bar was the focus, the magic of the place, with its gleaming, dented copper surface, bottles bristling in front of the mirrors on the wall behind. During the busy times, the place throbbed with life. Now it was quiet, dormant, turned off, waiting.

Ms Jakes indicated that Boyd should sit beside her. "Better view on this side of the table," she explained. She ordered a Vodka Gimlet. He ordered a Sam Adams Seasonal. She glanced at him when he requested this from the bar maid who tended to them, as if suggesting he order something stronger.

While they waited, she tapped those long, red fingernails on the table surface. "Click, click, click."

"So, Boyd, tell me about yourself."

Where do you start with a question like that in a situation like this? Was this a follow-up to a job interview? "Um," he stalled, "Harvard was okay. You know . . . law school. Cambridge. The Charles."

"Yup," she muttered. "No, I want to know more about you, Boyd. I want to know who I'm dealing with. What are your thoughts, your ideas, your passions? Do you have a girl friend?"

"There isn't exactly time for much of a social life," he smiled, briefly. Then he wondered if he should have said something like that. Did it sound like a complaint? "Not that I mind. I don't mind at all. I understand the dedication that it takes . . . ."

"Bullshit," she replied. "You have as much time as anyone else. It just depends on how you spend it. We all have needs outside of this business. We all have needs. You have needs. I have needs. How are you going to satisfy those needs?"

She sipped her drink and peered at him over the rim of the glass. "Um," he said and swallowed a slug of his beer. "I'm sure there will be time, but this case is . . . ."

"Tell me about yourself," she asked again, and then put her hand on his thigh.

He looked up from his beer to the glass walls of the bar, the shiny bar top, to the mirrors, to the bottles, the black and white pictures to the pipes on the ceiling, and then tried to shift gently a bit farther away, stood up and said, "Excuse me. Men's room." And he pointed toward the back.

"Christ," he said to himself as he stood at the urinal. He looked at the sports section of the paper that had been posted in a frame over the porcelain fixture. "RED SOX looking for a Spectacular year!" Having been brought up in New York State outside of Poughkeepsie, he found it very hard to support the Red Sox even though he had lived in the Boston area for more than three years and despite the fact that he had grown up almost a hundred miles north of the New York metropolitan area. He sometimes asked avid Red Sox fans if they would start rooting for the Yankees if they moved to New York. There was just too much rivalry between the sports teams of the two cities. He wasn't a die-hard sports fan, in any case. It was just one of those nagging little things that fired up the competitiveness in his blood. Sort of a marker of time. "How are the Red Sox doing?" Something like watching the grass grow but with less responsibility. Something to talk about other than the weather. "How about those Red Sox?" was always a good subject changer.

He gave it a shot when he got back to the table he asked, "So how about those Red Sox?"

"I don't pay attention to sports." Pause. "Sit over here."

He had moved to a seat on the opposite side of the table. The fact was that she was a remarkably attractive woman. Her high cheekbones somehow accentuated the color of her eyes and raised the corners of her mouth. She had somehow settled her blouse so that her necklace hung down into her cleavage. He hadn't noticed that she had cleavage before.

Her lips were shiny from the drink she sipped. Even her earrings were subtly provocative, dangly, shimmering, twisting as she moved her head.

"Um, I'm good," he said, trying not to stare. She tilted her head and adjusted her face into a pout.

There are those questions in life that no matter how you answer them or don't answer them will get you into trouble. "Don't you find me attractive?" was, particularly at that moment, one of those questions partly because Boyd did find her attractive and certainly because he truly had been working too many hours to have even moments for a relationship with anyone. Time is required to meet someone, but more than that, time is required to care about someone, to disconnect the working life from the personal life. Law school had been an all-encompassing exercise. He hadn't thought that it could get any more intense, but the pressures of working at Tittle and Baines and particularly of working for Ms Diamon Jakes went far beyond anything he had experienced before. He didn't know what color the walls were in the living room of his apartment. He couldn't remember the last time he turned on a television or took a walk for the mere pleasure of walking through the city. He couldn't remember reading a newspaper for anything except business issues related to cases that he was working on.

Now, here he was, seated across the table from a very attractive woman, with skin the color of chocolate and the texture of silk, with deep brown eyes, arched eyebrows, and lascivious, red lips who was smiling at him in a startlingly impish way. The fact was that all the pressures and frustrations and frenzy of his life made him want to throw restraint, checks and balances, decorum, rules, laws, all of it aside and say, "Fuck it! Let's do this thing!"

"Tap, tap, tap," she tapped her fingernail on the table. The "impish" look was gone.

He refocused.

"Boyd," she said, "you are an attractive young man. You're bright. You deliver. You have funny hair and big, blue eyes that I'm sure your mother loved to brag about. You have broad shoulders and the build of a football player. Were you a football player?"

"For a while," he mumbled. "High school. You know."

"High school," she summed it up. "High school. Where was that? Podunk?"

"Actually it was Spackenkill High School. In Poughkeepsie."

"Really? That's something. Hmm, hmm, hmm. Spankingkill, huh? Interesting. Didn't know you were into that sort of thing. You never know, do you?" She took a sip of her drink. "We're going to need a couple more of these," and she waved her hand to summon the barmaid.

"Poughkeepsie? That's in New York, isn't it? Where did you go from Spankingkill?"

"Vassar. I did my undergrad at Vassar."

"Really?" she said. "I thought that was an all-girls college."

"Actually there have been men at Vassar since 1969."

"Interesting. I don't know why I still have that image in my mind. So why Vassar? That's in that part of that world too, isn't it. Didn't you want to get out of town? I mean if you grew up there, didn't you want to get away? I wanted to get away from home as soon as I could. I mean DC is a hell of a place to spend much time. Particularly bad place to grow up. People aren't nice. You know that? People aren't always nice." She sipped her drink. "I'm babbling. I hate babbling. Jesus!"

"Vassar's a great school. I was lucky to go there."

"I'm sure," she replied, waving her hand, dismissing the subject, moving on. She straightened up in her seat, arching her back, pushing her chest out at him. "Scratch, scratch, scratch." She scratched and then massaged the smooth top of the table. "I was in a pageant once. My mother thought it would be good experience. I was pretty little. I don't know if she thought I might get a career in the movies or what. Mothers do that, you know. They get these ideas. Things they missed themselves growing up. Shirley Temple syndrome or something like that. 'Good ship, Lollipop'! I don't think she thought much of my going into the law. We haven't talked much in years. You haven't answered my question. Do you find me attractive?"

There it was again, and he still hadn't come up with a good answer even if there was a good answer. "Yes," he mumbled. It might not have been a good answer, but it was true. "But, no."

"What?"

"I mean you certainly are attractive, but, Jesus, you're my boss. I can't find you attractive."

"Why not? We're adults. This is a free country. Lincoln saw to that. What do you mean 'yes but no'? Make up your mind. Do you want to sleep with me or not?"

Slap! Down on the table! Right there between the two of them. He could no more look her in the eye at that moment than he could recite the Declaration of Independence backwards in Italian. His mind scrambled through scenarios of hot, pulsing sex, sheets flying, bed shaking, clothes all over the floor. He ripped his thoughts away from seeing Ms Diamon Jakes naked. Standing in the middle of the hallway at the office. What the Hell was she doing? Was this some sort of primordial test?

"No," he said. "We can't do this."

"Look," she said, "I'm going to the Ladies Room. They're shutting this place down anyway. I'm going to pee and then we're going to leave. You can leave with me or on your own." She paused, staring at him. "I can't tell you what tomorrow will bring, if you get my drift. You like your job, right?"

She stood up, did that little shifty twist to settle her attire, and then leaned over the table, into his face. "Think about it." She pursed her lips and blew gently into his nose. "Chance of a lifetime. These opportunities don't come more than once. These are real," she said, pointing to her breasts, and smiled. "What the fuck, eh? Why not?"

He was definitely sweating. How the hell had this happened? Too bad there was not a rewind on life. Back it up. Back it up. Change the scenario. Take a different path. Move in another direction. Fork in the road. Yogi Berra. Take it. When you come to a fork in the road, take it! Whoa.

Back it up. Job. Yes he liked his job. Consequences. What were the consequences? If he said yes? If he said no? Fork in the road? Hell! Fork in the pants! He could get up and walk out the door before she came back, but how would he come into work in the morning? He could just say no. Nancy Reagan said that he could. The former president's wife said he could. She gave him permission. Don't go there. Focus. She obviously had her mind set on getting in his pants. Not Nancy Reagan! Diamon Jakes! His pants. Guys would think he was crazy to turn this down. "I mean how many times do men get propositioned by women, women as good looking and powerful and, let's be honest, sexy, as her?" he thought. "If anyone at Tittle and Baines found out I'd accepted her proposition . . . . whoa. Would it be worse if they found out I turned her down?"

Time was not on his side. She would be returning momentarily. It seemed he had only fractions of a second to determine the future direction of his life. Human nature told him to go for it, but he couldn't see how his future would untwist from any sort of event or personal connection with her, what it would it mean to his job, his career, his future. He couldn't see how it would come out well. It wouldn't be long before she discarded the connection, looked at him as old shoes, and throw him out. Unless she did this sort of thing regularly!

No. He couldn't go there. It couldn't happen. He felt like one of those cartoons with the Boyd Devil on one shoulder and the Boyd Angel on the other. He knew guys that would have jumped at this chance without a second thought. But he wasn't one of those guys. Why not? If she wanted it, give it to her. If he didn't, he could lose his job. If he did, he could lose his job. He was definitely sweating.

No. It wasn't right. They would never be able to work professionally together. She was his boss. He had to show her respect as a professional. He had to treat her as his superior officer. Like in the army. You couldn't sleep with the general!

Then, there she was standing beside him, putting her arm around him, leaning down until her face was inches from his. "Well?" she purred.

Her touch on his shoulder made him shudder, but he jumped up almost tipping over his chair. "I can't," he said. "I can't do this. We can't do this. We're professionals. We're lawyers, for God's sake."

She looked surprised. "Ah," she replied, stepping back. "Uh, huh. Lawyers. Yup. We are. Okay then."

Pause.

"No," he said. "Don't take it that way."

"What way should I take it, Boyd? What way should I take it? Do you have a suggestion there? An alternative? A proposal? A brief? Do I have this wrong? What way should I take it? Do you think I'm out of line? You've thought about the consequences on both sides? Worked it out? Worked it through?"

Of course there really was nothing he could say, and it would have been crazy to try to explain. Things were not the same. The fork had split the road. Was it the right answer? Was it the wrong answer? Would she be grateful? Not a chance. The die was cast when she made the suggestion. They were standing just a few feet apart, but there was a solid wall between them. Moments before there was intimacy, their lives beginning to tangle, moving into the forest on a personal path. It had taken only seconds to split that apart.

"If I were you," she muttered finally, "I'd keep this to myself."

"Would you like me to walk you to your car?"

She looked at him incredulously. "Not a chance. Be there on time in the morning. Be there. Prepared," and she spun around and banged out the door.

Boyd stood his ground, looked down at his feet, and realized they hadn't paid for their drinks. He walked over to the bar and the barmaid handed him the bill and gave him a quick smile. "Problems?" she asked.

"Yes," Boyd said pulling out his Tittle and Baines credit card.

"We get a lot of that here," she replied. She passed him back the card after running it through the machine. He signed the slip and passed the bar's copy back to her.

+++++

It was pretty to clear to Boyd back in the office that Ms Jakes considered herself "a woman scorned", and he wondered if there was some way that he could have handled the situation better. She had been a tough but fair person to work for. Now she was just tough. Nothing was perfect enough for her. He now apparently personified all the traits she disliked in an associate. She had him get her coffee, and pick up her dry cleaning, but when she told him to go to the drug store and pick up tampons, he reached the limit and went to talk with Mr. Baines about the situation.

He had to set up an appointment and that took a couple of days. Ronald Baines was an impressive and intimidating person, living in a completely different world. He was not the sort of person that was easy to have a personal and somewhat intimate conversation with. But he said he didn't believe in having layers of bureaucracy between himself and the people who worked for his firm. He had a concept that it was a small firm even though over a hundred lawyers and staff worked there, and although he had staff who handled personnel issues, he wanted his associates and partners to know that he cared about them.

One of the problems, of course, was that he was an internationally recognized attorney with exceptionally egotistical clients who all knew they were the most important and wanted Ronald Baines to pay attention only to them whenever they wanted or needed him to unravel the complications they found themselves or their families in.

He presented himself impeccably from his hand-made Brioni suits to his hand-made John Lobb shoes to his collection of ultra-thin watches to his custom-made wire rimmed bifocals that were calculated to give him a grandfatherly look, indicating that he cared about the person he was talking to. He filled the suits well from too many corporate meals and not enough exercise. His hair was receding and his eye brows needed trimming.

Boyd had expressed the wish to speak with him about a personal issue and managed to get fifteen minutes of his time on a Tuesday morning at 10:25. Mr. Baines indicated that Boyd should take one of the leather seats in the more casual area of his office.

"So, how's it going, uh, Willis? How are you getting along? Settling in?" Boyd had been with the firm for over a year.

"Fine, sir. Fine. Thank you."

"Good," Baines replied, flashing a smile. "I'm glad it's working out." He paused for just a moment. "So what can I do for you? I'm glad you came to me. My door is always open, you know."

Boyd had been thinking about this conversation almost constantly since he had come to the decision that he had to talk with someone above Ms Jakes's head and the only person in that role was Ronald Baines. Now, here they were. Boyd felt the clock ticking like a bomb in his head. Once he expressed to the senior partner that she had harassed him, the next step in the drama would start to play out.

"This is a bit awkward, sir", Boyd began.

Baines looked at him expectantly.

"I'm having a bit of difficulty working with Ms Jakes."

"Why is that, Willis?"

Boyd hesitated. "She's been a bit personal, sir."

"Personal? How so?"

"Well, I don't want to stir up any trouble, you know. I just don't think we should be working together." He paused, waiting for questions that would ease the conversation forward. "She has made personal comments about my appearance and, um, suggestions that might lead to a more, you know, intimate association? Um, and when I declined, she made it very difficult for me to satisfy her professionally. Um. That might not be the right word."

The smile had disappeared from Ronald Baines's face. He leaned back. "Be careful what you say here, Willis. You're venturing into dangerous ground. Be very careful. Explain what you mean and be very clear."

It wasn't grandfatherly advice. It was more like the point of a sword. Boyd swallowed and forged ahead. "Well, sir, she sort of came on to me and the situation between us has become . . . awkward."

"Came on? Came on? What does that mean? You're a man, aren't you?"

"Of course, sir. I mean she's a very attractive woman and all but . . . ."

"What are you implying, Mr. Willis? I don't want implications. This sort of situation calls for facts, Mr. Willis. Explain yourself clearly."

"That's difficult to do, sir. I mean it's awkward. It's difficult. I mean we're co-workers, spend a lot of time together . . .."

"She's your boss, isn't she? Are you telling me that she is doing things she shouldn't be doing? If you can't handle your personal issues, then you have a problem. This is a business, Willis, a law firm, in case you have forgotten. You should keep your personal issues out of here, away from here. Personal issues are personal. Are you making a complaint against your boss?" He got up and closed his office door.

Boyd watched him. "Um. Well, I wasn't looking to do anything . . . you know, official. I am just suggesting that it is awkward for us to work together and be as productive as we should be . . . as I should be. It's, you know, distracting."

"Young man, Ms Jakes is one of the most productive and effective members of our team. If I understand you correctly, you are making a very serious allegation about her behavior, about her influence on your performance. Now you have a right to file a complaint, but my suggestion would be that you forget about all this, that you go back to work, and that you realize that this is all an illusion on your part. Nothing actually happened, did it?"

"Actually, sir. . .."

"I don't want to hear about it. You haven't talked with anyone else about this, have you?"

"No, sir."

"Good. Well, keep it that way. Say no more and we'll forget this whole thing. On the other hand, I'm going to sug-

gest . . . no require, that we get you enrolled in our sexual har-
assment-training program. Sounds to me like you need a bit
of freshening up in that regard. It's a good program. We take
this sort of thing very seriously at Tittle and Baines. Zero tol-
erance, you know."

"But, sir, she was actually . . .."

"Say no more, son," Baines flashed a smile. "Say no
more. Don't thank me. Least I could do. I see our time is up.
Let me know how it goes," and he ushered Boyd toward the
door.

Boyd did not find the outcome of this meeting satisfying.
Not unexpected, but certainly not satisfying. Boyd admitted
to himself that he was young. He admitted to himself that he
was naïve and, in fact, was proud of what he considered the
clean slate of youth – at least in certain parts of life. He had
experienced a small share of conflict in his life. It hadn't been
all smooth sailing. There was the period when his father's
landscape business had foundered in the early 80's and they
had to live off his mother's baking. He had worked his tail off
to get into Vassar and on to Harvard. He was considered a
"townie" at Vassar and had to put up with the skeptical looks
of the elite crowd that surrounded him.

His childhood had not been street gangs and living in the
back seats of cars, but it had toughened him up enough to not
be pushed around with equanimity. Baines's attitude had just
made him angry. So he attended the sexual harassment sensitivity training because he did what he was told, but he wrote
down notes on what had happened in the bar and the string of
events that had taken place before that. He kept the receipt
from the bar to mark the time. The sensitivity training taught
him what to look for and how to file a claim with the EEOC,
the Equal Employment Opportunity Commission, although he
decided against that path. He was grateful to Mr. Baines, with
his fancy suits and his fancy shoes, for that information.

The daily confrontations with Diamon Jakes piled up the
resentment in his mind. He hadn't done anything to cause this
situation, but from that night forward, she treated him like a
malodorous buffoon, demeaning him and his capabilities at

every turn, causing a decrease in the quality of his work, which made the castigation harsher.

His attitude toward his job declined to the point where he felt that he could no longer do it effectively, and despite the cachet of a Tittle and Baines position, he decided it was time to move on. There were other law firms in Boston. And time would tell. As his mother had said many times, "What goes around, comes around", and he knew better than to question his mother.

CHAPTER TWO

May 2011

For Augustus Sainte uncomfortable memories remained - the sounds, the smells, the taste of the dust in his mouth. They weren't exact. They weren't always sequential. They flared up, un-summoned. Always the heat, the baking, searing sun. Everything was hot. There was no shade. Even in the buildings with the AC running it was hot. The stench of the sweat was overpowering, sweat from the heat, sweat from the fear. Fear on both sides – guards and prisoners. They called them "detainees" as though they had just been pulled out of line at the border and were being delayed in their journey.

Right from the beginning, right from the first prisoner that he had helped drag down the concrete runway, what they called the sally port, between the fences, concrete that reminded Gus of a dog kennel that was hosed down on a daily basis, he knew the fear, the confusion, the uncertain, shifting mental ground. The prisoner was yelling in Arabic. The soldiers were yelling in English. Gus was the only one who understood both languages and the words were ugly, mostly noise, an unintelligible cacophony, the bottom of human communications.

There was hatred and fear on both sides and a complete lack of understanding. They were animals without even animal rules. There was a total misunderstanding of cultures, religions, and experiences. There was virtually nothing in common. The young soldiers, fresh off their suburban streets and T-ball afternoons, charged with dragging people as old as their grandparents down hot concrete dog runs under the blazing Cuban sun to yell at them to get them to stop flying more planes into more tall buildings and for no rational reason, killing hundreds, thousands of random men, women, and children who had done nothing other than live in a different culture. The young soldiers had never watched their brothers or sisters or fathers or mothers driven to their knees in front of them and executed as some of their detainees had. They didn't understand that forcing these prisoners to their knees surrounded by soldiers with guns might rekindle those images, images of the proximity of death.

The memory of the hot, putrid concrete block walled room where they had dragged the prisoners wouldn't leave him. The smells and the screams and the yelling of the soldiers wouldn't leave him. Holding up his hand, reminding him of holding up the Boy Scout sign at Pack meetings, he was able to quiet the room and ask the prisoner a handful of basic questions in Arabic, at least establishing rudimentary, human communications. It wasn't until much later that he realized that the dialect he was speaking might have been the dialect of the prisoner's enemies.

Then the noise returned as they forced the prisoner to lie on a board, raising and restraining his feet, restraining his hands, placing a towel over his face covering his eyes, and tucking a pocket of the towel into his mouth like something for a baby to suck on. It had flashed to Gus that it was like the worst kind of pacifier.

Then they gradually poured water over the towel while the prisoner violently thrashed against the restraints. Then they would stop. They would pull the cloth away and punch the prisoner in the stomach to force the water out. And once the prisoner stopped sputtering, Gus would ask the prisoner questions about who he knew and what he knew and what had been going on when he saw his friends, his terrorist friends. And then they would repeat the process.

The inflection point is that point on a curve where the direction of a line changes. There is a term in French *faisandee* where meat has aged just enough to have perfect taste and just before it becomes rotten and inedible. There is a level of physical and mental stress beyond which you can get people to say or do whatever it is that you want them to say or do. Their dignity is gone. Their self-worth is gone. They have been hammered into a soft, malleable, gelatinous blob.

Gus Sainte had been convinced by his superiors in general and Captain Hernando Crum in particular, that the process was necessary and important to protect innocent lives. The man strapped on his back on the board was evil. He wanted to hurt other people who simply wanted to live their own, quiet, peaceful lives. The visions of the twin towers, the fires, the crashing planes, the falling bodies were fresh in his mind. But even now, nine years later, the heat of the sun, the yelling in multiple languages, the splashing of the water, the smell of the cells was fresh in his mind and drove him forward, seeking another way to extract the truth. The fear, the adrenalin, the noise of war was not the way to hold a rational conversation and extract useful information.

Even under those conditions, Gus recognized that that sort of interrogation amplified, and in the process, masked all sorts of information that could have been extracted by more subtle means. He began wondering if there was a way of peeling back the layers of communication to get a better understanding of what they were saying or weren't saying even if they didn't want you to know what that was. It was clear to him that the information extracted by duress was as likely to be a lie as asking a detainee a simple question. "I'll say what you want me to say, just tell me what it is."

Driven on by the pent up anger of Captain Crum, the men under his command lost most of their humanity. The Captain was a stocky man with traces of Mexican heritage that put him just out of step with his neighbors and classmates in Queens, New York where he grew up. And his "crummy" last name didn't help with the teasing. He had a round face, brown eyes that squinted when he talked as though he needed glasses to see, and he would lean his head into people when he asked a question, sort of like a huge, round nosed chicken pecking for an answer. Then he would lean back and chew, open-mouthed on his gum while he waited. When he got an answer he didn't like, he would spin away as though he had been slapped.

Crum seemed particularly unhappy with Gus because Gus was the only one that knew what the detainees were talking about, and the Captain didn't want to believe his translations but he had to, just like he didn't want to believe that the Army wouldn't keep promoting him because he deserved it.

As the Captain hammered at them, he drove the compassion out of his men, more or less making most of them useless for returning to a suburban neighborhood life. He simply added to the miserable situation Gus found himself in. He wondered with men like Captain Crum leading the way, how it could be called Intelligence?

Gus thought that maybe he could find the answers in psychology, and when he left the Army, he enrolled in Boston University which wasn't all that far from his family home on Cape Cod. He had friends who had graduated from high school with him who had gone on to BU, but they had already graduated by the time he got there.

During his four years of studies he had come to appreciate the complexity of the human mind, the control some people had over their own realities, and the expression of those realities on their outward appearance and reflection. Truth and reality are different for different people. People live in a fantasy world, often not the pleasant fantasy of fairy queens and handsome princes, but a world of their own choosing and design nevertheless. It may, in fact, be hell on earth like the cages in Guantanamo. And it may be a world thrust upon them by the circumstances of their lives that they paint into a reality they can believe in.

It became clear to Gus that if people lived in their own reality with their own truth that it would be almost impossible to determine if what they considered truth would line up with what others consider truth. The key, he realized, was establishing the map, the coordinates, the bearings of the truth and reality of the subject's world.

In lengthy discussions he had with his fellow student, Allan Soberman, who was studying non-verbal communications or body language, he expounded on the idea that triangulation is used to find the source of a radio signal. It is also used to confirm an activity, verifying it with three different sources.

Allan was almost five years younger than Gus, but graduated a year ahead of him. They were both tall – Gus was six foot three and Allan was six foot four – but they came from very different backgrounds, which gave them very different points of view.

Auguste Marshall Sainte, known to one and all simply as Gus, was born on Cape Cod where his father was a developer, creating exceptionally luxurious homes that kissed the water as well as small boxes to shelter the working help that serviced those homes and taught the children and put out the fires. His mother was a Hospice Nurse who gave Gus a sense of the fragility as well as the resilience of life.

When he graduated from high school, he really couldn't care less about any of that. High school had not given him a passion to do anything but surf, hang out, drink beer, and drive ATVs through the sand pits. Girls liked him and he liked them and they were fun. Life was fun. His High School advisors hadn't done much to motivate him to further studies. He knew he could always get a job slinging a hammer on one of his father's projects. Why spoil it?

The events of September 11, 2001 had changed his carefree perspective. He had learned a rudimentary level of Arabic when his family had shared their home with a female exchange student named Cyrene Al-Masri from Kuwait during his sophomore year in high school. She was older. She was pretty. She was exotic, and he had a crush on her. He wanted to please her so he got her to teach him some of the basics of Arabic. He also learned some of the fundamental tenets of Islam.

When he went to talk to the Army recruiter, they welcomed him with open arms. Although they were a bit suspicious about his Moslem connections, they needed people with his skills. They guided him into the military police, refined his language skills, and he had ended up in Guantanamo.

Allan Soberman came from Austin, Texas. His Jewish father was a professor at the McCombs School of Business at the University of Texas in Austin. His mother descended from the Kickapoo Indians, and Allan had spent summers on their reservation. Allan's father wanted him to get into business, but Allan wanted to get out of Texas and chose Boston University, which was about as far away as he could get from Texas culture and mindset. During his anthropology studies at BU he heard a talk by the Director of the Center for Non-Verbal Studies and was intrigued.

Allan's ruddy face and big smile, high cheekbones, and big hands ingratiated him to people who met him despite his large size. He was quiet and listened intently, studying the speaker's face as though analyzing every nuance, which he was. He reminded Gus of the Chief in <u>One Flew Over the Cuckoo's Nest</u>. Allan embodied one of the key pieces of Gus's puzzle.

Gus had described the violence of his experiences at Guantanamo, and they had agreed that one man's truth is another man's fiction. "Finding the Truth," Gus had said, paraphrasing W.C. Fields, "is like trying to tie a hair ribbon on a bolt of lightning or put socks on a rooster! But maybe we can come at it from multiple directions, triangulate on it."

"The fact is," Gus explained one afternoon in the BU Cafeteria, "that there is only the reality that we agree on. We both have to recognize the same reality or it isn't there. They say that the only sure things in life are death and taxes. Take taxes, for instance, the government says we have to have our tax forms in by midnight April 15th. There are natural days and nights, but they certainly aren't divided by names like 'April' or numbers like fifteen. Even time. Midnight is only midnight because we say it is. It's a label, and we have to agree on labels or the society wouldn't function. Midnight on April fifteenth is only midnight on April fifteenth because we all agree that it is midnight on April fifteenth! That's what we'll call this moment.

"And what about death? We pour water over peoples' heads to make them believe that they are dying! But they're not. We convince them of the reality of their imminent approach to death, and then we change the reality. We pull the cloth away. We stop pouring the water. So where's the truth in that?"

Eventually Gus explained to Allan that he wanted to start a company that would develop a device or a system that would blend a variety of ways to discerning the "truth" that could non-violently solve many of the world's problems.

"Think about it," he said, "we could tell if someone was lying during a job interview or a suspect interrogation! Yeah, I know there are people doing stuff like this in a variety of ways, but none of them seem to be putting it together in one package. And with electronics and microprocessors, we could take the guesswork out of it. We could take the subjectivity out of it, the people out of it!"

Allan grunted agreement. "There are people out there, systems out there. Have been for a while. They teach courses in this stuff."

"But they're looking for liars," Gus said with a smile. "They're assuming that there is a truth."

"Heavy," Allan said. "Gus, I believe you have a point. You may be an idealist, but I think you have a point. I'm not sure my father would agree that you have a profitable business point, but I guess people have made money from weaker points."

It had taken Gus two years to move from that conversation to what became Blaytent, Inc. As he researched what already existed in the field of discerning the "truth" (he always thought of the word in quotes since he wasn't sure that such a thing existed), he determined that there were four leading technologies: the non-verbal communications that Allan was studying, Micro-Expressions that had gained popularity during the run of the TV Show "Lie To Me", Voice Stress Analysis, and Statement Analysis. Gus's concept was to blend the four of these technologies together into one smart machine that would see and hear and compare what it saw and heard against patterns, patterns developed and learned by the machine.

There was a forest of charlatans or perhaps, champions, depending on what you believed, who professed that their approach was the only one that had any value. And it was certain that some of them had already been used individually for profit from dating shows to police departments.

Gus had approached his father with the concept for the business and outlined what he had discovered about the four technologies. "Interesting," his father said. Gus hated it when he said that. It could mean anything.

"What do you think?" Gus asked.

"As I said: it's interesting. What would you do with it?"

"There are companies that use voice stress analysis on television to interview game contestants to determine if they are telling the truth. Like people going on dates or seeking mates. They ask questions of some macho guy like, 'Have you ever stood in front of a mirror naked and tucked your balls between your legs so you look like a woman' and they get a great audience reaction."

"That's crazy. It's a carnival act," his father said. "That's stuff's not real."

"Sure it is. I mean there's a basis of reality. I mean you can look at the person's face and tell whether they are lying or not. You can hear it in their voice."

"But where's the reality? Those people are actors or actresses or whatever or they're trying to be. Maybe that's not real either!" he laughed. "But where's the science? You're telling me that this stuff is scientific and you want to build a business with it. Then you tell me it isn't real."

"Well maybe how they're using it is an act, but the fact is that many fantastic ideas were first used as toys before their real value was realized. But here's the thing; each one of these techniques has good points and bad points. Each one has a definable degree of accuracy. If I put the good points together and add up their areas of accuracy, I can arrive at something that is much closer to the truth. It might even be the truth, who knows."

"Well, I think you should talk to some of those people, you know. Get a sense of who they are or what they are. I know you. I know what you've been through, at least in a small way. I know you wouldn't want to build a business on snake oil."

"But if someone really believes in what they are doing or have developed, how do you know that it isn't real? When you are dealing with discerning the truth, how do you know what isn't? These devices may be effective at accomplishing what their developers want them to accomplish. Like a divining rod. I mean, what if it effectively indicates a source of water 30% of the time? What if the swinging pendulum - that thing you see on YouTube with the ring on a string - what if it 'answers' your questions right some of the time? Is it the truth? How am I going to know?"

His father shrugged. "It's a matter of conviction. What you're suggesting is taking the human elements out of the equation; putting the decision into the computer circuits. How do you know that it isn't the human elements that make the divining rod work at all? How do you know that there isn't some sort of human connection to the earth? Oooh weee! Spooky! Ghosts made me do it!' And he laughed. "You are facing the crazy people and you are they, to paraphrase Pogo!"

The research Gus had done up to that point made him realize that at the heart of each of the four approaches there were the zealots who believed that what they were doing was the only way to do it. They presented that information so clearly and precisely and logically that made it difficult to question. Scientific proof was almost impossible. And since Gus was tapping into four different passions, linking them together and connecting them to electronic analysis, his father had a point. Would the conviction be there?

Another piece of the puzzle had fallen into place when he met Bob Thatcher. Bob was an acoustic engineer who was working on his PhD at BU. He had a round face and brown eyes and a receding hairline. He was a bit overweight which pushed out the belly of his black, sweater vest. And despite the fact that he was married and had three children, he continued to smoke no matter how hard people leaned on him to kick the habit.

Gus met him in the "Library" playing pool. The Library was a bar down Commonwealth Avenue from BU. The place was noisy as usual and the spilled popcorn covered the floor.

The pool cues were not exactly straight and the tables were not exactly level, but the place was not known for quiet dining and ambiance. It was a great place to tell your parents that you were going to the Library for the evening although not a lot of studying got done.

The bar was down a few steps from the street and the food was something that had been thrown in a microwave. The pitchers of beer were cheap and the free popcorn gave the place an extra crunch. Students moved the chairs into big groups and bitched about their courses, their professors, and the sucky job market. And they washed it all down with more beer and louder music on the jukebox. Someone always tried to sing along with Billy Joel and *Piano Man* until the place rocked along in joyous harmony or a shower of popcorn. There were hard wooden benches at the booths along the wall, with aging pictures of the campus and hockey teams and Paul Revere. There was often a dart tournament going on in the back room, driven on by shouts of missed shots and camaraderie.

Gus was shooting pool and drinking with Allan as Allan wound up his studies in the spring of 2009. Gus missed his shot on the eight ball leaving the table wide open for Allan to shut him down. Gus was sure that he shot better as he drank more, so he ordered another pitcher of beer and watched Allan lean over the table and line up his shot. Bob Thatcher was headed for the men's room looking the wrong way and bumped the end of Allan's cue.

"Hey!" Allan shouted. "Watch it!"

They couldn't hear what Bob said because of the noise level in the place and Bob mumbled.

Gus was sort of pleased because Allan had missed his shot and Gus was in a good position to finish off the table and Allan would have to buy the beer.

So out of the kindness of his heart, he said, "Allan, don't sweat it! I'm sure it was an accident wasn't it, sir?" and he winked at Bob. "Let's buy the man a beer."

Bob was five foot nine, but next to Gus and Allan he looked much shorter.

Bob mumbled his apologies and headed off to his original destination.

"Clumsy oaf," Allan said.

"Oh, come on, Allan. You weren't having much of a game anyway. 'It's just a game,' you always say!" Gus laughed, sank the eight ball, and said, "Rack 'em up!"

On his way back from the men's room Bob tried to ease past the table, but Gus called out, "Join us!"

Bob said, "No. Really. Thanks. I really should be going. Get home, you know. Face the music."

"One quick game," Gus said. "One quick game and tell us about it. I'm Gus and this is Allan."

Allan grunted.

"I'm Bob. I'm . . . ."

"Let's get you a glass and set you up. Anyone here with you we can team you with . . . ?"

"I'll sit this one out," Allan said.

"Allan doesn't like to lose," Gus explained.

With only a handful of further protests, Bob joined Gus at the table.

"Have you got a better place to be?" Gus asked.

"Yah. I should be studying. I should be home with my wife. I should be a responsible person. I should be . . . ."

"Whoa," said Gus, holding up his hand. "Man, you need to relax. After all, you're at the Library!"

Bob took a slug of his beer and scanned the table. Walked around the edge, chalking the tip of his cue. *Piano Man* had been replaced by *Sweet Caroline*. Bob missed his shot.

"So what are you studying, Bob?"

"Um, acoustics. Bio-acoustics. I'm a doctoral candidate."

"Really? You are slumming it tonight! Sounds like you should be studying. Where did you do your undergrad?"

"Northeastern."

"So does that mean you're an engineer?"

"Yah. I guess."

"What do you mean, you guess? You should be proud of that."

Leaning against the wall and sipping on his beer, Allan added, "Gus's a psych major. Analyzes everything."

"Acoustics are fascinating," Bob said. "It's great stuff, but, you know, I have to find a way to make it pay. My wife gets worried. We debate where this is going. Where the bills are going. How the kids are going to get fed. Where they're going."

"Don't worry about the beer. Allan's buying the beer. Won't cost you a thing," Gus laughed. "No. Seriously. I know what you mean. There's a difference between the academic side and the practical side. All this book learning is great, but how does it apply to the real world. And we all have to pay the bills, right?"

"Right."

"But you have to have fun too, right? It's been proven that you can absorb more if you relax and have fun too. Cramming it in doesn't always work, right?" Gus pushed his wire-rimmed glasses up his nose and peered at Bob. "So what kind of acoustics do you study, Bob? Underwater acoustics to position oil rigs? Concert hall acoustics? Designing hearing aids?"

"Bioacoustics. I study the sounds animals make. It's known as bioacoustics."

Gus thumped the end of his cue down on the floor, crushing some popcorn kernels. "Really?" He paused, looking at Bob. "Really? Why?"

It appeared that Bob was used to that sort of reaction. "I study how animals interpret sound, how they communicate with each other. Like crickets and birds. Bats use sound for guidance. It's known as echolocation. Elephants sense the low frequency vibrations in the ground. Some of the frequencies are beyond what the human ear can hear. We have equipment now that can 'hear' and measure things that we didn't have just a couple of years ago."

"What about the sound in here?" Allan shouted.

Bob turned to him and stepped back from the pool table. "Certainly. There are emotional impacts from the volume of sounds, a need to imbed the rhythms in our bodies. Patterns that affect how we feel and how we think."

"Or not think!" Gus said. "I think people come to a place like this to not think. They've thought too much. Or think they've thought too much!"

They danced around the table, lining up the shots, taking the shots, sipping the beer, cocooned by the noise and the heat and the crowd until Bob finally said, "I really gotta go. This isn't going to make things better with Anna. We gotta talk this out."

Gus put down his cue. "Bob, can you use this stuff, this bioacoustics, can you use it for people?"

"How do you mean?"

"Well, do people communicate in non-audible ways? I mean do people make sounds that they can't control, can't hear? Have you studied people?"

Bob looked kind of surprised. "Indirectly. I mean, it's animals. It's for, you know, environmental . . . you know. Saving animals."

Gus put his hand on Bob's shoulder and looked him in the eyes. "But people are animals, aren't they? Maybe you already know the answer to this, but do people hide things in their voices? Have you looked at that? Could you look at that?"

"I guess. But why? We're trying to determine if species are disappearing from the earth. We're trying to deal with diminishing diversity."

"Is there money in that?"

Bob's mouth flapped up and down. "Ya, but there's more to life than money."

"Sure there is. Sure there is, but money helps, doesn't it. We need to talk. Allan and I are working on a project and maybe you can help us. Think about it. Think about how what you are doing might be applied to people, to people's voices. Check out some of the stuff they're already doing in Israel. You might have your finger on the right place at the right time."

After that evening the project was solidifying in Gus's mind. It was moving from a concept, an interesting idea, into the realm of passion. He found it interesting how an idea that was a momentary flash at one point became an almost overwhelming freight train the next, an idea that was impossible for him to stop. He moved toward instilling that passion in people around him including Allan and then Bob.

It was clear that Bob's wife was not happy with him spending his time listening to crickets and fish. She appreciated what he was trying to do. She appreciated that he felt a need to help the world, but she also appreciated the fact that the banks wouldn't accept good feelings to pay their credit cards or mortgage. At first Bob wasn't particularly interested in what Gus was talking about. Voices certainly had wave forms and patterns, they certainly ranged over a variety of frequencies, but how could those frequencies be separated to extract patterns that would indicate stress or fear or love or lying? Bob was not convinced that the scientific evidence was there or could ever be there.

A year later when Gus graduated from BU, he had the full structure of the company formed in his head. He approached his father to work with him on the development of the business plan.

His father was intrigued. "I've seen some of this stuff on TV," he said. "Do you think it's real?"

"Maybe not in its present form, but I think we can do it better."

"It would be pretty valuable to some police departments," his father said. "Now that you mention it, I think I've heard some rumblings in the local press about it.

"You're going to need at least five million to get this thing off the ground. Better go for eight five or ten. They'll only give you half of it anyway. That's what these money people do. They figure you'll ask for twice as much as you really need. Then they're going to expect big results. Fast. You're going to be in this thing up to your neck. They're going to put you under the clock, you know that? You're going to need to prove that it works. Prove it. Show it. They're going to expect results. Can you do that?"

Gus was sure he could.

"How fast?" his father asked. "How long is it going to take to prove that this is a viable financial enterprise?"

"A couple of years, I guess."

"Jesus. You can't guess! You have to be sure. A couple of years is way too short. It would be stupid to estimate that short of time frame. You won't even know which way is out of the paper bag in that sort of time frame. You need to pull the people together, get facilities set up, all that stuff. You're going to be starry eyed with all the money for the first six months, spending it like a sailor."

"I have the people," Gus protested.

"Certainly not all of them. You're probably going to need fifty or so. Like your IT guy. The guy who handles all your computer systems. How are you going to handle that person? He or she is going to know everything about the company as well as everything about the computer systems. How would you ever get rid of them if they were incompetent? You're going to need policies for that. You're going to need policies for everything. Hiring. Firing. Petty cash. Payroll. Health insurance. Benefits. Taxes. You're going to have to find really good people. People you can trust. You need to find the personnel person. The person who is going to screen and interview all these people. Time is going to fly by. Think you need two years, figure on four."

Gus found a fraction of his enthusiasm ebbing away, and he wondered why it all had to be so damn complicated. He just wanted to do what he wanted to do and let someone else handle all the bureaucracy. Putting the business together was a puzzle. Each point had a process and a variety of answers. The trick in solving any puzzle is pulling together the parts and assembling them in an effective, reasonable and logical order. He remembered that Allan's father taught at the McCombs School of Business in Austin.

Allan had gone back to Texas after graduating the year before and found himself drifting. When Gus called him and told him that he would like to get some advice from his father on setting up the business, Allan knew that life was likely to get a bit more interesting. "You still on that kick?" he asked.

Gus assured him that he was and was getting ready to go out for funding and that he wanted Allan to be a part of it.

When Gus met Allan's parents in Texas, he was intrigued. They were unlike any couple he had encountered before.

They were an amazing pairing of Jewish and Native American values and ideas and they welcomed him into their home. Gus wondered if they were eager to get Allan on some sort of track and out of the house.

Allan had described his home as a "ranch", but it didn't look like what Gus had pictured as a Texas ranch, and it certainly didn't look like the grand home pictured in *Dynasty*. It was at a corner of a couple of flat, straight highways that headed off to the horizon in both directions. Yellow, dried up grass and a dirt turnaround with no markings were all that signified an entrance. The house itself was tucked back among some trees, making it difficult to see from the road. Gus was not at all sure he had found the right place, but he had followed Allan's directions carefully and this was the right road and there was the house number on a mailbox. He parked the rental car and followed a path through the brush until it opened up to display a graying two story ranch house with a wide, wrap around porch, some rusty roofed out-buildings, and a decaying tractor.

There are those moments in travel where the next connection has yet to be made when one is not sure if this is the right place, the right city, the right hotel, the right hour. There is a disconnect from one surety to another – home to car – to airport – to plane – airport – to car – to hotel, each element coupled to the next like train cars. For moments or hours you can be sure of where you are and then you hope that you are in the right place at the right time, and they accept your ticket at the gate or find your reservation in the hotel computer or come striding down the porch steps, hand outstretched to greet you and welcome you to your next surety and you leave the linking moments of uncertainty behind.

As Gus walked toward the house a dog began to bark, and he paused. He had no desire to be confronted by some farmer's wild dog. Suddenly a non-descript hound came bounding through the screen door, down the stairs and across the yard, ears flying, tongue flapping the wind. Gus held his ground. A woman followed the hound through the screen door.

"Blanche!" she yelled at the hound. "Blanche! Stop!"
She saw Gus, and said, "Oh!"

"Hi," Gus called over the barking. "Hi. Is this the Soberman's? Are you Allan's mother?"
The hound was eagerly smelling Gus's pant legs. The woman came walking toward Gus. "You must be Gus," she said as she approached. "We've heard a lot about you."

Gus was neither a painter nor a photographer but even he would have categorized her as having a "wonderful face", a face that told a thousand stories, a face that would have been wonderful to photograph. She had high cheekbones and a broad nose and deep, earth brown eyes, and her face was covered with a party of laugh lines and creases and freckles, and it all lit up with a big smile with the remarkably straight and even teeth of a model.

Gus couldn't help but smile back. "And you must be Allan's mother. I've heard a lot about you too."

"Hearing is listening," she replied, "and listening is wise. I'm Sara; it's a pleasure to finally meet you. Let's get out of the hot sun. Blanche! Come!" The hound trotted off happily ahead of them, smelling and marking her territory.

Allan's mother pulled open the front door and yelled, "Allan! Your pal Gus is here. Get out here and take care of him."

The inside of the farmhouse was cooling and dim in contrast to the bright sunshine outside. The old wooden floors creaked. The front door opened to the stairs, sunlight lit rooms on the right and left, and the kitchen in the distance in the back. There was a small table in the hall at the bottom of the stairs with a vase filled with flowers.

It was an old house that spoke of historical but not thermal constancy. There was no central air conditioning so the temperature changed with the seasons, but the response was sheltered by the structure, absorbing some of the heat during the day, tempering the desert cooling during the night. It smelled of heat and dust and baking.

Allan's big hulk darkened the light from the rooms to Gus's right. "Hey," he said. "you made it."

Sara headed back toward the kitchen while Allan guided Gus on a quick tour of the downstairs, then they strolled back out to Gus's car to get his bag.

Gus asked Allan if he had found the meaning of life yet, and Allan snorted. Gossip and small talk weren't the friends' style, and they had kept in touch through the electronic social media so there wasn't much need to catch up.

"So they let you graduate?" Allan asked.

"Wanted me out of there," Gus laughed. "Yup. That's done. Time to move on. Real life."

They walked for a while. "So this is where you grew up?"

"Sort of. We moved around a lot when I was little. Dad's time in the Army. Then I guess he found his path in business and teaching, and we settled in."

"So you don't farm this 'ranch' . . . raise cattle . . . grow stuff?"

"Dad's not a rancher. I'm not sure he knows one end of a cow from another, and I can't see him riding horses off across the plains. He lets other people use the land. He's figured out some way to make that pay, get the tax credits, invests in equipment and leases it. It's sort of remote control ranching, I guess. He's good with that stuff. I suppose he should be since he teaches it every day. Mom grows some vegetables. She's the farmer."

They settled into a couple of rockers on the porch, and watched the light fade. It was a pleasant separation from the rush of airplanes and airports and rental cars, and Gus could feel some of the tension leaving him. He understood why they wouldn't want to live in the heart of the city. Austin was not a quiet town.

When Allan's father arrived, he vigorously shook Gus's hand. "Call me Nat," he said with a grin. "Sit! Sit! I'll just get a drink and join you."

Nat Soberman was not a big man. Gus briefly wondered how two short people could create a son the size of Allan, but nature had its ways. His hairline was receding and he sported a graying beard, but his eyes twinkled behind his glasses.

When he returned and had settled into a rocker beside them, Gus asked Nat about what he taught. "Allan was telling me how you run the ranch."

Nat laughed. "How to be a rancher without wearing chaps and riding a horse! Not exactly old west, is it? Wouldn't see me in the movies! But I did get the girl." Sara had appeared on the porch.

"Let's eat," she said. "I'm sure you're hungry, Gus. Couple of hours different from home? Never know how those time zones will affect the body. Still think it is a bit unnatural travelling at those speeds."

It was not a formal dining room. It was a large space adjacent to the living room and open to the kitchen. A casual chandelier hung over the middle of a long table covered with bowls of potatoes and vegetables and salad and a stack of steaks and plates of homemade bread and pitchers of ice water and ice tea. The double hung windows were open to the night air and Gus could hear bugs slamming into the screens seeking entry. The smell of the baked bread blended with the warm wood smells of the house and the night air to create an almost soporific perfume, but Gus knew he wouldn't be sleeping through this meal.

Nat came back into the room and the less than gentle strains of Coltrane's saxophone merged into the background. "Now," he said. "Sit. Let's eat this stuff!"

As they ate they talked about all manner of things – living in Austin, living in Boston, national politics, local politics, the weather, the climate, music, food – a convivial blend of conversational topics. Gus asked Nat why he had chosen a career with the Army.

"Growing up is confusing for most of us just getting through the basic schooling. I've always looked at the basic school years as a kind of flight of stairs. You get through the elementary years, junior high, high school, and college, if you care, and then you're at the top landing. And you stand there, looking around, wondering, 'Now what?' It should be liberating, but to many, it's not. Before that getting to that landing you have a specific path that you have to get through. Now you can move in any direction. The Army offers what appears to be a safe alternative to the confusion. Funny, isn't it. Thinking of the Army as safe. Being trained to kill people. Being trained to risk your life. Thinking of that as safe!

"It wasn't bad, though," he continued, "it let me travel around. It wasn't a particularly tough period for the military. Vietnam was over. They didn't need me to shoot anybody. They wanted my accounting skills. They love paperwork, don't they, Gus?"

"They do," Gus agreed.

"What about you?" Nat asked. "Allan said that your experiences in Guantanamo led you to this truth and lying stuff."

Gus explained the gut wrenching experience of trying to extract confessions by means that he considered torture. "What is the reliability of the information that is extracted when someone believes they are going to die? I believe there is a mental threshold that the subject stands at where, thinking that they are going to die they can carry their information with them. If they think they can save themselves, they might say something to end the pain. But if they think they're going to die, what difference does it make to them what they say? So what is the reliability of their information? Is it the truth?"

"That's horrible," Sara said. "They . . . I mean, we . . . really did that?"

Gus nodded. "Versions of water-boarding have been around for centuries. It's not new. But I started thinking about it, not in terms of the torture stuff, which is certainly horrible, but in terms of getting to real information. Truth. And there certainly other ways, and that's what I want to work on, that's the company that I am pulling together."

"Something other than torture, I hope," Nat said. "Being in the torture business would be difficult to promote! Although I guess it worked for the Inquisition!"

Gus laughed, "No way! No, I'm talking about pulling together a variety of approaches and then using electronics to harmonize their information to improve the odds of getting an accurate and usable result. I'm looking at four different approaches: voice stress analysis, micro-expressions, statement analysis, and non-verbal communications. Non-verbal communications may be the most difficult to reduce to markers that a computer can analyze, but the others have reasonable paths through computer analysis."

Nat pushed his chair away from the table and leaned back. "What would you use this for?"

"There are millions of applications for a device that can reveal the truth of a statement; everything from every day job interviews to suspect interrogation to more humane military applications. Personally, we use these techniques constantly without even knowing it. We study people's faces when we are talking to them for clues as to how they are receiving the information we are trying to get across. We listen to the changes in their voices. We listen to their speech patterns. Sometimes we get the signals right and sometimes we don't. Some people are good at hiding the truth. Some people are good at lying, but I believe that if we assembled all of those signals into one package and let a computer disassemble it, we could get the right answers."

Allan said, "Gus has been talking about this stuff for years!"

"And we've had some great discussions over a few pitchers of beer!"

"Different cultures are certainly more physically expressive than others," Sara said. "I haven't met a lot of Italians, but they say they like to talk with their hands. Poker faces, playing poker there are 'tells' that people have. Do you really think it could be computerized? That's kind of a terrible thought."

Gus was surprised. "Why?" he asked.

"You are reducing one more human element, one more element of expression to machine language. We photograph everything. We express everything on social media. We are changing the speed with which we communicate, reducing everything to machine elements. We are losing our humanity."

Gus had thought about it in the opposite direction, that he was improving the humanity, removing the torture, eliminating the lies.

"It's an unfortunate part of being human," Sara said. "Lying is human."

The four of them were quiet for a moment. "Lying is human," she repeated, "It's unfortunate. It's not honorable, but it is part of being human. Keeping secrets. It's a layer of personal mystery. If that is no longer hidden, we lose a part of humanity."

"Why do people lie?" Gus asked.

"People lie to change the course of history, to alter the future," Sara responded. "Think about it. You get arrested for killing someone and the policeman asks, 'Did you kill that man?' and you say, 'No. I didn't do that thing.' You know what the consequences would be if you said yes! Or what about if your mother calls you and asks if you picked up milk like she asked you to and you haven't and you say, 'Sure. Did you think I'd forget?' And then you stop and buy the milk. You don't want her to be mad at you. You don't want the future to go that way. You don't want to take that path."

"I've never thought about people predicting and altering the future," Gus replied.

"That's what business plans are," Nat laughed. "Tales of the future. 'This is how it will be if you invest in my company.'"

"So are business plans lies?" Gus asked.

"That's a bad word. The word 'lie' implies something negative."

Allan said, "They're not the same. Just because you're forecasting something that might happen in the future doesn't mean that you are lying. They're different things. There's a line there."

"Where?" asked Sara. "Where is the line? How are you going to be able to define the difference between when someone is lying and when someone is just unsure of the outcome of future events? How are you going to be sure that the truth you reveal really is the truth?"

"The truth we are interested in," Gus said, "is in the past. Did you steal from this company? Did you break the law? Did you plan to blow up that building? Did you molest that woman or man? It's in the past!"

"But their answer impacts the future. Intuitively they know that they can't change the past. Maybe they did that thing, but it's done, and now the human mind has to protect what happens next."

"Our business ethics courses have to deal with this all the time," Nat said. "No one can be one hundred per cent sure of anything! And certainly different people project their own levels of certainty on every problem. If you borrow money from a bank, the bank forms want you to say that there is no chance that they will lose their money and it is a one hundred percent sure thing that they will get paid back. Of course they want collateral too, just in case you're wrong! But how can anyone be one hundred percent sure? It's a lie. The bank wants to lend you the money because that's how they make money. In a sense, they want you to lie!"

"Wait a second," Allan said. "Banks want you to lie, Dad? Really? No, there's a difference. And I think it's pretty clear."

"Oh?" Nat said, leaning back away from the table and crossing his arms.

"Yeah. It's pretty clear. The line between lying and think-ing about the future. Those are intentions. Intentions about the future are different than lying about the past. There's a difference."

"But what Sara is saying," Nat continued, "is that people lie to change the path of their future. Where does the line be-tween intention and lies get drawn? 'Are you hiding a fugitive in your basement?' 'Oh, no, officer. There's no one here but me and the chickens!'"

"Right!" Allan said. "You made my point. That's differ-ent than, 'It's my intention to set up a fugitive refuge in my basement.'"

"But you wouldn't tell anyone that," Sara said. "You'd keep that to yourself. This machine you're talking about building would reveal that sort of truth. It would be one more thing that tore off the layers of personal privacy. Like all this social networking which is really just a way for companies to sell you stuff because they know all about you."

"Sara doesn't like Twitter," Nat laughed. "She thinks it's Big Brother come to life. Orwell had the timing off. It's a bit after 1984, but come to life nevertheless."

Gus stared at his beer. It was a comfortable space. Intelligent people surrounded him. He had been welcomed into their home. The crickets chirped outside in the night. "Are you saying we shouldn't do this?" he asked finally.

"Not at all," Sara smiled. "I'm just saying be careful."

"Here's the thing," Gus said. "Whether we like it or not, people are always going to seek to know what other people are thinking, what other people know. Do they care about the truth when they do it? Sometimes. I don't think the torturers during the Inquisition really cared if they were extracting the truth or not, but finding out when a terrorist event might occur, could save a lot of people. Finding out if a sports coach is a child molester . . . or not, might put a guilty man in jail or keep an innocent man out."

"Good things," Nat said.

"There are certainly times when people get snowballed into acting in ways they wouldn't if they knew the 'Truth' like Ponzi schemes. We can't always trust our own senses to reveal liars. Some people are so good at lying because the liar has convinced himself that it is the truth!"

"The Kickapoo," Sara said when Gus paused, "have a mythical character called Wisaka who is a trickster. Unlike Ponzi schemers, we think of him as benevolent. His tricks are not dangerous but they make people confront truths about themselves that they would otherwise ignore." She paused. "I think the Truth is that we should have desert!"

After they were comfortably settled on the porch, Nat said, "So tell me about the business. What's your plan? Do you have a business plan?"

"It's coming together," Gus said, and I'd love you to look at it. "But in general what we're going to do is build an electronic analyzer that will take input from our four sources. Sources – horses! Four horses!" He laughed. "Horses of the Apocalypse. Hope that's not right! The summation of all that input will be a determination of the veracity of the subject. What you might call, the Truth."

"I wouldn't call it that!" Nat laughed. "But it would be good for marketing. I'll have to think about the ethics of the process."

"The machine will use sophisticated video reception for the micro-expressions and the non-verbal or NVC so it won't have to be connected to the subject at all. In fact, it may be possible that the subject won't even know it's happening. The voice stress and statement analysis would be acoustic, done with microphones. The statement analysis would compare the subject's statements to a database of expressions and patterns. My plan is to have four teams working on each of these technologies and a fifth group working on the electronics, the packaging and output. I'd like Allan to lead the NVC team, and I think we can get Bob Thatcher, an acoustic guy Allan and I met, to lead the voice stress team."

"Have you figured out how much money you're going to need and how long it's going to take?"

"I was figuring five million and a couple of years."

"Wow!" Nat said. "What did you study at BU?"

"Psychology."

"You're going to need a lot more than that! You need to go for ten million in the first round. And you should plan on four or five years of development time before you have a viable and marketable product."

"There are a bunch of products in the field that are being sold to police groups for interrogation. Some of the voice stress things are being used in entertainment. It seems that there are an endless number of markets."

"Well, you're going to need to focus that. What's the difference between what you are doing and what is being done already? Are you going to get a different truth? Is it going to be more convenient?"

"Here's the thing, Nat," Gus said leaning forward, "none of these things are one hundred percent accurate, right? I mean, honestly, they're a bit like Ouija boards; they can point to whatever they want to. As I said earlier about prisoners being tortured, they will tell you what you want to hear. People get stressed by these situations. They'll tell you pretty much anything to get them over with. Tests, interviews, interrogations; they're incredibly stressful. More so for some people than for others. What I figure is that by not connecting our device to the subject and by analyzing four different parameters we can triangulate . . . or I guess it would be quad-rangulate . . . on what they really mean, what they may not say. The other approaches are single elements."

"That makes your device much more complicated, obviously."

"True."

"You're going to have to prove that it works. You're going to have to make your investors, your clients, and your markets believe it."

"I know."

"And you're going to be under intense time pressure. As soon as you get your hands on venture capital money to fund the project, they're going to want to see results. They're going to want to watch what you're doing all the way along. They're going to own you until you double their money. They're going to own your soul."

"Yup. I know."

"And you still want to do it?"

"I do," Gus said. "I do. I believe in this. I believe that there is a better way to get at the truth."

"Oh, for God's sake!" Nat blurted. "Gus, this is business. We're talking about business. It's good to believe in what you're doing. It really is. But it's business. I teach ethics in business, for God's sake, but when it comes right down to it, in business, God is in the dollars! There are very few occasions where losing money is a blessing or looked upon as one."

"But I do think that getting at the truth is a good thing."

"Of course it is," Nat replied. "Of course it is. But you can't take this personally. You can't. You can't start out that way. You can believe in what you're doing as something that is good for mankind, and then stuff those feelings away somewhere. If it succeeds, great you'll achieve your dreams and make some money at the same time. If it fails, oh well, it's business. You'll lose money. It's just business either way. Do you understand that?"

"I think so."

"It's just business. It doesn't reflect on the kind of person you are or how smart you are or how great the project is for

mankind. It's just business. You have to draw the line between wanting to do good and wanting to make money."
   "But I'm not doing it just to make money!"
   "Of course, you're not. Of course you're not. But frankly
that's the bottom line. It's business. You can't take it personally. You have to draw the line. It's like being a general in
battle. You have to draw the line between all those young
men who are going to die and get maimed and winning the
battle for your country or your cause. Too many generals fail
because they take it personally."
   "But how do you keep going if you just treat it that way?"
   "It's tough. You have to have the passion for what you're
doing. Passion is critical, but you have to focus the passion
on having the business succeed and making business not personal decisions. It's a struggle. You'll ask yourself why a lot.
And four or five years from now, maybe you'll know!"
   Gus sat back to absorb what Nat was telling him. He
didn't want to believe that the whole thing was a mercenary
exercise. Nat had some good points, but he was an academic.
He didn't have to face these things in the real world. As an
academic, he had the books to tell him what happened, but he
didn't have to face his passion on a daily basis.
   "Have you thought about getting some government
money? Perhaps a grant or one of the innovative research
things? How about DARPA, the Defense Advanced Research
Projects Agency? I think they'd like to participate in something like this."
   "I don't want the government's fingers in this. What they
are doing with prisoners is what led me to get this going."
   "So what are you going to call this exercise?"
   "I am calling it 'Blaytent'. That's my working name."
   "Good one – like a blatant liar. I like it. Better get it regis-
tered before someone steals it."
   For the next couple of days, Gus worked with Nat and Allan and Sara to develop the plans for the business and the
approaches he would make to funding sources. Gus convinced Allan to head up to the Center for Non-Verbal Studies
in Washington when he found himself sucked into Gus's pas-

sionate vortex for his project. It was going to be an interesting five years.

CHAPTER THREE

June 2011

Waiting. Waiting with a known positive result is anticipation, like waiting for your birthday when you're a kid or waiting for the delivery of your first car or waiting for your wedding day or the birth of your first child. Sometimes waiting is anticipation of a negative result like waiting to be executed or waiting for a loan to come due when you haven't got the money to pay it.

And then there is the waiting when you don't know what the result is going to be. It may be positive or it may be negative. You try to steel yourself to the negative result and tell yourself that you don't really care either way. That if the result is negative, you'll just have to move on in a different direction. It would be better, easier, more fun if the result was positive, but it won't be the end of the world if it's not.

Most of the time, waiting depends on other people to make up their minds, make a decision, throw the switch on your life. Which track will your train run down? Gus had put himself and his ideas on the venture capital funding track. He had built the train, stoked up the engine and approached the venture capital switch. They could decide if he kept going or switched onto a siding and had to start again. They had their own process to make that decision, and Gus thought he had explained things in a way that would make sense to them, but you never know.

It's just business. Remember that, he told himself. Don't take it personally. It's just business. Venture capital firms are created to make money. They provide capital to entrepreneurs who have business ideas. The entrepreneur develops the business, the value of the capital increases, the venture capital firm gets double their investment back and everybody is happy. If the idea doesn't succeed, nobody's happy, but it's just business. The venture firm wants to do everything it can to invest in ideas that will be successful.

Obviously the success of a new idea is virtually impossible to prove. It's new! The art is knowing how close you can get to proven success while going a step beyond. There are secondary levels, of course, when the idea is proven, the company is working, but needs more capital to grow. But that's not where Gus was.

Blaytent, Inc. was a start-up. Gus had put in some of his own money, and added enough from his family to get office space, and bring in Allan Soberman and Bob Thatcher to get things started. He had hired an attorney, Boyd Willis, to help him put the package together and take it to Avitas Capital, a firm that Allan's father had recommended.

Putting the business plan together was a learning exercise that helped him focus his thoughts. He had to create development plans and marketing plans and forecast the financials for the next five years. And he had to make sure that there was enough enthusiasm and positive belief in the success of the venture while providing enough sobering reality. He had to develop all the reasons why it would not succeed and then counter them.

He had projected that the system would be developed in stages as the four technologies were blended together, and he would be able to have a fully workable, integrated device in five years.

"Four," said Maria Gudmudgion, the partner from Avitas who had been assigned to him. "It needs to be done in four years. Not five."

Maria had a long, Modigliani type of face, straight, auburn hair that she kept resisting touching, straightening, adjusting.

She stared at Gus through her glasses, challenging him to disagree.

"So you're saying that Avitas would back the project if we could do it in four years instead of five?"

"No, I'm saying that we won't consider the project unless you can do it in four. This is just too much vaporware; too many risks. We can see the potential, certainly from police departments to the military. But it borders on the fanciful. Have any of these technologies been proven valid?"

"Certainly facial recognition has been used extensively throughout the world."

"Is that what you are doing?"

"Not exactly. But we are using some of the same technologies. Some of the same approaches."

"So let me get this straight," Gudmudgion said, crossing her legs. She wore the sharpest heels. Gus couldn't help but wonder how people could walk in shoes like that. "Make this clear for me."

"We are going to combine the fundamental techniques that have been developed for voice stress analysis, micro-expressions, statement analysis, and non-verbal communications into one device that will be able to provide a higher degree of accuracy than any of these techniques used on their own."

"That will be able to reveal the truth of what the subject is saying."

Gus hesitated. "Or close to it," he said. "There are very few events or situations that one could say were absolutely True or absolutely False. What the system will be able to reveal is the intention or what the subject believes is the truth."

"So you want us to provide you with ten millions dollars to help you to develop a futuristic Ouija board."

Gus bristled at this definition even though he had thought that himself, but refrained from commenting. He watched her green eyes restlessly twitch around the room.

"I mean how close to the Truth do you think you will be able to get?"

"Voice stress technology devices, for example, have been used for all sorts of flashy purposes like TV shows and love connections and suspect interrogations. That's not what we want to accomplish. Our project will create a device that will provide much more information than just whether or not two people are compatible. We're not developing something that is just smoke and mirrors. This is not a party trick."

She didn't reply.

"Facial recognition technology is developing almost as fast as we can talk about it."

"But you say that's not what you're doing either."

"No. We're interested in the movement of the muscles in the face, and we can do that without touching the subject."

"What about ethnic accents? What about social mores? Society impacts how people move, their expressions, their language?"

"I did address all of this in the plan," Gus couldn't resist saying.

"Humor me," she replied.

"For the voice stress we're not looking at the sound of the language but the frequencies that are components of the sounds, acoustic riders that are created by micro-muscle tremors which are impossible to hear by the human ear. And again, by combining the technologies, we believe that we can bypass any one dominant trait and any training that the subject might have. Also, some people are extraordinarily good at lying or prevaricating or hiding their knowledge. I certainly experienced that with the prisoners in Guantanamo. I think we can generate a very high degree of accuracy."

"Sounds expensive and risky. We need to feel comfortable about the return. And on top of that, have any of you actually run a business before? None of you have business credentials. Before we can seriously consider this you need to plug some of the management holes. You need someone with business experience. And I don't see how you're going to put the system together without a computer or technical expert. You say you are going to integrate the technologies. How? Who's going to do it? Why don't you get back to me on that?"

At least Gudmudgion hadn't said no. She had given him more work to do. He had an internal reaction to Ms Gudmudgion; that she was an idiot and didn't read the information she was given. But he was able to push that aside because he recognized that she had some good points. He was concerned, however, that even if Avitas provided the capital could he work with her leaning over his shoulder, questioning his every move? Just business, he kept telling himself. It's just business.

Back in the Blaytent office Bob Thatcher sat across the desk from Gus and leaned back in his chair. It wasn't much of an office, but it was a start.

"I don't want to reinvent the wheel with the voice stress stuff," Gus said. "I hate reinventing the wheel. It doesn't get any rounder. At least to start with."

"What's out there has a pretty spotty reputation," Bob replied. "Some voice stress systems are surprisingly comprehensive, however. They look at as many as twenty-two different parameters including pure frequencies and combinations, very low frequencies and their relationship to stress, the stability of the frequencies as a reaction to emotional intensity and cognitive effort."

"Okay, then," Gus said. "That's what you're here for. Some of the companies have been around for a while, right. They must be doing something right. Can we get one of the devices or software and play with it? I have to have something to show the investors. They know it is the beginning. We'll use it to tell them how much better our approach will be. It'll be great."

"We can't tell one of these companies that we are going to be taking their software apart. Can't even hint at something like that. They'll sue our ass till we can't move. I've heard that some of these companies are vicious. And how can we tell them anything that isn't true? They're supposed to be able to tell!"

Gus laughed. "That would be rich, wouldn't it? If we made up a story and they couldn't tell. Wham! Bad news Bears!"

They sat in silence for a while. Finally Bob said, "Maybe we could find some organization that is thinking of buying one of these things, and we could borrow it?"

"Even better," Gus replied, slamming the front legs of his chair back down on the floor, "even better we could get them to pay us to analyze whether or not they should invest in the technology! Hmm? What do you think? We can be pretty professional. We have the credentials, right? Like a police department. That will be great. Who do we know that has an in with a police department?"

Another period of silence.

"While you're thinking about that," Gus said, "put together a plan to review the existing technology. Something scientific. How long will it take? What equipment do you need? All that stuff. I'll see if I can dig out any requests for proposal, any RFPs, looking for this stuff. Maybe we'll get lucky"

He recognized that it was best to start locally. He recalled his father mentioning a connection to the Barnstable police department on the Cape. Maybe they'd be interested. In fact, maybe they were already thinking about it.

The Barnstable Police Department was interested in improving their interrogation tools. Cape Cod was getting beyond the small town-crime-is-rare condition. More people meant more crime. Tough economics for many people meant there were more break-ins of unoccupied trophy homes, more theft of copper piping from outdoor showers and compressors, and more violent crimes. The courts were crowded and the police were interested in improving the elimination of suspects. Some sort of device or system that could be used efficiently in this process would be welcomed, but only if the courts could accept it. Gus proposed that Blaytent could evaluate the available technologies and research and secure grants that might be available through the Bureau of Justice Assistance or other programs to secure both equipment and training.

Charles Allen, the chief, was an old golfing partner of Gus's father. He had an athlete's build, close cropped graying hair and large ears. Gus knew he could be intimidating, but he was also a sensible sort who could listen to reason. He had the intelligence to take his time making up his mind about something, but once it was locked in, it was difficult to dislodge it.

Gus, Chief Allen, and Gus's father, Bob, met at the golf club for lunch. Gus's father had always tried to convince Gus that you could do more business on a golf course than you could in an office, but somehow Gus just couldn't get his head wrapped around that concept. There didn't seem to be enough time in the day to ride a cart around a manicured lawn, whacking at an expensive little white ball and trying to avoid valleys of sand and sink holes of water. Like any other sport, to be reasonably good at it, you had to practice, and Gus couldn't find the time for practicing. But he had to admit that in this case, it was particularly useful.

He also had to admit that the course was a beautiful place. The rolling hills of close-cropped grass were amazing. The course had been sculpted out of acres of farmland decades before. The clubhouse was an old building situated on a hill strategically located near the first tee and the green for the eighteenth hole. Golf carts hummed out from the locker room area. The starter stood near the first tee, pacing the launch of each group according to the schedule on his clipboard.

The club's maître d' guided them out to a table on the patio overlooking the course. They were seated in metal chairs with curved arms at a metal table with a glass top and a deployed, green umbrella for shade. The chairs didn't slide easily over the stone patio surface with carefully cut grass growing between the stones.

Gus was seated between the two older men and after a few of the usual pleasantries Chief Allen asked Gus what he had in mind.

Gus explained the basic thinking behind the voice stress analysis component of his project.

"I've heard about that," the chief said settling back in his chair and turning to look out at a golfer with an awkward swing on the first tee. "Sounds a bit like bullshit to me, though. Getting at the truth is a matter of hard work, good questions, and intuition."

Gus agreed. "People believe all sorts of things though, Chief; Tarot cards, palm readers, tealeaves. It just means that they have to believe. If they think you know when they're lying, doesn't that help?"

"I don't want to trick people into telling the truth."

"I think it's more than a trick," Gus said. "I think there are physical manifestations of mendaciousness. I'm trying to determine ways to get at those manifestations, and I think that some of that can be revealed in people's voices; unintentionally perhaps. And that is ideal because the subject won't even know that they are doing it. I would suggest that it would be worth looking into. I think we could get there without any cost to the department so there wouldn't be anything to lose."

"Reputation?"

"We could keep it to ourselves."

The chief laughed. "Really? You think we could keep something like this a secret?"

"Well, even if it did come out that you were exploring the possibilities, would it be all that bad? Police departments around the world are using these techniques. I'm not saying you have to spend town money on mumbo-jumbo. Don't you think it's important to at least explore techniques that will make the department more efficient?"

The chief leaned forward on the table, making it rock on uneven feet. "This guy's good, Bob," he said to Gus's father. "What do you think?"

"I'm biased," Bob said. "He is my son. He's been to school for this stuff. He's been to war with interrogation techniques, and frankly I think he's right to try to find better ways."

Gus looked at his father and pushed his glasses up his nose. His father looked relaxed and comfortable in his polo shirt and shorts. The white hair from his chest stuck out of the open neck of his shirt.

"Better ways to find the truth?" the chief asked.

"I mean, come on, Charley. Technology is changing faster than you and I can keep up with it. Dick Tracy was way ahead of his time. You have to stay up with it or it will snow you under."

"Okay," he said finally. "Write me up a proposal, and I'll take it from there."

So Gus took on the role of consultant for the Barnstable police department, which was the truth. He flew to Fayetteville, Arkansas to visit the *International Institute to Discern the Truth*. It appealed to Gus that this particular, computer voice analysis technology required training. Not only that, but they had developed all the peripheral services and used the peripherals to make the core technology real even if it wasn't. How could it not be real if it was supported by an "Institute"? With organizations of substance like the Institute of Contemporary Art, the Massachusetts Institute of Technology, the Dana Farber Cancer Institute, the Institute of Official Cheer, why not an International Institute to Discern the Truth (IIDT)? "I heard about it on the Internet. It has to be true."

They also had a support group for trained analysts that had ranks starting with Voice Stress Analyst Associate (VSAA), Voice Stress Analyst Professional (VSAP), and with time and experience, Voice Stress Analyst Master (VSAM). You could buy their equipment, get the training, and then join the group and be part of the *Institute*. People, particularly men, like ranking and badges of their experience that others can look at and admire. It is a magic that locks them in and keeps them engaged. "I have to reach that next level. Just one more month and I'll have six stars!" It's hypnotic.

Gus flew to Fayetteville, Arkansas, rented a car and headed off to his hotel. It was hot. The air was heavy and still. It was not conducive to strolling about. It didn't appear to be in a part of town where people actually did much strolling at any time, in any weather. The streets were straight lines and right angles. There were plenty of fast food restaurants and fitness centers and billboards for lawyers to handle your divorce or your death.

The next morning he headed out to find the Institute that was located in a partially occupied strip mall about three miles from his hotel. He found the address but there was no sign identifying the company. He pushed through the double glass doors and was confronted by a perky receptionist. She asked him who he was and when he identified himself, she said, "Oh, yes," as though she had been told to expect him.

She asked him to take a seat and someone would be with him momentarily. It wasn't exactly a waiting room. The space in the mini-mall was limited, reducing the size of the reception area, pushing everything together. It was three steps from the receptionist's desk to a group of four, orange, plastic chairs and a small table. The sun streamed in through the glass front of the space, raising the temperature even that early in the morning. When Gus dropped down into one of the chairs, it squeaked in protest.

Moments later a man in a short-sleeved yellow shirt with a pocket protector pushed through a door beside the reception-ist's desk. He didn't look at Gus, but glanced toward the receptionist who nodded her head in Gus's direction. The man had a round, reddish face, dark rimmed glasses, receding hairline, and a belly that stuck out over his belt. He turned toward Gus without a smile on his face.

"Yes?" he asked.

Gus wasn't at all sure what he meant. When he stood up, he towered over the man. "I'm Gus Sainte," he said.

"Yes," the man replied. "I know,"

"This is the International Institute to Discern the Truth? The IIDT?"

"Yes," said the man deliberately. "Yes, it is."

"I have an appointment. With Mr. John Flack."

"I'm Johnny Flack." He looked at Gus appraisingly. "And why are you here, Mr. Sainte? Why exactly? Could I see some identification?"

It was not the reception that Gus had expected. He had been under the impression from what he had seen on the In-ternet that this was a place that was eager to sell their equipment and promote their process. He expected to be wel-comed, not interrogated. He was on a legitimate mission and had received a grant from the Bureau of Justice Assistance to accomplish it. He didn't appreciate the flipping of the power roles.

"Look," he said finally, "I set up an appointment with you for this morning. I flew all the way down here from Boston to discuss your . . . whatever . . . representing the Barnstable police department. If you're not interested, then I guess that's that!"

Flack handed Gus his driver's license back to him and smiled. "Good," he said holding out his hand. "Good. I'm pleased to meet you, Mr. Sainte. Glad you're here. Linda," he said to the receptionist with a smooth, Southern drawl, "get Mr. Sainte coffee, water, sweet tea? What's your pleasure? Will you come with me?"

Gus followed the man out through the door next to the reception desk wondering at the weird reception.

The space they walked into was a hodge-podge of display area, offices and a quasi classroom. The fluorescent light glared down at them and warehouse fans oscillated above, slowly circulating the air. Flack strode ahead of him across the concrete floor and then pushed open the door to one of the small offices and ushered Gus inside. The difference in temperature was startling.

"So, how's Boston this time of year?" Flack asked. "Never been there myself. Thought about going. Thought about taking the wife up for one of those fall foliage things. See the leaves drop. They say it's spectacular."

"It is something to see," Gus replied.

"So how can we help you, Mr. Sainte? How can we help you here at IIDT?"

"Gus, will work for me."

"Gus, then. What can IIDT do for the Barnstable police department? Is it the BAHNstable police department or the BARNstable police department?"

If this was a clever process to make the customer feel off balance, then it was neither clever nor successful. Gus doubted the cleverness, but he decided to go along with the dumb northerner role and see where things went. So he laughed. "People do like to make fun of us for the JFK accent, don't they? Paahk the caah in Haahvaahd Yaahd! Don't baahthuh your faahthuh when he's baahbequing in the back yaahd! All of us don't actually talk like that, but it's a signature sound. Is that what y'all do down hereuh?"

Flack creaked back in his chair. "Yup. You do sound authentic. So you are evaluating voice stress technologies for them? They're paying you to do that? Normally, you know, we like to work directly with the client. But caution is a good thing. There are some systems out there that, between you and me, really don't do what they claim."

"Really?" Gus asked in what he hoped was realistic amazement. "Really? That's why I'm doing what I'm doing, you know?"

"There are systems that are really nothing more than white noise attached to a computer. I mean, people will believe anything when it comes off a computer."

"I'm sure you're right," Gus replied.

"So what other systems are you thinking about maybe I can give you some guidance and save you some time?"

Gus didn't want to go down that path. When sales people start talking about how bad the competition is it means that they don't have a lot of good things to say about their own product. "We really haven't gotten much beyond IIDT to tell you the truth," he said. "Would you recommend I look at any particular product . . . to compare to yours?"

Flack flipped open the file folder he had on the top of this desk and Gus noticed that the letter of introduction from Chief Allen was on top. Going back to the thought that this was some sort of preplanned, clever process, Gus wondered if Flack had the company's system running on his computer, evaluating each of Gus's comments. But Flack didn't seem to pay any attention to his monitor.

Flack looked at the papers in the file. "So you signed up for our two day training course?"

"I thought that would be the best way to get to know your product first hand."

"Mmhm, hmm," Flack seemed to agree. He looked up. "Then what?"

"Sorry?" Gus asked.

"Then what? Once you go through our training what will you do with the information? We take this very seriously, Mr. Sainte . . . Gus. This is not a game. We make serious equip-ment for a serious purpose, and we're proud of what we do. We're proud of the clarity we bring to extracting the truth. We lift the burden of suspicion from the innocent and place it where it truly belongs. All across this great country. This is not a game, Gus."

"No, I am serious. I am."

"Ah, good," Flack said closing the folder and leaning on his desk and peering at Gus, his glasses expanding the size of his eyes, giving Gus the impression of a large bug with a pocket protector. Gus resisted smiling. "What do you know about VSA? What do you know about polygraphs?"

"Lie detectors? We did some of that in Gitmo."

"Ah, you were in the army?"

"Yes. Military police."

"Ah, good. So you know something about this. Here's the thing, Gus, as you know there is no such thing as a true 'lie detector'. Lying is a whole bunch of stuff. It's complicated. It relates to how people are feeling, thinking, their upbringing, background and friends. It's not just one thing. People see things differently, experience things differently. Two people might both be in exactly the same place at the same time and witness the same event and report it so differently that you wouldn't know it was the same event. You'd think it was something else entirely. Would one of them be lying? Would both of them be lying? That's what we need to find out. Right?"

Gus nodded.

"As you probably know, so called lie detectors, polygraphs, are not really all that reliable because they rely on the operator to interpret all those squiggly lines!" Flack tipped back in his chair again and flipped his hands out to either side in mock amazement. "How accurate can that be? The squiggly lines could look one way to you and another way to me, right?"

"Sure," Gus agreed.

"Where's the 'truth' in that? VSA is not a random process, particularly our patented application of it. You probably didn't know that lying causes tremors in the vocal chords that are uncontrollable. They are micro-muscle tremors that are impossible to hear with the human ear. You can't hear them. I can't hear them. A dog can't hear them!" He laughed. "Actually I don't know if a dog can't hear them. Never been a dog." "Ha, ha!

"So what we've done," Flack continued, "is we utilize these inaudible tremors in the six to fourteen Hertz range to detect high stress in the speaker's words. When the consequences for the subject are high, these high stress micro tremors are a reliable and involuntary indication of lying, prevarication, uncontrollable stress. A great deal of research was done on this by the Department of Defense (maybe you know this) and it was used pretty effectively during the Vietnam War. Saved a lot of time over the polygraph approach and got much better results."

"I didn't know that," Gus said.

"The dumb thing is that the polygraph boys were threatened by our technology. Jumped all over us like a cheap suit. Tried to say we were liars ourselves," he laughed. "They painted us as used car salesmen, but we knew we had the truth by the short and curlies so we really didn't care. Police departments believed us. The Army believed us. We really didn't care what the other guys thought. Business, as they say, is business.

"You know a Greek character, mythological character, or maybe he was a philosopher, called Diogenes? He had this thing about liars. He didn't think there was an honest man anywhere, so he got a lantern and said he was going to walk around the world with his lantern until he found one honest man. At least that's what I hear. Some people in this business developed an approach they named after Diogenes. *Diogenes's Lantern.* Clever, eh? Sounds scientific. *Scienterrific*, I say. That's why I'm telling you there are a bunch of things out there that you can't believe."

"What about yours? What about IIDT?"

"Wait a sec. Let me give you our promotional packet. You've already paid for the course, right?" He handed Gus a slick presentation folder with the IIDT seal on the cover. Gus idly flipped it open and noted all the fancy color brochures tucked into the pockets including a sticker with a police shield on it to stick on a car window.

"We rely on the micro tremors," Flack continued, "but we require . . . and I mean require . . . training to understand what you're looking at. The voice patterns have a huge amount of information, but you have to know what you're looking it. Like an X-Ray: I can't tell what those things are when they hold them up to the light, you know. Is that a tumor or what I had for lunch or a baby? I don't know. I haven't been trained to know. But hopefully the technicians, who are reading those things, know what they're looking at and can interpret them correctly. That's what we're doing. We are producing the equivalent of X-Rays of the voice and that can tell us a lot if we know what we're looking at.

"There is a history here, but you probably already know that. The technology behind this has been around since the eighties, but it certainly goes back farther than that. And, as I'm sure you know, there is a bunch of knock-offs of our technology even though we have patents. It's a tough world, Gus. You can't be too careful."

Flack sat back in his chair with a satisfied squeak and crossed arms. Gus looked around the small office. Through the small window he saw an unkempt field and a distant street. There was a tan, metal bookcase that had stacks of papers on it in moderate disarray along with a handful of miscellaneous books and magazines.

Gus twisted on his metal chair. This was a bit like an interrogation room. Flack looked smug leaning back in his chair. "So, Johnny, where do we go from here?" Gus asked.

"Our technology was developed in conjunction with the military, you know?"

"Ah," said Gus.

"They use it. They work with us. In fact we have a representative of the Defense Advanced Research – DARPA with us now. Maybe you can see how they feel about our equipment and training. That might help you with your decision for the Barnstable Police Department. The BPD. Do you call it the BPD? Must be a bunch of those. Birmingham Police Department. Baltimore Police Department. Baxter Police Department."

Gus didn't respond. He had the sense that Flack wanted to start singing.

"Sure," Flack continued. "We have you signed up for two days of introductory training, is that right?" he asked looking at his computer monitor.

"Yes."

Flack pushed back his chair and jumped up. "Any more basic questions? Are we good to move on? Let's get you situated. Get you some information. Time's wastin'!"

Gus didn't feel as though he really had learned much of anything from Johnny Flack, and he hoped that maybe somebody else would be leading the introductory training. He had actually learned more on the Internet! He needed to know the heart of the system. All the fluff around the outside – the training, the poofy descriptions, the seriousness, the emblems – all that stuff was interesting, but Gus needed to know how it worked. He needed to know how it worked so that he could, well not exactly copy it, but at least duplicate the steps that had already been taken and improve on them. He needed to know what IIDT was doing right and where the flaws were that could be corrected. His mind was still open that maybe they had it completely right in which case Blaytent would have to come to terms with IIDT to integrate the technology, but Gus was confident that Blaytent could go further, but he had to know where they were starting from.

They left Flack's little office and were greeted by the heat in the warehouse space. "Let me show you around a bit," Johnny said.

The IIDT facilities did not really produce anything. What they sold was a computer program. They packaged it in a moderately high-end, ruggedized laptop computer and sold microphones and earphones and portable printers and other accessories for inflated prices. So the warehouse wasn't filled with industrious workers assembling anything.

Flack guided him past some glassed in rooms with sealed doors with technicians working with a variety of computers. They were sitting at tables surrounded by monitors, their faces flickering blues and greens and whites in the artificial light.

Flack didn't let him linger there. Perhaps he thought Gus
would read the keystrokes their fingers were making.

They pushed through some swinging doors and walked
into a dimly lit corridor. "Down there at the end is the little
boy's room if you need it, but right here is our training room
where you'll be spending the next couple of days."

Flack pushed open a black, door with a glass insert and
they stepped into a moderately sized classroom space that had
no windows, lit by the glare of the overhead fluorescents.
Four rows of tables were aligned along the length of the room,
three chairs to a table. Three laptops were arrayed on each
table with power and network cables running down to floor
outlets. At the front of the room there were two very large
monitors, and between them was one of those electronic white
boards where the instructor could write things, which would
be transferred to the monitors and documented in the system.

"State of the art," Flack said proudly.

"Impressive," Gus replied.

Flack waited for more, but none was forthcoming. "So
why don't you pick a seat. A couple more folks will be join-
ing us today. I'll be starting the training in about fifteen
minutes."

Gus flipped his folder down on one of the tables in the
second row, glanced around the room and dropped into the
chair. Flack left the room. Gus was tempted to try to fire up
the computer and see what he could see, but thought the better
of it.

He opened the folder and began reading about the history
of IIDT, its founder, and much of the same information about
the technology that Johnny Flack had already recited. The
fact was that Gus wanted to believe that there was science
behind this technique, but it bothered him that it wasn't coming across as something legitimate. Gus realized that it was
because it was frighteningly near the edge of extremism. At
the extreme edges of society reality gets a bit murky. In the
middle, everyone believes the same stuff – the world is round,
time flies, people drive on the same side of the road (at least
by country), and money has value. But when you venture out
to the extremes you get other beliefs and a fair amount of

paranoia: Martians, conspiracies, and Ouija boards. It was then that Gus realized that his biggest challenge was going to be moving Blaytent's technology from the fringe at least partly into the middle, and he wasn't at all sure where IIDT fit into the extremist spectrum. It was clear from the data that he had read that police departments and law enforcement officials in many parts of the country already used voice stress technology. It was also clear that police departments were often paranoid simply due to being surrounded day in and day out by criminals who hated them. If criminals populate your daily world, it is hard to think of there being anything but criminals in the world. If politicians populate your world, it is hard to think that there are anything but politicians in the world. And so on. If the same people doing the same dance every day surround you, it's hard to imagine that there is anything else in the world. That is reality. That is truth.

So out on the fringe of paranoia everyone and every thing is a threat and a liar until proven otherwise. Hand in hand with that are the fellow travelers, others with the same paranoia who believe the same way. And there are the heroes, the ones who champion the same thinking and make devices or sell products or tools like IIDT that prove, beyond a shadow of a doubt that you were right! There really are Martians! JFK was killed by a power mad, wealthy cabal! Everyone's a liar . . . except you and me, and I'm not so sure about you!

He was lost in the swamp of these thoughts when he heard a familiar voice behind him. "Well, well, well. Look what the cat dragged in!"

Gus swiveled around quickly in his seat and found himself facing an unpleasantly familiar face. For a moment he suffered from a disconnect of the environment and the attire, but then it connected. He jumped to his feet in an uncontrolled reaction.

"Captain Crum! This is indeed a surprise. No uniform?"

"Major now."

"Congratulations, sir."

The two men eyed each other. Crum was dressed in a casual, khaki suit, white shirt, but the collar open at the neck and without a tie. His military crew cut was thinning and he had tucked on some weight in the five years that had elapsed since Gus left the Army. His face was flushed and a thin film of sweat glowed on his upper lip.

"Hmm. Yes. Well, seems like civilian life is treating you well, Sainte. I am surprised to see you here."

"Me as well, sir," Gus found himself saying. His mind was struggling to connect the situation. "Are you still with the Army?"

"Absolutely. Lifer. Intelligence. Still."

"Ah," Gus replied. "Are you IIDT's DARPA connection?"

"Can't admit to that," Crum said. "Can't admit to anything."

"Ah," said Gus.

"So Flack tells me you're evaluating their technology? For a police department? In Massachusetts? Up there with the liberal pansies?"

Gus paused. "Yes. The police department part is right."

"What do you want to know? I know more about this stuff than Flack cares to know or could ever know. You know my thinking about this, Sainte. Interrogation under pressure is the only way to get at the real stuff. But if you have to be *gentle* about it," and he slurred the word 'gentle', "this is one way to do it. People can't hide, Sainte. They just can't. We know what they're thinking. We know what you're thinking. You think my being here is a coincidence?"

"Did someone tell you I was coming here?"

"Can't say, Sainte. Can't admit to that. Can't admit to anything. So what do you want to know?"

"I want to know how it works. In fact, I want to know if it works. Some people say this sort of approach is hocus pocus."

"Does it work? Of course it works. Why else would I be here? Why else would the government be pouring all sorts of money into it? The government doesn't pour money into things that don't work . . . except when it comes from uninformed . . . uh, people."

"Good to know," Gus replied.

"This stuff works because it ignores how the subject is feeling, what they're thinking about, whether they've had a fight with their girlfriend, or whether their checks bounce. It doesn't care if they're nervous or innocent or guilty. It just cares about little, teeny fluctuations in the frequencies in their speech and the patterns of those frequencies." He illustrated the small size of the frequencies by making a gap between his thumb and forefinger.

"Do they do this with . . . .?"

"Don't interrupt, Sainte. You were always a great one for interrupting your superiors. Let me illuminate you and then you can go home."

"I didn't sign up for this class, sir, to go home. I have no such intention. The Barnstable Police Department would not welcome that."

"Ah, the Barnstable Police Department. That's right you come from that hoity-toity community up there in Liberal Land. Cape *Cawd*. Wasn't that where those pansy Kennedys hailed from?"

"Excuse me, Captain . . . uh . . . Major. You're language is unacceptable!" Gus was a good six inches taller than Crum and they were close enough for Gus to see into the thinning hair follicles on the top of his head. "Your association with this organization," he continued, "is enough of a negative to want me to support an alternative approach."

"What connection do you have with the police anyway?" Crum asked. "I thought you hated law and order."

Gus didn't reply.

"Well, let me tell you something, Mr. Sainte. We know. We know what you're up to. So watch your step. I represent the power of the most powerful nation in the world and, frankly, we don't like people messing around where they shouldn't be." He nodded as though to make sure his point had been made and then he smiled and stepped back. It was one of those weird, fake, Santa Claus smiles.

"Can you tell me anything about this technology or not?" Gus asked.

"All right. Stick around and see for yourself. Good to see you, Sainte. Remember what I said. Watch your step you're treading on thin ice." He turned and left the room.

Gus sat back down and found that his hand was shaking when he rested it on the table in front of him. "That was weird," he said to himself. Where the hell had that guy come from? Was it coincidence? The guy is a freak.

Gradually other people floated into the room, glanced at him, and took seats. Several of them were wearing police uniforms. Gus struggled to get his mind back into the subject at hand, but it kept drifting. He arranged his folder in front of him and tried to dig into the contents. But it was clear that he was in hostile territory. Seminars sometimes started out that way. People didn't know each other and had no connections but they chose a seat and then kept coming back to it every day. If there were social occasions – breaks, lunch – they might strike up a conversation, but Gus definitely felt like he was an outsider and was going to remain so.

Johnny Flack strode back into the room and headed for the front. He tossed down a binder, looked up at the room, smiled, and said, "Welcome. Welcome one and all. How are you doing this morning?"

There was a general affirmative murmur throughout the room.

"Good. Good to hear it. I want to start off with some housekeeping issues." He went on to outline the schedule and where the bathroom was and where the exits were and what was supposed to happen in case of a terrorist attack or if someone had a heart attack. "We're a little out of the way here," he said, "so we've arranged to have some lunch brought in. That'll kind of speed things up anyway. Any questions before we get started?"

Gus was surprised that they hadn't gone around the room introducing themselves the way most of these training sessions, seminars, groups start, but then he realized that it all had to do with privacy. Maybe they weren't supposed to know who was there or why they were there.

Flack leaned over and pushed some keys on the computer in front of him and the two big monitors fired up displaying the IIDT logo. Gus glanced around at the other participants. They seemed to be looking at their folders. A couple of them had notebooks that they had flipped open and were making notes.

An image of the building they were in flashed up on the screen. It looked a lot more impressive than it actually was. It was identified as "IIDT World Headquarters", otherwise known as "The Institute" as though it were the only Institute in the world. Then there was an image of a man who was identified as the founder of the company who was portrayed as the 'Alberts' (Einstein and Schweitzer) of the Truth extraction world. Flack droned on about all the innovations the man had made to advance the technology.

Then he put a page of what appeared to be text written in a different alphabet up on the screen and stood back and crossed his arms.

و الارض السموات الله خلق البدء في.

"What the heck does this mean?" he asked smugly.

There were general murmurings. And then without really thinking about it, Gus said, "*In the beginning God created the heavens and the earth.* From the Bible." As soon as the words came out of his mouth, he wanted to retract them. Flack did not look happy. Gus had stolen his punch line.

Flack's eyes widened and he stared at Gus, and then looked around the room for confirmation of his amazement. "Yes, well, okay. To most of us these look like a bunch of unintelligible, squiggly lines. They don't mean anything. But then we run into someone who can read Arabic."

Gus glanced around the room with a slight smile. No one smiled back.

Flack looked at Gus expectantly.

"Army," Gus said. "Guantanamo. Military police."

"Ah, right," Flack replied. He paused and looked down at his computer keyboard. "What I was going to say is that these squiggly lines which <u>are</u> in fact from the Bible look as meaningless . . . to most of us . . . as these squiggly lines." And he put an image of acoustic patterns on the screen. "Most of us have to learn to read these lines just the same way, and what they reveal can be as meaningful and intense as those other foreign scratchings. You just have to learn the lingo, as they say! That's what we're going to teach . . . most of you."

Flack had them fire up the computers on their tables, then he went around the room, asked each of them to turn away as he entered a password, connecting the computers to IIDT's system. In the middle of each screen a large button appeared after the IIDT's logo drifted away. The button was labeled "FATE".

"Now before I have you determine your fate," Flack smiled, "I want you to think about something. How often in your line of work have you had a sense that what your subject was saying was clearly different from what he should have been saying, different from what he really meant? How often? The fact is that the human ear can detect things in people's voices that the speakers don't even know are there. Right?"

A few students were nodding.

"But you can't take 'feelings' into the courtroom, can you? In the courtroom you need facts! And what you were hearing may have been fact to you, but until someone scientific says it's fact . . . it isn't. Right?

"So here's the deal. Our system, which we call FATE for Frequency Analysis Testing Environment, is a fact. It's scientific. It's been proven to be fact in thousands of situations. Way beyond cases. Situations. From Army personnel interviews to legal interrogations. Fact. And we have the documentation to prove it!"

A couple of people were writing down notes. *Facts. Must be facts!*

"All right," Flack continue, "I want you to click on that big FATE button on your screen."

Gus's screen flickered and blinked and came up with a warning box with an agreement check box.

"Go ahead and click OKAY there," Flack said.

Gus wondered what he was agreeing to, but he always did when he was going to new websites and opening new programs. They could put anything into that boilerplate, legal language. Who would know? Who has time to read that stuff? Then he told himself to focus on this particular problem.

The screen opened up to a sort of desktop. Flack began to describe what he called the "Dashboard". Where you turned things on and off, where information was stored, where they could find the report, the basic functions of the software.

They went through a variety of questions and Flack described the responses. "What the system is doing is building a pair of comparative models of the subject," he said. "One model is the actual subject. The other model is what the FATE knows would be the honest answers to the questions. It then compares the two and will provide a report on the level of certainty that the subject is telling the truth and, of course, the level of honesty behind each answer. So you'll notice that there are questions like, 'Are you the Queen of England?' The system knows that the answer to that is 'No!' unless you are truly interviewing the Queen of England which seems pretty unlikely!" He laughed and the students chuckled. "You need to work through the questions in order. They have been carefully designed to build a usable model. Any questions?"

Gus asked, "How does your program know what the truthful answers should be so it can build that comparative model?

Flack looked at him. "Ah," he said. "Yes. Good question. That's part of magic of FATE. I can't tell you that or I'd have to kill you!" He laughed and the other students smiled.

"Seems to me that's sort of the heart of your system, right?" Gus asked.

"Part of it," Flack replied, moving over toward Gus.

"And it seems like . . . I mean it's very clever . . . but the software is giving us the answer. There really isn't a whole lot for the operator to do except ask the questions and get a print out of the answers."

"Exactly!" Flack replied. "That's part of what makes this such a great system." He paused. "But wait, as they say on TV, but wait there's more! A pilot can rely on the automatic systems most of the time. If they could rely on it all the time, we wouldn't need pilots, would we? And that's true here as well. There has to be a pilot, a knowledgeable officer sitting at that screen. As you so clearly pointed out, the machine can't know everything about the subject. It requires some understanding of the graphs on the left side of the screen. We didn't just put them there because they're pretty! You can't be lazy about this."

Gus was not convinced. It seemed to him that you couldn't just start from scratch, without giving the system any sort of information about the subject being questioned and have it build some sort of ideal model of what a perfectly honest version of that person would be. Interesting concept, though; something to think about.

They broke for lunch. The students drifted out, some of them stepping outside to smoke, some of them making calls on their cell phones. Gus found himself standing in front of a table with the makings of sandwiches – cold cuts, bread, cheese, mayonnaise, pickles, lettuce –while standing next to the officer from the front row.

"Interesting stuff, eh?" Gus asked.

"Yup," the officer answered.

"Have you used this sort of thing before?"

"Not really."

"Where are you from?"

"Albuquerque," the officer replied.

"Ah," Gus said.

"You?" the officer asked, spreading mayonnaise on his bread.

"Boston," Gus said. "Massachusetts. But actually I'm checking the system out for a police force on Cape Cod. Barnstable."

"Never been to Cape Cod," the officer replied. "Might go. Someday. Vacation."

Having completed the assembly of their sandwiches they grabbed the cans of soft drinks that were resting in a plastic tub of ice and tried to go back to their tables in the classroom.

"Sorry, guys. Can't eat in here. Computers, right?"

There was no way that Gus was going to stand around in the heat outside the building, so he found a chair, put his drink can on the floor and tried not to spill his sandwich on his pants.

On the IIDT website, the Institute promoted the hundreds of police departments that they were working with and had trained. It was hard to believe that they had all gone through this space. They did say they would bring the training to you so Gus supposed that was possible. This seemed like bogus international headquarters.

When they returned to the classroom Flack said, "This morning you saw how the computer interpreted some of the results. What we want to look at now is how the operator can enhance those interpretations and improve the accuracy of the results even more, right?" He showed them how to access the list of questions and select any one of them to pursue the answer further. "This will show you the flexibility of the software.

"For example," he continued, "you know the perp's name isn't Daffy Duck." Ha, ha, ha. He leaned over his keyboard, and started typing, the words appearing on all the monitors and the two big screens. *You said your name was Daffy Duck. Is that correct?* He asked the officer from Albuquerque to read the question.

Flack answered, "Whatever, man!"

Again, Flack leaned over his keyboard and typed, *That's an unusual name, Daffy. Is Duck your family name?*

Flack waved his hand to the officer who repeated the question out loud.

Flack answered, "Rhymes with . . . ! I'm sure you occasionally get a hostile subject?

"So you could pursue a series of questions to dig into anything that your subject brings up, and as you get deeper into the layers, it's common for the subject's stress to increase as you get closer to the heart of the lie. Of course, you're probably saying to yourself, I don't want to type in these questions in the middle of an interrogation! My typing sucks." Ha, ha, ha. "The system uses voice recognition and will record your questions for you so you end up with a complete record of the questions and the answers as well as the voice patterns for both you and the subject. You would have to 'voice train' your machine, of course so it clearly recognizes the way you talk."

He stood back. "Pretty impressive, right?"

One of the participants said, "Perps . . . I mean subjects, almost always have unusual speech patterns. How's it going to get those right?"

"Not important for this process. That's not important. As far as the subject goes what's important is what's behind the speech pattern not the actual answer. I understand that the answer is important to you. That's what the questioning is all about, right? Getting answers you can work with. But you're right, it just can't cut through all the jive of every slurred word."

Flack looked around the room for further questions, and when there were none he said, "All right, so let's try an unrehearsed, real example. Any volunteers?" No one responded. "Okay," he said, "how about you, Gus or Mr. Sainte? Would you care to step up?"

Gus did not relish the idea, but he was curious. As the subject he would certainly know whether or not he was being truthful, so he said, "Sure."

"Step right up and take the witness box," Flack said pointing to a chair in the front of the room. He started to recite, "Do you swear to tell the truth, the whole truth and nothing but . . . except for the occasional . . . untruth so we can see if the machine is working?"

There were some chuckles from the audience.

"Yah. Sure," Gus replied.

"Notice, of course, that I don't have to connect anything to him: nothing to measure his heart rate or body temperature. I just need this microphone near him . . . just near him . . . to pick up his answers, right? So now we'll reset the system for a new subject. It automatically files away the previous one to a secure server. If I don't give it a name it will file it under 'Daffy Duck' with the date automatically." Ha, ha, ha.

Gus felt pretty relaxed at this point. It was sort of a game, sort of cool, certainly interesting, and certainly about as far from water boarding as you can get. If this really worked, it was at least a significant piece of his puzzle.

"All right," Flack finally said, stepping back from his computer screen. "Let's get started. Ready?"

"Sure," Gus replied.

"Is your name Gus Sainte?"

"Yes," Gus replied, and then he realized that wasn't his full name. Should he say his full name? It wasn't quite true that his name was just Gus Sainte. That was what people called him. So he amended his answer, "Augustus Marshall Sainte."

"Where are you from, Gus?" Flack asked, then he leaned over and tapped a key on his computer. "See, you don't have to have specific questions looking for specific answers. You can have a conversation. As far as the software is concerned, the actual words don't matter. It's looking at small acoustical patterns." He tapped the key to continue. "So where are you from?"

"Boston . . . Massachusetts." Well that wasn't totally true either. He lived in Boston, but he was born on Cape Cod. What did the question mean?

"Why are you here, Gus?"

Gus paused. How was he going to answer that one? "I'm here for the Barnstable Police Department to evaluate this software."

Flack tapped the key on his laptop. "Notice that a couple of things happened there. There was the pause as the subject thought about the question and shaped his answer and notice the reaction of the system. Also notice that the system is not having trouble with Mr. Sainte's *Bahstun* accent!"

Flack leaned over and tapped his keyboard again. "Are you a member of the Barnstable Police Department?"

"No," Gus said, sure of the answer.

"Have you ever represented yourself as a member of the Barnstable Police Department?"

"No," Gus replied.

"Have you ever smoked dope?"

A whole bucket of thoughts dumped into Gus's head with that one. It was certainly unexpected. His thinking had been skating along the path ahead of Flack, attempting to anticipate where he was going next, what sort of picture he was trying to draw. This question was the sort of thing where an attorney should jump up and say, "Objection! Relevance?" Gus momentarily admired the technique and then returned to coming up with an answer, so he said, "Objection! Relevance?"

Flack looked at him and then looked at the audience with a smile crossing his face. "Kind of answers that question, doesn't it?" Ha, ha, ha!

Then he continued, "Were you in the military?"

"Yes." Gus was on alert now.

"Do you plan to tell the Barnstable Police Department that the IIDT system is what they should buy?"

Gus hesitated. "The jury's out," he replied.

"Where were you last night?"

"Uhm, in my hotel room. Here in Fayetteville."

"That's not entirely true, is it, Gus? My equipment tells me that isn't entirely true."

Gus paused. "Your equipment is wrong."

"Well, maybe. So you spent the whole evening in your room?"

"No, I did have to go out to eat."

"Ah." Flack turned to the audience. "Did you see that little shade of not quite the whole truth? Those little shade of not-the-whole-truths can lead you to deeper questions or to something you can ignore."

Gus wished he could see these patterns on the screens. It would have been helpful to be able to see how the machine was working, but there was no screen visible from where he was sitting. He supposed that was part of the set up. If the subject couldn't see what the operator was seeing, the operator could say he was seeing whatever he wanted the subject to think he was seeing. It didn't really have to be there at all. There were so many layers in what was actually going on that may or may not be important.

At that point the door opened and Major Crum slipped into the back of the room, and stood against the back wall with his arms folded and a slight smirk on his face. Flack didn't acknowledge his presence.

"Have you ever been part of a police force?" he asked.

"Yes. Military police."

"Were you honorably discharged?"

"Yes."

"Why did you leave the military?"

"I wanted to get on with my life."

"Did you always obey orders?"

Gus looked at Crum. "Yes," he said.

"Did you respect your superior officers?"

Gus looked away from Crum. "Yes. It's part of the code of conduct."

Flack tapped his keyboard and turned to the audience. "There are a million ways to go with questioning, as you all know. Some of those directions are useful, some of them are interesting, some of them are a waste of time, and some of them will help you to get to the point you are trying to get to. With a system like FATE it's a bit like being on the Internet – every answer you get, every page you open might lead you to some other interesting place. What you have to learn to do as the operator, as the questioner, is learn to guide the process to the information that you need. If you do it right, you will be able to see inside parts of the subjects' brain and turn over rocks that they don't even know are there!

"Gus," he said, "work with us a bit more. This has been very helpful." Flack smiled. "You didn't come here just to evaluate our system for the Barnstable Police, did you?"

"Um, yes."

"You had another reason?"

Gus paused. "Is that a question?"

Flack looked at Crum who nodded almost imperceptibly.

"Your work with the Barnstable Police is a cover, isn't it?"

"Did your machine tell you that?" Gus paused. "Wow," he said finally. Flack looked smug. Gus looked at Crum at the back of the room with his arms folded and glaring. Gus drew the silence out until he knew that Flack was about to crack. "I can't tell you," he said finally. "It's classified. Government stuff."

Flack looked at him blankly. There was a level of paranoia that made it hard for him to see beyond that barrier. Gus realized at that moment that there was a level of looking for answers that the operator expected. Paul Simon's line came into his head about a man disregarding what he doesn't want to hear. The really valuable moments were when you did get answers that you don't expect because that is lifting a veil. Is it true? Probably not. But is it a road map toward the truth? Highly likely. But if the operator is of the opinion that everyone is a criminal, everyone is out to cheat the system, everyone has a plot or is part of a plot, then you expect those answers, answers that reinforce that opinion. People are confident that they are smarter than the technology and certainly much of the time they are or should be. But there is little point in developing something to give you an answer and then ignoring the answer because it doesn't agree with your thinking. In that circumstance, you are creating a device to confirm what you already know.

"My program is interested in IIDT," Gus continued, enjoying the ride. "We need to know how your technology will impact the security of the country." He kept his face straight and level. If the machine was doing its job it should be flagging these comments. But apparently something wasn't working because Flack looked confused.

He looked at Crum who shrugged.

"What government? The CIA? Central Intelligence?"

"Something like that." Gus was having a hard time believing that Flack was apparently buying this. "I think I've probably said enough," and he got up and walked back to his seat.

There was general silence. When Gus looked up to the screens displaying his answers, it was obvious to him that the machine thought he was full of shit! The damn thing really worked.

Flack, on the other hand, was at a loss, which was quite stunning to Gus. Flack was in a bit of a hole simply because he didn't know whether or not to pay attention to his own technology. He had achieved his goal of having his subject reveal a truth, but then he didn't know what to do with it.

Ignoring the problem he finally said, "All right. Let's move on. Thank you, Mr. Sainte. That was, uh, very illuminating."

Gus was impressed that the system worked, and he had begun to think about how Blaytent could improve upon it by limiting the operator issues. Crum was still hanging around and pulled him aside at the next break.

"What the hell was that all about?" Crum asked.

"What?" Gus asked innocently.

"You don't work for the fucking CIA or any government agency."

"I don't? How do you know?"

"Oh, I know. I know a lot more than you want to think."

"Okay," Gus replied, stepping back. "Is there a point?" He was looking into the top of Crum's hair again and realized how it was thinning and turning grey. He wondered how far the man was from retirement. He never got close to a bullets-flying level of conflict to shut him up. But someone might shoot him just to make the world a better place. Gus wondered if he should be having such thoughts in a place like this where they had a machine to read your mind without being connected to you.

"I think you should move on, Mr. Sainte."

"Hey," Gus said, "we're not in Guantanamo any more, Major. I voluntarily subjected myself to questioning to demonstrate the technology, which I could have declined. You, Major Crum, are not the boss of me!"

Flack stepped up to the two of them, "Well, that was interesting. Very interesting. Is there anything more we can do for you?" It sounded clearly like a dismissal.

"I thought this went on for another day?" Gus said. "Do you actually get into how FATE does what it does?"

Crum was glaring at him, standing back with his arms crossed, his crew cut standing up like the bristles on a porcupine.

"Uh, not really," Flack said. "Mostly operator training stuff for people who actually have the technology. It's probably a waste of your valuable time. We'll get you a reimbursement for your enrollment fee." He smiled.

Gus looked at the two of them. What a pair! Thick as slimy thieves. "You're sure you don't have anything more for me to report to the Barnstable Police Department? I don't really work for the CIA, you know. But your machine told you that, didn't it?"

"Of course," Flack smiled again. "Of course. We'd be happy to come up and visit with the department and answer any questions they might have. I've never been to Cape Cod. Been promising myself to get there one day. This might be the opportunity."

"Can't say it's been good to see you, Crum. Brings back memories I thought were long behind me."

"Feeling's mutual," Crum grumbled.

On his way back to Boston, Gus wondered about where he was going with this project and whether or not he really wanted to be working in a world that was populated by people like Crum and Flack. There was such an incredible miasma of distrust he wondered how they could get up every morning and smile about the good things that happened in the world. They were the sorts of people you expected to eat their young.

On the other hand, the technology did have promise, and it was very much like surfing someone's brain. He still had the problems that had been posed to him by Avitas to find the people that Blaytent needed.

Chapter Four

2011

B oston was a world away from Arkansas and the world surrounding IIDT. Talking about truth technology with someone like Bob Thatcher was refreshingly less radical and more grounded. Bob had met with a competing technology for voice analysis in London and had an international version of Gus's experience.

"They wouldn't tell me much of anything," Bob said. "At least anything useful. They use their technology for commercial applications as well as military and police. You know those things on TV, on the so-called, 'Reality' shows. They ask people rude questions and then the audience gets to see if they are 'lying' or not. You know questions like a babe asking a hunk if he's ever stood in front of a mirror dressed in drag!"

"What does that get them?"

"Laughs," said Bob. "It gets them laughs and that gets them ratings. The equipment doesn't actually have to do anything. It could be, and may be, completely pre-programmed to provide the answers they want. But it sounds like the IIDT stuff actually does something."

"The interesting thing is building a model of the honest subject to provide a baseline. What do you think?" Gus asked. "It seems like a natural follow-on to what we've been talking about. The face recognition technologies use the Ei-gen-faces technique using a library of faces and expressions and comparing the subject to those, couldn't we do the same thing with voices, statements, micro-expressions, and non-verbal communication?"

"I can see it working with everything except voice stress. How are you going to build something to compare a voice to?"

"Think about it," Gus said. "Isn't that what we're doing anyway? I mean we're taking the pattern of the sound and then evaluating what that pattern means. The operator is doing that from experience, right? The operator looks for certain peaks and, . . .forgive my non-technical description . . . peaks and squiggles and knows from experience (or think he knows) what they mean. What I'm suggesting is that we figure out a way to build that knowledge base, that experience into the system and take the operator involvement out."

Bob thought about it. They were sitting in Gus's office in what they hoped was temporary space. It was essentially in a basement that could have been anywhere in the world. There were no windows, and the fluorescent lights glared down from the ceiling. They had rented the offices furnished and the furnishings were minimal.

Bob was skeptical. "I'm not sure that would work," he said. "It still goes back to what's 'true' and what's not. Who's going to tell the machine which patterns represent truth?"

"That's not what we're doing though, remember. We're just looking for indications of what . . . stress? Indications in the patterns indicative of . . . I'm not sure what to call it. Remember people are systems. Speech is part of the system."

"I don't know," Bob said. "I mean we didn't put that in the business plan. What if Avitas doesn't like it? It might screw up the whole thing. We told them we knew what we were doing and now we're changing things."

"We're bound to change things, Bob. If we knew exactly what we were doing, we'd have the working device now."

"I don't know. What if we don't get the funding?"

"We'll be fine, Bob. Really. Don't worry about it. You really need to find a way to relax and give up smoking. You're going to kill yourself."

They needed to address Avitas' question about business experience, and they needed to fill the personnel holes for micro-expressions and statement analysis, the remaining technologies. Maybe they could combine a couple of the skills to keep the overhead down. And they needed to do it quickly so they could get the package back to them.

"Let's get Allan and Boyd in here and see where we stand."

When they were all assembled, Gus described what he had been talking about with Bob and Bob's concern about giving Avitas updated information.

"He has a point," Boyd said. "I'm not sure Avitas is all that adventurous." Boyd had more experience than any of them working with money firms which was why they had hired him. He had contacts and connections as well as experience. He was almost ten years older than Gus, but his blond crew cut still bristled. Gus liked him because he seemed down-to-earth and practical and not full of himself and he seemed to know what he was talking about.

"It's hard to believe you can run a successful venture capital firm and not be adventurous," Gus said. "I suppose you have to moderate your level of risk."

"Going to Avitas came from your father, Allan, right?" Boyd asked.

Allan nodded.

"Does he have any particular experience with them? Any personal leverage we can exert?"

"It's all through McCombs, dad's school," Allan said. I don't think he has any more pull than the intro that he already did for us."

Boyd asked, "Where are you on the other technologies?"

Allan said, "I met with the people from a program that teaches non-verbal communications. It is certainly possible to load a facial recognition program into the computer and perform a modified version of PCA or principal component analysis using standard face ingredients. But you have read all of that in our proposal. I have been able to take it a bit further and gotten into the "Fisherfaces" technologies, which is an active appearance model which will help us when the face is not directly facing the camera.

"Speech is only a small part of our communication. The fact is that we have come to rely on speech to define our world, but that is only the conscious component. Many more links in communication came from our innate knowledge of the world around us including colors and smells and sounds as well as body language and positions. Smiles or polite grins, for example, can be forced but a zygomatic smile which causes the zygomaticus major muscle to contract is the sign of genuine pleasure and may be traced back to a primate's grin of fear."

Boyd looked at Allan blankly, "Uh, yup. It's not important that I know what all that means. I'll check with Ms Gudmudgion and see where they are. Chances are good that they are having someone outside the firm evaluating the technologies and that might take a bit of time. There's nothing there they might run off with, is there?"

"They did sign the confidentiality agreements, right?" Gus asked.

"Absolutely. It's a good sign that they are taking their time. They must have some interest."

Bob said, "It's important that they support us. I mean what will we do if they don't? We've given up other possibilities, you know, to be here. What do you think our chances are, Boyd? You've had experience with these things. How often do the venture guys agree?"

"Frankly, Bob, not often. There are a million people with ideas out there. Good ones. Money people have money because they pick more winners than losers. But I think you have a good shot at it."

"Oh, Christ," Bob mumbled. "I just wish they would make up their minds."

"They can't make up their minds, Bob, until we answer their questions," Gus said. "We still have to bring in someone that has business experience. We need the statement analysis role filled. And we need a tech person to put it all together. And we have to put that together fast so we can resubmit."

Boyd replied, "I think this is good though. I think it shows that you're addressing their issues and making progress. I think you've got enough capital for the short term at least to make those things happen."

"Don't you have enough business experience, Gus?" Bob asked. "Why do they need more?"

"I've never run a business and never studied business, Bob. I can fumble my way through a balance sheet or an income statement, but before talking with Boyd, I had no idea what a ten year projected Pro-Forma was! As much as I'm not fond of Ms Gudmudgion, she's got a point."

"Boyd can help us with that, right, Boyd? And what about Avitas? Don't they stick their noses in our books?"

"That's one of the points. We want them to know what we are doing so they let us get it done with minimal interference. We need to get the word out. Any resumes? Any contacts? How do we find these people?"

Bob said, "They have a good graduate placement program at Northeastern. I'll see what I can do."

"And let's talk to BU too. Might as well tap the old almamaters."

Allan said, "Let me look into micro-expression research. Maybe we can turn over a graduate student."

The interview process is not a fun one and Gus wished that he had his machine already so that he could delve more deeply into the characters that sat across his desk from him without trying to figure them out. Allan's input was invaluable in terms of body language and how candidates dressed and how they held their hands and angled their heads or crossed their arms.

He read their resumes but that barely gave him a snap shot of their credentials and little insight into who they were or what their thinking was. It would be like trying to get married to someone after reading his or her history on paper. Where they were born, where they went to school, what degrees they have, how successful they portray themselves certainly doesn't tell you if you are going get along, not have arguments, agree on child raising, agree on major political or historical issues, or even if you both root for the Red Sox!

Developing a product is certainly a child rearing process and the political and historical issues will impact the product's distribution or financial support and help to agree on what to call it! Yet you are supposed to read a description of the person and then talk to them and get to know them well enough to be able to work together for years!

And what does the potential employee know? They know they want a job. They want to get paid, paid well enough to meet their needs. They don't know much about the people they will be working with or whether their mental or emotional needs will be met. Gus thought maybe they would need to develop an 'app' down the road that would be able to be portable so that people could take them to interviews and on dates.

With the job market as tough as it was at that moment in history, even the hint of an available job brought out anyone and everyone. It was overwhelming; hundreds and hundreds of applications, far too many to get back to individually. They could smell the desperation in many of them. If they had all been paper, it would have been impossible to even look through them, but the vast majority came in electronically and were sorted through by algorithms in the software looking for keywords like 'business', 'leader', 'statement analysis', 'micro-expressions', 'electronic engineer', 'software engineer', and 'imagination'. It also looked at the dates in employment history for longevity of employment, and it generated an approximation of the candidate's age. How many times could you read, "I'm a people person" or "I doubled the income flow of the company" or "I'm the person you're looking for"?

They were all individual people. They had lives and families and stories to tell and experiences and knowledge and weaknesses and strengths. They were all trying to stand out and be selected to fill the job. But if everyone is standing up, the one you notice will be sitting down. But you may not like that one.

So you let the computers thin things out and many great candidates are missed. It occurred to Gus that there were similarities to Blaytent's pending machine. They would be allowing a machine to determine the truth. These employment machines were determining the character of people. The problem was data. There was just so much data that humans can handle. Machines are needed for defining the winners. Maybe in the future the machines will decide who runs the country, sorting out all the candidates for President and then selecting the best. But who would define what the word 'best' meant?

They did get some applications that stood out from the rest and required face-to-face interviews. In some cases the machine had done a relatively poor job. It must have missed a key word or been fed through the sort algorithm wrong. One guy that came in was so nervous his hands shook and the sweat poured off his forehead. He had been the chief financial officer of a company that had closed its doors a year before. Gus estimated that he was just under fifty years old from the data on his resume. The company's name had been *Great Amaginations*. When Gus asked about the name, the candidate had merely shrugged, and Gus thought he detected a small sneer. "They said it was a combination of *Amazing* and *Imagination*. I didn't get it." Having been sensitized to non-verbal communications, micro-expressions, and voice stress analysis, Gus found himself watching a candidate's every move. He realized that he probably wasn't as subtle about it as he should have been and that only made the candidate more nervous. He wondered how they were ever going to sort through that level of nervousness when the person being interviewed was guilty of a crime.

One woman he talked to insisted on talking all about her family, immediate and extended, which began to sound like she was running a boarding house. It seemed as though she was needed to drive people from one medical appointment to another, that her car was needed constantly, that she was truly a "people person", and several of her relations wouldn't last the winter. And when she described the band that practiced nightly in her living room, he was ready to move on to the next candidate.

On a first date, there is a lot of ground that needs to be covered quickly to create a snapshot that can be followed up further and developed over time. In a job interview, the applicant must be able to establish the fact that he or she can do the job. The personal issues must be set aside and limited to indicate that the candidate has them under control.

Gus was glad that Allan was sharing in the interview process. His observations about body language and qualifications were invaluable. He finally referred Gus to one candidate that seemed to have it all. Her name was Julia Medici. She was a short, heavy, attractive woman with hazel eyes and curly, brown hair. On the qualifications for the job side she had graduated from Northeastern in 2004 from the School of Criminality and Criminal Justice. She had developed a comparative database of terms that could be applied to statements that flag discrepancies and key terms that indicate issues and provided proof for what she said was the *Undeutsch* Hypothesis. She said it supported the Statement Validity Analysis or SVA.

"Can you give me a quick layman's overview of what you are talking about?" Gus asked.

"It's grammar really. Pronouns are important and the tense of the verbs. Changing the structure of what you say or what was said. If I am talking about a person, and I use the past tense for example, "My husband always liked to fish" it means that I believe that he no longer exists. He's no long alive and maybe I am the killer!"

"Oh, great. You're not, are you? Did you have a husband?"

"If I describe my day talking about myself in the first person – 'I did this' or 'I did that' – and then I drop the pronoun – 'Went to buy a newspaper and a quart of milk' – that's suspicious. Did I think someone else bought the newspaper or the milk? Why did I drop the pronoun?"

"Okay."

"People move in and out of their realities just like in a book. You can't describe every second of every scene so you include what you think is important or interesting and edit out the rest. When a person describes an event they may add little details like that coffee cup you're holding that probably holds lukewarm coffee by now."

Gus looked down at his cup.

"They think that by adding those details they make their story more truthful. But maybe the cup wasn't there. Maybe the table wasn't there. The subject reveals the truth in his or her own words.

"So if you interview someone like me, and I start talking about your company in the first person plural, like, 'We're going to do great things here at Blaytent', you know that I have mentally already joined the team."

"I guess I'm going to have to be careful with what I say around you."

"See. You are assuming that we will have more conversations meaning that I'm doing okay." She smiled, and it lit up her face and made her eyes sparkle.

"All right, then. What about business experience?" Gus asked.

"I minored in Business," she said. "On the one hand it helped me with my father's restaurant and on the other it allowed me to intern for a profiling analysis company."

Gus paused. "You're pretty good at this interview process?"

She laughed and her eyes flared and squeezed up at the corners. "It's a bit of an advantage," she said.

She was relaxed and confident and presented herself well. There were no misspellings on her resume, and it was neat and carefully laid out. "Where's your father's restaurant?" he asked.

"The North End: Northern Italian cuisine. He is truly a chef and not all that great at business."

"Restaurants are hard," Gus said. "Not that I know firsthand. I mean I imagine that they are hard because of keeping the right amount of inventory. There must be a lot of waste." He subconsciously noticed that she had pushed the dominant balance of the conversation over to her side. He felt like he was being interviewed.

"With a good system, it is manageable," she said. "It means keeping good records, working with suppliers, keeping the customers happy, keeping the equipment running."

"Doesn't he miss your help?"

"Hey," she said, "we're Italians. We're family! I see him all the time and get him back on track when he strays!" She laughed again. Gus realized he liked her laugh.

"So with your skill at reading people and what they say and how they say it, why are you still looking for a job?"

She looked at him, challenging him, testing him. "Because until now I hadn't found the right company to match my skills."

So that was why they hired Julia Medici to join the team. She didn't have an enormous amount of business experience, but she did offer a unique blend and perhaps she would satisfy Avitas. She could help them adjust the wording in their Business Plan.

To fill the other hole on the team they hired Arya Satyam Jain, a computer science graduate from the Indian Institute of Technology. Arya was five foot six inches tall and weighed in at one hundred and sixty pounds. He had been studying facial recognition techniques for security systems particularly in airports.

Allan was surprised at his sense of humor. It took him a few moments to realize that there were times when his facial expressions were being read and Arya was chuckling quietly to himself. It was unnerving. Like having someone looking into the contents of your brain, mindreading of sorts. Allan's Texas sense of humor was noticeably different from Gus's New England dry wit but what amused Arya's was way different.

Arya had spent most of his life in India but had done his graduate work at MIT. He had struggled to immerse himself in Boston culture which sometimes had unusual results like when he talked about 'parking the car' in a combination of Indian British and Boston English which came out something like 'paaking thuh caa'.

He wore horn-rimmed glasses that made him look a bit like Mahatma Gandhi with spiked hair. He loved hot food and craft beer although he knew that it would not be good for his Karma. Clearly Arya had a passion for electronic hardware and software. He told Allan about a circuit he had designed where he had used the waste heat generated by a microprocessor to alter the output of components on the other side of the circuit board. Then he sat back in his chair and laughed while Allan smiled in perplexity. He went on to describe a camera he had worked on whose resolution was such that he could tell if the subject had washed his face that morning. "And he didn't have to be close to the camera at all! The software was so fast that it could detect the smallest of winces or twinkles. Creating an electronic device is like creating life. You invent the idea, put the parts together, add the spark of electricity, and then the software makes it think! You can make it do whatever you want it to do. It doesn't bleed when you open it up the way a body does. It's much cleaner, more logical, more understandable, but once in a while it does surprising things that you don't expect."

Allan was exhausted after talking to Arya. The man was clearly infatuated with what he did and after checking his records, it was also clear that what he did he did very well. "Why would you want to work for a small company like Blaytent," Allan asked. Arya probably could have worked for a multitude of companies.

"I like Boston's beer," he replied. "And I like the Red Sox."

It was as simple as that. With the addition of Julia and Arya, Gus and Allan felt that the team had been completed. They modified the business plan but more than that, they both felt more confident about the outcome of actually producing a working product. Before, the plan neatly reflected all the hypothetical income, product development, marketing, and a fictional future income stream, but it was flat and lifeless; interesting but lifeless.

Julia helped them develop policies to address a company constant improvement process. She guided them through an internal audit. She helped them define a management structure and system for maintaining privacy and records and all the mundane stuff that neither Gus nor Allan was interested in doing.

They were crowded into their temporary spaces and they needed equipment for Arya to work his magic on, and they needed to do more research into the technologies so that they could map out how to advance them beyond the existing state of the art. But they couldn't do any of those things until they got the funding. Gus was not fond of socializing, but he knew it had to be done and he knew that he was the one that had to do it. His father had developed a friendship with Robert Adams who had lived not merely in Chestnut Hill but actually on Chestnut Hill in Brookline in a very beautiful but subtle home that had a wonderful view of the city stretched out below. Bob Sainte liked to cite the Harvard toast:

"And this is good old Boston,
The home of the bean and the cod,
Where the Lowells talk only to Cabots,
And the Cabots talk only to God."

Robert Adams was not a Lowell or a Cabot, but he knew them and rubbed elbows with them. Gus had grown up with the Adams children, and at one point had a crush on Rebecca Adams. But early on he discovered that there was always a division between the city mouse and country mouse. The city mouse had the sophistication and the worldliness. The country mouse was never quite the same. Rebecca was very definitely a city mouse. Falmouth is a nice place, but it is not Boston. Rebecca went to boarding school. Gus went to Falmouth High. They were different worlds and Rebecca let him know that in her own, sophisticated, subtle way.

But business was business and Robert Adams was a man of business, a man of many businesses, in fact, from trucking to clothing to television. When Gus told him about Blaytent, Mr. Adams suggested that Gus attend a small cocktail party at the Chestnut Hill house where he could meet some people who might be able to help him. "What firm are you working with?" Mr. Adams asked.

Gus assumed that he was asking about his Venture Capital firm. "Avitas," he said.

"Ah. Good. Maria will be here too. She knows what she's about."

Gus drove up the winding roads to the top of the hill and the ivy covered wall that protected the Adams' house from prying eyes. He pulled his car onto the pea stone gravel covered circular driveway in front of the house, listening to the crunch under his tires. The edge of the drive was already lined with impressive high-end automobiles. Gus found a spot near the end of the line for his unimpressive, aging vehicle, got out, locked the car just in case, and sauntered back toward the brick arched entrance to the house.

There are parts of New England towns that have special committees that are in charge of trying to keep the town from changing, to keep them quaint, New Englandy, and frozen in time. Gus looked up at that façade of this house on Chestnut Hill and thought that in a neighborhood like this you didn't need a committee to keep things frozen in time. Every once in awhile some character came along who had new money and no taste and would buy one of these homes, tear it down and build some modern design or paint it a garish, unacceptable color. But rarely would it slip through. This house had not changed in all the years that Gus had known the Adams family, and it wasn't likely to change as long as the "Cabots spoke only to God".

To underline that fact, as Gus approached the front door, it was swung open by a familiar older man with thinning, graying hair wearing a white jacket and black pants, with a thin welcome smile. "Good evening, Mr. Sainte," he said.

"Good evening, Joe. Good to see you again. You're looking well."

"Thank you, sir. You as well."

Joe had been a part of the Adams family as long as Gus had known them. When he was small, Gus had found Joe to be a scary kind of guy. He didn't talk much. He seemed to know where everyone was, what doors needed to be opened, what drinks needed to be poured, without being seen. Gus was sure that he was filled with family secrets like the time Joe had interrupted him making out with Rebecca in the bushes but never said a word. Gus had fantasized that Joe had been created when the house was created and wasn't really real. Gus had no idea what his last name was or where he was born of if he had a family of his own. It flashed through

Gus's mind that Joe would be an interesting character to test Blaytent's product.

"They're in the Chinese garden, sir," Joe said holding the door open for him.

Gus moved through the dim light and old furniture smells of the living room of the house and out onto the patio, turned right and walked across the grass toward the sounds of conversation and laughter. He paused for a moment to turn to his left and look out through the trees to the glittering lights of the city that seemed so far away. Gus had always had the sense that as comfortable and secure a place like this must be for the occupants who had staff to maintain it and keep it fixed in a moment in time, the very subtlety of it was enough to put visitors in their proper place. That was a feeling that could never be bought. The flash and flair of mega-yachts and mega-homes could never duplicate that power.

Suddenly Gus's thoughts were interrupted by Joe who had appeared at his side with a silver tray supporting a lovely Steuben beer glass with a perfectly poured beer with a perfectly sized head. "Sir?" Joe said.

"Ah. Thank you, Joe."

And then he was gone. Like smoke, Gus thought.

Gus pushed his glasses up his nose and holding his beer he moved on toward the conversation and the laughter in the Chinese garden.

Gus wasn't sure what qualified it as Chinese, but it was Robert Adams' favorite part of the house. Gus had been told that Mr. Adams liked to maintain it himself, although Gus found that hard to believe. Gus had never seen him not wearing a tie. Although it was probably possible to garden wearing a tie, it wasn't something that Gus was ever likely to try. Mr. Adams probably spent time with what he would call his secateurs trimming the roses or pulling a few weeds.

As Gus approached the garden entrance a woman in a flowing, flowered, white dress floated toward him with her arms outstretched. Tanny Adams, Robert's wife, had battled alcoholism and was in and out of rehab, and Gus found her very real and very down to earth. Her real name was Florence, and he had no idea where the Tanny had come from, but he certainly didn't question it.

"Gus!" she bubbled. "So good of you to come. We've missed you!"

"Thank you, Ms Adams. It was wonderful of you to invite me. The house looks great. Never changes."

Tanny Adams smiled. "We do what we can." She smiled again and pushed her arm through Gus's and guided him back into the garden. "Rebecca's in London. She'll be sorry she missed you. I hear you are working on a new venture?"

"Just trying to stay out of trouble," Gus said with a chuckle.

One of the problems of Gus's project was that he found himself overwhelmed with input he would have missed before. Because of his brief conversations with Julia, he found himself listening for changes in pronouns and missing words. Allan had indoctrinated him with seeing body language that he would never have consciously noted before – people leaning toward or away from each other, hand gestures, eye brow twitches. He tried to hear voice patterns or changes in pitch. It was difficult for him to concentrate on what was actually being said while he consciously tried to decipher what should have been unconscious communications. At the same time he was acutely aware of familiar smells of perfume and food and roses as well as the cool, dryness of a late May evening. On top of all that was the complexity of performing in the role of an adult in a place and among people he had known as a child. He told himself to focus on the goal of funding, making connections for his business. He wasn't here to ask for an ice cream cone or to stay up late.

Tanny did the rounds with him, and he was grateful that she minimized the childhood connections. She introduced him as a longtime family friend and a graduate of Boston University. "Get him to tell you about his latest project," she said to a smiling couple. Lowering her voice she said, "But be careful. I hear that he knows when you are not telling the truth!" She leaned away from them with a light laugh and disappeared into the group.

Gus smiled at the couple who looked at him with expectant faces. "Yes, well," Gus started. One of the things he had learned in his discussions with Boyd Willis and others was that he needed what Boyd called an "elevator pitch". He needed a description of the business that could be executed during the course of a short elevator ride. It needed to engage, intrigue, and explain in less than sixty seconds (Boyd said fifty six seconds and no more than two hundred and thirty words).

Of course Gus hated formulas like that. He wanted to do it his own way, so he launched into a rambling and vague description of what he was working on at Blaytent, spiced up with a brief mention of his experiences in Guantanamo.

"Where are you from, son?" the man asked when Gus paused.

"Cape Cod, sir," Gus replied.

"Ah, yes. We have a house down there. Chatham. Love it down there. We might retire there. Getting a bit touristy, though." He turned to his wife and smiled. "Good luck with your project, though." They turned away to another couple who approached them, grinning, hands outstretched. "So good to see you . . . ."

"Thank you," Gus said, and tried to move on with a purpose and not seem like he had been snubbed. He surveyed the guests looking for Mr. Adams to thank him for the invitation and Maria Gudmudgion to update her on the status, and he noticed a distinguished looking, dark skinned woman who looked vaguely familiar.

Tanny magically appeared at his side, and Gus again wondered how people learned to do that sort of thing. Was that something they taught in what used to be called "finishing school"? Were there classes in being a hostess, of keeping conversations going, of knowing how to avoid unpleasant situations, to put interesting people together? It certainly wasn't something Gus had ever learned. Maybe it was the country-mouse/city-mouse thing.

She said, "Bob tells me that you are working with Maria. Interesting woman. Very smart. She just arrived. Let's get you together, but remember," she said in a motherly fashion, "keep the business conversation light. I don't have to tell you this, but there is a line between business and social occasions." She looked up at him and smiled and then locked her arm through his and guided him over to Maria who was just accepting a glass of wine from a silver tray.

"Maria!" Tanny said, reaching out to take her hand in both of hers. "So good of you to come. You're looking wonderful tonight."

"Thank you, Tanny. You're looking splendid as well. And this is such a beautiful house. And it's good to see you again, Mr. Sainte."

Gus smiled and held out his hand. This was another of those business/social situations where sometimes people hugged each other and sometimes they shook hands. Body language. He wished this stuff came naturally to him.

"Well, I know you two have a few things to talk about, but let's not have all business tonight," Tanny said starting to turn away. "Maria," she said, pausing, "I've known Gus a long time, and if he needs an endorsement to get your support, I'll be glad to give it." And then she was gone.

Gus was trying to read Maria's body language. She was standing relatively close to him, leaning back, her right arm across her waste with her right hand under her left elbow, holding her drink elevated in her left hand. Her feet were planted firmly on the ground; spread about eight inches apart, both the soles and her ubiquitous spike heels resting on the stone and not on the grass between the stones. Nothing surprising there, Gus thought. She's protecting herself. Her green eyes blazed looking up at him through the lenses of her glasses and her shoulders and eyebrows were raised, indicating tension. "This woman is wound tighter than a mainspring," Gus thought.

"Mr. Sainte, I make it a rule not to talk about business at social occasions, but, of course, occasions such as this tread lightly on the border between the two." She almost smiled.

He tried to keep his own posture open and welcoming. "Well, you asked us to reinforce some elements of our plan, and I believe we have done that. Of course, it is putting a strain on our start-up capital to bring more people in."

"Not too much, I hope?" Maria responded, stepping back. Defensive, but challenging move, Gus thought. On the one hand he had to demonstrate that Blaytent really didn't need Avitas money in order to keep Blaytent in the driver's seat. On the other hand, if Blaytent didn't need the money, why had it asked for it? Gus had to show that Blaytent would be fine on its own, but by teaming up with Avitas both organizations would reach their goals.

Gus resisted putting his left hand in his pocket. Instead he put it around to the small of his back, still holding his beer in his right hand. He had to put this conscious positioning or acting out of his mind. It would appear that he was having some sort of mental breakdown.

He decided that the best approach would be a straightforward delivery. He knew Maria Gudmudgion was smart. She had the credentials – MIT graduate, MBA from Harvard and a partner at one of the best venture capital firms in Boston. She was probably pretty good at reading body language herself. The successful start-up companies did not often come from bullshit artists. He also knew that clear facts would be the only thing that would appeal to her.

"On your suggestion we have hired a programmer from the Indian Institute of Technology called Arya Jain both for programming and to handle the micro-expressions part of the project. We have also hired Julia Medici for both her business and her Statement Analysis skills. I have to watch what I am saying around her . . . because of the way she takes sentences apart!" He smiled.

"What business school did she go to?"

"She got her BS from the School of Criminality and Criminal Justice at Northeastern. She minored in Business. Her practical business experience comes from helping her father run his Italian Restaurant in the North End."

Gus saw Maria's eyebrows twitch, but then she leaned more toward him. "What made you think that your approach in developing this system would actually work when you didn't have all the pieces when you started? Why something so complicated? Why not make it simple and focus on one? Why four?"

"Because one of these elements alone doesn't work," Gus replied, getting into his groove. "When you read the research on these technologies, each one of them will eventually confess to only leading the questioning, pointing out a line of inquiry that should be followed. And they are heavily reliant on the knowledge and skill of the questioner. If we remove the questioner from the equation and let the machine interpret the input, the most significant unreliable variable is removed."

"The government might be interested in what you are working on. With your army experience, maybe you can make a connection there to support your efforts?"

"That would be giving it away," Gus bristled. "If they funded it, we would get buried in a mound of bureaucratic paperwork, and then they would bury it. They would much prefer the more traditional techniques."

"Don't abandon any path out of hand. I <u>have</u> read the research, Mr. Sainte, and I am convinced that there is a significant market for what you are working on among law enforcement agencies and others. I am also convinced that most of the work is crap. The only legal basis I have found is *Terry vs Ohio* relating to the Supreme Course decision about body language and the police. We're going to have to go up against all of the established lie detection industry. They're not going to be pleased."

"Bingo! A change to first person plural!" Gus thought. One little change in one little pronoun. Thank you, Julia! "We're going to have to go up against . . . ." instead of "you're going to have to go up against . . . ." Was that conscious?

"There is no denying the skill and the judgment that comes from years of experience in any profession," Gus continued. "I have always admired dedicated professionals in any trade across the board, no matter what they do. But I also know that machines can learn much faster than people. Machines can make connections more quickly, relating one disparate element to another. Machines don't forget and if their internal memory fills up, we can give them more."

"But no formal business school training? This person you just hired?"

"No, but you should talk to her. I'm sure you would be impressed."

Maria carefully stepped back on the stones. "Well, send me your updated information and we'll set up a time to get together. By the way," she said leaning into him again and looking over his right shoulder, "do you know if that is Judge Jakes?"

Gus turned so he could see where she was looking. He noticed the African-American woman who was talking with another woman that he did recognize from her press. "I see Senator Perkins there, but I don't know who Judge Jakes is."

"Bob Adams knows how to bring the right people together. Excuse me, Mr. Sainte. Send me that information and we'll talk again," and, heels clicking on the stones, she moved off in the direction of Senator Perkins and the person Gus assumed must be Judge Jakes.

Joe appeared at his side to replace his beer. Gus thanked him, and shrugged. Judges were not on his agenda, at least not at this point.

+++++

The following week he delivered an updated version of the Blaytent plan to Maria. After reading it, she visited the office and sat down with Julia and rest of the team.

After the meeting Bob was still nervous, still in his doom and gloom mode. "We should have tested her," he said. "We should have asked her if she was going to give us the money with the microphones rolling. I could have told you right away whether or not she is just stringing us along." And then he stepped outside for a cigarette.

But they hadn't tested her, and so they waited. Research was performed, the project rolled along, money rolled out of the bank account, and days went by. Gus began to wonder himself if he had misjudged, if he should have started with another venture firm at the same time despite the fact that he had been told that would kill the deal. He tried to figure out if there was another way he could piece the project together, if he could tap into family friends but the kind of money they needed would be asking a lot. Could they reduce the amount of money they needed? Did they really need to be so ambitious? Maybe Gudmudgion was right? Then again, maybe that was what she was driving at and she was going to come back to them offering less money to fund part of the project.

Three weeks went by before Maria called. "Good news," she started. Gus geared himself up to what that might mean. It was better than starting off with the alternative, but it still might be just the flavor not the whole lollipop.

"Avitas is going to back your project, with a few conditions. The product has to show successful commercial viability in four years, inside your projections. Blaytent has to be able to clearly demonstrate the viability of the process by that time."

"We can do that," Gus said. They'd already talked about that. No surprise there.

"We will be involved in your financials. Julia seems competent, but we want to watch more closely. I'm going to have Chris Pinel from our office stop by so you can meet him, and get to know him. He works for us, but I want him to be working with you."

"Is that necessary?" Gus asked.

"We think so. I think you'll find Chris quite helpful."

"Okay."

"We're going to provide you with access to four million."

Less than half of what he had asked for. Money was good. They certainly couldn't get there without it, but could they get there with a fraction of what they had said they needed? Why did they ask for all the detail based on a higher number if they were going to provide less anyway? Gus had inflated their needs because he had been told that he would get half of what he asked for, but he hadn't inflated them that much. "That's less than what we were looking for." It was an obvious statement, but it just came out.

"We will be controlling sixty-eight percent of the company, and we want to be sure that our money is carefully spent."

"Sixty-eight percent!" Gus nearly shrieked. "That's more than we talked about."

"We think the risk is high. That offers potentially good returns which is why we are backing you, but it is still smoke and mirrors at this point. You're going to have to convince us . . . and everyone else, that there is strong scientific backing for what you are doing. Palm readers don't get venture capital, Gus."

So now we were 'Gus' and 'Maria' now that he had been robbed! Gus tried to refocus. This wasn't going to work if he thought that way. "Sixty-eight percent is going to be tough for the team to swallow. They have been working mostly on promised equity."

"Challenge to your leadership capabilities, Gus. Show that a smaller part of something is better than a large part of nothing."

Gus internally bristled again. There wasn't anything about that he liked. Platitudes. "This is going to hurt me more than it hurts you." What a lie! Put that doctor on a polygraph!

Gudmudgion waited, dragging out the silence on the other end of the phone. Gus scanned through his options. Less money. Less ownership. Less time. Unhappy crew. Could he turn it down? Should he turn it down? If he said he didn't think that would work, would that be considered a sign of weakness?

"We have to have an option for more funding if we need it and a down the road buyout," he said. "If the crew goes for this, they have to know there will be a reward for success."

"We can look at that."

"No," he said. "It has to be part of the package. When we make this a success under these conditions with less money and less time than we asked for, we need to know that we'll be able to get rewarded in the end."

Maria paused. "All right," she said finally, "I'll write it up."

Gus didn't want admit that Gudmudgion was right about convincing the crew, but she was. It wasn't a great deal, but it was a deal, and it allowed them to move forward. "It's only business," he kept telling himself. "It's only business."

Gus explained the arrangement with Avitas the way Gudmudgion had explained it to him. "I got some good news! We got funding." Smiles and cheers all around. "It wasn't all the funding we asked for and Avitas will have control of the business so our ownership has been diluted." He explained that he would get together with them individually and explain the impact.

"When we make a success of this, in four years we can get ownership back. And that," he said, "is what I intend to do. Both of those things! Make it a success and get ownership back. But for now we have the fuel to move forward. Right?"

After Chris Pinel got together with Julia the following week, Gus asked her how it went. "All right, I guess. He seems to know book-learned business pretty well. I don't think he ever actually took a company from concept to reality."

"Well, don't let him get in your way."

Chapter Five

2013

For Boyd Willis, the best thing that had developed out of his two plus years of work with Blaytent was his relationship with Julia Medici. He found the corny phrase, "You light up my life" to be absolutely true. She was awesome. He wouldn't have said it to her, but she was a fireball. She was amazingly smart and bubbling over with energy. Like all the experts at Blaytent, he found her ability to take apart the things that he said and did and extract what he really meant to be unnerving. And she was nine years his junior but that could be both a positive and a negative.

Sitting up in bed, he watched her bustle around the apartment, picking up clothes, opening the shades, closing the windows. She never stopped, and it made him smile. She whistled to herself while she bustled and tidied.

"Didn't Allan say that whistling to yourself was a form of calming? Are you nervous about something?" he asked.

She stopped and looked at him. "Don't start. Stick to the law, buster. Don't try to venture onto my patch."

"I wouldn't dare," he replied swinging his legs out of the bed and heading for the bathroom to shower.

While he showered he thought about the amazing colors that his association with Blaytent and Julia had brought into his life. He felt a swell of happiness and comfort surge up inside of him. What Gus Sainte had started was amazing. It could do a lot for the world. He had pulled together an exceptional team of people and for the most part they worked well together. Boyd enjoyed learning about the various technologies, and they seemed to enjoy explaining them to him.

And then there was Julia. She wasn't a raving beauty, but that really didn't matter to him. She was just five foot three, and he guessed that she weighed nearly two hundred pounds. She had the most amazing hazel eyes that twinkled and sparkled and flared when she got angry. Her Italian family background was extremely different from his upbringing along the Hudson River. Her family was large and loud and loved to eat. Her father's north-end restaurant was always full of great smells and Italian music and laughter.

Washing his face under the cascading water from the shower, he experienced a twinge of guilt at the feeling that he shouldn't be this close to a client. Not that Blaytent had any serious legal issues. He looked around for some wood to knock on. But still. He had other clients. He had a responsibility to his firm. Nevertheless, try as hard as he could, he couldn't suppress the happiness that he felt. "That's what we need," he thought to himself, "a little Catholic guilt to spoil the day! Forgive me father for I have sinned and so on."

He stepped out of the bathroom and smelled the coffee. In the little kitchen, she had spread out some breads from her father's restaurant, prosciutto and slices of fruit. Boyd put a hand on her back and leaned over and kissed her forehead. "One of these days, I'm going to cook you a real New England breakfast," he said.

"I've had those. Makes me feel bloated and heavy and weighted down. Don't look at me that way! Are you calling me fat?"

"I didn't say a word," he said, stepping back and holding his hands out to express his innocence.

"It's not what you said. It's what you didn't say! It's the look. I know I should do something about it. Maybe I'll take up jogging."

The vision of Julia jogging almost caused him to smile. She was probably reading him anyway. You couldn't get away with anything.

"Take your coffee and have a brioche and stop grimacing," she said.

"How's the project going," Boyd asked, sitting down at the table.

"Well," she replied. "Time is tight. More for Bob and Arya than for me. I don't know how Arya is going to pull all of the electronics together. Mine is mostly gathering the list of words, but the timing of the analysis is critical. Before we started working together on this, I didn't realize how interrelated all of these elements were. Gus is great at understanding the psychology behind it all. Knowing what to look and listen for is one thing, but understanding what the subject is expressing and understanding how the operator understands and interprets all that is something else. Replacing that layer of human interpretation with a machine's artificial intelligence is almost cold. But I guess that's what we are trying to do."

"Is the truth cold?"

"That's the expression, isn't it," she replied. "The cold, hard truth."

"How's the business going?"

"Seems to be okay. It's all outlay at the moment with nothing coming in of course since we're not selling anything. It should be simple, but there is something going on that I can't put my finger on. But I'm not that worried about it because everything we do is reviewed by Avitas, by Chris. It's really his problem if there is one."

"Is Gus thinking about hiring the technology out?"

"He doesn't want to do that, but it might make some sense," she said. "We could test it that way. I guess it depends to some extent on what Arya comes up with."

"You know, we should talk about other things when we're not working."

"Like what?" she asked.

"I don't know. Like music or art or food or anything that isn't related to the law or telling the truth!"

"We could just sit around and lie to each. That would be fun. I hate you."

He paused. "What?"

"No. I don't. I was just practicing lying."

"You hate me? How am I supposed to know? You're the expert!"

She got up and came around and hugged his head to her breast. "Better?"

"Is that body language? I didn't see that in any of Allan's notes."

She cuffed the back of his head. "Smart-ass," she replied putting her dishes in the sink. "Gus did say something about TV. I guess Bob says that the British company that he talked to is using their voice stress analysis with some game show, sort of a reality game show. Know what I mean?"

"I don't like those shows."

"I know you don't. But, you know, they're a bit like the old soap operas. People watch them because the fictional lives are much more disastrous than the viewers' real lives."

"But in the 'reality' shows, it's supposed to be real life. If that's real life, then I'm not at all sure that I want to be alive."

"But you know what we are doing is lot like the circus side show to people. We can magically see inside peoples' brains. We're mind readers of a sort." She sat down at the table again.

"It's interesting," he said, "but I think that's the point. What Blaytent is doing is serious. I think that you guys want to avoid being circus freaks. The problem with polygraphs is they are just not interesting products. The public can't look at the squiggles on a piece of paper and have a clue what they mean!"

"'Oh look, honey! Boyd Willis is lying when he says he loves me!'" she laughed. "'I can tell by the squiggles on this piece of paper!'"

"You know that's not true without a polygraph! But that's the point. Just because a machine draws squiggles, doesn't make it a fact."

"None of these things are really fact, Boyd. You know that, right?" she asked. "Not yet at least."

"I guess. But that's just the point. You guys need to be careful about the image of the technology. Keep it away from the side show."

"It may not be up to us," she said. "We have this eco-
nomic watch dog hanging around the office. It's a pain."
"What's he like? I mean Chris. What's he like?"
"He's all right, I guess. More coffee?"
"No, thanks. I really need to go."
She poured herself a bit more. "See you later?"
"You bet," he replied. "If not sooner."

When Julia got to the office, there was the usual controlled
mayhem. The project had moved forward, but two of their
four years had passed and it seemed like the more they did the
more there was to do. Electronics technology moved at light
speed.

Arya had resolved that the system needed five cameras to
watch the subject: one watching the face for his micro-
expressions, one aimed at the subject's shoulders, one at the
torso and the hands, one at the legs, and one at the feet. The
beauty was that these cameras could have exceptional resolution and still be exceptionally small. The positioning motors
could angle them to point in any direction on a hemispherical
arc. But then Arya ran into the positioning problem of having
the cameras not interfere with each other and any image dis-
tortion that might occur through a transparent housing.
Before Arya had to dedicate a vast amount of time trying to
sort this all out, he realized that some of the commercially
produced game consoles could do pretty much everything that
he needed! It was workable to use an off-the-shelf solution
that could do almost everything he needed and advanced the
project by a massive leap forward.

The software was something else. Julia's part was fundamentally simple. She had already developed the basic verbal
structure that Statement Analysis was based on – at least in
English. It wasn't always the actual words that mattered so
much as the transitions in pronouns and tense and sentence
structure. From that, she built a verbal model that would anticipate what the subject would be expected to say next, and
then a means to calculate the variance from that model. If the
subject said, "The grass was green" the system might anticipate that the next sentence would be related, like "the sun was
shining" or "the sky was blue". But if the subject said, "I had

lasagna for dinner", the variation, the subject change would be significant. Dealing with that significance was the point.

The software would have to break down the acoustical patterns into words and sentences and compare them to the database of words, sentence structures, and phrases that Julia was compiling. It would also have to parse the sounds to get a contextual meaning because of accents and slurred speech – a Texan's 'titty bar' might not have quite the same meaning as a Canadian's 'teddy bear'! The system would have to be able to understand that a child would not be likely to hug a 'titty bar' in the edifice meaning of the words!

Julia had watched Allan's efforts for mapping body language, non-verbal communications, or NVC. He was using the techniques they use for athletes to map their movements, developing universal stick figure video snippets to map the pacifying motions that people use to comfort themselves during times of stress. He too was building a reference library of fundamental body 'tells' that indicate when people are uncomfortable or under stress or avoiding something.

"We are so good at reading this stuff mentally," he said, "it's difficult to extract that knowledge and put it down on paper, or in this case on film. It's really intuitive. It sort of demeans it. But at least for our needs it is limited to captive interviews, someone sitting down, alone. That helps. If I had to do this for males chest bumping or group behavior, there would be no end to it."

The linkage and timing between the 'tell' and what triggered it was crucial. The software would have to link the question and the context to the body language that followed, compare the body language to the library, and then link it back to the question to try to anticipate what the subject was wrestling with.

Bob Thatcher was working with an array of acoustic issues from choosing the microphones to filtering out background noises to his primary task of cataloguing the inaudible micro tremors as well as the audible components of speech that vary in pitch and tone.

"We don't want this to work in just a sound studio," Gus said. "It has to work in other places like court rooms or press conferences."

"Without the subject wearing a microphone?" Bob asked. "We're not going to be able to get there."

"Try," Gus replied. "You can do it, Bob."

"I don't know. It's hard enough already. Nobody does it without external mics."

"That's what makes Blaytent different. We do things other people don't. And I'm not saying that we shouldn't allow external mic capability. I just don't want any wires connected to the subject."

Arya's task was the toughest. He had not only to create the hardware and the software that pulled it all together, he also had to catalog the array of micro expressions that were more subtle than Allan's NVC movements. He had to focus on the muscles of the face that are associated with sadness, happiness, surprise, or deception. Micro-expressions occur in fractions of a second. Recognizing the difference between a twitch that meant nothing and a twitch that meant something that happens in a fraction of a second with a live subject in real time was daunting.

When Gus got them all together and said, "We've got to demonstrate this thing (and we have to find a name for it). We've got show the investors we're making progress", there was general shock. They knew that was going to happen eventually, but this was sooner rather than later.

"When?" Allan asked.

"What can we show them and how soon can we do it? We seem to be going through our funding faster than anyone anticipated."

"Not that surprising," Bob said, holding his head as though he had a headache.

"We're making good progress," Allan said. "The challenge, as you know, is converting an operator reliant system to a computer reliant system. We have to get the computers to see and hear and understand and interpret."

Gus was pacing. He stopped, crossed his arms and leaned back against the wall. It was a small conference room that looked out across a patch of green lawn. The building was relatively new – boxy, glassed, industrial. It had fluorescent lights and a weak heating and cooling system. Rooms were either too hot or too cold and the air didn't seem to move and the windows didn't open.

The team sat around the conference table and watched Gus who was looking out the windows.

"Yes," he said eventually. "I know that."

Julia added, "Each of these technologies are already being used, right? For better or for worse. Each of us obviously has a good handle on our specialty, but it doesn't show much if I just sit down with a subject and start to analyze what he says. Even if I get it right."

A nervous chuckle went around the room. "You better get it right," Arya added.

"But that doesn't show anything, right? The machine has to get it right."

They all looked at Arya. "Well," he said. "It's not easy."

"And," Bob added, "and we said all four techniques would be working together!"

"I know," Gus said, turning to the room and putting both hands on the table and looking at them. "I know."

Bob looked down at his hands.

"But what can we show them? Have we got anything working, Arya? Can we concentrate on . . . .SA, for example?" He looked at Julia. Can we get that one piece working? Here's the thing: the fact is that we have to make this thing work. If we get it working one technology at a time, adding one to the next, we can move on to the step of comparing the results. But until we get one working, what have we got?"

There was general silence.

"The fact is," Gus continued, "that I know that you have all done amazing work. I also know that we are all perfectionists. We think that it could always be better." He smiled. "But at some point something usable has to come out of all this work."

Arya looked at Julia. "I think we're close for Statement Analysis, don't you, Julia?"

"Yes. I think we're close. I'm not sure about the accent discriminator yet. But Arya has employed some state-of-the-art voice recognition software. So, yes I think we're close."

"What do you need for a demonstration?" Gus asked.

"We have to show that the result is accurate, right? So we have to start out with someone who is lying. Maybe it would be best to have a videotape? The machine needs to listen and interpret. Maybe we could get a tape of someone who was thought to be innocent and was later found guilty? Don't police departments video tape interrogations?"

"I don't know," Bob said. "Is that enough? Would that be enough to convince anyone that SA works?"

Allan noticed movement in Bob's shoulders and the twitching of his shirt. Although he couldn't see Bob's feet under the table, he knew that they were dancing around. "What's the problem, Bob?" he asked.

"I don't know," Bob said. "We have to be convincing. That's the point of a demonstration. SA is a good process," he looked at Julia and gave a smile, which was more of grimace. "It's a good process, don't get me wrong, but is it enough? I mean on its own?"

"Bob has a point," Allan said. "What we are trying to show is how the combination of technologies increase the odds of getting it right. Arya, are you ready for anything else? Are you and Bob ready with VSA?"

Arya looked at Bob and then leaned back in his chair. Bob's shoulders indicated that his feet were still dancing. "This stuff is hard," Bob said. "Building the baseline, the true model means understanding what that particular person at that particular time knows to be true."

"Of course, it's hard!" Gus said. "We knew that when we started. You knew that. That's what's going to make it so spectacular when we get it together and we've been at it for two years! It's time we started . . . not just talking about progress, but actually showing progress. So the question is, Bob and Arya, can you do it? How about three weeks?"

"No way!" Bob exclaimed. "Certainly not from a videotape. I can't get the frequencies. It has to be live."

"If it's live," Allan said, "how are we going to prove if the system works?"

"That's very true," Gus replied. "But then how does anyone know for sure if a subject is lying? Just because the jury finds him guilty doesn't mean that the jury is right. It's still just their opinion."

"There's always DNA and confessions to back that up," Julia added.

"But we can't do that on a short term, demo basis." Gus said. There were a few moments of silence. "What if we hired someone like an actor, to play the role of a suspect?"

"Of course we'd know they were lying. That wouldn't prove much," Bob said.

"Okay. What if we hired three or five actors? Like a line-up? One of them is guilty."

Allan leaned back in his chair and put his hands behind his head. "I don't know if that would work. I mean they're not really going to be guilty. Wouldn't that just prove that our system doesn't work? That people can fake it?"

"That might be bad," Arya said.

The room was silent. "We can't exactly have someone go out and commit a crime so we can catch them," Julia added. "Interesting thought, though. I wonder how the courts would deal with that one."

"That's it, Julia!" Gus said. "Brilliant."

"What? That we hire someone to commit a crime in the name of progress?"

There was a round of nervous laughter.

"No. That would not help our cause with the investors. No. We hire four actors and one criminal, someone who has already committed a crime and is in jail, serving time. Maybe even confessed. Even better. We don't know which one it is and we pick out the guilty party!"

"What if we pick the wrong one?" Bob asked.

"That would be bad," Arya said.

"Maybe they're really innocent. Have you thought about that?" Bob asked. "So none of them come out guilty."

"Well," Gus said, "that would be . . . uhm interesting."

"This is only a trial. I mean a test," Bob said. "We're not really ready. We don't have the whole thing together. We could easily screw this up."

"Could we get the court to go along with this?" Allan asked.

"Well, what do you all think of the idea?" Gus asked. "Julia, you think the SA component is pretty much there?"

Julia nodded. "It's not completely where I want it to be, but I think it's close enough."

"Bob? What about VSA?"

"Oh, Jesus," Bob replied. "I need more time."

"How much time? Can we set this up for a month from now?"

"A month! I don't think Arya can get the software resolved in a month, can you?"

Arya replied. "It's tight. It's definitely tight. Let me see where we are."

"If we commit to this, we're going to do it, come hell or high water. I'm not going to be a vaporware company, continuously promising stuff and not delivering. I'll do my best to play down the expectations with the investors. I'll just let them know that this is a trial run, an incomplete trial run and they can witness the results. Everybody agreed? We're going to do this thing!" He paused, and then added, "Remember to keep all this stuff to yourselves. You've heard this before, but we have to be sure that our thoughts, ideas, progress, etc. are secret and secure if we are ever going to be able to get patents on any of it. Okay? It's a pain to work with, but those are the rules."

When Bob got back to his office, his wife, Annabelle called, sobbing, to tell him that their thirteen-year-old son, Zack, had just announced that he was gay. "He just bounced in through the back door, threw down his books, and said, 'Mom, I'm gay.'"

"What?" Bob replied, uncomprehending. "What are you telling me?"

"He says he's gay, Bob! That's what I'm trying to tell you!"

"That can't be right! Look, I don't have time for this right now. Gus just slammed us with a deadline that I don't think is possible. This is going to have to wait."

"You want me to go tell your son that he's going to have to wait to be gay while you meet a deadline?"

He had nothing to say to that. He pulled the phone away from his ear and looked at it as though he was looking at his wife. He realized that it was easier to look at his phone at that particular point.

"You're going to have to talk with him," she said. "This is a male thing!"

"I really don't need this right now," he mumbled. "You can tell him we'll talk when I get home." After he hung up, he left the building for a cigarette. Standing outside in the sun, he wondered why life had to throw curve balls at you. What's that all about? Gay? Really? Where the hell had that come from? No one in his family was gay. He'd never even known anyone who was gay.

He was Dr. Bob. He had his PhD. He got married to Annabelle when he was nineteen and an undergrad at Northeastern. He did the math quickly. They'd been married for seventeen years. Seventeen years! Jesus. He had more hair and a smaller waist when they married. Where had the years gone? Where was the fun? When was that supposed to happen? Where was the time that he could concentrate on bioacoustics? He was definitely working on that here at Blaytent, but he couldn't concentrate when this other stuff kept coming up. Was that a lot to ask? Kids were expensive. They were, in fact, a luxury.

He realized that it was good thing that Annabelle couldn't see thoughts like this inside his brain. She would not have been happy with him. Annabelle was such a great name. Blaytent was working on revealing the thoughts inside people's brains. What was going to happen to marriages then? What if they made a home version of the device and everyone had one and you could see what was really going on in your spouse's brain?

Gay? Bob stubbed out his cigarette. Maybe he should test his technology on his son. Could voice analysis reveal if a person was really gay or not? That would be an interesting test. The fact was that he was finding it impossible to bifurcate his brain. The stuff they did at Blaytent was as much a part of life as the stuff he did at home, and Bob found it difficult to separate the two. And on top of that, Gus had told them to keep it secret, and where did that come in when it came to wives and families? If your brain was filled with acoustic wave patterns that reflect how people really thought, how could you talk to anyone about life without talking about acoustic wave patterns? Was that boring? Annabelle would say it was. It made it somewhat easier that she was simply not interested in what he was working on. Never had been and never would be. It wasn't hard to keep a secret if the people you were talking to didn't care. Even little kids know that! "I know a secret, and I won't tell!" "Who cares?" they say and walk away. No fun there!

When he got home, his oldest daughter, Christa was in the kitchen talking to Annabelle. "Hi dad," she greeted him and then vanished.

Annabelle was cooking. "Well?" she asked not looking at him.

"Gus wants us to demonstrate the project for investors in a few weeks."

"That's not what I was referring to," she said, turning to look at him and putting down the spatula.

"Oh," he said. "Zack."

"You have to talk to him. It's just peer pressure. It's a tough time of life."

"When isn't?" he mumbled turning away.

"It's like a tattoo."

He spun back around. "Who's got a tattoo?"

"No one," she replied. "No one. I was just saying."

"I don't understand why kids get tattoos and piercings and all that other stuff they do to their bodies. Don't they know that stuff is permanent? How are you going to get a job with a dragon on your neck or a snake on your arm? At least when they were dyeing their hair green or emulating a Mohawk Indian it would grow out. But tattoos are permanent."

She didn't answer him. She'd heard the rant before. "Being gay is permanent too," she finally said quietly.

"Don't understand that either," he replied.

The following silence and the look from Annabelle weighed on him. "All right!" he said. "All right. I'll talk to him. Jesus. You know I don't have time for this right now. I'm under a lot of pressure at work. Why does he have to choose now to tell us this? I mean he's just thirteen! How can he even know what being gay is all about? He doesn't have a boy friend does he?"

"I don't know," she said. "That's why you have to talk to him."

"Yah. Great. Father/son thing. I have a pansy for a son."

She snapped. "Don't say that! Don't even think that word! No matter what, he's still your son! Don't start using words like that. He may hear!"

"All right. All right," he said, holding his hands up to stop her. "I'll talk to him. I'll talk to him."

Bob slouched up the stairs to his son's room and knocked on the door. He heard a muffled, "Yeah?" from inside.

"It's your dad," Bob called opening the door.

Zack scrambled into a sitting position on the floor beside his bed. Bob wondered what he had been doing, but put the thought from his mind.

"Hey," he said. "What's going on?"

"Nothing," Zack replied.

"Your mother said you had some news to share with us?"

"Nah," Zack said.

"You don't have news or your mother didn't say that?"

"It's not news. It's just something."

Bob looked at him. Thirteen. Skinny. Growing like a weed. Big ears. Expressions changing like lightening. Bob watched his feet because Allan had said that feet were the most honest part of the body. Right now they were splayed out on the floor and that didn't tell him anything or at least he couldn't understand what they were saying if they were indeed saying anything. Bob was impatient to get this over with, but he knew how important silence was and so he waited for Zack to explain further.

Zack jumped up and walked over to the window. His room was in its usual mess. Bob resisted an expression of disgust with the dirty clothes on the floor, the magazines spread open, the building blocks scattered about, the stuffed animals hanging off shelves, the unmade bed. He tried to find a place to sit and eventually settled on a relatively clear spot on the bed, straddling a car racing game sticking out from underneath, and he remembered the cost of it, but he didn't say anything about that either.

"I think I'm gay," Zack said finally.

"You <u>think</u> you're gay? You're not sure?"

"Yeah."

"You think you're gay, but you're not sure?"

"Yeah."

"Zack, you're thirteen! Do you know what being gay means? When I was thirteen I don't think I knew what girls were. They were barely interesting."

"That was a long time ago, dad. Things are different."

"Not that long ago," Bob said. "Why are things different? There are still boys and girls. There's still a lot of growing up to do."

Zack dropped back down to the floor on his knees. "Kids do stuff sooner now."

"How do you know that?"

"Everybody knows that. You watch it on the news. It's on the Internet."

"Oh, right," Bob said. "Because it's on the Internet, it must be true."

"But it is true," Zack replied looking at his father's face. "Kids I know have sex."

Bob was stunned. "What? Thirteen-year-old kids have sex? Do you even know what having sex means? When I was thirteen . . .."

Zack cut him off. "I know what it means even if we haven't had that, you know, talk that parents are supposed to have with their children."

"I thought it was too soon. I had no idea . . .. There's no 'Parents' Handbook', you know." He tried to laugh. "Why gay, though? What makes you think that?"

Zack walked over to his closet and began trying to shove things in so that the door would close.

"I don't know."

"I've never been gay," Bob said. "I like girls. I love your mother. Always have. So tell me what you're thinking."

"I don't know."

"So what makes you think you're gay? You must know something."

"I said, 'I don't know'!" Zack almost shouted.

Bob didn't need a machine to tell him that this was not going well. He didn't want to be having this conversation any more than his son obviously did. It wasn't that he didn't care. He did. He was also curious in a scientific way, and he couldn't help thinking about all the things that they worked on at Blaytent every day – Zack's body language, his words, the tone of his voice, and even the expressions that flew across his face. He tried very hard to focus on what his son was going through, what he was struggling to express which was obviously a major transition or could be a major transition in his life. He felt like he was observing himself having a discussion in a laboratory and that none of this was real. Did parents really have discussions like this? It occurred to him that good ones probably did, as he mentally patted himself on the back for being a good parent. But if he was a good parent, why was his son proclaiming to be gay? If his son was gay, didn't that mean that somehow he hadn't done a good job of portraying a positive, male role model? Didn't that mean as parents they hadn't defined the wonders of a male/female relationship? But he wasn't at home during the day. Was it Annabelle's fault for not being more of a woman? At least they talked about it. Not like some parents who just seemed to ignore their children and whatever it is they were going through, parents who stick their heads in the sand and assume or know that it is all going to go away, that it's just some passing stage their children are going through. They probably read that on the Internet! "Don't worry about the fact that your kid is a drug user or murderer or . . . or gay. It will pass. Some famous Doctor says so."

He shook himself out of it. "Look," he said finally. "I'm sure you're going through a lot right now. We can talk about this later."

Zack turned to his father. "It's not going to go away."

"I know," Bob said. "That's why we're talking about it." They looked at each other and Bob found in Zack's appraising gaze that he, Bob, Dr. Bob, husband, dad, was getting older. He was only thirty-six, for God's sake, but admittedly he smoked too much, he didn't get enough exercise, he didn't sleep well, his brain always seemed to be exploding from stress. And his son was looking at him as though he should be in a nursing home!

There was a war going on in Bob's brain. Work and family were not blending well together: neither was easy and neither was simple. It occurred to him that on the surface the fundamental question was whether or not Zack was gay. That question could be resolved by Blaytent's machine – if it was working! Could he suggest that they use his son as a test subject? That might make clinical sense but it certainly didn't make family sense!

Was the truth the issue here? Was sexual orientation a fact and if it was, could it be cured? Of course, that would mean that there was a right and a wrong sexual orientation and that led to philosophy and God and other meanings of the Truth!

None of that got Bob beyond this particular impasse. "Tell you what," he said finally, "we need to have a father/son thing. We'll spend some time together. We'll talk. Maybe we'll have lunch. How would that be?"

Zack shrugged and turned away.

"I'll take that as a 'yes'," Bob said.

"Why?" Zack asked.

Bob looked at him. "Because you're my son. Talking about this stuff is a good thing."

"Whatever," Zack shrugged.

"Do you like school?"

Zack shrugged. "This is stupid."

"No, seriously. That's a serious question. I really want to know if you like school."

"It's okay."

He was starting to think of this as an interview; something perfectly suited to his lab. It would have been so much easier to put a device between them and to put the responsibility on the machine. "Do you have a favorite class?"

"No," Zack said quickly.

"You don't have a favorite subject or class? Math or science or English or . . . drama."

"No."

"What about your friends?"

"What about them?" Zack looked up at his father.

"I mean do they have favorite classes?"

"How should I know? Why don't you ask them?"

"I know you're going through a tough time right now," he said, "but it is important to talk about it."

Zack shrugged.

"Are you getting a lot of pressure? High School is a tough time and kids can certainly be mean."

Zack shrugged.

"Why don't you tell me about some of the things you like about school? Like maybe the building or the teachers or . . . maybe even the smell?"

"The smell? It smells like sweaty kids and floor wax!"

"Are there are lot of kids?"

"Yes."

"Zack, what did you mean when you say you think you're gay?"

Zack was momentarily surprised by the changed in direction. "What do you mean? I meant that I was gay!"

"But do you even know what that means?"

"Duh, dad. Yeah. Everybody knows what that means."

"You don't like girls? Nobody likes girls at your age."

"Well, that's certainly not true. Not for other guys. There are guys and girls hanging all over each other. It's all over the place."

"I'm just trying to think about what it was like when I was your age."

"It's different! I'm trying to tell you that it's different now."

"Of course it is."

"It's not that I don't like girls. They're okay. Kids are so stupid. Most guys just want to get into girls' pants."

Bob was stunned.

"But some guys are . . . different. But they're the same as me. Understand?"

"These are tough times for you. Tough age. You're going through a lot of changes."

"No, dad. This isn't something that I'll just grow out of. I'm sure."

"Jesus, Zack! How can you be sure? You're only thirteen!" Bob's head was spinning. He wanted to have his machine to turn to, to reveal to him how his thirteen-year-old son could be so sure that he was gay. How could anyone be really sure? Love of the opposite sex is hard enough. Love of the same sex went against the social norms. Loving the same sex was like loving yourself; at least that was how Bob thought he understood it. How can you understand or prove love? He wondered if Love was something his machine could define for him. It was as amorphous as a lie.

He told himself to focus. He wanted desperately to avoid this conversation and to retreat into the science of his technology, but he knew this was important. It was a crossroad for his son and for his relationship with his son that would impact the rest of their lives together. He wanted to retreat into a cigarette. He reminded himself that he was supposed to be the mature one, that he was supposed to know what to do. Once again he wished that children came with an operations manual that would tell him "How to deal with your son when he tells you he's gay!"

"When did you first know you felt this way?" Bob looked around the room and not at his son.

"What way?" Zack asked.

"You know. Different." He didn't want to have 'the sex conversation' with his son. No one had ever done that for him. Maybe he should have. Maybe that's why Zack was this way?

"Have you been on a date?"

"No. You said I was too young."

"You are too young. But maybe I was wrong. Is anyone picking on you at school?"

Pause. "No."

"Is there a bully? Should I talk to the school?"

"No, dad. It's just kids."

They looked at each other and then turned away. Bob was at a loss. He mentally retreated into the science. It was clear that taking the emotions of the interviewer out of the dissection of sounds for analysis was as important as removing the background noise. The emotions of the subject would be influenced by environment, the room that the interview took place in. That was evident in the police interviews on TV with the bright light shining in the suspect's eyes. Taking a subject from a comfortable, home environment and bringing them to the police station, surrounding them with sounds and smells of crime and suspicion, as well as burly, threatening men in uniform impacted the stress patterns in their voices. The subject's feedback from the interviewer in response to their answers from facial expressions to other, subconscious, non-verbal communications impacted their answers. But how much? Did it make the answers invalid? Or were they invalid without that feedback, without that external stress? Was it different for every subject? Would the purity of response be more accurate from subjects if they were talking to a blank wall? Was it even possible to subtract the external influences and extract the pure, clear truth – the truth, the whole truth, and nothing but the truth?

But then Zack turned to his father, looked him in the eye and said, "Thanks, Dad" and left the room without another word.

Bob felt his heart make a little thump.

Chapter Six

September 2013

"I'd like to arrange for some actors to talk about a burglary," Gus said into his phone.

"Excuse me?" the voice on the other end replied.

"Yah. I guess that sounded a bit weird didn't it. I'd like to hire some actors for a demonstration we're doing. Maybe I should come in and talk about it?"

The clock was running on the demonstration of the technology that Gus had suggested. He needed to line up the characters – the actors and the real criminal, someone who had been found guilty so that guilt would be revealed by the technology. He needed to find the criminal so that he could describe the crime to the actors so that they could fabricate their stories. He had to figure out how to have the criminal released so that he would be able to participate in the project. He had decided that his cast of characters would be male and the crime would probably be a minor burglary of some sort, and he figured that he would probably need to talk with a judge to get the release. So he had called Exceptional Talent Management (ETM), a casting agency and set up a time to come in and talk with the CEO, Blythe Perry, about what they were trying to accomplish.

Stepping into the ETM offices was like stepping into another reality. Gus had seen these places on TV and in movies, but there were images of actors all over the walls and hopefuls hanging out in the waiting area. The women smiled at him and tilted their heads and the men scowled and tried to look fierce. None of them knew when he walked in whether he was competition or potential employer so they tried to cover both ends.

He gave his name to the receptionist and moments later a tall, elegant woman stepped into the room and there was a general shuffling and straightening up, like a flock of birds on alert.

"Hiiiii," said the woman, drawing out the sound and holding out a well-manicured hand. "I'm Blythe."

Gus wanted to say, "Of course you are," but refrained, introducing himself instead.

Back in her office they settled into a comfortable sitting area, and she asked, "So you're looking for burglars?" and laughed a dry, shallow laugh.

"Not real burglars, of course," Gus chuckled in return. "No. We are developing a product, kind of like a polygraph, and we need to be able to clearly demonstrate that we can discern the truth, if you know what I mean."

"Tell me more!"

"We want to set up a panel of three or four actors and one real, convicted criminal, interview them individually, and then have the technology tell the difference. In this case the criminal will be the one telling the truth – hopefully! The actors will be lying!"

"Interesting. Yes, interesting. Sounds like fun!"

"Well, it's pretty serious for us. It's really for our investors . . . as well as ourselves."

"So your technology can do this?"

"We hope so. We're counting on it."

"Is there a name for the technology? Something like a Liedoscope?"

"No," Gus smiled. "No name at the moment. Actually that name has already been used."

"Really! So what sort of actors are you looking for? Young, old, male, female, tall, short, beautiful, plain? You have a lot of choices."

"I don't know," Gus replied. "Male, I guess. Plain. Actors that look like burglars. We are going to use the acoustics of their voices and their words and how they say them as the 'tells', the indicators of their truth or lies. So we don't want their appearance to factor into the equation. In fact, if anything we want their appearance to do the opposite, if you know what I mean. If they appear to the witnesses or audience as the burglar, but the technology says they're not . . . I don't know. That might be okay."

"Maybe they should all look pretty much the same? Can I see what your convicted criminal looks like?"

"We haven't lined that up yet."

"It sounds pretty scary," Blythe replied. "I'm not sure about our insurance in subjecting our clients to a convicted criminal." She crossed her legs and leaned toward him.

"He won't be a killer," Gus laughed, leaning back. Blythe Perry was an attractive woman, he thought. She would have to be, wouldn't she, being surrounded by actresses and actors all day long? He wondered about her background. Had she been in the business herself? What signals was she sending him? He had become almost too sensitized to non-verbal communications. He had to reign in these thoughts and focus on the task at hand.

"Well, Extraordinary Talent Management, is a full service talent agency," she almost winked at him. "We can offer you an array of options. We are the best in the Boston area."

"You were highly recommended," Gus replied. He'd found ETM on-line.

"I'd certainly be interested in knowing what you've heard about us," she said, smiling at him and putting her hand on the amulet that hung over her décolletage.

Gus didn't have recommendations to pass along so he simply replied, "Nothing but good stuff, really," and smiled. He found that he was definitely distracted and was having a hard time coming up with a clear path.

"Are you going to film this interaction?" she asked.

"We'll definitely be documenting it. Why?"

"Actors get different compensation for different roles – speaking, acting, filming. We will need to spell out in their contracts what they are expected to do and what they will be paid for doing."

"Ah," Gus replied.

"Do you have a script?"

"No. I guess we can give them an outline of what is required, but we hadn't intended to actually write a script. You know? We want them to use their own words."

"So you need actors who can ad lib? Improv actors."

"I guess that's right." She had nice hair. She could probably arrange it in all sorts of different ways for different looks. "Have you ever acted? I mean you look like it." The words just came out.

She laughed and leaned back in her chair. "Thank you. I guess? Are you suggesting that I look like a washed up actor?"

"No! No! Of course not. I mean I was assuming that to run a business like this you have to have acting experience. I was wondering I had seen you in any movies?"

This was one of those times when Gus realized how fast all these interactions moved. He would love to have been able to pull back, scan through the film, think about what the best conversational gambits would be, analyze their future impact, and then say the right thing. But when it happened in real time, all of that analysis had to happen instantaneously, and he wondered if he had started on the wrong path. And then he retreated into wondering, "the wrong path for what?" Was he looking for a date or a business transaction? Why did issues like this have to have multiple, potential outcomes?

"Wow! Is that a pickup line, Mr. Sainte?" She smiled and sat forward in her chair, her hand back on her amulet.

He reached up to straighten his tie. "Professional question," he replied smiling.

Her hand moved up to run through her hair. "All right, then. I have been in a few things, but I found that people who want to get into the acting business are not very good at the business end of things. They want to concentrate on the acting part. When they get into the business end, they act like they know what they are doing, but they don't. But the good ones are good at faking it. And they get screwed. Both literally and economically."

"Ah," he replied.

She looked at him expectantly and the pause was deafening. Eventually she said, "So, you don't have a script. You need three or was it four, actors, improv actors that can come across as burglars. Male, improv actors. Right? And you need them when?"

"We're planning for this to happen in about four weeks."

"And how long do you need them for?"

"Well, I think the actual event may take a couple of hours, but . . . a day, maybe?"

"Any rehearsal? It's improv but they should at least get the lay of the land."

"I would think just the day will work if they know what they're doing," Gus said.

"They'll know," she replied. "We have the best."

They talked about timing and fees and contracts and Blythe pulled out a book of pictures and asked him to point out some face types that might work for him. It annoyed him that she distracted him although he enjoyed her smile. He pulled back, jumped up, and said, "All right. Great. Why don't you send some information over to my office?" He dropped his card on her desk.

"Fine," she replied, "Mr. Sainte."

"Gus. Call me Gus, please."

"Fine, Gus. Take a look and let me know what you need." She smiled.

Gus was really too big to scurry, but it felt like he was scrambling for the door to her office and that embarrassed him. It just wasn't cool.

Back at the office, Gus called Maria Gudmudgion to tell her the demonstration plan. "Sounds like a great idea," she said. "Glad to hear it's progressing well. I've been a bit concerned about the economics. Chris Pinel has been keeping me updated."

He had more or less forgotten about Pinel. He made a mental note to check with Julia and find out if the man was helping or hurting. Gus asked Maria if she had any thoughts on how they might line up a convicted criminal to participate because they needed a control character. She thought for a moment and then said, "How about I ask Judge Jakes if she has any suggestions? Or maybe you should ask your attorney, Boyd Willis, to speak to her. She might be interested in the project. That would give us another layer of credibility. You don't need someone who is actually serving time do you?"

"I guess not. Criminals don't really go stale when you take them out of jail! What they did, they did."

"I don't know what she can do if she can do anything, but I think it is worth asking. She and I have been working together on a couple of projects. She's an extraordinary woman."

"Good idea. Let me see if Boyd has any connection with Judge Jakes. We need to be sure our legal tail is covered – liability and such – before we bring a convicted felon into the office."

"Well, get back to me," Gudmudgion replied.

Gus called Boyd to see how he felt about contacting Judge Jakes and helping to find a felon they could work with. "That would be an odd request to make to a judge," Boyd said after hesitantly agreeing that he did know Judge Jakes, but it had been quite a while. He agreed to try to talk with her, but that Ms Gudmudgion's connection might be a more direct path.

"Let me know how it works out," Gus replied. "We need to get this set up."

Boyd said, "Look, Gus, I'm not backing out of your request. I'll do whatever you want me to do, but there is some old history there that I would rather not stir up. Tell you what, why don't you let Ms Gudmudgion handle it? If it doesn't work for her, let me know, and I'll give it a shot."

"Fine, Boyd. No problem. I'll let you know."

Gus called Maria back and asked her if that would work for her schedule. After he hung up the phone he pulled his time line management software up on his computer screen to see how they were doing, then he called Julia to get an update on Chris Pinel.

"Maria thinks we're not paying enough attention to our numbers," he said.

"There is something happening, but I can't put my finger on it," Julia replied. "But there's a lot going on."

"I know. I'm asking a lot of you. The demonstration and all."

"No. It's fine. I can handle it."

"What's the guy like? I've barely talked to him?"

"Who? Chris?"

"Yeah."

"He's here. You want to talk to him?"

"Sounds like it might be a good idea."

"I'll send him to your office."

A few moments later Chris Pinel stepped into Gus's office and stood by the door. "You wanted to see me?" he asked.

"Yes, Chris. You've been here awhile now. I thought it might be good if we got to know each other a bit better. Sit. Sit. Coffee?"

Chris Pinel was about average height and greater than average weight. His hair was turning grey and receding and his glasses needed cleaning. He wore a short sleeve white shirt and non-descript tie and his somewhat chubby face was flushed. His forehead was creased with wrinkles and the fingers of his hands were stubby like a carpenter's. In response to the question about coffee he mumbled that he was 'all set'.

"So, how's it going?" Gus asked.

"Okay, I guess," Pinel replied.

"Got everything you need?"

"Sure."

Gus waited to hear more but when it wasn't forthcoming he asked, "So how do you like working with Maria?"

"You mean Ms Gudmudgion? Fine," Pinel said. "She's fine to work with."

Gus wondered what Maria saw in this person. Avitas Capital was one of the most aggressive venture firms in Boston. They chose cutting edge companies to work with, and they demanded exceptional performance. Partially because Avitas was part of his team, Gus expected only the best from them, and was Chris Pinel really part of the best?

He sat with his legs tucked under his chair and his arms crossed and looked at Gus as though to challenge the quality of Maria Gudmudgion. There must be more to the man than

Gus was seeing. Maybe he was one of those hidden person-
alities that Allan had expressed concern about.

Gus tipped back in his chair and put his hands behind his
head. "Are you from the Boston area, Chris?"

"All my life," Chris replied. "JP. Jamaica Plain."

"And you went to school here too?"

"UMass Boston undergrad and Boston University School
of Management for my Masters."

"Ah," Gus replied. "Did you ever want to get out? See
the world? Join the Army?"

"Not the Army. They don't pay well. But the long-term
benefits could be good. Scholarships and such. But my
grades were good enough to get decent scholarship benefits."

"Good," Gus said.

"Julia said you were in the Army?"

"Yes. Yes I was. Did she tell you any more than that?"

"Not much. Just that you were in Gitmo. Military Intelligence."

Pinel nodded and crossed his legs and put his hands on the
arms of the chair.

"So, Maria seems to think that we are going through our
finances too fast. Any thoughts on that?"

Pinel put his legs back under the chair and re-crossed his
arms. "No," he said. "Seems okay to me. I mean it's all going out at this point, right? It's all investment. I can't offer
an opinion on if you are directing that investment correctly. I
don't know enough about what Blaytent is working on."

"But you know the economics? Why would she be concerned?"

"Oh, I don't think she is. I don't think she is. I think . . .
well that's her role. This is development period. I'm sure we
all get a little nervous at this point wondering if it's going to
work the way you say it will. Wondering if people will be
interested in buying the technology. All that stuff. Venture is
an adventure!" he laughed.

Gus sat forward and leaned on his desk toward the man in
front of him. "Really?" he asked.

Pinel snapped his mouth shut and compressed his lips until
they turned white. "What?" he asked.

Gus didn't reply for a moment as he studied Pinel. 'Nope,' he thought. 'I don't see it. I don't see what Maria sees in him. Maybe he's just good at pushing the numbers around.' Out loud he said, "Good." He smiled. "Good. I'm glad we had this chance to talk." He stood up. "I hope you will join us for our little demonstration in a couple of weeks."

Pinel jumped out of his chair and backed toward the door. "Yes. Good. Thanks."

Gus shook his head and sat back down. 'What the hell was that? How can some people seem to simply have no personality? Invisible? Maybe the FBI could use him.' He wondered how Julia, who was one of the most colorful and vivacious people he knew could work with him. Maybe that was another side to her character.

+++++

About two weeks before the demonstration, Gus realized that the scenario they had described was backward. The idea had been to put up four people, three were innocent and one was a convicted felon. All four would say they didn't do it. 'Which of these things is not like the others?' But only one of them could actually say they had done it because only one of them was actually guilty. So instead of all of them saying that they hadn't done it, they would all have to say that they had done it and only one of them would be telling the truth. Three of them would be liars and the one telling the truth would be the guilty party, the opposite of what is supposed to happen in a court. Then he realized that it didn't matter what they said. It was the combination. If they said they hadn't done it and it was the truth, then that participant could be eliminated. If they said they had done it and it was the truth, then that was the guilty party.

A lie is a lie, he thought. Was that right? In a real case, the criminal says he or she didn't do it. Would the lies be the same if they said they did do it? Would the key words for Julia's Statement Analysis algorithms be the same? Would the voice stress indications be the same? Was it as stressful to be innocent and lie about being guilty? Was this test going to work or would the whole thing fail miserably in front of a critical audience? Was a lie truly a lie no matter what?

That was what made conspiracy theories so intriguing. There were layers of truth as a story was told. Was it a fact that men walked on the moon or was that all done on a film stage in Area 51? That's why it was called a 'cover-up'; story layers are laid on top of story layers, enhanced and embellished by the telling of the tale over time. Digging down deep enough, Neil Armstrong really knows whether he flew to the moon, walked on its surface, and came back or if he just put on the space suit and bounced around on a stage in Nevada. If that was a lie, it was a very detailed lie with a lot of people involved. So all the questions that arise have to be explained by the conspiracy theorists that layer one explanation over the other, obfuscating the truth! The amazing thing is that at some point even Neil Armstrong might begin to believe that it was a sound stage in Nevada!

So if I'm innocent, Gus thought, and I lie to protect someone and say that I'm guilty will the software be able to pick that up as easily as if I'm guilty and I say that I am innocent? He thought back to the incredible stress that the prisoners in Guantanamo had been under, fearing for their lives. It seemed to be the case that there were people who had difficulty telling the slimmest lie; "Yes, dear. I know it's our anniversary!" All it takes is a wife with hands on her hips, feet spread apart, her lips compressed and that LOOK at the doorway to shake the truth out.

What role does the consequences of telling the truth play? These actors are being hired to lie. There was certainly pressure on the staff of Blaytent to have this work, but the actors would get paid either way. Did they need to put more pressure on the actors? Gus had the fleeting thought that they would tell the actors that their children were being held hostage and would be harmed unless they performed well. Would that make their lies more realistic, their performances more effective, put more stress in their voices? And would it be the right kind of stress? Just because someone is under stress because of situation 'A' does that mean that they are lying about situation 'B'? A person who is under economic stress and afraid they might lose his house and be out on the street may lie about hitting a pedestrian while driving into work. Like most things in life, it's all connected. It's a system. The economic stress may cause him to be distracted which caused him to hit the pedestrian and then lie about it because of the consequences, which would impact his economic situation. Stress layered on top of stress. "I can't deal with this right now!" Diogenes, the ancient Greek cynic that Johnny Flack had told him about, who famously went out with his lantern to find "one honest man". Maybe he needed to find one man who was not under stress! It would have been just as difficult.

As he thought about it, Gus realized that the Guantanamo prisoners had been given a clear choice: tell us what we want to know or die. Water boarding clearly indicated that death was imminent at least to the person being water boarded. If you get to a point where it's black and white like that, is it easier to lie, to say whatever it is that you think you should say and does that make what you say the truth? Does the mental switch of right and wrong, truth or lie get switched off when you are that close to the edge of life? What happens to the truth as you back away from that edge? Gus wanted to believe that the threat of imminent death made no difference to the veracity of the response. It was just a response.

In any case, they couldn't put their participants under that kind of stress, and that was hypothetically a serious concern. Would the lies be too thin, too delicate for the systems to detect and if there was such a threshold, where was it and was it the same for everyone? These thoughts greatly increased Gus's own stress levels.

Gus left his desk and dropped in on Julia. She always brightened up his day. Her office often smelled of fresh bread, emitted from some goody or other that she had brought in from the family restaurant. "Hey, Julia," he said as he stepped into her office, "how's it going? Going to be ready?"

"Good, boss," she replied as she looked up from her computer. "Just wrapping up some of the last details for Arya to work into his software."

"How long's the list of words?"

"The trick is not the words themselves but their relationship to other words in the same statement. A word like 'never' is pretty clear on its own. 'I never inhaled.'" She laughed. "You can never use the word never without it being a lie – at least at some level."

"Ah. I'll have to think about that."

"'Three' is another tell-tale word. Oddly enough, when people want to make up a detail about something they use the number 'three': three people, three guns, three o'clock. I don't know. It comes across like a real number for some reason. So when you hear the number three in a statement, it's a flag to look for something else. So the software has to recognize that and branch off."

Gus nodded.

"And then there are words like 'began' and 'started' which are not words that people use in regular conversation. They're story-telling words. 'It all began when I . . . .' So the system has to pay attention to those as well.

"And then there are the pronouns. Shifting from 'I' to 'we' is a major tell in a conversation. It indicates a serious shift in point of view, transfer from a personal to a general way of thinking about an event."

"I'll have to watch what words I use," Gus snorted.

"The words on their own are innocent enough, as I say, but in context and in a statement they can be damning – or not. And it happens in real time. That's what makes our project so cool. The computer can handle real time a lot better than we can. If you have to do this without the computer assistance, you have to get the statement and mark it up to flag the words and reveal the truth or the lie. By that time the interview has ended, and you can't ask questions derived from the tells, the flags."

"And Arya has all this down?"

"You'll have to talk to him about it, but he seems to be on top of it. Having that state-of-the-art game console to serve as the basis for the transducer cut the development time down dramatically."

"It is great for us to have had a major corporation develop a significant piece of what we needed. I'm glad people like to play games."

He headed off to Bob Thatcher's office and found him peering at an oscilloscope. "Hey, Dr. Bob," Gus said in greeting, "how's it going? Peering into your crystal ball?"

"That's not funny," Bob replied with a scowl. "I'm not getting the right patterns."

"What are the 'right' patterns?"

"Something is screwy with the frequencies. I don't know if it's the microphones or interference from something. It may even be cell phones in the building."

"Seriously? We can't be that susceptible to surrounding issues. It has to be robust."

"I know that," Bob said in exasperation. "But sound is sound. It comes from everywhere. It bounces around, and at the frequencies that are difficult to filter. When you get down into the infrasound range where we are working, below twenty Hertz, below where people can identifiably hear, things get strange. This is what they use in *ballistocardiography* when they are working with the ballistic forces of the heart, for Christ's sake. But you know that."

"Uh, huh," said Gus.

"These frequencies get the sound around obstacles. They use it for charting rock formations below the earth. Research has shown that these low frequency sounds introduce unidentifiable fear in people. It may be what people sense in 'haunted' houses that freaks them out!"

"Where would it come from in a 'haunted' house? Is it just randomly created?" Gus asked. "It's surprising that you can find the same frequencies in human speech."

"And there are a lot of different patterns. Thousands of them! Cataloging the ones that are important and the ones that aren't is incredibly time consuming. And that's what makes this so difficult." He looked up from his work and took off his glasses and fixed his eyes on Gus. "I honestly don't know if I can have this ready. It's never been done this way before."

"Never?" Gus asked.

"Well, never this way."

"I'm sure you can handle it, Bob. If anyone can, you can. The fact is that we really don't have a choice." And then he slipped out of the room.

Gus discounted Bob's concerns because that was the way Bob was. It wasn't exactly crying 'Wolf!' but it was close. Gus needed this demonstration to work. They all did. So he had to believe that it was just Bob whining.

For a moment Gus paused as he was walking toward Arya's laboratory and looked around. All of this was to realize the fulfillment of his creation. All these people working, creating, and moving in the same direction was because of him. He stood still listening to the sounds, smelling the smells, feeling the air like a bear in the woods. It wasn't egotistical or a feeling of power. It was a feeling of awe that from a single point, a single idea, a single person so much can emerge and become real. He was honored to be the mother of all of this creativity.

At the same time all of this, all of these lives, all this money was his responsibility as well. If it failed, it was on him. If you're holding the coin, you're responsible for both sides.

Arya was responsible for the thousands of lines of computer code that were required to pull all the information together that the others on the team were giving him. He, in turn, had a team of twelve who were concentrating on the different components. In some respects it reminded Gus of the teams digging the tunnel under the English Channel, the Chunnel. The team working from the English side and the team working from the French side had to end up in the same place. It was even more complex than that. That was a matter of keeping the engineering straight. This was more like a Frankenstein monster with different people working on different body parts that had to function as a coherent person, like a fairy godmother in the end. If a committee of computer engineers had designed the fairy godmother in Cinderella, the pumpkin might have turned into a pimped-out tractor-trailer rather than a beautiful carriage, the glass slipper might have ended up as a diver's swim fin and the story would have had a very different ending.

Gus shook off those thoughts as he came into Arya's lab and found him running with a bunch of papers in his hands. Gus stepped back to stay out of the way.

Arya threw the papers down in front of one of the other engineers. "Here!" Arya shouted. "It's in here. You missed something. It's in your section of the code. You've got to find it. It's screwing all the rest of it up!"

Arya looked up and saw Gus standing there. "Problem?" Gus asked.

"It's nothing," Arya replied. "Literally. A missing ellipsis or an 'O' where there should have been a '0'. Computers want specific information. What they do with it is sometimes a mystery, but it is a specific mystery." He smiled.

"Well, I'm certainly glad it's nothing!" Gus smiled back. "We've only got twelve and half days to have something that works in front of witnesses."

"I am aware of that," Arya replied.

Gus looked at him expectantly, hoping for a more detailed report.

"Yah, well, all I can say is we're getting there," Arya said finally. "I don't have much time to work on the micro expressions, but . . .."

"But we don't need that for this demonstration."

"A good thing. But integrating just the two is hard enough. And getting the software to develop readable questions can be horrible. Sometimes what it asks makes no sense . . . at least to humans. Here look at this."

He energized his computer screen. The image was the human interface of the program with the areas segmented for the speech patterns, test and candidate name and other identifying information, a graphical display of the questions in percentages of truth certainties, buttons to press for previous questions, and the present question to ask: "Did you put butter on the porch?"

Gus had seen the screen before, but it took him a moment before his eyes arrived on the question box. He laughed. "What?"

"Exactly," Arya replied.

"What the hell does that mean? How would it know those words? Why would it put them together? Did you ask it about porches or butter?"

"Not at all. At least it's speaking English today."

"You mean it knows other languages?"

"Well, sort of. Sometimes it makes up its own language. By the way, we've got to find it a name. Can't keep calling it 'It'. We're calling it 'Cranky Franky' now. After Franken-stein."

"Funny you should say that. I was just having similar thought. But I don't think we can use that for marketing."

"But it certainly is developing a personality."

"You guys are in here in the dark staring at computer screens all day. It must be a bit unsettling when things like this pop up."

"Tell me about it. At least you haven't asked us to make it talk."

"So what do we do?"

Arya shrugged. "We're trying to have an escape option so that if something like this comes up, the questioner can move on to the next question. The problem is that sometimes Franky gets . . . well cranky and won't let you move on or will rephrase the question so you're still stuck. Here let's see what it does today." He clicked on the NEXT QUESTION button on the screen.

Franky printed: "Is today Thursday?"

Gus looked at Arya. "That's actually good," Arya said. "That's a preprogrammed truth question. I mean it is Thurs-day so if the subject answered 'Yes' that would give us a marker for them telling the truth. It's not supposed to be a logical, conversational sequence." Arya clicked on the NEXT QUESTION button again.

Franky printed: "Is the button on the Porsche?"

"Yah," Arya said. "This is the sort of thing that is driving me to drink. See part of the problem is that it's difficult to pin down who is responding when there are multiple people in the room. It could have picked this up from something else somebody said. Getting Franky to tune in to just one particu-lar sound source has been a challenge particularly when we get into the stuff Dr. Bob is working on. His infrasound stuff is off the charts. Want me to show you what Franky thinks about that?"

This was not making Gus feel comfortable. He realized that whoever was reading the questions was going to have to be pretty tolerant and understanding to make this thing work in the best light. "No," he said, "I believe you. In fact, I think I'll leave you to it."

"It should be interesting," Arya replied.

"Good choice of words."

+++++

On the following Monday Gus received a call from Gudmudgion saying that Judge Jakes had connected her with a candidate for the convicted felon role. His name was Derron Willigan and he had served his time for whacking another golfer with his driver. Apparently the victim had been harassing him for his lack of golfing expertise and pushing him to move on more rapidly on the course.

"He went to jail for a golfing incident? Really?"

"Well, I guess you should have seen the victim. He nearly killed him."

"Wow. And Mr. Willigan is back out on the course now?"

"Well, I don't know if he is back out playing golf," Gudmudgion laughed. "But he's out of jail and willing to talk about it. In fact he has been encouraged, shall we say, to discuss his anger issues more openly."

"Could I get some case information that I could review so I can have a background to provide to the other participants?"

"I'll see what I can do. Do you want to meet him?"

"That would probably be a good idea," Gus replied. "I don't know if we have the time. We're less than ten days away from the demo now."

Gudmudgion gave Gus Derron's phone number. "He needs to know more about what he is getting into anyway, don't you think. I mean this is sort of like a public confessional. Who knows how the guy will react?"

"Well, that's true, of course. I'll ask him to come in."

When Gus went to greet Derron Willigan in the Blaytent waiting area a couple of days later, he was surprised at what he saw. Although he never would have admitted it, Gus had an image of a convicted felon in his mind and Derron did not comply with that image. He did not look big or mean or have a visible tattoo or an earring. He looked more like a banker on vacation, and it flew through Gus's mind how the man had survived in prison. Didn't only particular people go to jail? Old people are always old. Kids are always kids. And crooks are always crooks. Each and every one of them is born into the role. Old people are trained to be old people and they know how to do it well. The same old people are around now as were around when Gus was a kid. A few come and go to keep it real. The same people gather at accident scenes. Every time. They're just there. In the crowd. None of these people are real just like in the Ray Bradbury story: *The Crowd*. Derron Willigan was the first real convicted felon that Gus had ever met.

"Mr. Willigan," Gus said holding out his hand in an overly effusive greeting, "so glad you could come and help us out."

As Willigan stood, Gus realized that he was bigger than he had assumed him to be. Not as tall as Gus, about six foot one, weighing two hundred plus. He was slumping - shoulders forward, hair thinning, pale skin, unshaven.

"Thanks for inviting me," Willigan replied.

Gus guided him to his office and offered him coffee or water. Willigan accepted the coffee.

Then he asked, "How can I help you?" His voice was deep but sharp.

Gus smiled. "Well, we're working on this project. We're developing a product, you could call it, that will help to determine if people are telling the truth."

"I did what they say I did. I already admitted that."

"I just . . . I started this company because I didn't think interrogation techniques were very humane or fair or even accurate."

"So what's this? Like a polygraph?"

"We think it is a lot better than that, Mr. Willigan."

"Derron. Call me Derron."

"We think it is a lot better than that, Derron. A polygraph relies on the skills of the operator. What we're doing is trying to remove the operator element and at the same time our product will use four different approaches to analyzing the responses of the subject, not just one. We think we can greatly improve the accuracy."

"A lie detector."

"Sort of . . . but lies are more a state of mind than anything else. What we are striving for is to come as close to facts as we can. 'Just the facts, ma'am,' as Sergeant Friday said." Gus smiled again.

"So what do you need me for?" Willigan asked.

"Well, we want to see if it works. The fact is, Derron, you have admitted to doing what you were convicted of and a jury believed you and . . . uhm, found you guilty as well."

"Yes."

"So, if you'll forgive me, we're going on the assumption that you are telling the truth and that the jury felt you were telling the truth. So we're going to ask you to tell your story to our machine. Then we're going to let three other people tell your story and other stories to the machine and see if it can tell us who is telling the truth."

"But the other people don't know my story, do they?"

"Well, no. But we are hiring three actors to tell your story or something like your story and since they are not you and haven't done what you have done, it should be relatively simple for the machine to indicate that they are not telling the truth."

"So you're hiring people to lie. And I'm the honest one. That's ironic. What if I were to say I didn't do it and the machine says that's the truth?"

Gus paused for a moment, not quite sure how to respond. "But you did do it. You just said so. You said so in court and the jury believed you."

Willigan smiled, a enigmatic, Mona Lisa type of smile. "I'm just sayin'. What if?"

"We're counting on you to tell the truth . . . and be guilty!"

"Well, maybe if I say I'm innocent and your machine confirms it then I can go back in court and get all this stuff reversed."

"Derron. We can't reverse time. You've already been convicted and done your time in jail. For this demonstration to work we have to be able to count on you to tell the truth."

"The truth as the court saw it. The truth as those fine people on the jury saw it. The truth that took away my life. For you, Mr. Sainte, this is a business experiment. This is proving a gadget. For me, this was my life. This wasn't an experiment or a game although it started as a game; a simple day on the golf course. I don't even like golf. But my former friends . . . notice I say former 'cause they didn't hang around after this . . . convinced me to play. And this asshole said I took his parking place. That was just the beginning. Then he follows us around, hole after hole, nagging at us to hurry up. Golf balls are expensive, Mr. Sainte, and mine kept going off into the bushes and the ponds and getting lost, and I wasn't about to keep buying more balls because Mr. Impatient, Mr. Type A was in a hurry. This is supposed to be relaxing. You're supposed to play golf to relax. How relaxing could it be if you're constantly trying to get it done, to get to the end? Why not just go to the eighteenth hole, sit down and have a beer right from the start, for Christ's sake?

"So finally I couldn't take it any more. He was in my face nagging at me like a bitch in heat. I had my driver in my hand, and I don't know, I just hit him, maybe a couple of times. Just to shut him up, you know? He spoiled my day. I couldn't relax with that in my face. That 'game' spoiled my life. I had a good job. I was living a comfortable living, and in a moment it was over. Done. Finished. For him and me. I didn't mean to hit him so hard. I just wanted him to shut up. Teach him a lesson. You know. I'm really not a violent guy."

"You didn't kill him, did you?"

"Nah. He's just not the same. He's not nagging anyone any more or so I'm told. I wonder if he learned anything from the experience." Derron shrugged.

"Well, okay," Gus replied. "You sure you want to go through this? You want to tell this story again to a bunch of people?"

"Yah. I'm okay with that. What happened happened, you know?" He looked away from Gus and out the windows.

"So what we're going to do is to give the basic outline of your story to these three actors. They do improv."

"I like improv. It's amazing what those guys do."

"They'll try to convince our software that they did it. You just tell the truth. Tell your story."

"Yah. Okay. I can do that. And I get paid for it, right."

"Yes. Absolutely."

"More than the actors, right? I mean they didn't do it, did they? They're going to be telling my story. It's my story so I should be paid more than they are."

"Yes. You're getting paid more than they are."

"Now?"

"Now? You want me to pay you now? In advance?"

"Yah. In advance. I got something you want: a story. You need me."

"Well, yes. That's true. But . . . . Look, I'll have our attorney draw up an agreement and get you an advance. We want to make sure you'll come back," Gus laughed a shallow laugh. "We want to make this legal."

"Yah. Legal. We wouldn't want to do anything illegal, would we? Can we get that done today? A man's got to eat, you know. The employment scene is not looking all that rosy right now."

Despite the fact that Gus was sympathetic to the man's condition, he had the strongest desire to have him out of his office. It fluttered through his mind to wonder how the man had arrived at this point in his life and how the rest of his life would flow. Had he always been angry? Did he want to put this incident behind him or did he want to tease it constantly in his consciousness? Gus and Blaytent wanted to use the story for something completely abstract. Derron was right: for them it was a game. When the demonstration was over, they could leave the details of the event behind. The actors would play with the story. They might even make it funny. For Derron it was everything.

But it was a serious game for Blaytent, and Gus wanted to be sure that Derron was going to be there when he was needed to tell his tale. "Sure," he said, "come back at three, Derron, and meet with our attorney, Boyd Willis. He'll have an agreement for you and a check for three hundred. We'll get you the rest when our session is over on the twenty-fifth. Okay?"

Derron shrugged. "I guess." The lack of conviction behind that response did not make Gus comfortable that the man would be there when he was needed.

Chapter Seven

September 25, 2013

Whehen the three improv actors assembled in the Blaytent conference room, Gus tried to compare them to Derron. Blythe had told them in rough terms what the project was all about and so they had come dressed as they thought a convicted felon would dress. Gus and Allan Soberman greeted them, got them coffee and seated them across the table.

Guy Marzolla was dark skinned and chunky. He had a round, pumpkin face and an obvious nose. He was what might be termed a 'character actor'. He had the looks of Karl Malden and not the handsome leading man. Jake Leiker was skinny, and he had dressed to emphasize that. His clothes hung off him. His arms drooped down and his eyes had bags under them as though he hadn't slept in days. He wore wire-rimmed glasses and his hair was retreating and turning gray. Randall Garvey, on the other hand, reminded Gus of Santa Claus. He was fat, cheerful, and smiled a lot. He had Santa Claus's round face and round body, but unlike Santa Claus, he was clean-shaven. His face seemed shiny and smooth. He wore a polo shirt.

Gus thanked them all for coming in. "So you all do improv acting?" They nodded. "Have you worked with each other?"

Guy and Randall had worked together in a small theater for six months with a group of others. Jake had done most of his work in Montreal before coming to Boston six months before. "Is it different working alone than in a group? I mean, for this project you will essentially be on your own, being interviewed. Making up the story as you go along."

"That's very different," Randall replied. "Working with a group of actors you're working off each other and the energy of the audience." He looked at his fellow actors who nodded. "So why don't you describe what you need us to do?"

Allan said, "Here's the motivation. I think that's the right term. You are playing the role of a convicted felon. You went to the golf course with your buddies. You had the bad luck of pulling into a parking place that another driver was planning on parking in. The two of you have angry words and proceed to the course. The other guy ends up playing in a foursome that is following you. You are not a good golfer. Are any of you golfers?"

Jake Leiker shifted uneasily in his chair, but they all shook their heads.

Allan continued. "All around the course this guy is on your case until you get to a point where he is literally yelling at you in your face. You happen to have your driver in your hand and you hit him with it; a couple of times. You are arrested on an assault and battery charge, tried, convicted by the jury, and you served your time. You are here to bare your soul and let the world know that it is a bad idea to lose your temper no matter what is happening."

"That's a pretty complete story," Jake said.

"And we will also be interviewing the man who actually experienced all of that – Derron Willigan."

"So you want us to tell this story as though we were Mr. Willigan?" Guy asked. "'Will the real Willigan please stand up?' That sort of thing."

"That's right," Gus replied. "You can add your own details – the type of car, the brand of driver, the color of the grass. Whatever you want. The point for us is that our machine will be able to tell who the real felon is."

"Do you want us to 'be' Derron Willigan, name and all?" Jake asked.

"No. When our interviewer – who will be a local police chief, by the way – when he asks you your name, we want you to give your real name. That will establish what we believe is an element of truth. Like a benchmark."

"The idea," Allan added, "is that our machine should be able to tell if you're telling the truth or 'lying'."

"We're acting. We're not lying," Randall said.

"We know that," Allan said. "As far as humans know there is a difference between acting and lying, but the software can't tell the difference. Or at least we hope so!" Allan looked at Gus. "I'm not sure that we've thought about that before."

Gus meditated, "Is an accomplished actor the same as an accomplished liar?"

"I'll bet there are books on that subject," Allan said.

"So you want us to try to fool your machine?" Randall asked.

"Or not," Allan replied. "The machine should be able to tell the difference. So if you are more comfortable telling the truth and just telling your own story that would be okay too. The machine should tell the difference. It would be like if you are accused of the crime and you said you weren't even there. Telling the truth or telling a lie: the machine should be able to tell the difference and either include you or eliminate you as a suspect, or in this case as a participant."

Jake Leiker said, "That's pretty freaky."

Gus smiled. "We hope we're that accurate. This is a test remember? It's only part of the machine."

"What do you mean?" Jake asked.

"Oh, we're only testing two of the four technologies that will eventually be integrated into the software. It will be using SA or Statement Analysis, which will analyze what you say – the words you use and their context. And it will be analyzing inaudible acoustic traces in your speech."

"Is it going to hurt?" Randall said seriously.

Gus looked at him. "Hurt? Certainly not physically! Nothing will be touching you. Each one of you will be individually in the room with the moderator who will be working with the machine. There will also be a bunch of observers."

"Wow! Kind of personal performance, right?" Randall asked. "There's a whole new line of acting for us. We can go to people's homes and play whatever role they want – rich uncle, burglar, the guy from Publisher's Clearing House delivering the check! Wow! Great concept."

"So we have an idea of where you guys want to take this," Allan asked, "will you all try to take on Derron's story or will you be telling your own?"

The three actors looked at each other. "I'm going with Derron's," Randall said. "A convicted felon is a good gig."

"I will too," said Guy.

"I don't know," Jake added. "When did this occur?"

"In the spring of 2010," Gus said.

"Jesus. I don't remember what I was doing in the spring of 2010! Where was I? So this was a few years ago?"

"Well, it had to be, didn't it?" Guy asked. "The man was convicted and spent a couple of years in jail, right?"

Gus nodded.

"Can I think about it?" Jake asked.

"Not for long," Gus replied. "It's show time in just seven days!"

"How do you want us to dress? What sort of costume?" Randall asked. He looked at the other two and leaned back in his chair as though he had scored a significant point.

"How would you imagine an ex-convicted felon would dress? As an improv, what would you do for the role of a felon?"

Guy thought about that for a minute and Gus watched his face gradually become another person. When he spoke, his voice was lower and his speech was slower. "As a felon, I've paid my dues to society. I can dress any way I want. I choose to be subtle rather than flamboyant. I choose to be gray rather than orange or purple. I might even wear a tie." His forehead crinkled and his eyebrow went up on this last note as though challenging anyone to refute his right to act as he pleased.

The other two actors watched him create this personage. "That's nuts," Jake said in a higher pitch than he had used before. It was more of a whine. "You get out of jail you don't have any money. You can't buy clothes. You look pathetic. And that's okay because you are pathetic. You're a loser. You've been stupid and you should be punished. How you dress will certainly reflect that."

Randall laughed. "Really?" he said. "Really? You're going to act like a poor, mistreated soul that has been given a bum deal by society? Not me. I'm proud of what I did. Oh, yes. The guy was a jerk and deserved what he got. Society's got a right to punish me, but that's over. That's done. Kaput! C'est tout! That's all. Fini! I don't think a felon looks any different than the rest of us. We're all felons in a way. Most of us never get caught. Ha, ha, ha!" he snorted. "We get away with it and that's the point isn't it? It isn't a crime if we get away with it."

Gus and Allan looked at each other. "That was interesting," Gus said. "This ought to be an interesting test. You guys are good."

+++++

The afternoon before the demonstration Gus received a call from Blythe at Exceptional Talent. "I've got some bad news," she said.

"That's not what I want to hear. The demonstration's tomorrow! I don't need any bad news."

"I know," she replied. "I know. But Randall's in the hospital. He's obviously not going to be able to be there."

"Oh, come on, Blythe! Really? What the hell's wrong with him?"

"Some sort of stomach thing."

"Must be serious if he's in the hospital."

"I guess. I don't know details."

"Well, send us someone else."

"That's the bad news," she said. "I haven't got another talent available for tomorrow. I'm really sorry, Gus. I know this is important for you. Can you do it with just the two?"

Gus thought for a moment. "Shit," he said. "Juggling all this stuff was tough before. This adds an issue that I really didn't need."

"I know," she said. "I know. Wish I could give you better news."

"We'll have to. We'll have to do it with just the two. I have to get on this. Just make sure they're both here."

"Absolutely."

After Gus hung up the phone he tipped back in his chair and stared up at the ceiling. He pictured the old poster that a friend had on his wall in college that said something like: "When you're up to your ass in alligators, it's tough to remember why you drained the swamp." He wondered why he had started down this path. The business plan had a Vision Statement and a Mission Statement and those were nice and motivating – yada, yada, yada. He sat upright in his chair and told himself that he was really full of it.

"Allan," he shouted because he knew Allan was in his office next door. "We have a problem! Remember that fat, jolly actor that was here? One of the improv guys? He's in the damn hospital!"

Allan walked into Gus's office and dropped down into a chair. "Well, let's do it with just the two actors and Derron. Why did we need three in the first place? This will save us some money."

"We're set up for three. Think about it. We have to prove that our system works better, is more accurate than random chance. If we have only two people, we'll have a fifty-fifty chance of getting it right which wouldn't prove anything. If we have three people, we have a probability of one in three with just two to one odds. Still not all that difficult. If we increase it to four people, we have a one in four chance with three to one odds. I mean if we only have three people, we're not going to be proving much. We know one of them is guilty. One of them's the winner!"

They sat in silence for a moment. "So what do we do?" Allan asked.

Gus didn't respond.

"What if one of us does it?" Allan asked.

Gus looked up at him, with his eyebrows going up. "Can't do it," he said. "We know this stuff too well. They'll say we scammed the test."

"Well, how about if someone who doesn't know the system were to do it?"

"Like who?" Gus asked.

"I don't know. We have a lot of people around here who are employees who aren't intimately familiar with how the system works. What about that guy from Gudmudgion's office?"

"Who? Oh, you mean that pasty-faced spy that she has working with Julia?"

"Jesus, Gus. Keep your voice down."

"Close the door. That's a good idea. Does he have to know the story, Derron's story?"

"No. That's the point isn't it? Hey, maybe we could actually get some extra mileage out of this. We have another layer of test here. We have the real felon. We have two actors who could have rehearsed their stories. And we have a guy 'off the street', as they say, who's just speaking his mind! Could be good."

"Think he'll do it?"

"He will if Gudmudgion tells him to."

"Good idea, Allan. I knew there was a reason I kept you around."

Gus called Maria and told her their problem and asked her if they could use Chris Pinel as their fourth subject. Maria said she didn't have any problem with that as long as it helped the demonstration prove the value of the project. She said she'd talk with Chris.

She called back a half hour later and said that he'd agreed to do it. "He isn't happy about it," she said. "He's not the most outgoing person."

"I've noticed that," Gus said. "But that's kind of good for this. Franky will have to pull it out of him."

"Who?"

"Oh, yeah. The guys in the back are calling our project 'Cranky Franky'. You know. After Frankenstein." Gus regretted that slip of the tongue as soon as it left his mouth. When it came to the projects they were funding, money people seemed to lose their sense of humor.

"Your guys think you're building a monster?"

"Affectionately. You know. In-house stuff. The system needs a name and we haven't come up with a better one yet."

"Why 'cranky'?"

"Um. Because it has a mind of its own? Sometimes. I mean we have it under control. But remember it's not finished yet."

"I know that," Gudmudgion replied. "I am well aware of that."

"It's a joke, Maria. It's going to be fine. Really."

Jesus, Gus thought as he hung up the phone. Alligators. Everywhere. Alligators to the right of him. Alligators to the left of him. Into the valley of death rode the six hundred. That's not how it went. Apologies to Lord Tennyson. Gus shrugged and went out to be sure that Arya had a tight leash on Cranky Franky.

+++++

Next morning he was back in his office at six-thirty. The demonstration was scheduled to start at nine-thirty, and he was the first one there. He enjoyed the office space in these early hours. The roads into the industrial area were quiet. There were the occasional garbage trucks, forking up the dumpsters. The food people were opening up the small lunch places, making the coffee, putting out the danishes and donuts. The odds and ends of workers like Gus, getting in early to get ahead of the day.

The Blaytent offices were quiet. There had been a major rush the evening before to get the demonstration room set up. Gus had created a descriptive piece that the staff had printed and arrayed on a table outside the demonstration room. Nametags had been created for all the visitors and the staff who would be attending. Chairs had been arrayed in the demonstration room, computer equipment set up.

Gus passed through the reception area and opened the inner door with his cell phone's *Keypass* app and walked down the hall to his office at the corner of the building. He had lots of windows that looked out on the limited but manicured lawn of the industrial complex, looking across to the next building. As a kid, he had admired those lavish offices in the old movies that looked like ballrooms, with wood paneling and fireplaces with the powerful boss, putting his golf ball across his rug into a cup. But he wasn't trying to reproduce that. His office was comfortable and practical. At a Salvation Army center he had found an old desk that obviously had a history. It was massively heavy, beautiful oak, with hand turned corners, and big surface area that he had managed to cover with papers and files. He struggled to keep the growing stacks at bay, filing what was obvious, but stacking what didn't have an immediate home to get to later. It was easy to get rid of the advertising flyers for printer cartridges, but there were technical papers on the workings of the mind that he wanted to not only read but also file someplace where he could find them again later. So the piles grew. He had bookcases of binders and reference books and technical journals. He had black lateral file cabinets with labeled drawers. There was a sofa and chairs in the sitting area and interview chairs across from the desk. There was a conference table that he was able to keep clear, primarily because it was used frequently.

On the morning of the demonstration he set his coffee and danish down on his desk and set his messenger bag with his laptop in it on the floor, picked up his coffee again and walked over to look out the windows at the front of the building and watch the neighborhood come to life.

His mind darted from image to image as he thought about the day ahead, about the people who worked at Blaytent, about finding the truth, about water boarding and Captain Crum (he would always be a Captain to Gus), about how well the machine would perform, and a million other things related and unrelated. He wondered for a moment if he should try taking Blythe Perry out for dinner. She was certainly attractive enough, but when would they find the time? It would be a distraction. Would all the people he had invited to be there actually show up, particularly Mr. Willigan? Maybe they shouldn't have invited other people to come to this demonstration. Maybe they should just have used it for an in-house test. But it was too late to go back now. The train had left the station.

He walked back out of his office and strolled through the empty hallways and past the empty offices, thinking about all the thinking and talking and interactions that occurred there each day when the place was humming. They had put a good team together – smart people who were passionate about what they did and what they were creating. He turned into the hallway in front of the two test studios and stepped into the one where they would be spending much of the day. It was quiet now but in a couple of hours it would be full of people and vibrating with energy like a classroom of eager students. The chairs and tables had been arranged in rows along the back for the observers, a table and chair for the interviewer (or interrogator) with a small computer monitor and keyboard and the transducer that was pointed at the 'subject's' chair which sat about six feet from the desk and about six feet from the wall which had been covered with a green-screen photographic backdrop. The rest of the walls were a pale, off-white. The ceiling was nine feet up, lower than the sixteen-foot ceiling in the hallways and development areas. There was a large flat screen monitor that was aimed so that the audience could see it but the subject could not. It would display the output or result portion of the interrogator's screen. The room backed up to Arya's electronics laboratory so there were cables running through the wall. There was an array of small video cameras and microphones in the four corners of the room to monitor and record everything that went on. The spotlight that was aimed at the 'subject's' chair could be regulated from moderate to intense. The rest of the room would be in reduced light. There was a smell of clean technology in the room, far different from the smell in the interrogation rooms in Guantanamo that reeked of sweat and fear. For Gus, this room was like an operating room before a major surgery. He wondered how much of a role smell played in interrogation.

He glanced into the second studio, which had a large expanse of glass, some comfortable chairs and was set up as a waiting room. The actors would wait in there and be brought into the demonstration room one at a time. The activities in that room would also be recorded.

He walked back to his office and sipped his coffee and took a bite of the Danish, fired up his desktop computer, and rolled through his email.

Forty-five minutes later Allan appeared in his doorway. There were times when Allan moved like smoke and really freaked Gus out when he would just appear.

"Hey," Allan said.

"Hey," Gus replied. "You ready for this?"

"Sure. Why not?"

"Do you think we made a mistake bringing Gudmudgion and crew in? Maybe we should have done this in-house first."

"Yah. Maybe. But we didn't."

"Thanks. That's reassuring. I'm not convinced that Cranky Franky isn't going to come up with some real winner questions."

"Chief Allen can handle them." They had asked Barnstable Police Chief Allen to be their interviewer.

"I'm sure," Gus replied. "We've just never done anything in front of an audience before."

"They know that. They know this is as much a test as it is a preliminary demonstration. If it's perfect, then why do we need another two years to finish the development?"

"There is certainly logic behind that. I'm just not convinced that investors are always logical. What about Pinel?"

"He wasn't happy about it," Allan replied. "Claims to never have done any acting in his life not even a school play. He said he handled the costumes. That was as close as he got."

"Yeah, but this isn't acting," Gus replied. "He doesn't even have to talk about the crime. He just has to tell the truth. Hopefully the machine will recognize that."

"Let's hope."

"You have doubts it will work?"

"Always."

"Oh, that's good. You're just full of reassurance this morning."

"You asked!" Allan said with a smile.

As the hours crept forward, people arrived and populated their offices, the pace quickened. The two actors arrived an hour before the demonstration. Gus greeted them in the reception area. Guy Marzolla wore a narrow, black and brown tie, beige jacket, a white shirt with a button down collar, and black pants. His hair was slicked back and he had added a pair of black-rimmed glasses that sat on the bulb of his nose. Jake Leiker had chosen to emphasize his skinny frame and looked like he had just been dragged out from under a car, wrinkled, disheveled, and not quite dirty. He kept running his hand back through his hair, making Gus hesitate to shake it.

When Chief Allen arrived, Gus guided him through the building to the demonstration room, and showed him how the system worked and what they needed him to do. "The monitor will prompt you with questions, but you can certainly add your own. It's a little like GPS guidance," Gus said. "If you choose to go a different way, the system will adjust."

"'Recalculating'!" Chief Allen smiled. "Should be interesting. Hope you're serious about this."

"We are, Chief. We definitely are."

Maria Gudmudgion and several other members of her firm arrived. Blaytent staff fussed over them, ushered them temporarily into the conference room, and got them coffee.

Pinel took Gus aside in the hallway. "Look," he said. "I know I agreed to do this, but I don't think I can. I don't know how to act. I don't know what I am supposed to do."

Gus laid his hand reassuringly on Pinel's shoulder. "All you have to do, Chris, is sit in a chair and answer some basic questions like your name, today's date, what you do for a living. That sort of thing. You don't have to make anything up. You don't have to act. I know people are always saying, 'just be yourself'. Well in this case that's all we want. We really appreciate you sitting in. You're going to be fine." Gus thought he looked particularly gray and drawn.

Finally, just minutes before the demonstration was about to begin Derron arrived. Gus mentally checked off one more hurdle crossed. Derron was dressed as he had been when they had first met. Gus guided him to the second demonstration room where the other subjects were waiting, turned and went back into the first demonstration room, which was now lively and buzzing. Altogether there were about a dozen people there. Most of them were friendly. All of them wanted the demonstration to succeed including the investors.

Gus walked to the front of the room by the subject's chair and looked over the people. He thanked them for coming and helping Blaytent with the first live test of their system. Although most of the participants knew about the Blaytent system, he explained that when the system was complete there would be four, integrated technologies, what they called 'the Quadrangulation of truth', but that at this point they were testing the first two – Statement Analysis and Voice Stress. He introduced Julia and Bob as the geniuses behind these approaches, and asked them to describe their creations. And then he introduced Arya as the electronics and programming brain who was putting it all together. Then he introduced them to Chief Allen.

"Chief Allen is an experienced interrogator. Extracting information from a witness or suspect is nothing new to him, but we have asked him to work with our system to interview four participants. Two of them are accomplished improv actors. One of them is a stand-in that some of you might recognize. One of them is a convicted felon, and he will tell you all about what he did. We haven't told any of these men what to say, although we have told them what we are working on and that we want some of them to try to lie. Our technology will prompt Chief Allen with the questions to ask that will drill down to determine if they are telling tales or telling the truth.

"On that monitor," he pointed to the flat screen that was facing the audience and displayed the Blaytent logo, "you will be able to see what the software thinks of the subject's response as well as the likelihood of it being the truth. So let's get started."

There was some nervous shifting of positions as Guy Marzolla walked into the room and took his position in the witness chair. He looked smug, smiling at the audience, adjusting his tie, pulling down his sleeves.

Chief Allen adjusted his own position so that he could clearly see the computer screen as well as the witness. His monitor was adjusted so that the witness couldn't see it. The image on the audience monitor changed to the program's output quadrant with a neutral background.

"Let's get right to this, shall we," the chief said without a preamble. "Is your name Guy Marzolla?"

"Guy," Guy replied. "It's Guy. I'm the guy!"

"Right," replied the chief. "Is today Thursday?" he read off his screen.

"If you say so," Marzolla replied. "I know that because I'm here. Normally, you know, I don't pay much attention to what day it is. I mean, who cares? Right? Days are days. They're here whether you want them to be or not!"

"Let's stick to the questions, shall we?" the chief said gruffly.

"You're right there, Governor!"

Gus worried he was hamming it up a bit too much. Nerves, maybe. Opening scene. All three bars were a pale blue.

"What can you tell us about yourself, Guy?"

"Well, let's see. I'm handsome. I'm smart. I come from a long line of smart people. My father was a judge, you know?"

"How do you make your living?" the chief asked.

"How? Living? Who says I make a living? This and that. I do this and that. Whatever is required, you know."

"Could you be more specific than that?"

"I work for a telephone company."

"What company is that?"

"Um. Vonage. It's called Vonage. You know the one that had the ads."

"And what do you do there, Guy?"

"I sell stuff. I'm a salesman for Vonage, you know?"

"How long have you worked there?"

"Hm. Let me see. Seems like a long time. Couple of years, I guess."

"Could you be more specific than that?"

"Nope. Couldn't be. Days are days as I said before. I don't pay attention."

"Were you working there two years ago?"

"I guess. Seems like a long time."

"Were you working there four years ago?"

"That's a really long time. Where were you four years ago?"

"I'm asking the questions, Guy. Just answer them," the chief said.

"To tell you the truth, I don't remember."

"Do you play golf, Guy?"

Marzolla smiled a thin smile. "Yeah. I play golf. No let me change that. Can I change that? I know you have all this equipment here telling you about me. You want to talk about the 'golf episode'. Yeah, I used to play golf, but you know that already, don't you? I used to play golf until some ass hole got in my face and I had to shut him up, you know?"

"Tell me about that."

"It wasn't my fault. Yeah, I was there. Yeah, I had a club, but it was his fault. He started it. It began when he got pissed off about a parking place, you know? Parking place! So you have to walk a couple more feet. Big deal. You're about to walk around a couple of miles of grass chasing a little ball. What's a couple of feet? Of course people don't walk around golf courses any more. But you'd think he owned the place, you know? Don't get all worked up about it! There were four of us there, me and three buddies. Gotta have a foursome, don't you? I wasn't a big golfer. They just thought it would be a fun day out. Nice way to enjoy the spring weather. That didn't turn out so well, did it?"

"What color shirt was he wearing?"

"Um, blue. Blue with one of those little horsey guys over his left tit. He had a big gut too. Didn't look to me like he was in any shape 'to participate in an athletic event'," he narrated.

"Are you sure of that? What he was wearing? That's pretty specific."

"Yeah, I'm sure. He reminded me of that fat comedian who played in that golfing movie they keep bringing back. Dangerfield, that's him. Rodney Dangerfield."

"He was bigger than you?"

"Fatter! Sure. Lard ass!"

"Did you feel threatened by him? Did he make you mad?"

"Actually, no. No he was just a loud mouth. That's all. No more no less."

"So what happened?"

"To tell you the truth, sir, it's kind of a blur, you know? It happened a long time ago and so much other stuff happened since then, it's kind of a blur. But I'll tell you this, my buddies and I were having a good day on the course, not a good golf day, really because I kept hitting the ball in the woods and in the water, but the weather was nice, the grass was green, and it was pleasant, you know?"

"What were the names of your 'buddies'?"

"They're not my buddies any more, you know? Things have happened."

"What were their names?"

"I don't remember. What difference does it make? People. Friends. Men. You want to know their actual names?"

"Yes."

"All right. All right then. Let's see. There was uh, Huey Mazzeo, Tommy Pilgrim, and I'm trying to think of the other guy . . .. Oh, yeah, Neal. Neal was there."

"Then what happened?" the Chief asked.

"After I hit the guy, he fell down, and that's about all."

Julia, Bob, and Arya had not met any of the participants except Chris Pinel specifically because they wanted to watch how their systems worked at unraveling the lies and truths. They knew that there was a golfing incident involved, but they didn't know who had done it. And as Julia watched her computer monitor, she tried to subtract her own personal biases about the tales Guy was telling from the information Statement Analysis was interpreting. The output was not clear.

There was surprisingly little stress indication in Marzolla's voice and that in itself was unusual. Bob Thatcher wasn't able to tell that he was lying, but just the lack of the stress indicated something. He expected that anyone under stress would exhibit some unusual patterns. This wasn't a true interrogation. It was more like an act on stage for an audience. He needed something to verify his results and be sure that the system was working. He leaned over to Arya and whispered, "Can I prompt it?"

Arya scratched out some instructions on a piece of paper and passed it to him. Bob entered the information into his system.

When the information appeared on the chief's screen, he looked back at Julia, Bob, and Arya as if to ask, "Really?"

They nodded and the chief shrugged and asked, "Tell me, Guy, did you wet your bed at night when you were a teenager?"

For a moment Marzolla didn't respond. He looked at the chief. He looked at the audience. "That's none of your business."

"But would you answer the question please?"

"That's none of your business," Marzolla replied, his voice rising. "That has nothing to do with this situation."

The stress indications were clearly showing on Bob Thatcher's monitor.

"All right, then. We'll take that as a yes. Just a simple question."

"Anything else you want to know about the goddamned golfing incident or are we through here?"

The chief looked at the three scientists who nodded their heads.

"Yes. I think we've heard enough. Just don't leave. We might want to talk to you again," and he smiled.

Marzolla slid out of the room.

Gus stood up and said, "So what we'd like you to do is to put down on the paper that we gave you when you came in whether Mr. Marzolla was generally telling the truth or lying. Imagine that you're a jury."

Derron came in next and Gus indicated the witness chair and the chief began again by asking him his name and what he had been doing for a living four years ago and Derron described the events at the golf course.

"I didn't mean to hurt him," Derron said. "I just wanted to shut the fucking ass-hole up."

"You hit him with your golf club but you didn't mean to hurt him?" the Chief asked.

"That's right. It was just a reaction. Something that happened."

"Which golf club?"

"The goddamned driver. My driver."

"You sure it was your driver? Not your putter?"

Derron looked at him. "Of course I'm sure. Who the fuck would drive with a putter?"

"Then what happened?"

"Well, you know, Eric checked him out. Eric was on my case to leave the guy alone. Worse than a fuckin' mother. Nag, nag, nag."

"Who's Eric," the chief asked.

"The guy that talked me into playing golf! Jesus, if I hadn't listened to him, I wouldn't have been there and my life wouldn't have gotten so fucked up."

"Was it just the two of you?"

"Nah. Phil was there too. Phil. Phil Zhou. I think Eric thought he was some sort of doctor. He got some medical training in the Army or some such. Wanted to be a medic or some fuckin' thing. We were out there. Minding our own business."

"What was the victim's name?"

"Victim?! Victim, my ass! The jerk was no victim. Well, I guess he was. I mean, I hit him and all. What was his name? Petty: Mark fuckin' Petty. I couldn't forget that name or that face. Surprise! I saw the surprise in his eyes when I hit him. I think in the last second he knew it was coming."

Derron's face lit up as he said this. He went on to describe the police coming and taking him away, and started to get into his legal trials.

Julia's computer screen was telling her that the man was telling the truth. The structure of his story was perfectly balanced: twenty-five percent before the incident, fifty percent describing the incident, and twenty-five percent for the aftermath. The details were clear and his reactions quick. His use of swear words underlined the emotion in his statements.

The emotions were also clear to Bob. The Voice Stress patterns indicated true stress, true emotion. Derron had experienced these events. There was no doubt in Bob's mind.

Again, Gus asked the observers to write down their impressions of Derron's story whether it was true or false.

After Derron left, Jake Leiker slouched to the chair, sat down and glared at the audience. He slowly swiveled his head to stare at Chief Allen who glanced up at him, the glow from his computer monitor illuminating his face in a ghostly, pale blue.

Jake ran his hand through his hair. "What do you want to know?" he asked.

"Tell us your name."

"Mark Petty. P-E-T-T-Y. Petty."

There was a slight gasp from the observers, several of whom glanced up from their cell phones to see if Jake was kidding and would smile. These first questions were meant to establish a line of truthfulness that the software could use as a baseline – something to which they could compare other patterns. Obviously Julia and Bob knew that this was a lie, but the software didn't and if Franky considered that answer to be true, then the veracity behind all the following statements would be reversed. They looked at each other and shrugged.

The chief continued, "Is today, Thursday?"

"Yes," Jake replied.

"What do you do for a living, Mr. . . .uh . . . Petty?"

"I'm a plumber."

"Licensed?"

"Sure."

"How long have you been a plumber?"

"About thirteen years."

"Do you work for yourself or do you work for a company?"

"I'm independent. I work for myself. Do it all. Books, parts, jobs, all of it."

"Do you play golf?"

"What?"

"I asked you if you played golf?"

"Nope."

This was one of those points in a person-to-person interview where the interrogator would be scrambling to find the relevance of the witness, but Cranky Franky didn't care. It put together the little information that it had gathered from the past seven questions as well as the vast body of information about people on the Internet and popped up the next question on the chief's screen: "How long have you lived in Newton?"

"What? I don't live in Newton! I live in Dorchester."

"What's your relationship to Julia Petty?"

"I don't know any Julia Petty."

"When was the last time you were in Garland, Texas to visit your parents?"

"What? My parents don't live in Garland, Texas!"

"Were you born in 1973?"

"No. I was born in 1981."

"You're not Mark Petty, are you?"

Jake ran his hand back through his hair and looked around the room before turning back to the chief and admitting, "No. Actually I'm the Green Hornet! You found me out. Curses!"

"Did you know Mark Petty?"

"Mark who?"

"Please tell us your real name," the chief asked.

"Jake. Jake Leiker. L-E-I-K-E-R."

"What's a cable jetter?" the chief read tentatively off his screen.

"A what?"

"What's a cable jetter? It's a plumbing tool."

"I have no clue. This is weird. These questions are weird. I'm actually an actor that they hired to come in here and talk to you. I live in Dorchester and have done for the past seven years. I don't play golf. I just said my name was Mark Petty because I was talking to one of the other actors, and I thought that would be interesting. I'm sorry if I screwed up your lie detector experiment. But I am not a plumber. This is the truth. Maybe I'm not a very good actor, but it's a living, know what I mean?"

"Did you grow up in Kansas?"

"As a matter of fact, I did."

"Did you run a stop sign when you were under the influence and leaving the Worlds of Fun amusement park in Kansas City and subsequently hit a bicycle?"

"I'm not sure what that has to do with any of this. 'Relevance' the lawyers are always saying on TV. I'm not saying I did or I didn't, but if it says so on the Internet, it must be true."

The chief looked up from his computer and Gus got up from his seat. "Thank you, Mr. Leiker," he said. "That was very interesting."

"Weird," said Leiker as he left the room.

Gus looked at the expectant faces in front of him. "So you see," he said after sucking in a deep breath, "it is simple enough for us to tap into that vast electronic information pool during an interrogation to check facts, to open new lines of questioning, to compare the witness's response to criminal records, driving records, marriage records, credit records, anything that is known about a person, and we can do it in real time. And we can verify it with our own technology."

"The questions are a bit awkward," the chief said. "It is certainly not the line of questioning I would have ever used in an interrogation room."

"How so, chief?"

"Well first of all, in a real interrogation there would have been a purpose. We would have been trying to solve a particular crime. Here, we're more or less just talking. There isn't a particular problem to solve. These people are just telling their stories. Who they are, what they do, that sort of thing. So the questions that we ask them are more or less sequential; you say this and that leads to that. These questions are random. Really random!"

"All right. So let's do this. We have one more subject for you. Walk him through the questions as you normally would. We don't really have a crime for you to solve," he laughed. "At least I don't think so. I don't know if he's guilty of anything at all. There is no reason why you can't go 'off script'. Our system is meant as a guide. All of the information that the subject relates will be analyzed in any case. You can take the occasional clue from the system as you wish."

Chris Pinel came into the room and took the witness chair. Maria Gudmudgion's eyebrows went up when she saw him, but she didn't say anything.

"Would you tell us your name, please?" the chief asked.

"Pinel. P-I-N-E-L. Chris Pinel."

"And Mr. Pinel, is today Thursday?"

"Uh, yes."

"What is your occupation?"

"Accountant. I'm a CPA. I work for Avitas Capital."

Chief Allen looked at Gus who nodded in confirmation.

"Do you play golf, Mr. Pinel?"

"What? No."

"Do you know a man called Mark Petty?"

"No."

"How about Huey Mazzeo or Tommy Pilgrim?"

"No."

"How about Derron Willigan?"

"No. Wait. He was one of the people in other room. You talked to him already."

"Did you ever know him before today?"

"I don't know him. Wait. I think I saw his name on some paperwork."

"Paperwork? What sort of paperwork?"

"Well, not really paperwork. On the computer."

"What computer, Mr. Pinel?"

"You know. Blaytent Corporation paperwork, I mean computer."

"Why would you be looking at Blaytent's computers?"

"Because that's what I do. I'm here checking Blaytent's financials. For Avitas. That's what I do. Financials." He smiled at the audience.

"Are you saying that Blaytent paid Mr. Willigan to be here?"

"Well, I can't be sure. But I think that's where I saw his name before."

"Do you have access to all of Blaytent's financial information?"

"Certainly. That's the only way I can do my job."

"And the accounts?"

Bob Thatcher noticed an increase in Voice Stress tremors on his monitor.

"Yes. Certainly. Avitas wants to be able to keep a close eye on things."

Chief Allen looked at Gus, who stood up. "It's okay chief. Everyone here has a stake in how we are doing so you can go ahead and ask."

"How are things?" the chief asked Pinel.

"Fine. I guess."

"Excuse me? You guess? Aren't you supposed to know?"

"Well, I don't really want to say anything negative, but . . . you know. Like living beyond their means. Expenses exceed income."

"I understood that there is no income at this point."

"That's true. I guess that's part of the problem."

"What else?"

Bob wondered what was going on. The tremors were getting dramatic. The questions were moving in on something. He looked over at Julia who shook her head.

"Can you describe the situation a bit more for us?" Chief Allen asked.

"Well, we just seem to be going through funds more quickly than we should be given the situation."

Julia noted Pinel's pronoun transition

"What situation is that, Chris?"

"I know there's a deadline for a product launch. Are we making any progress? Really? I don't know. No one tells me anything. I just look at numbers. Numbers don't lie. All this lying and truth stuff. Is there any substance to it? I don't get paid enough to baby sit. I can't do anything really, can I? I can't help it."

"Can't help what?"

"You can tell, can't you? You can see what's going on. You just get into these things and you can't get out. And maybe you want to walk away, you want to quit but you can't because there are all these strings. And every time you try to get away, you get pulled back in."

"Excuse me? What are you talking about?" the chief was confused. He looked at his computer monitor, and the question popped up in front of him. **"Are you siphoning money**

from Blaytent?" He looked at Gus, and then asked the question.

"What? No! Of course not!"

"Is Blaytent leaking money into your own account? What did you mean when you said, 'I can't help it'?"

"Nothing. It's just a figure of speech."

Chief Allen looked at him, confronting him with the sword of silence. Pinel squirmed in his seat. Looked down at this hands and rubbed them along the top of his legs. His feet slid back under his chair, locking his ankles around the front legs. Finally his head came up and looked at the chief in defiance. "Do you have a question? I thought that was what this was all about."

"All right. Let me put this to you bluntly, Mr. Pinel: Are you stealing money from Blaytent?"

"No! No, I am not *stealing* money from Blaytent. I'm not." He looked up at Maria. "I'm borrowing money. It's more like borrowing. I'm going to put it back!"

Maria was out of her chair. "I think that's enough for now! I've heard all I need."

Gus wasn't sure what had happened. It seemed like the system worked pretty well, but was it the machine or just the presence of the machine? He knew that sometimes interrogators could get confessions when there was just the presence of an all-knowing entity. Police had been known to use radios or other basic electronic devices to convince suspects that they couldn't lie. He thought to himself, "If it works it works. Does it matter *how* it works?" But that was a cheap rationalization.

+++++

They had to break the episode down and so after the visitors had left, and they had released the 'suspects', Gus, Allan, Julia, Bob, and Arya got together to evaluate what they had learned.

"Well," Gus began, "what did you think?"

"That first guy . . . what was his name?" Bob Thatcher asked.

"Marzolla. Guy Marzolla."

"Yeah, him. He wasn't showing any voice stress at all! There was nothing in his voice that would have indicated that he was lying. That's why I requested that out of sequence question."

"About wetting the bed?"

"Yeah. That did get a rise from him. Obviously."

"But there were red flags all over his statements," Julia added. "He used words like 'about', 'began', and 'so' which are storytelling words. He had three friends . . . three is a liar's number . . . but of course they played in a foursome, which is typical in golf."

"What was the audience's judgment?" Allan asked.

Gus thumbed through the handwritten pages produced by the participants and then looked up. "They were pretty neutral. Some thought he was telling the truth. Most of them weren't sure. I wonder if we should have had a larger audience?"

"So an actor could fool Franky at this point. Right?" Arya said.

"What about Derron?" Gus asked.

"He was the real felon, right?" Julia asked. "His swearing underlined his emotions, giving them some truth. He didn't hesitate with the names of his friends the way Marzolla did. Just listening to him, you knew it was a real story."

"But did the machine know? I mean it's great that you could tell. I think we all could tell that he was telling the real story, but could the software? That's the real point. We need to be able to tell with certainty that we are not just guessing about the truth. That's the point."

"It was also clear in the Voice Stress," Bob added. "Yeah. It was clear. He was stressed."

"Sure he was stressed," Julia said, "but how do we separate the stress of sitting in an interrogation room in front of a bunch of strange people from talking about an actual violent episode that put you in jail?"

"That's one of the reasons we put Pinel up there," Gus said. "We wanted to get a baseline for ordinary stage stress."

"That worked out strangely," Allan commented.

"Before we get to Chris, let's go back to Jake Leiker," Julia said. "What was that all about? I'm not even sure what I'm going to find with his answers!"

"Again," Gus said, "the way he tripped over everything and started off with that blatant lie about his own name, I think everyone knew he was lying. But the interesting thing was the way you had the machine connected to the Internet, Arya. Wow. It's like a fifth technology! We're going to have to get Boyd to check out the legal issues of being connected to all those sources of information and when and where we can reveal them."

Arya said, "It's not really fast enough for real time. Yet. Remember 'Watson', that computer they put on the TV show, *Jeopardy*? It answered questions faster than the brains who had won all that money before."

"We'll have to smooth out that connection, but why not use it? There may be legal issues, but we'll let Boyd look into that. It's another layer. It's not down to the detail of asking about feelings, but it can certainly tell us if someone is lying about publicly reported activities."

"Not yet," Arya smiled. "But there are a lot of feelings out there on the social networks. People don't hide anything. 'I just took a great shit! It felt so good!' Stuff like that. 'I just asked Betty-Lou to marry me! I'm so happy!' That's how people relate now. They log on and reveal what's on their minds. A lot of it is bullshit but you can certainly tap into how they are feeling!"

"Isn't that stuff supposed to be private?" Allan asked.

"Some of it is more difficult to get to than others. But it's amazing that people somehow seem to think that it's all private and don't pay much attention to what is private and what is public. How many people read the instructions on how to put up the security barriers?"

"It's like the world has become a small town where everyone knows everything about you," Allan said.

"So what about our friend, Pinel?" Gus asked.

Julia replied, "I didn't see that coming. I probably should have. I worked with him enough. But I trusted him. I mean he works for the people who give us money! Why would he be taking it?"

"Because it was there," Allan answered.

"I don't know how he did it. It certainly wasn't obvious. The two of us looked at those numbers constantly."

"We don't even know how much he siphoned off, do we?" Gus said. "Practically, that's going to be an interesting issue to get straightened out. But on the positive side, our exercise revealed a truth that we might not have come across otherwise."

"The guy was unstable," Bob said. "I knew that from the first time I saw him. He was definitely unstable."

"What does that mean for our money situation?" Allan asked.

"I don't know," Gus replied. "I'll have to work that out with Maria. But she must be impressed with how things worked out. I'll have to put together a report. I mean from our conversation here, the results from the audience, and the events of the morning, I can't say that our technology positively revealed the truth in any of the statements from the participants. Marzolla was generally lying. Willigan was generally telling the truth. Who knows what Leiker was trying to do although he was generally lying? And then there was Chris Pinel! I'm not sure we're ahead of the coin toss results yet! We'll have to see what happens next."

Chapter Eight

December 11, 2013

Maria was not impressed. Gus was surprised by her reaction. He supposed that there was an inherent anger at her own inability to discern the machinations of her own employee. It left her on shaky ground. If she couldn't trust the people who worked for her to provide a true economic picture of the companies she invested in, whom could she trust? And so she blamed that on Gus and Blaytent.

On top of that, she seemed to feel that they had not gotten beyond the Ouija Board technology. Lights and graphics were all very interesting and probably something that could be promoted as a toy, but hardly a clear and scientific revelation of the truth! The project was interesting, certainly, but she was no longer certain that it was worth the millions of dollars invested in it.

Pinel's confession, Gudmudgion seem to feel, was merely the pressure of the venue and the threatening nature of the technology. He must have been convinced that they could see inside his brain to his most personal thoughts. There was no place for him to hide. That sort of intimidation might work for some people, but it wasn't proof of any advancement in technology that would have a high probability of working a high percentage of the time.

Gus tried to reassure her. He observed that this had been an initial trial run in front of an audience. He emphasized the fact that they had only been using two of their technologies.

He agreed that it had not been the clearest of results, but assured her that it would get better. He also asked her to step back and realize that they had never promised to deliver the 'absolute' truth because there was no such thing. He reminded her that truth was not an object like an apple.

"That's what scares me," Maria said. "I need to know that what you produce is reliable. That it will reliably reveal reality. I suppose that charlatans do make money from phony technology, but that's not what Avitas Capital is all about. "

"Neither are we," Gus replied.

That left Gus hanging in another moment of uncertainty, but he sucked in his breath and moved forward. One of the really interesting things about life is the way the past can sometimes just pop back into the present. Years before, it was a chance encounter that caused Gus's parents to invite an exchange student into their home for a year. That invitation led Gus to learn and appreciate another culture and another language. That knowledge and those skills led to his experiences at Guantanamo. And that experience led him to start Blaytent. Finally, weaving the thread back into the pattern that made up the colorful tapestry of his life, Cyrene Al-Masri walked back into this life. And she took his breath away.

She just appeared. She didn't call first. She just appeared at his office on the Monday before Thanksgiving. The receptionist let Gus know that there was someone who had asked to meet with him.

"Who is it?" he asked, annoyed at being interrupted.

"She wouldn't say. She says she's an old friend."

Gus thought for a moment, flipping through the Rolodex® in his mind of 'old friends', sighed and made his way out to the reception area. Just for a moment he didn't recognize her. His brain fluttered to put her into context. So familiar. So very familiar. Older, yes, but just as beautiful as he remembered her, and he was momentarily rendered speechless. Allan would have pointed out that a true, zygomatic smile had plastered itself across his face.

"Cyrene!" he mumbled. "Where? How?"

Cyrene's return smile was equally genuine. "Gus! I wanted to surprise you!"

"Oh, my god. You did! And you did," he said, regaining
his balance, moving forward, and hugging her. For a moment
it felt like coming home. No questions. No doubts, just a
genuine surge of emotion. And then a flood of thoughts
flowed through his head in an uncontrolled Tsunami of issues.
He stepped back.

"Come back to my office. Do you have time? How did
you find me? What are you doing here?"

She laughed in that light, musical way that had always indicated that she enjoyed his enthusiasm.

"I do have time," she said. "I came to see you. Do you
have time for me?

He paused, processing her presence, and blurted out, "Certainly! It's just wonderful to see you!"

She walked beside him down the hallway to his office and
he was acutely aware of how her body moved, that she was
only slightly shorter than he was, the swish and smell of her
luminous black hair, and the familiar scent of her perfume.

"Wow," he said. "I'm babbling."

She took his hand, and he felt a ripple go up his spine, the
smoothness and softness of her skin, and the remarkable
length of her fingers.

"Can I get you anything? Coffee, tea, water?"

She waved him off. "No, nothing," she said. "Sit," she
ordered. And so they sat, across from each other.

"How are you?" she asked.

"Fine," he replied. "I'm fine. Older. But seeing you
makes it seem like just yesterday."

"Don't be silly," she said. "It's been years. Almost fourteen years. We're much older. I'm much older."

"But you look great!"

She smiled. "Tell me what you've been doing."

And so they talked like the best of old friends, talked as
they had on the porch of the Sainte's Cape Cod house in the
dark, talked as they had on beach in the warmth of the spring,
talked as they had nudging next to each other in the cold of
the bleachers at a high school football game when he tried to
explain American football to her, and she would laugh at the
'crazy Americans'!

The passage of fourteen years was a long time. They had exchanged a few letters. It seemed extraordinary now, but Facebook hadn't even started until five years after Cyrene had left the U.S. Communication depended on writing letters and waiting for replies and long distance contact broke down as he moved around and she moved around and they had lost touch.

She told him that she had lived in England for a while.

"Oh, that's right! You were going to go to Cambridge."

"I did. And made it through. Things were certainly not peaceful at home. They're still not!"

"No," he replied. "Although we don't get a lot of news about places that we are not at war with. Are you married?"

"No," she said, looking down at her hands. "I was. He was a professor, but a fierce believer in politics, and he couldn't stand by in England while what you call the 'Arab Spring' was raging. He was killed. By a bomb, a roadside bomb."

"That's terrible, Cyrene."

She smiled for his sympathy. "And you?" she asked. "I didn't see anything about wife and children in your profile."

"You were looking at me on-line? And you never contacted me?"

"How do you think I found you?"

"No. No wife. No children. No time."

"Aw," she sympathized. "Poor boy. Doesn't have time for girls!"

She controlled him with a word. He wanted to prove himself to her. Impress her. He was thirty-one years old! He owned a multi-million dollar company. And yet . . . and yet she could reduce him to feeling like an embarrassed small boy with a phrase, a handful of words, and a small, sympathetic smile. He both hated and loved that she had that sort of power over him. He wanted to rush off and solve all the problems in the Middle East or fire somebody or win the Nobel Prize. Something, anything to impress her. All this roared through him in a moment. She smiled, and it was over.

They talked about families. She asked after his parents and his sister. "Does your mother still work at Hospice?"

He told her she did. He didn't know how she could watch people dying day after day, year after year; watching their families dealing with the loss.

"My sister . . . Julia . . .?"

"I remember," she said.

". . . is married. Two years ago, I guess. I'm an uncle!"

"Congratulations!"

"She's teaching. Still in Falmouth. Hasn't been able to get out."

"Not such a bad place," Cyrene replied. "You got out, as you say. But no girl friend?"

"No. Nothing lasting. I guess I just got swept along. People used to try to set me up, but . . ." he shrugged. "I think they may have given up."

"And now?" she asked.

He looked at her, not knowing what she was asking and not knowing how to ask her. He always thought that she could look into the back of his mind, could see what he was thinking before he knew himself. It was as if she could tell the future, knew what would happen next, knew what he would say before he said it. He imagined what her husband must have been like. He must have had a close-cropped beard, impeccably dressed, powerful build, with fire in his eyes, and a soul that blazed with justice and integrity.

"Now?" he asked. "Now . . . I have Blaytent. Do you know what we do?" He wanted to ask her why she was here. This couldn't have been just a coincidence. But he didn't ask. She would tell him when she was ready.

"Tell me," she said.

He told her that they were fundamentally trying to find ways of revealing the truth without pain or torture. "For example," he said, "if we knew that a crime suspect was telling the truth, we wouldn't put innocent people in jail. It would be so much simpler. You could ask them if they did it and they would simply tell you! And you would know it was the truth."

"How could you be so sure?"

"Well . . . that's what we're working on."

"Do you always want to know the truth? Aren't there times when it is better not to know?"

"What do you mean?"

"What about privacy?"

"It's a new tool. The interesting thing about new tools is that we can see things and do things and ask questions that we never could see, do, or ask before. We don't even know what those questions are. We don't know what they will reveal."

She smiled.

"What?" he asked. "What are you thinking?"

"I'm thinking that it is great to see you again."

"Why?" he asked. "No, I don't mean why 'is it great to see me again'. I mean why did you . . .. I mean why are you here? Why didn't you call me? It's great to see you again too. I'm just curious. What are you doing now?"

"I'm an engineer, a computer engineer."

"Really?"

"You're surprised? You don't think I can be an engineer? Girls shouldn't be engineers?"

"No! No! I think women can be anything they want. I thought you were into the classics . . . language and literature. I thought you would be a teacher or a professor."

"I like those things. I do. You were a good student. Your Arabic served you well?"

He told her about his experiences in Guantanamo.

"Terrible," she said looking down. "But necessary? To stop more bloodshed? These demons must be controlled!"

"I don't know. I guess some of the information helped to stop other terrorist acts. I'm not sure we couldn't have uncovered the same information in a different way."

"The classics are important, certainly," she said, "but they are a luxury."

"'Those who ignore the past, as they say, are condemned to repeat it.'"

"I think we repeat it anyway."

He looked at her, still wondering. "But you still haven't told me why you're here."

"Do I have to have a reason? Can't old friends just get together and visit? You know, Gus, I think you need to do things that may not be perfectly focused on what you are doing. It might give you a different perspective."

He gave up. It was clear she wasn't going to provide a more detailed explanation. "Are you going to be around for a while, or will you just disappear again like a rainbow?"

"No. Actually, I'm working here for now."

"That's great," he said. "Can we have dinner? Where are you working?"

She smiled her enigmatic, shy smile. "I'd love to have dinner with you."

They arranged to meet at a small, local Italian restaurant. "I'll meet you there," she said, leaving Gus feeling like the bus from the past had just hit him, a million unanswered questions rushing through his mind. She was even better looking than he remembered her, as though she was maturing like a fine wine. He hadn't seen her in more than a decade! She sweeps in, bang! And leaves with a promise to meet later. What was he supposed to do while he waited? It was as though his entire momentum of moving forward had been stopped and had to be restarted. He hadn't even vaguely realized that he had such strong feelings for her. How was it that people could unbalance his life that way? How was it that with some people he could be 'the boss', with others 'the colleague', and with others, even at this late date in his life, he felt like 'the child'? With Cyrene, he didn't know what role he was meant to play.

He tried to recover what he had been doing before she had arrived, and he was surprised to find that she had only been in his office for forty minutes. This feeling of childishness and disorientation and lack of control was not part of his character, and he wondered how she had accomplished that. It crossed his mind to wonder what he might discover if he could get her on the machine.

He got to the restaurant early, to be sure that he didn't miss her, got a table facing the door, and waited for her, looking at his watch with an unnecessary frequency. Waiting again. Seemed like that was what life was all about. Waiting for other people. The restaurant was steadily busy with business customers, entertaining clients. Locals dropped in and greeted the staff as old friends. The atmosphere was warm and welcoming. The wooden floors creaked as the staff scurried between the tables, taking orders, carrying menus, delivering food and drinks. Italian music painted the air. Candles and flowers in small vases decorated the red tablecloth covered tables.

Finally she arrived. He saw her talking to the maître d' at the door, looking around the room, seeing him, smiling and gliding toward him, swinging her hips as she navigated the obstacles of patrons and tables. She had changed into a scoop necked 'little black dress'. The rich dark colors in her long hair glowed in the subdued lighting, her hoop earrings popping in and out of sight. And she was smiling.

He jumped up from the table and guided her into a seat.

"Such a gentleman," she said.

They ordered wine. They ordered food. They chatted about the year they had spent together in school. They laughed about the time she had spilled her clam chowder on him when she turned quickly in the cafeteria. His fault, she claimed, for startling her. It was hard for him to think of her as a gawky girl in a grey, high school sweatshirt. Was she ever that person?

"What about your family?" he asked. "You never talk much about them."

"They're well," she replied. "Mum's getting fat at home. Gossiping with her friends, hoping for grandchildren as mothers do."

'Grandchildren?' he thought.

"My father is busy as usual. The politics of the world keep him that way. It is not peaceful there. It seems like people are always squabbling over one thing or another. But maybe that's true everywhere."

"What does your father do?"

"Oil," she said, "and other things."

They drank their wine. They ate their soup. They laughed. Two old friends revisiting old times, exploring memories that may never have even happened. Neither of them were the people they talked about. Not any more. He remembered when they had first met. His family had driven

up from the Cape to a hotel not far from where they now sat.
Other families were there to pick up their exchange students.
His mother and father were up front. Gus and his sister, Julia,
hung back, not quite sure of how they felt about another family member interrupting their lives.

When Cyrene had walked into the room, Gus could only
see her dark eyes, shadowed by the *hijab* she wore over her
head. "This is going to be fun," he thought sarcastically. He
was just entering his junior year in High School and that was
no time to be saddled with some foreign girl that didn't know
her ass from a hole in the ground. It was going to be like
wearing a party hat all the time and having other kids point
out how stupid you were. High school was a war zone. What
would the girls think? They would get the wrong impression
about his relationship with this bimbo. She would cramp his
style. She would dress funny, talk funny, and have all the
wrong ideas about music and movies and know nothing about
American culture. It was going to be miserable; another
dandy idea starring mom and dad.

In the family van during the hour-long ride back to the
Cape, Gus, Julia and Cyrene sat in the back seat with Julia in
the middle. Gus stared out the window, studying the scenery.
Gus's mother tried to generate a conversation: "How was your
trip? Was your family sad to see you go? What's it like in
Kuwait now? Have things settled back down since the war?"

Cyrene was being grilled, Gus thought. 'Let her be,' he
thought. 'Let her breathe.' Periodically he snuck glances
over at her to see how she was taking it, but he couldn't see
much of her face. Julia sat quietly in the middle, hands folded
in her lap, staring straight ahead, with a smile plastered on her
face. Gus could tell she wanted to plug the earphones from
her MP3 player into her ears and just tune out of the conversation. But she restrained herself.

They had fixed up the guest room in the house for her, to
give her a private space. She had space for her clothes and
books, a desk for homework and a comfortable chair to retreat
to.

She had gradually lowered the *hijab* and Gus was capti-
vated. She was exotic. He decided that her voice was like

clear water in a stream – joyous, subtle, and powerful. She was smart. She was clever, and she talked about things he had never thought about before. He had never known a girl as a friend before. It was an odd relationship: she wasn't really . . . a girl. She was sort of another sister. Sort of . . . he didn't know what else, and life was already confusing. But over the course of the year, Cyrene had become more Americanized.

Sitting in the restaurant in Waltham now, they laughed as they remembered the warm fall day that a group of girls standing around outside the High School began abusing Cyrene as a 'towel head' while she was waiting to be picked up, looking at each other, giggling, egging each other on. One of the girls took off her scarf and swept it around her own head in a poor imitation of a turban, bringing it down over her eyes like a blindfold. She fumbled around her group, hands groping out in front of her, making babbling noises in a twaddle of nonsense.

Cyrene stepped over to the girl, grabbed her by the shoulders, and whipped her around until they were face to face. She spun the scarf off the girl's head, and said, "Here. Let me help you." With a few deft flicks of her hands she swept the scarf into an expert turban.

But almost before she was finished, the girl had stepped back, away from her, simultaneously brushing the scarf off her head. "My uncle died for you!" the girl yelled at her. "My uncle died in that filthy country, in the desert, and for what? So you could come over here and take up space in our school and eat our food and . . . and . . . you shouldn't be here!"

"I'm sorry to hear about your uncle," Cyrene replied quietly.

Gus walked up behind her, just hearing the end of the confrontation.

"My brother died in that war too," Cyrene said.

"Yeah? Well, so what?" the other girl said. "He was just another filthy towel head. You people should stay there and get your own lives straightened out." She looked at her friends for confirmation. "Why do we have to do your dirty work for you? Why? You're just a bunch of greasy, greedy butchers. All of you!"

"Back off, Chelsea," Gus said, guiding Cyrene away from the group.

"It just sucks!" the girl said. "You stink. Get out of my face!" And she turned on her heel and stormed away with her friends in tow.

"Until that point, I never knew you had a brother," Gus said as they sipped their wine, over the remnants of their desert.

"I didn't," Cyrene replied.

"What? You made that up?"

"Sure. She deserved it. What ever happened to her anyway?"

"Not sure. I'd have to check a more reliable source. I think she's working at a sandwich place in Falmouth."

Gus looked at her and gently shook his head. "You're amazing."

"How so?" she asked smiling.

"I don't know. You're just amazing; so much hatred. So much anger and you just walk through it like it's not even there. Doesn't it get to you?"

She reached across the table and took his hand. "Sure I feel the anger. People can be intensely stupid on both sides. But life's too short, Gus. You have to grab for the good as it gets close to you." He felt her foot touch his under the table. Allan had told him that feet were the most reliable parts of the body, that they told the most honest tales and that communication often indicated the most honest touching between people. And the electricity moving up his leg was pretty honest, and he realized that he should stop listening to the voices of the colleagues and technologies in his head and make the moves on this extraordinarily attractive woman who was sitting at the table with him and looking through his eyes into the back of his head!

He took a sip of his wine, set down the glass, and asked, "Where are you staying?"

"Yes," was her only reply, and he took her back to her hotel.

Chapter Nine

February 2014

It was big news, but when he read it, Gus had no concept that Blaytent would be involved in the man's interrogation. "AL-QAEDA LEADER CAPTURED IN DARING RAID!" An FBI raid in Jamaica Plain, a Boston suburb, secured the capture of Mustapha Kadah, a suspected terrorist in a plot to bomb several electrical generation systems in Canada, which would have cut the power to numerous east coast U.S. cities.

In early February Gus received a phone call from the FBI requesting his presence at a field office. When Gus arrived at the office, he was quickly ushered into a small conference room that smelled of sweat and blazed with harsh lighting. It brought back uncomfortable memories.

"We hear you are developing a device that can assist in revealing the truth of a suspect's statements."

"Really?" Gus asked.

"We'd like you to assist us."

"I'm afraid you've been misled," Gus replied warily. "May I ask who told you this?"

"We're not at liberty to say. Will you do it?"

"I'm sorry. Do what?"

"Don't play dumb with us, Mr. Sainte. We are well aware of what Blaytent is working on. We have an urgent need for your assistance. There is little time."

"Sir," Gus had forgotten the agent's name, "what my company is working on is proprietary. It is also under development and incomplete. Even if I could help you I couldn't."

The agent looked at him. The man had the blank face of a fish and the nose of a fox. He was losing his hair, and he had fat fingers that he wove into his crossed arms. "That's too bad," he said. "That's just too bad."

He leaned back in his chair and closed his mouth tightly. "We know you were a soldier. We know you were in the military police. We know you interrogated prisoners before, and we know you didn't like it much."

"Not much news there," Gus replied.

"We heard, unofficially, that you visited IIDT in Arkansas and that Major Crum was your commanding officer when you were in the Army."

"Lucky me."

"So it's too bad."

"Why is that, sir?"

"Well we could use their technology instead. We've heard, again unofficially, that you admired their technology and that you went there under what might be called false pretenses while you were developing your own company."

Gus had learned a lot about non-verbal communications and micro expressions and many other generally uncontrollable body 'tells' so he did his best to keep his countenance neutral. But his nose itched, and he was forced to scratch it and reposition his glasses.

"There was no false pretense," he said.

"Ah," the agent replied. "And what would you call it then?"

"Research. That's what I told them and that was the truth. The Barnstable Sheriff's office was considering purchasing their equipment."

"And did they?"

"Well, no. I advised them against it."

"Why? Because you thought you could get them to buy your own?"

"Really! What is this all about?"

"Look," the agent said, "it's simple. We need to get information. His name is Mustapha Kadah. We know you speak Arabic. We know you know a lot about truth technology, and we need to get this information fast or we may all be working in the dark for a long time."

"You're scaring me," Gus said. "You're being reasonable."

The agent didn't reply.

"How much time do I have to set this up?"

"We can give you two days."

"Two days? Shit!"

"Well if you don't have the technology, two days or two weeks or two months shouldn't make a difference!"

"I want to bring in someone else to assist in the translating."

"We'll have our own translator. Who is this person?"

"Someone I have known for almost fifteen years."

"Oh, sure. Ms Al-Masri."

"How . . . ?"

The agent smiled. "She's very attractive, isn't she, Mr. Sainte?"

Gus was stunned, but he kept it to himself. There didn't seem to be anything that these people didn't know. He would have to try to be more careful.

He agreed to have the prisoner brought to the Blaytent offices in two days, and then he scrambled back to the office to alert his team. This would be an opportunity for them to explore the readiness of Arya's micro-expressions component. Statement analysis would be difficult because of the language issue. Julia hadn't yet gotten translation details down.

Bob said, "I haven't got a clue how VSA will work with Arabic. We haven't tried it. There are a lot of facets of that language that are not in English."

"I know, Bob," Gus replied.

"I'm just saying, I don't know if it will work."

"It will be a good test then, won't it?"

Arya was more sanguine. "We have moved ahead of the *eigenfaces* and *fisherfaces* approaches, combining them with an *Active Appearance Model* to allow us to perform the analysis in different lights and different projections of the face since we can use an *eigenface* decomposition after we warp the image."

"What?" Gus asked.

"We've talked about this before," Arya said.

"I guess I forgot."

"*Eigenfaces* are a set of standardized face ingredients. If we put these ingredients together we can come up with virtually any human face. We are not working from digital pictures but just mathematical values. The Active Appearance Model allows us to get accurate facial recognition by mathematically warping the image to visualize it in different positions and different light. This is pretty standard stuff."

"Ah," Gus said.

"On top of that we have a mathematical library of micro-expressions. People can make more than seven thousand expressions with the forty-four muscles in their faces. Micro-expressions can happen in one twenty-fifth of a second. Just a flicker."

"Uh, huh."

"So the key is to be able to almost instantly capture that micro-expression and connect it to the response to the question that was just asked."

"And how is Franky handling this? By the way, as we bring this concept to reality, it deserves a better name. We're giving it life!"

"True enough. But I'd say it's handling things pretty well."

"Pretty well? Pretty? How close are we, Arya? Is this going to be a disaster?"

"No. I don't think so. Once in a while . . ." Arya shrugged, "he does something strange."

"How so 'strange'?"

"Well, there are still the odd responses." Arya shrugged again.

Gus was getting a bit frustrated. "Arya, the machine doesn't put on party hats and dance around, right? It is passive. It responds in the ways you have programmed it to respond. It may be smarter than the average human, but it is still a machine. Isn't it?"

"It's laughed."

"What? Laughed?"

"It has, actually. Laughed. Not acoustically. It doesn't start making 'Ho, ho, ho' sounds. We haven't provided it with a voice. But it probably would if it could. It prints 'Ha, ha, ha' on the feedback screen!"

"How the hell does it know how to do that? Someone must have told it how to do that. It can't have a sense of humor. Can it?"

"It seems to assemble the facial expressions that it is reading and then respond with an approximation of the subject's feelings."

"That's just plain creepy!" Gus said. "So it is reading the micro-expressions and then responding in a suitable, emotional way."

"Well, not always suitable. It depends on what you mean by 'suitable'."

"Oh, Christ! This should be interesting. Will the interrogator see any of this? This is going to be a really serious interrogation, Arya. This is a vicious guy they're bringing in. It wouldn't be good if the computer starts laughing!"

"We'll try to filter the output."

"That sort of output would be very confusing. One other thing, the interrogation will be in Arabic, I'm assuming that it is only programmed to ask English questions? Although I probably shouldn't assume anything at this point!"

"Yes. English only. We should be able to get to questions in other languages, but then we will have to get Julia's assistance to frame the linguistic structures so that we have the idiom right. Even in British English a simple things like 'pants' or 'rubbers' in the U.S. are different than 'pants' or 'rubbers' in the U.K. so it should get interesting."

"Later. Let's not start that now. We'll let the human translators handle that stuff."

+++++

Gus called Maria to let her know about this incident. She wasn't surprised. "I was approached by Judge Jakes. She knows about Blaytent. We had talked before, you know before the Derron Willigan, the golfer . . . thing."

"This is confidential, right?" Gus asked.

"Absolutely," Gudmudgion replied. "The government doesn't want it to be known that it uses experimental techniques . . .. I know you're going to say they're benign. The government doesn't want anyone to know prisoners are being experimented on."

"So how does this benefit us?"

"I thought you'd welcome the opportunity, Gus. After that last fiasco, maybe you can prove this idea. Time is running out here."

"And how is this going to be off the radar? This guy, this alleged terrorist, has been big news in the press ever since they grabbed him. How are we supposed to keep this little event to ourselves?"

"The in-house logistics are going to be up to you. The FBI is going to have to handle moving him and the rest."

"Wonderful," Gus replied.

After hanging up, Gus leaned back in his chair and stared out at the sky and wondered once again what he had gotten himself into. It seemed like every path he walked down, every corner he turned, the problems got more complex. It was also remarkable to him how good people are at naturally 'reading' other people. All of the signals that people send about what they are thinking, how they are feeling, what they really mean are there to be read. People are good at sending conflicting signals, conflicting messages with their words and their expressions and the tones of their voices. Which one is the real one? Gus supposed that was why actors were able to portray completely different people than who they really are. "Look me in the eyes and tell me that you love me!" That was the sort of test that people used to reveal the 'truth'.

Was it the same in different languages and different cultures? The military had assumed that the fear of imminent death would work on anyone; the carrot of the cessation of pain would work on anyone. Was that because certain feelings and experiences were universal? And what about the imminent death or suffering of another person like a loved one? Did interrogation have to focus on the baser, common feelings?

He wondered if there was a scale. On the one hand there was heaven or paradise or Nirvana. On the other hand there was hell. We are somewhere in between. Did someone need to be pushed toward those extremes in order to reveal the truth? Was there some sort of magic inflection point, the French *faisandee*, the point that Somerset Maugham referred to as "The Razor's Edge", the balance point, what Goldilocks referred to as "Just right!"? Maybe Goldilocks would be a better name for the device than 'Cranky Franky'!

He told himself to focus. When you're on the roller coaster, it is not the time for second-guessing whether it was a good idea or not. He had to pull together the staff and emphasize the confidential nature of what was going to be happening. He debated if he should tell them all or limit the news. Security would be tight, and there was certainly an inherent level of risk for all of them. There were those who felt that those associated or hinted to be associated with Al-Qaeda did not deserve to be alive, and if the U.S. Justice department wouldn't do the job, they would just have to take care of it personally.

And there was the problem of the press. No one wanted the building to be overrun with reporters and TV trucks and cameras. "Film at Eleven!" They didn't have prepared statements. They didn't want to discuss the work they were doing. It wasn't ready for prime time.

He assigned Julia the task of handling the press and preparing a brief statement if it came down to that. "What am I supposed to say?" she asked. "How much can I tell them?"

"As little as possible," he replied. "Our job is primarily to get the system to work and get as much information from Kadah as we can. Beyond that the government is going to have to deal with the logistics."

"Are we going to get paid for this or are we just doing our civic duty?" Allan asked.

"We'll let Boyd work that out. If this works, it means a lot. It means that we have the system working in multiple cultures and languages. It will demonstrate some of Arya's micro-expression input – one more component. So let's get it right."

"It's going to be like a war zone," Bob said. "This place is going to be overrun with cops and agents and guns. I think this is a bad idea!"

"Bad idea or not," Gus replied patiently, "we haven't got a choice here. It's going to happen so let's make the best of it."

"What have we got for security? I think we should let the local police know what's going to be happening just in case," Bob advised. "Maybe they could do an extra drive-by or send a squad car or something."

"We're going to start this very early in the morning. The FBI will bring Kadah here at four AM so he gets here in the dark. We'll bring him in through the back into Room Two. We have to be here and ready to go at three."

"Three AM!" Arya said. "Wow. There goes my beauty sleep. Are we going to have any observers?"

"Not that I know of. They want to keep this as quiet as possible."

"What kind of results are they looking for?" Julia asked.

Gus paused and sighed. "I don't know. I don't know if they know. That's one of the issues of interrogation of terrorists, and why I think that some of the violent approaches don't work. They want to know if there are any imminent plots. They want to know whom the suspect knows. They want to know what they don't know. It's like that line from Donald Rumsfeld, 'There are known knowns and there are known unknowns, but there are also unknown unknowns, the ones we don't know we don't know. It is the latter category that tends to be the difficult ones.' I'm misquoting him but you get the essence."

"Could you repeat that?" Allan asked.

"No," Gus replied. "Oh, and Cyrene will be here to help interpret for us."

The crew gave each other a quick round of smirks.

"The FBI seems to know who she is. I don't know how, but they had no objection when I said I want her here to interpret for us. They'll be bringing their own interpreter . . . maybe more than one, of course. But I want to make sure that we know what the guy is saying. AND I want to know how his answers are being interpreted both by the humans and by the machine whatever we're calling it now."

"This is getting serious," Allan said with a smile.

"She's an old friend," Gus replied.

"Yup. Sure. We believe you," Allan said.

"Three AM!" Arya said again.

"Yah. Three AM. Wide-awake and ready to rock. You still have a day to get things squared away and set up. Make the most of it."

+++++

Two AM that Thursday morning found Gus in his office trying to shake the cobwebs out of his head. He hadn't been able to sleep even though he had put himself to bed early after a quiet evening trying to relax. He had to trust his team. He had to trust their development. He had to believe that the machine wouldn't start laughing or asking about the 'buttons on the porch' or some other weird thing. There were just too many variables! Even though they were struggling to remove the people element from the interrogation process, emotions and interpretations and pre-conceived notions swirled throughout the process. It was somewhat like asking the machine for the meaning of life. The answer was likely to come back, 'It depends', and they were trying to define all the dependencies!

Gus's head was full of 'what if's'. Not the least of which were his own 'what if's' like what if he'd stayed in Falmouth and built houses with his father? What if he had just started practicing psychology? He probably could have had a nice quiet practice on the Cape. Maybe he could have gone to work in one of the schools. Other people had lives like that. Why did he have to wrestle this monster?

It was when he moved on to the 'why' questions that he got up from his desk and started pacing around the office, and pacing the hallways, he found that Arya had stayed around all night. He was in his lab with his face focused on his computer screen. "Have you been here all night?" Gus asked him.

"Why not?" Arya replied. "You didn't happen to bring donuts, did you?"

Gus shook his head.

"The good thing about machines is that they don't need food and they don't need sleep. They're equally crazy any time of the day or night."

"That's not reassuring," Gus said.

Arya shrugged. "True though."

"So how are we going to do this thing?" Gus asked.

"You tell me. You're the shrink."

"We put Kadah in the chair and the interrogator at the desk with the computer. Lights are bright, right? Not like the sort of serene scene that we did before. We'll bring the room temperature up. The interrogator asks a question. As the machine hears that it is also looking for the micro-expressions and analyzing the voice stress. It puts that information together and indicates to the interrogator if the question exerted unusual stress on the subject. Right?"

"Right."

"The problem is . . . I mean the first problem is that if it is exerting stress on the subject, we don't know why. Right?"

"Right."

"It's a bit like that old game of 'Huckle, Buckle, Beanstalk."

"Right. What?"

"Huckle, Buckle, Beanstalk. Didn't you ever play that when you were a kid? Someone hides something and everyone else runs around trying to find it, and as they get closer, the person that hid it starts saying 'warmer, warmer, warmer' or 'colder, colder' until they find it."

"Didn't know that game had a name."

"But it's like that. The machine is reading the clues given by the subject as the interrogator gets closer and closer to the truth or whatever. So as the computer recognizes that the subject is getting nervous, the interrogator keeps refining their questions to get to the source of the anxiety. Right?"

"Of course that still leaves us with the interrogator in the middle," Arya said.

"I know. But in this case it is definitely a language thing. But if we can lead the questions to useful answers, I think we will have definitely succeeded on this round. Can you brief the interrogator on what the computer is telling him?"

"I'll have to show him how to interpret the graph. It's too late to program in your huckly, buckly thing."

Gus smiled. "The graph will be fine."

+++++

The sun doesn't rise until about a quarter to seven on February thirteenth in Boston so it was hard to think about this as being 'day time'. It was pitch black outside when the first of the FBI team showed up and banged on the front door at three fifteen. He flashed his badge at Allan who let him in. The agent told Allan that he had to sweep the building before they brought the prisoner over. Allan gave him the guided tour.

Julia arrived looking rumpled and sleepy, but she brightened up quickly and following Arya guidance, adjusted the chairs and monitors in Room 2.

More agents showed up and posted themselves by the front and side doors. "We'll bring him in through the back," the first agent said.

Cyrene showed up at just after three thirty and the agent at the front door waved her off without opening the door. She attempted to identify herself through the glass, but he wasn't interested or feigned not being able to understand her. So she stepped back from the door and called Gus's cell phone.

"She's part of the process," Gus told the agent who reluctantly let her in. Although his expressions were pretty dead pan, it was still clear that he was not fond of the idea of having anyone who might be in any way related to the subject in thought or race or religion in the same building. Even without saying a word, the agent was clearly profiling Cyrene.

She flashed a brief smile at him as she preceded Gus into the back of the building.

"What do they know about this man?" she asked Gus as they walked. "They haven't told me much. Just 'need to know' stuff."

"Have they said where he is from? That would be useful in interpreting his dialect."

"Nope. I'm sure they know a lot more about him than they are willing to share. I can't tell if they think this whole process is a good idea or not. I think they might have been forced into bringing him here."

Cyrene stopped and turned to Gus. "Who would do that?"

Gus shrugged.

"Have they told you what they want to know?" she asked.

"No, but I imagine it's the usual stuff, you know, who does he know? What are they doing? When were they planning on doing it? That sort of thing. They were apparently planning on crippling the electrical systems on the east coast."

Cyrene looked at him, waiting for further information. She had a creepy sort of way of doing that, watching his face, seemingly reading his mind. They had spent a fair amount of time together since that first night in December. They were both busy although he still wasn't sure what she was working on. But he enjoyed her attention.

The agent in charge met them near the entrance to Room 2. He introduced them to a pale man in black-rimmed glasses that the agent said would be the translator and interrogator. Gus thought he fit the part well. One of those people that you would pass on the street and not even see, but if you did see them, he would raise the hair on the back of your neck for some reason that you don't even understand, one of those pre-historic feelings that alert you to beware.

"Has Arya shown you the system?" Gus asked.

"Yes," the man replied. "I have my own technique though."

"I'm sure," Gus said, "but the reason we're doing this here is to determine if our equipment can assist in the process."

"I'm aware of that." The man paused looking at Cyrene. "I am well aware of that. I have been briefed."

"This is Cyrene Al-Masri," Gus introduced her. "She will also be interpreting what is said."

"Why?" the man asked.

Gus hesitated. "Why? Not because we have any doubts that you will understand or do this right. No. No, we just need to know the relationship between what is said and how our system is functioning."

The man continued looking at Cyrene.

"Where is the subject from?" Cyrene asked.

The agent-in-charge said, "He said he was born in Egypt. He's been living in the Boston area for a while. We've been watching him for about a year. So he probably knows more English than he is willing to reveal. We haven't gotten a great deal from him and we're running out of time. They want him in the court system. No pressure. People will die if you don't get anything from him. But do what you can."

The man stood back looking smug. It was obvious to Gus that he didn't want to be there. He reminded Gus of Crum's attitude toward the violent and sadistic nature of "enhanced interrogation techniques". He was sure that this agent just wanted to put Kadah on a rack and extract information from him between his screams of agony.

But, no, maybe he wasn't that way at all. Maybe he was a nice guy with a tough job that had to be done to protect his nation and its people. They would see.

"What do you want to know?" Gus asked.

"Kadah was implicated in a plot to disrupt the electrical supplies on the East Coast of the U.S. We want to get the names of all the people he was working with so that we can be sure that we have disrupted it and that it won't reappear. We want to know how he was planning on doing it, when he was planning on doing it, and obviously, where."

"Obviously," Gus replied. Cyrene looked at him. "How much of this have you been able to figure out so far?"

"Some," the agent replied. "But even if he repeats himself, it will help to confirm what we know."

"It would be helpful to secure more information if we can start with things that he has revealed already," Gus said.

"Trying to make it easy on yourself? Let's just go at this from a clean slate and see what happens, shall we?"

"Great," Gus replied sarcastically. "An enigma inside an enigma."

There were two basic types of information that the interrogation could reveal. One was if what was known so far was the truth. For that it would have been extremely helpful to know what was actually already known! The other was revealing new information derived from information already known. Gus's initial concept for Blaytent was the former –

revealing the truth. Uncovering the unknown was a side benefit.

By four AM agents manned all the building entrances. On a signal the back door was opened and two agents came in with Kadah between them, a black bag over his head. One of those weird and wonderful random thoughts flashed through Gus's head about where they had gotten the bag. Was there a spy store where you could buy things like that or had it come through a government contract, purchased for hundreds of dollars? Or had one of the agents sewn it at night in his hotel room after he had darned his socks?

Kadah was shackled and shuffled awkwardly down the hallway between the two agents, turning left toward the inter-rogation rooms, and left again into Room 2. They removed the black bag and one of the agents stuffed it into his back pocket.

Gus was struck again by how normal the man looked. His expression was a mixture of defiance and fear. His brown eyes were sunken under his fierce, black eyebrows. His skin was a light brown, and he had a well-trimmed line of a beard that ran from his ear to his chin to his other ear. He was al-most six feet tall, with a thin, muscular build. His mouth was tightly clenched in either anger or pain. Gus couldn't tell which.

The agents guided him to his seat. His eyes darted around the room, like a hawk.

The agent who was to serve as the interrogator was sitting at Blaytent's computer monitor. Gus and Cyrene sat behind him, and Arya, Allan, Bob, and Julia sat at a table behind them, each with his or her own monitor.

And the interrogation began. The interrogator fired off a handful of basic questions, and Kadah didn't respond, looking down at his hands. Allan made some notes of his body posi-tions, but because his hands and feet were shackled, he couldn't tell much. Allan leaned forward and asked Gus to ask if the man could be unshackled.

Gus passed the request along to the agent-in-charge who wasn't happy with the concept. "Look," Gus said, "if you want us to get everything we can from this process we need to take advantage of everything. If the man is uncomfortable, he won't relax. He won't let his guard down. We'll miss a large part of his communication. It's just another barrier. Of course if you guys don't think you have this situation under control, that's another story."

So they released him. Kadah rubbed his wrists, but didn't change his position in his chair. His feet were planted squarely on the floor.

The interrogator asked the same questions again.

Julia had integrated a translator into the system. It wasn't perfect, but it gave them a reasonable sense of what was being said. It was like removing the violins from a symphony. The tune was there, but it was harder to detect.

Some dialog began to flow. It started as a small monotone. No emotion.

Bob watched the voice patterns on his monitor. The language was different but the indications of stress were there.

Julia was distracted at first by the quality of the computerized translator. A simple question like "Where are you from?" became "Where are you?" A question like, "Do you know the muffin man", however, was still, "Do you know the muffin man?" The inconsistencies of the translations made tracking changes in tense or pronouns next to impossible.

Allan was noting the way Kadah moved his feet, the way he rubbed his hands on his thighs, the way he crossed his arms, the way he stroked his chin. The actual words may not have been clear but Allan believed that the body language was universal. Some cultures were much more demonstrative with their hands, but their feet sent clearer, less societal messages.

Even without the words, Kadah's micro-expressions were declarative. Portrait painters throughout history had struggled to capture the expressions and the emotions of their subjects. Perhaps more than anything, freezing the looks of power or love in the face of a model revealed whom the portrait portrayed. People look at an image and say, "Oh, that's really got him, doesn't it?"

Arya's computer screen zeroed in on Kadah's face, watching the perspiration on his skin, the pulse in his neck, the flickering of his eyebrows, and his *orbicularis oculi* muscles around his eyes, pulsing quick flashes of emotion that he couldn't control. Arya had programmed the machine to categorize these flickers of expression in general ways as pleasure, pain, anger, frustration, hatred, or fear. Fear led him to send an indication to the interrogator's computer monitor that he should pursue the questioning along that line, guiding him to further depths.

The interrogator started with simple questions, generating a rhythm in the words, increasing in complexity – who are you, where are you, when are you, why are you. Are you married? Were you ever married? Do you have children? How old are they? Do you love them? Do you love Allah? Have you been on a Hajj? What is the frequency of U.S. power? What is the transmission voltage? What is telemetry? What is the Eastern Interconnection? Where is the ISO Northeast Campus?

These questions led to related connections – where are your children, where is your wife, when were you on your Hajj? How is the power frequency controlled? Why is the U.S. frequency different than the European frequency? How can you measure it? What would happen if it changed?

Arya signaled the interrogator to pursue that line of questioning. Kadah had said he didn't know.

Bob noticed the tone of exasperation at the end of the phrase. Just the sound of the words would only have told him that the man was tired. It was the voice stress explosion on the screen that told him there was something more to it.

The interrogator asked Kadah what he expected to accomplish by altering the electrical frequency, who was going to assist him, how he was going to accomplish it, when they were going to do it, why were they going to do it? Why did he hate Americans?

They could all tell that Kadah was getting agitated. Gus sent a message to the interrogator to slow down the pace of questioning. The interrogator looked back at him, shrugged, and asked Kadah, "Where is the money coming from?" He waited for an answer that came in the form of a shrug and a shuffling of his feet.

"What day is it?"

Kadah responded by asking which calendar – Gregorian or Islamic? Did he belong to Al-Qaida? Kadah laughed. Arya's computer screen said, "Ha, ha, ha." Pursue that. Why is that funny? What is funny about Al-Qaida? Kadah responded that it was a Western club concept, deriving from the need to categorize things, put them into neat little boxes and tie them up with ribbons. Or put them on sports teams, winners and losers. The interrogator asked him if he liked sports. Kadah laughed again. Arya's computer screen said, "Ha, ha, ha." The interrogator asked Kadah if this was a game to him? Kadah responded that this was life. Allah be praised. The interrogator asked him if he liked the Red Sox? Kadah looked puzzled. This was not an expected question. "Yes," he replied in English and smiled. "Big Papi!" Arya's computer screen said, "Ha, ha, ha."

The interrogator asked him if he had been to a Red Sox game, did he like Fenway Park, where the Red Sox played? Kadah replied that it was the temple of evil, the center of Satanic revelation . . . except for Big Papi.

The interrogator asked why he liked Big Papi, David Ortiz? Had he seen him play? Would he like to see him play again?

Kadah answered that he would never see him play again.

Arya's computer screen said, "Ha, ha, ha." Arya thought there might be a mistake, that the system might have misinterpreted Kadah's expression.

The interrogator forged on knowing that Kadah would be in jail and would certainly never be in Fenway Park in the spring to see Ortiz or anyone else play.

Kadah crossed his arms and leaned back.

The interrogator pursued the questions of where and who and where the money came from, but Kadah didn't elaborate.

In the interrogation room there were a lot of computers with lots of lightning fast microprocessors that made a myriad of connections to data and concepts and histories. There were a lot of extremely intelligent minds that were doing the same. All of that information was moving at the speed of thought. The results of all of that brainpower were based on preconceived notions of what the results of the interrogation should be and because of that, they almost missed the result that they were hoping for.

Arya was distracted about why his computer would interpret Kadah's expression in response to seeing David Ortiz as being funny. Maybe it was something else. And then he thought about the opening of the baseball season. What would be more disruptive, a greater terror causing, US symbolic event than opening day for the World Champion Boston Red Sox? What would be result of a major explosion in the ballpark and the power shutting down in the Northeast, paralyzing emergency vehicles, blacking out the news? Another emergency tied to sports in Boston.

Arya did a quick Internet search to find out when opening day at Fenway would be in April. He sent a message to the interrogator, "Ask him about April 4th." He sent another message to Gus, "Opening day at Fenway!"

"What's happening on April 4th . . . on the Gregorian calendar?" the interrogator asked.

Allan saw Kadah's pulse rate increase as he locked his feet behind the front legs of his chair.

Arya watched Kadah's face droop slightly, his eyes twitching down.

Kadah responded noncommittally. He shrugged and looked up at the interrogator. Don't know. Nothing. Don't know what you mean.

"You know exactly what he means!" Cyrene fired off in Arabic.

The interrogator spun around to face her. Gus laid a restraining hand on her arm. They were all stunned by her outburst.

Arya recognized the complexity of pulling off such an event. Was Kadah really the mastermind? This would definitely not be a one-man show . . . if it were what Kadah was working on.

"Are you planning to set off an explosion at Fenway Park? On opening day?" the interrogator asked.

Arya's system was not laughing any more.

Cyrene jumped up and stood in front of Kadah, glaring down at him. Agents moved toward her. "Tell us who else is involved! Tell us where you meet! Who is doing the planning? Surely it is not you. You are too stupid for that!"

Before anyone could stop him, Kadah leapt up out of his chair and grabbed Cyrene by the throat. Gus knocked over chairs getting to them. He slammed the edge of his hand down on Kadah's arms breaking his hold on Cyrene who staggered back. Two agents grabbed Kadah from either side and forced him to the floor.

Gus pulled Cyrene out of the room. "What the hell?" Gus hissed. "Why did you do that?"

"Sorry!" she said. "He was pissing me off! The man is an idiot and a dog!"

"But that was no reason to confront him like that! That was foolish! He was wound up! Do you know him?"

"What is 'Opening Day' anyway?"

Gus was breathing heavily and trying to be sure everything was back in order. "Baseball. Opening day of the baseball season at Fenway Park."

The agent-in-charge burst out of the room. He was a couple of inches shorter than Gus, so he had to look up at him. "What . . . was . . . that?"

"She lost her temper," Gus said.

"Has she got some personal beef with the guy?"

"No, of course not. She's just emotional, that's all."

"I'm sorry," Cyrene said. "The man is an idiot!"

The agent glared at her. "You interfered with the interrogation! Is that how you work here?"

"Of course not," Gus replied. "We got information! We connected Kadah to the Red Sox."

"Yah! Great! We're going to have to find another way to confirm this because she stopped it! Why? We're going to have to talk to her. Is she a U.S. Citizen? She was out of line!"

"I'll talk to her," Gus said, trying to calm things down.

The agent glared at Cyrene, turned away and then stepped back in front of Gus. "Why? You have to ask why, don't you? We were getting close to something and she forced it to stop, didn't she? And you have to ask why."

"Don't make more of it than an emotional outburst," Gus insisted. "She's been through a lot. She's emotional. That's all. You're blowing this out of proportion."

Agents escorted Kadah out of Room 2 with his black hood over his head. Gus and the agent-in-charge watched in silence. When they had disappeared down the hallway, the agent said, "You haven't heard the end of this," and turned away.

Gus went back into the room. Cyrene was sitting in a chair next to the wall, looking at her hands. The interrogator was packing up his notes. The other agents had left.

"Make sure they're all out of here," Gus said to Allan who headed out of the room. "Let's go to my office," Gus said to Cyrene.

He closed the door when they got there.

"I'm sorry," she said as she took a seat in front of his desk.

He fired up his computer.

"I don't know what happened. He just pissed me off."

"You said that already," Gus replied, looking up at her.

"Well, it's true. You care about truth."

"Kadah is a very dangerous man."

"Pfsfht!" Cyrene hissed.

"What did he say that set you off? I wasn't getting all of it."

"He's just a fool. He should have known that he wouldn't get away with what he was trying to do! He should go back to whatever hole he crawled out of!"

"But that's the point, Cyrene. We don't really know what he was trying to do because we didn't get a chance to finish it. You stopped it."

"Pfsfht!" Cyrene spat again. "I didn't stop anything."

"You did. The system had revealed something that was obviously making Kadah anxious. If we could have continued,, we could have drilled down farther, maybe uncovering the people he was working with or where the money was coming from or some of the rest of the network. But you stopped it, and you know that doesn't look good to those agents. They said they would have to talk to you further. Maybe me. It may have put our whole project in jeopardy."

"They could have kept going! That was a minor interruption. Confrontation is what these people understand. Just when things got tough . . . .."

"'These people'? Who are 'these people', Cyrene?"

"Scum. Dogs. Fanatics. People like Kadah who have no connection with reality! All they understand is violence and confrontation not a namby-pamby, hand-holding 'conversation'!"

Gus looked at her. She had been a vision in the back of his mind for years. That vision had come back to life when she had walked into his office. It had grown into what he had thought was a strong relationship, a reality over the past couple of months. Now he wondered if he had been blinded by the past and hadn't really seen her at all.

It was clear that she recognized that she had gone too far. "I'm sorry, Gus," she said, coming around to his side of the desk to lay a hand on his shoulder. "I didn't mean that. I know this is important to you. They just make me angry. They are so stupid. They are making so much of life miserable for so many people."

He stood up and stepped away from her. "I'm not sure that you understand what we are trying to do. I'm just not sure who you are or what you are thinking or even why you are here. It doesn't matter how you feel. It doesn't. What matters is that we know what people like Kadah are thinking so that we can stop them from killing other people. Of course it is stupid. It's pointless. To us it's pointless. To them . . . who knows? They think it is everything. Maybe it's Allah. Maybe it's God. Maybe it's Money. Maybe it's Power. Who knows? It doesn't matter! It doesn't matter what we think. We have to know what <u>they</u> think. So we can stop them. And we have to stop them."

Cyrene looked down at Gus's desk.

"It is emotion. It is passion. It is hatred and fear and greed that have caused these conflicts and innocent people get caught in the middle just trying to live their lives. And they blow off legs and arms and destroy whole families well beyond the direct victims. We have to stop them."

"I know," Cyrene said. "And I'm sorry. I should have controlled myself."

"I'm going to have to see if I can limit the damage," Gus said and left her standing in his office.

+++++

Later that day he was talking with Arya about the session, when the front desk buzzed him and said there was a man here to see him. "Who is he?" Gus asked.

"He won't say, but he says he has papers here for you to sign."

Gus reluctantly walked up to the reception area and saw a messenger with a pack slung across his back, and he knew that it was definitely not Santa Claus!

The messenger asked, "Augustus Sainte?"

"That's me," Gus replied.

The messenger handed him a small clipboard and some papers and said, "Sign here, please."

Gus's eyes opened wider as he accepted the package, turned and walked back into the heart of the building. He walked as he opened the pages, and stopped as he scanned the titles. IIDT was threatening to sue them for patent infringement.

June 2014

The path to a goal is rarely straight. It was hardly in Gus's mind that he would be making a device that would be suitable for use at home, an add-on to a video game console so that people could play an electronic version of "Truth or Dare"! Gus wanted to make the world a better place. Blaytent's investors wanted him to make money. At board meetings, Gus had insisted that the two goals were not incompatible, but the board wanted him to explore that possibility. "Why not?" they asked. "You're already using the Kinect device. You could tap into a vast market. How hard could it be?" It might not be that difficult, but it was distracting and time consuming. Gus asked Julia to look into it.

She was reasonably satisfied with the English version of the Statement Analysis work, and she was confident that she would be able to more or less 'plug and play' other languages and other syntax into the system, but not without help from other language experts. There would always be the issue of timing because the Blaytent system did not afford the luxury of a completed statement, but was performing the analysis on the fly in real time.

Chris Pinel hadn't been seen since his confession. Ms Gudmudgion was relying on Julia to provide reports on Blaytent's economics that were still all flowing out with nothing flowing in. Julia could clearly see the bottom of their economic 'well' now. The thought of actually producing a marketable device struck her as being a great idea. She wasn't clear on how they would produce it or promote it, but that was someone else's problem. She turned her thoughts toward how to package the technology that they were developing into something anyone could use. Much of that had to do with providing user-friendly interpretations of all the graphs and other scientific squiggles that Cranky Franky produced. And they would have to come up with a better marketing name for the product. The fact that the artificial intelligence (although she was nervous about calling it artificial for fear of offending what she thought of as the creature behind the curtain) . . . actually found some things funny and would randomly put words together, intrigued her.

Back in her apartment, there was certainly more talk about work than either Julia or Boyd would have liked. Boyd was spending a significant amount of time trying to unravel where IIDT was coming from in their threatened suit. Since he had to bill Blaytent for his time and Julia had to review those costs, it added another gnarl to their relationship. But they couldn't talk about that.

One evening in early June after they had finished another simple but tasty and filling meal that Julia had concocted and they were sitting back sipping a nice Chianti, Boyd asked how the consumer version project was going.

"Fine," Julia responded.

"What's the thought on how you're going to bring it to market? It's almost too late for the Christmas products."

"Christmas? Jesus. It's only June!"

"That's the way the markets work. People wouldn't be shopping for the thing now, but it would have to be in the retail pipeline."

"People may be looking at Christmas stuff now. Seems to get earlier and earlier every year. They start telling you about Lay-Away!"

"Is Gus looking to team up with Microsoft to package it?"

"I haven't got a clue," Julia replied.

"How far along is it?"

"My stuff?"

"Yeah."

"My stuff is progressing. I've got to get some time with Arya to get it programmed."

"Are you making it a game, or what?" Boyd took a sip of his wine while he studied her face. He wondered what she was thinking about him. They had occasionally had brief conversations about where their relationship was going. But both of them seemed to be enjoying the status quo, but he knew that he was not always good at interpreting what women were thinking. Maybe this thing that Julia was working on would be useful. Maybe it would reveal what women really wanted! He told himself not to go there.

"I'm exploring a number of ways to use it. It's electronic so it's not like Chutes and Ladders. There isn't a beginning or an ending point. Well, I suppose there is, but they are not clearly defined. Maybe it's more democratic, you know. Like there is no winner or loser."

"Well that goes along pretty well with Truth or Dare, right?" Boyd asked. "I mean there really isn't a winner per se in that game either."

"The trick is making it fun," Julia replied. "If it's just going to determine if someone is telling the truth, that may not be exactly fun or even funny. It could get nasty."

"I guess. It certainly could get personal. So you have to have rules that limit how revealing the questions can be. I'm sure you could work that in. Can the software interpret what people are actually saying?"

"That's what I do, Boyd. I have it instantly interpret the meaning and structure of what people are saying."

"Whoa! That's freaky!"

"You knew that. I told you that. Don't you listen?" She got up from the table and started clearing the dishes off.

"Of course I do," he said, coming up behind her and putting his arms around her. "Every word. Sometimes I just don't remember."

"Bull shit," she replied. "Maybe I'll bring it home and we can see where the truth really lies!"

"Uhmm."

"We have to test it. We could do that."

Boyd was not convinced that would be a good idea. Maybe this wouldn't be the best product to get out on the retail market. "What kind of truth would it . . . reveal?"

"Truth *truth*," she replied, moving the rinsed dishes from the sink to the dishwasher.

He sat back down and poured himself a bit more wine. "I mean lawyers and truth . . . you know. Remember that movie with Dustin Hoffman, 'Liar, liar'?"

"That wasn't Dustin Hoffman. That was Jim Carrey."

"Oh, yeah. Right. Well, you remember how hard it was for him to tell the truth? The results weren't pretty, as I recall. And what about that line from that other movie . . . about not handling the truth?"

"That was Jack Nicholson in 'A Few Good Men'," she added.

"Well he meant it, didn't he? I mean if you start revealing the stuff you'd rather not reveal that could . . . ." He stopped. It was clear that he had worked himself into a place that he probably shouldn't have gone. She was looking at him while leaning on the edge of the sink. "What?" he asked innocently. It was one of those looks that can wilt a victim in a heartbeat.

"Is there something that you would like to tell me?" she asked with just a touch of lemon on her tone.

"What? No. I was just saying, you know, in general terms. Now don't make this personal. This was a general conversation. We were discussing the thing you guys are working on, and I was just saying that in some cases, not ours of course, it could reveal awkward stuff. It could."

"Ah," she said, still looking at him.

"I mean people never say everything that they're thinking, right? I mean if a woman asks a man something like, 'Does this make me look fat?', the man would be a fool to answer, 'Yes' even if it <u>was</u> the truth." Oh, my God, Boyd thought. I have done it now!

"Is there something you'd like to tell me, Boyd?" Her expression had frothed up like a latte that had gone rancid. "Are you calling me fat?"

On the one hand Boyd was terrified about what might happen next. He had no clue how he could find his way out of this conundrum. On the other hand he could see that there was likely to be a great deal of new legal business if Blaytent's product got out to the general public! But first he had to survive this conversation and second he had to figure out some way to not get the product home, into this particular home anyway. There was absolutely no way on the face of the earth or the span of time that he wanted to mess with something that could reveal everything that he was thinking in real time with no filter and no rules in a prototype condition. But at the moment he was sitting at the table, his face as white as a sheet and his mouth open like a cod at a fish market.

Maybe if he took the offensive. "Stop it!" he commanded. It didn't look like that was quite the right approach.

"I'm serious, Boyd. Do you think I'm fat?"

This was one of those times when he wished that he could rewind the tape, take time back to a spot where he could have chosen a better path. Maybe not talking about the truth at all? "Of course not," he said. "I love you just the way you are."

"That's not what I asked," she replied.

Lawyers are taught never to ask questions that they don't know the answer to before they ask it. "That's an unfair question," he said.

"Oh? Why is it unfair? It's a simple question. Yes or no?"

"No," he replied and held his breath.

Julia knew that she was probably taking things farther than she should have taken them. She knew that if she pushed too much further that it might result in unnecessarily serious consequences, but it was all that she could do not to ask him to explain his single word answer. She could feel her temperature rising. She took a deep breath and turned back to the sink.

Boyd took a large gulp of his wine and scrambled for a way to change the subject. "How can you interpret language in real time?"

She didn't answer him for what seemed like an infinite amount of time. Finally she replied, "People do."

"Yah, but it's people. We're supposed to be able to do that."

"Franky has all the inputs, at least virtually all the inputs that people have while not being clouded by emotion." She looked at him.

"How much of what people say to each other is based on emotion do you think?" he asked. "You can't exactly program emotion into your machine, can you?"

"It's hard to know what people are thinking, Boyd," she said, sitting down and picking up her wine glass. "How much of the truth is just emotion?"

"I suppose that's why people are so bad at communicating with email and text messages. The emotion is pretty much removed. You can't tell what they're thinking. That's why people use those little smiley face things. What do they call them? Emoticons?"

"Sometimes I wonder if people are going to forget how to talk," Julia replied.

He got up and poured some more wine in her glass. "I'm sorry," he said.

"For what?" she asked.

"Don't start," he replied.

+++++

The International Institute to Discern Truth (IIDT) was claiming that Gus had come to Arkansas to their offices with the specific purpose of stealing their interrogation technology. They demanded that Blaytent cease and desist everything they were doing.

Like two battleships lobbing shells at each other, that was IIDT's opening salvo. Boyd responded to IIDT's lawyers that that was not the case at all. That Mr. Sainte had visited the IIDT offices for legitimate purposes and what Blaytent was doing was far more comprehensive than anything IIDT had ever even considered, and that IIDT's patent was extremely limited and barely covered the paper it was printed on.

IIDT shot back with the fact that their technology was partly supported by the Defense Advanced Research Projects Administration (DARPA) and that Blaytent should check out that connection before they made any further moves. Blaytent should consider its position carefully.

Boyd responded that that was very nice for IIDT, and they were lucky to have that backing, but that DARPA supported numerous research projects and that a multitude of companies had made advances in voice stress technologies. IIDT replied that they had an obligation to defend their patent and they would do so to the fullest extent possible.

All of this, of course, was written in the finest legalese, using language that could be debated and argued for years if there was money in the budget for legal fees. Gus was well aware that this dance could tie them up endlessly. If he hadn't been aware of that, it was made clear to him by Maria Gudmudgion who wanted to know the meaning of all this and how it would impact the launch of Blaytent's product line. He reminded her that he had indeed visited the IIDT offices as a legitimate representative of the Barnstable Police Department to review the IIDT equipment and their F.A.T.E. technology.

She added that Blaytent's connection to the government through their FBI episode had not gone all that smoothly.

Gus pointed out that it had been successful to the point where they had determined the date of a planned attack and the Red Sox had had an uneventful opening day except that their playing had not been up to World Champion caliber since then, as he tried to add a bit of humor into the situation.

Gudmudgion was not amused, however. "Time is running out. This sort of distraction can be harmful if the investors get nervous. Make it go away."

That, of course, was much easier said than done. It occurred to Gus that there was at least a remote chance that he could get IIDT to back off if he could convince Major Crum that he was barking up the wrong tree. After all, Crum was the connection to DARPA, or he had been several years ago. Gus asked Boyd to dig through the paperwork and see if there was some sort of contact information for Major Hernando Crum.

"If there is," Boyd advised, "I don't know if it is the best idea for you two to discuss this case."

"We need to end this," Gus said. "I need to find out who's pushing whom to stir up all these problems. Maybe Crum

has an ownership interest. I can't believe that the government
wants us asking for confidential documents."

"And you certainly don't want to turn over all the research
you guys have been doing."

"Jesus, no!" Gus replied

"Is this Major Crum friendly?"

"Not exactly. He was my C.O. in Gitmo."

"Oh, yeah. I think you told me about him. He was a hard
ass and a bit unbalanced, as I think you described him."

"Maybe he's mellowed," Gus replied hopefully.

"Well, they haven't actually filed the suit yet," Boyd said.
"So maybe they just want to shake your resolve."

"We need to find out what they really want then. Is there a
legal way to do that or should I try Crum?"

Boyd said, "Let me see if I can get some contact information for you and if there is anything else we can turn up on the
Major and IIDT. It would be good to know where their funding is coming from. We need to know what we're dealing
with."

+++++

It was June and the city hadn't started heating up yet. Students from the multitude of colleges and universities
throughout the city were leaving their apartments and heading
home. The weather was, in fact, quite beautiful, warm enough
to leave the coat behind. It was the sort of weather that stuck
its tongue out at you when you were trapped inside the same
building in the same climate all year 'round and went, "Nyah,
nyah, nyah. You should be out here. You really should. You
shouldn't be behind that desk in that funky old artificially
controlled environment. It's a beautiful day. It really is.
You're wasting your time. You won't get many more of
these. Nyah, nyah, nyah!" But of course, Gus couldn't get
out there and enjoy the day. The clock was winding down on
his deadline with Avitas Capital to prove that the system
worked. There was less than a year left. And they'd had to
slow down after the inroads that Pinel had made on their resources. And then there was this pending lawsuit with IIDT.

So the beautiful, late spring weather would have to wait.
The time wasn't right for him to take Cyrene out to lie on the

new mown grass on a hillside somewhere and define the white, fluffy clouds that floated by overhead. The bucolic side of life would just have to wait.

This mournful reverie was disturbed by a call from Blythe Perry from Extraordinary Talent asking if Gus would be interested in some TV exposure. After the usual introductory pleasantries Gus asked, "What's going on?"

"These morning shows are always looking for good local stories and I thought of you and your lie detector," she said with a laugh.

Gus snorted. "It's not really a lie detector."

"Well your truth teller or whatever it is. Would you be interested in showing it off?"

"It's not really ready for prime time," Gus replied.

"Oh, this isn't prime time," Blythe laughed again. "We're talking about a morning show. You know, that time of day when people turn on their TVs while they're getting ready to go to work and the anchors are all laughing and chatting and hummy-chummy with each other."

"I never watch TV in the morning," Gus said.

"Well, let me tell you. It's there. Every day! They could even get one of the anchors to answer some questions. Is it photogenic? I mean are there graphics that people can see or is it just a black box or your basic computer monitor? Oh, and is it portable? I mean they could come to your building, but it would be much better if you could come to the studio."

"We've been asked to develop a consumer packaged version."

"Perfect!" Blythe gushed. "That's perfect!"

Gus was not at all sure about that. Problems and conflicts and lawyers and patents danced through his head like out of season sugar plum fairies. This sort of exposure would be great if they had a finished product that was ready for market, but it wasn't. They had finally managed to get all four technologies working together although none of the Blaytent team was quite sure that the results were reliable. But they weren't working with a black and white technology to begin with. Would putting it on TV help or damn their cause with IIDT? What other loonies would come crawling out of the woodwork if they thought there was a 'game' product that could tell the truth? There were those who might think that if it could divine the truth it could tell the future like the Oracle at Delphi! Maybe it could predict the stock market? Who knew what rocks it might turn over? There were as many reasons to tell her no, they couldn't do it, as there were, yes, they could. His gut told him it was stupid to expose the system now, as it stood.

"What are the details?" he asked.

"So you'll do it?"

"I don't know yet, but give me the details and I'll run it by my team."

"This will be great exposure for you!" Blythe blathered. "They've had things like this on before, you know. Lie detectors. You know these dating shows that expose the hunks and the babes to the truth about each other. The audience loves it! Loves it! They ask them horrible, personal questions and the contestant has to answer and the audience gets to see if they are telling the truth or not! They have had that show on Fox for a season. Like 'Who wants to be a millionaire' that you had to answer more and more personal questions. This will be great. Yours does more than that, right? Besides all that," she added, "this will be great for me and E Talent. You're a gem!" She told him to call Pooch Williams at the station and he would give him all the details and left him with his mind and his jaw flapping.

When he talked to the team about it, Bob said, "They're making this into a side-show gimmick. 'Visit the fortune-teller' sort of thing. We're creating something serious. It's not a toy. I never liked the idea of a home game version."

"It's not really a game," Allan added. "I suppose it could be."

"Yah, well we've talked about the game part of this thing," Julia injected. "It could lead to problems."

"Truth can do that to you," Arya added. "Sometimes it hurts!"

"Aren't you full of it?" Julia said.

They were gathered in the seating area in Gus's office. It was late in the day and they were all pretty tired. Bob was pacing. Allan was relaxed with his long legs stretched out in front of him, ankles crossed with his left hand stroking his chin. Arya sat forward on his chair with his legs tucked underneath, hands locked onto the edges of the seat. Julia watched Bob pace, her legs crossed, her hands clasped as though she were praying.

"The question is, should we take this opportunity or not?" Gus asked. "There are a lot of good points particularly for our investors. This would be great exposure."

"What about the bad points?" Bob asked. "What about the lawsuit?"

"It isn't a suit yet," Gus said. "They haven't actually sued us. Maybe this will prove how different we are."

"What about our patents? Isn't this going to reveal all of our technology to everyone? You could just say no."

"Well, I could, I guess," Gus replied, "but the patents we are applying for would cover the algorithms in the programming. Internal. We'll just be revealing the external stuff, the output. I'll talk to our legal genius about it before I agree one way or the other. I need to know that if we go ahead and do this, that we're ready, that we're not going to look like idiots. It's got to work."

Arya said, "Well, it's not far away. I mean it's mostly there."

"That's not exactly reassuring," Gus smiled.

"Even if we're just showing off the external," Bob pursued, "this will show off the look and feel. Arya's done a great job of that. What if someone decides to copy that before we have the whole system complete?"

"Bob, you worry too much," Julia said. "You're going to raise your blood pressure."

"Bob, we have to come out of the closet someday," Gus added. "At some point we have to start selling stuff if Blaytent is going to survive. At some point we have to tell as many people about it as we can. This may be a bit premature, but we have to take the opportunities as they come along. Look, what I want to do is see where we are. Can you show me that tomorrow morning, Arya? I'll talk to Boyd and make sure we're reasonably covered and not treading in bad places with the IIDT folks. I'll get the TV people in here and see what they have in mind. How does that sound?"

"I can show you now," Arya said.

"No, tomorrow's fine. We're all beat. Time to go home. Time to get at least a moment or two of this beautiful weather. So let's call it a day."

After they had left him alone in his office, Gus stood in front of his windows, looking out across the short lawn at the neighboring building. It was a metal and glass box that contained a controlled atmosphere, where dozens maybe hundreds of people spun out the hours of their lives. Even when he was little he had wondered what the meaning of all this was, if there was an ultimate purpose, or was the only meaning whatever we put on it, day to day, week to week, month to month, year to year. And Bingo! That was the lifetime. You're done. You're toast. You're through. So what? Was someone going to deliver an evaluation when all this was over? He'd seen those billboards that proclaimed that when you die, "You're going to meet God!" Well, that would give it a purpose, wouldn't it? You're going to sit down with God and talk things over.

"So how'd it go for you?" God might ask.

And what would be the purpose to that conversation? Were you supposed to be able to go back and do things better? Were you going to get a scorecard or a critic? What comes after that conversation?

It seemed as though the more he pursued this finding the truth concept the more complicated it became. He felt like he would choose one door and push through it only to find a dozen more. He loved the huckle, buckle idea of getting warmer as they approached the truth, but which truth? If they knew what they were trying to find out to begin with, they could use the technology to confirm their suspicions. But if they had no clue what they were looking for and ventured into someone's mind unrestricted, they could go anywhere. It would truly be like the feelings he had gotten when he was in Arkansas with IIDT, surfing the Internet of a subject's mind!

No. They had no choice but to find ways to restrict or focus the path. The search had to have a primary purpose and the closer it was to the final destination, the better off they would be. It could flick open doors along the way, but they had to restrain themselves. The risk with that, of course, was that the primary purpose might be completely wrong! It might work if they were asking a suspect if they killed a person. Yes. No. I wasn't even there. No problem.

But what if they were interrogating someone like Kadah and the questions weren't even remotely close to resulting in yes or no answers? Perhaps that was the difference between a lie and a story. The difference between "did you do it?" and "who did it with you?" or, even worse, "<u>why</u> did you do it?" What if they thought Kadah had a plot to blow up Fenway Park, and they were trying to figure out when and who else was involved? The point of torture was to beat it out of him until he confessed to make the torture stop. That might or might not be the truth. Maybe he was just in the wrong place at the wrong time.

Gus had to stop thinking about all those possibilities. It was time to move on.

+++++

Pooch Williams was the director of the morning news program at the local Fox Network TV station. He had tried to improve their ratings by creating an elaborate set that the anchors moved around in, leaving their Plexiglas desk, moving to the cooking area or the living room couch area or the multitude of video screens for the live connections to the field reporters or the weather. Pooch was convinced that since television was a moving medium that the subjects shouldn't be snapshots or stills, that they should do something and not just sit there like a talking head. The cameras were robotic and followed the cast around under the direction of the human beings in the control room.

Although Pooch was only thirty-one he prided himself on his knowledge of what he thought of as the classics of the early days of television, and when Blythe had suggested Blaytent's technology as a segment for the show, he had immediately thought of Gary Moore and "I've Got a Secret". It crossed his mind that perhaps they should shift the show to a black and white segment, but the station brass was not happy with that idea.

"What about that idea? Doing it like a game show?" Pooch asked Gus when he visited the station with Cyrene to work out the details.

"I guess," Gus replied. "I mean this isn't a toy."

"I know. I know. I know," Pooch replied. "But people love this truth or lie stuff. They eat it up! No, I know you're serious about this. What about you, sweetheart?" he asked addressing Cyrene. "You have any secrets?"

Cyrene flicked him a quick smile to humor him.

"No, seriously. We need someone with a secret that we can reveal to the audience like they did on that old show, and we swear to the audience that your machine or the machine's operator doesn't know it. Doesn't know it. Doesn't have a clue!"

Gus nodded while the man sped on.

"How many questions do you need? How many questions? On that show they had four celebrities and a hundred dollars. Each celebrity asked questions until their time ran out and the pot went down by twenty bucks! Can you believe it? A hundred bucks! People wouldn't step on the stage for a hundred bucks these days. Have to be thousands. Millions. Billions someday soon! A hundred bucks! Wow!"

He put his arm around Cyrene's shoulders and guided her between the screens and the sofas and the other locations on the set. "Here, let me show you around. This is pretty cool isn't it? Been in a TV studio before, sweetheart? You could be a star, you know? You have the looks for it. You do. I'm not just saying that."

Cyrene shrugged his arm off and stepped back to Gus. "So how does this work, Mr. Williams?" Gus asked.

"Pooch. You have to call me Pooch. I mean it's my name, right? I'm not ashamed of it. How does this work? Well, let's see. What does your gadget look like?"

"Physically? Physically, it's not much to look at. The heart of the hardware is the Kinect from Microsoft."

"Shit. No! There's no visual there. Everybody knows what those things look like. Why are we even discussing this?

I need something like that big robot from *Lost in Space*. Something like that. Waving its arms and blinking lights. Something like that."

"Sorry to disappoint you, uh, Pooch."

"What else you got? What else? How the hell does the thing know you're telling lies? Does it at least talk or something? 'Warning! Warning! Warning, Will Robinson! I loved that show. God was it hokey. Horrible sets. Horrible. Corny as a corn-dog at a country fair. Americana. Early days. They did some pretty amazing stuff. Even then. So what does it do? How are we going to make this work?"

"The information comes from the computer screen. Did anyone explain this to you? What we do, I mean? We have four different technologies all working together. It's not like a polygraph. Well, it is and it isn't."

"So what do we need?"

"A polygraph only looks at one thing. We look at four. Things like body position, micro-expressions, what people say and how they say it. From there we zero in on what they're actually saying."

"Yah. Great. Whatever. The question," Pooch said, "is what we can put on the screen? Huh? Know what I mean? Where's the entertainment value? There is nothing new in a computer screen, my friend. Nothing. We look at them every day. All day. Don't take our eyes off them. They rule our lives. Nothing new there. That is certainly not entertaining."

He stood back and put his hands on his hips and glared at Gus as though Gus had insulted him. Gus looked at Cyrene. They stood there, motionless in the middle of the studio amongst scenes that imitated life – the comfortable living room isolated in darkness with equipment and wires and lights all around, the window on the city that was nowhere close to the outside of the building, the cozy kitchen with a fake window looking out on the ocean beyond. None of it real. Ersatz life. They stood there in this simulated world talking about how a machine could reveal reality.

"We need a lie or a liar or someone with a secret," Gus said.

"Okay," Pooch replied, turning away. "Okay. We can do that. I'm with you so far."

"And we can use our technology to reveal that lie or secret."

"Like the old TV show. Great idea. Wish I'd thought of it. How do you do that?"

Gus thought for a moment. "Well, seems like it would be pretty simple to connect the output up to your monitors to broadcast on the air."

"That's probably true. And what does your . . . technology look like?"

"Tough to describe. I mean it's the output from the various . . .."

"Is it interesting for people to look at? Does it change colors or something? Does it flash when people lie? What does it do? It's got to do something!"

"It's not a game, Pooch."

"If it's not entertaining, it's a waste of my time. Waste. Of. My. Time. I mean 'I've Got a Secret' wasn't particularly interesting in terms of what they revealed. Stupid stuff life kids eating bugs or Johnny Carson shooting an arrow off Gary Moore's head! They didn't ask questions about people wetting the bed or wearing woman's clothing or any of the sexual questions they ask now. And the questions didn't go on very long and didn't reveal much. They ended up laughing at each other and that is always entertaining. And they had a couple of babes asking questions. Eye candy. The story might not have been all that interesting but the visuals were good even in black and white. What about you, sweetheart? Want to ask the questions? The camera would love looking at you!"

Cyrene looked at Gus. "I don't think so," she said.

"Oh, come on," Pooch pleaded. "That would make it work. You ask a few questions, the machine figures out the answer, the audience which is mainly the crew, gasp in appreciation, baddah bing, baddah boom! Life is good. We move on to the next segment. You get your publicity. We go to commercial. What do you say?"

"I don't think so," Cyrene repeated.

"How many questions do you need? Did I ask you that before? Does it seem like we're in a time warp? Ooh, wee, ooh," Pooch hummed. "Seems like I've asked these questions before. Did you give me answers or was I just not listening? Don't answer that. How many questions do you need?"

"There isn't a set number," Gus replied, trying to remain calm. His instinct told him to walk out now before this madness went any further. "Maybe ten."

"Fantastic! Fantastic! 'I can name that lie in ten questions!' New show. New show. Game show. Those things are so simple and they make so much money, and I have to be doing this morning stint with dull people with dull stories to tell . . . no offense."

"Well, if you don't think this will fit your needs," Gus started to say.

"Nonsense! Nonsense! I can work with anything. The duller the better. I'm a genius with these things. And we have her. Nudge, nudge."

Cyrene's normal, gently bronze facial color was beginning to turn white. Her intense brown eyes were glaring like an eagle's at Pooch. She looked as though she were about to either spit on him or slap him. Gus putting a restraining hand on her arm. "A little respect, Pooch," he said.

"Oh! I'm sorry. I'm out of line. I do that. I get carried away. Didn't mean anything. Just trying to put the show together. Forgive me. It's show business. Even here in this limited form. It's still show business. We still appreciate beauty."

"Fine," said Gus. "So what're the details? Will you get someone with a secret? Sit the person down. We'll ask some questions. The audience can see the questions on the computer screen."

"So what do you think? Five minutes. Will it take longer than five minutes?"

"Five minutes? You want us to uncover a fabrication in five minute?"

"What did you think? We were going to give you a couple of hours? This is a morning show. Short attention span. Between the baby and kissing the hubby on the way out the door

and morning vacuuming. Five minutes is forever! I doubt if
we can hold them for half that time."

"Just seems longer when you're watching."

"That's the magic of TV. It does strange things to time.
Compresses it. Stretches it. We do what we want with it.
We do what the audience wants us to do with it."

Gus said he would have to talk to his team.

Pooch whipped out his smart phone and finger flipped to
his schedule. "Next week. Tuesday. The seventeenth. We
have a slot. Let me know by tomorrow morning if you're in
or out."

+++++

Against Gus's better judgment, they were 'in'. Arya confirmed with the technicians at the TV studio that he would be
able to connect the Blaytent equipment to the broadcast system. He had bubbafied the output display so that it was
simpler to understand as well as to protect some of the information that defined how they were handling the information.
Despite that fact, Boyd had some releases signed by the station to cover the disclosure of proprietary information and the
ownership of the broadcast material.

Gus considered Pooch's suggestion of using Cyrene as the
interrogator. At first, she had said categorically, no! Wasn't
going to happen!

"Well, let's just talk about it," Gus had suggested. "Who
else would do it?"

Cyrene pointed out that she didn't work for Blaytent. She
didn't know the equipment. She didn't know the system. No.
Allan could do it or Boyd or Julia. No. Why would she?

"To help us out. Look, Cyrene, it's just reading a series of
questions. Franky will create them. You don't have to do
anything but read them. And there is no question that of all of
us, you have the best stage presence! You're a natural!
You're the 'wow' factor!"

"Hmmf," Cyrene grunted. "You're blowing smoke up my
ass, Gus."

Gus was astounded, but he was pleased because he knew
she would do it. The primary question remaining was would
it work or would Franky be a national, or at least local, dis-

grace? Pooch had proposed that the show's anchor, Phil Gerber, would use a marker to write a secret on a piece of paper. One of the cameras would shoot an image of it so the audience could see it but it would be kept from the Blaytent team.

"Not exactly high tech," Pooch explained, "but this isn't some high priced game show. We'll try to make it casual, like we just thought it up. Maybe our co-anchor, Betty Ray, will be talking with you on the couch set, asking about the system and stuff, and then she'll suddenly suggest that you demonstrate it. Like it just came to her! Flash of brilliance! Know what I mean? We'll fumble around for a moment looking for a piece of paper and a marker. She'll have Phil write down his secret and your machine will figure out what it is!"

"Does he know he's going to do this?"

"Phil's a pro. He's had to deal with animals and little children and lots of whackos on the show. He's used to it."

"I mean does he have a secret in mind?"

"We'll tell him what he has to do just before the show; more spontaneous. More off the cuff. Better television. More to the point, can your gadget do it? Fast? We have a very tight time frame. It's got to happen like clockwork. Secret. Question. Question. Question. Surprise! Answer! Yay. Crystal clear. Audience claps. Fade to commercial."

"We're working with real stuff here," Gus said. "I don't know how long it will take. It depends on Mr. Gerber's secret."

"All right. Ten questions. Get the answer in ten questions. Maybe we can go over one commercial break. That might be good. 'Phil's secret when we come back. Don't go away!' That might be good. Although it might look a little fake, you know? Like we gave you the answer while we were on break?"

They went on to thrash through some of the details. Pooch informed Gus that, "You never know what will happen on live television," something that was pretty obvious to Gus. This was obviously a song and dance routine – a little show, a little drama, and a quick result. It had nothing to do with showing off their technology. If (he wanted to think 'when') it did work, it would probably look fake anyway. If it didn't work, it would be more realistic certainly, but it would not be good for Blaytent to say the least. But it was only a local show. Gus would have preferred a more serious presentation where they could have discussed the input from the various technologies and how they interacted to produce a verified result. But this ersatz demonstration was much better from the legal standpoint. It would reveal very little of what they had actually created.

So they arrived at the studio early enough for Arya to set up the equipment and make the connections to the broadcast system. He spent some time with Cyrene on how to follow along with Franky's questions, what buttons to push, and what the display meant.

She needed little assistance from the station's make-up artists to make her appealing to the cameras. She had highlighted the intensity of her eyes and the elevation of her cheekbones. Her hair glistened and she had dressed to show off the natural curves of her body.

Gus felt dowdy beside her. Although he was a foot taller than she was, he felt he needed to slouch along behind her as they came into the studio. The staff bustled around getting them in the right spots, working through the timing, and then guiding them to a dressing room where they were to stay until the right moment.

It was fifteen foot by fifteen-foot box with yellow walls, fluorescent lights on the ceiling, a large digital clock, oversized mirrors and a flat screen TV. An old sofa and a handful of chairs faced the TV. The air smelled stale and dusty. There was a light fixture that looked like a bulb in a glass jar by the door. Gus flopped down into one of the chairs. Cyrene alighted on the sofa.

"So what am I supposed to say?" she asked.

"I don't even know what I'm supposed to say," Gus replied. "It would have been good to meet this Phil guy before we started talking on camera. I think I've seen him on TV, but I'm not a morning show kind of guy."

"I'm sure we'll see him on that big screen up there."

They sat in silence for a few moments, listening to the sounds of the studio around them. "Ever done this before?" Gus asked. "I mean been on TV."

"No," she replied.

More silence. At least an analog clock might have ticked.

Gus jumped up and went to the TV. "I'm going to turn this thing on. Maybe we can see what's going on out there." He started running his hand along the edge, feeling for the power button.

"But what am I supposed to say?" Cyrene asked.

"You just have to read the questions that Franky puts on your screen. Done any interrogating before?" Gus smiled.

But there was a pause before Cyrene replied quietly, "Yes. A little."

Gus found the power switch and stepped back as the TV popped to life. It was more of a studio monitor than a TV. It had one channel and that was this studio here and now. It provided a window for them to watch the set up. Gus settled down beside her.

"Well. I don't know," he said. "I mean we're supposed to find out what the secret is. I'm hoping that Franky will behave while he reads all the subject's inputs and leads the questions to the answer. Franky is really the one on the spot here. Arya has it set up so that there is a graphic of the subject and as the questions get closer to the answer, the subject image gets redder, simulating getting warmer. If the subject image gets bluer, the questions are moving farther away."

"Cute," Cyrene replied.

"That's not what will be on the serious version, but I think it's a graphic that a morning TV audience can understand."

It seemed as though the walls of the studio were decorated with TV monitors like some of the bars Gus had visited over the years. He wondered if anyone paid attention to any of those stations. Was it supposed to be like the old Teletype machines that rattled in the background, bringing "you news from around the world"? It provided a living and colorful backdrop. Did people really need all that input to keep them interested – the scroll bar on the bottom of the screen with stocks and news and sports?

They saw the male and female anchors take their seats in front of the long desk. Makeup artists put on the finishing touches. The light by their door came on, indicating that the show had started, and they watched the anchors launch into the news. "That must be Phil Gerber," Gus said.

A staff member with a headset on stuck her head in the door and announced that they would be third segment. "We'll let you know five minutes ahead of time. Let's get you hooked up to your microphones." She smiled and helped them guide the wires from the small lavaliere microphones through their clothing to the transmitters. It was easy for Gus to clip it on his belt. It was more of a challenge to find a spot on Cyrene. Her dress did not leave much room for anything except her. The staff member did a quick sound check and then slipped out again.

Time crept along. "I hate waiting," Cyrene said. "I hate it. If they're going to shoot me, I'd much rather they just did it quickly and get it over with."

"No one's going to shoot you," Gus replied with a smile. "It's just a TV show. It's just a local TV show. Think of all those people in their kitchens making breakfast barely listening to this. You could start talking Arabic, and I don't think anyone would notice."

"Want me to?"

"No. That would probably not be a good idea."

"Should I wave to the family back home?" She smiled.

"Just be pretty. Serious but pretty."

She blinked her eyelashes at him demurely.

Finally the staff member came back and guided them out to the set. They waited at the edge of the lights until the commercial break then Cyrene took the seat she had been guided to previously and Pooch indicated that Gus should take a spot on a sofa, under the lights. The show's co-anchor, Betty Ray, shook his hand as she settled down beside him, quickly introducing herself. She was attractive in a garish sort of way that appealed to cameras. Her face had been plastered on with lots of make-up and her hair was mostly glued in place with just enough loose to provide a little motion with the occasional flick of her head.

Gus mumbled a greeting, his head pivoting around like a bird surveying where an attack might come from. Phil Gerber remained at his place at the anchor desk and on cue, introduced the segment.

"So I'm going to write a secret on this white board while Betty talks with Gus Sainte, the inventor of this technology," Phil said after an awkward description of the Blaytent project. "I haven't told this to anyone here, so it should come as a bit of a surprise! Betty?"

The lights glared on the sofa illuminating Gus and Betty. "So, Gus, you have invented some new kind of lie detector? Don't they call those polygraphs? How did you come up with the idea?"

"The fact is, Betty, it's not exactly a lie detector. There really isn't a good term for this technology. We developed it to assist in getting to the reality of a subject's story."

"You were involved in water boarding in Guantanamo I was told."

Gus was momentarily taken back. He didn't even like to think that he was attached to that process. "I was in military intelligence. There. Yes."

"That must have been an ugly experience," Betty pursued.

"It was. I mean, it is."

"Is it still going on?" She didn't give him time to answer before pushing on. "And that led you to seek out a better way?"

"It did. There are various ways that interrogators in effect read people and what they say to get to things that they may not necessarily willingly reveal like body language or micro-expressions that have been popularized recently on TV shows."

"Oh, yeah, like 'Lie to Me'! Loved that show." She bounced up on the sofa. "Okay, so tell me about your system. How does it work? How is it going to reveal Phil's secret? This is exciting!"

"What it does is use a series of cameras and microphones all built into the same sort of array that Microsoft builds for the game consoles and interprets all that information, puts it together, and tells when we are getting closer to the information that we want to discover."

"Ah," Betty replied.

"We have to give it a hint, if you will, because a lot of things go on in people's minds, and you could wander about in lots of irrelevant areas like looking for stuff on the internet."

"I know what you're saying. We don't really want to know everything that is going on in Phil's mind, do we?" She laughed. "And then your machine tells us when Phil is telling the truth?"

"Actually, truth is relative, you know. But Phil will tell us when we are getting close. Maybe he won't actually say it in words, but other actions will tell us from how he moves, the sound of his words, the formation of his sentences. All that stuff is pretty revealing. And a good interrogator knows that. In fact, Betty, people are pretty good intuitively at knowing and interpreting this stuff. Just like intuitively we know what time it is but we look at a clock to confirm it."

"Well, let's see how this works, Gus. Phil, have you got your secret written down?"

"I do, Betty. I'll hold it up so the camera can see it and so our audience can see it, and then I'll take the hot seat and let Gus's assistant, Cyrene, ask me some questions and see how this thing works."

He held up his white board, and the camera focused in on his scrawled message: "*My wife is having a baby.*"

People in the studio gasped and tittered.

"Please," Betty shushed them. "We don't want to give it away, do we?" You couldn't see that, Gus? Right? I know I couldn't see it. So let's see if your machine can get it. We have to give it a hint. What's the subject of your secret, Phil?"

"It's personal," he said.

The other people in the room sniggered again.

"Okay," Betty replied. "But you have to give us a hint."

"That's the hint, Betty. It's personal!" He got up from the anchor desk and moved to a comfortable chair that had been placed near Cyrene and her computer system.

Cyrene smiled at Phil as he settled into his seat. The TV camera was kind to him, a kind of grinning manikin with a hairline that was threatening to recede despite the gel. He was attempting to combine the looks of Geraldo Rivera and Walter Cronkite and it wasn't working well. He wanted to portray a vibrant youthful image tempered by sage wisdom, truthfulness, and honesty. Cyrene thought he just looked tired and getting fat. She asked him if he was ready?

He squirmed at bit, grinned and said he was. "Always! I'm always ready!"

Cyrene looked at her screen and the human silhouetted figure. She typed in 'personal' as Arya had showed her, and the form of the figure flowed into a pale yellow.

"Okay," she said to Phil, "please tell us your name."

Phil shifted in his chair, and said "Phil Gerber."

Cyrene's screen figure put on a pale bluish tint.

Phil squirmed a bit, looked away from Cyrene, twitched his plastic grin a fraction and asked, "My whole name? Phillip Hatley Gerber."

The TV image shifted over to Betty. "Oh," she said. "We're going to learn all sorts of things, aren't we, Gus? Is that the secret? That's personal!"

Cyrene's screen prompted her to ask where Phil was from.

"Indiana," Phil admitted. "Valparaiso, Indiana. Born and raised. Heart of the country."

The screen figure had shifted back through the pale yellow into a light, pale salmon.

Phil shifted around in his chair and didn't seem to know what to do with his hands but he kept his feet still.

"Where do you live now?" Cyrene asked.

"Boston, of course," Phil said. "My home town. Go, Red Sox!"

The screen figure drifted back toward the yellow again.

"Boston's a big city," Cyrene said. "Can you be more specific, Mr. Gerber?"

"Phil, please. Or the machine won't like me. Ha. Ha." He laughed. He was trying to decide if he would alienate some part of his audience if he identified just one part of the city, but he finally said, "To tell you the truth, we live in Southie.

South Boston. It's where my wife's family's from. Big family. She has a big family. She actually has three brothers. You're right. It's a big city. Lot's of wonderful people everywhere."

"How long have you been married, uh, Phil?" Cyrene asked.

Phil looked around the studio again. His feet shifted back to the front legs of his chair. "A year. One year. One wonderful year," he grinned.

The screen figure had shifted to a light pink.

"Any children?"

Phil looked at Cyrene. "No," he said drawing out the word. "Not yet."

"How old is your wife?" Cyrene asked.

"Do I have to answer that? Ha, ha, ha!" Phil asked the camera. "She's going to kill me. 'Sorry, honey. It's an experiment. It's for work, okay? I can't lie.'" He paused as though expecting an answer to rise up out of the floor. With a very subtle shrug he finally said, "She's thirty." His feet were dancing a silent soft shoe step in front of his chair.

The studio had gotten very quiet as the staff put things down and stopped moving around, listening to the exchange and watching the monitors as the figure gradually darkened in intensity.

"Are you a religious man, Phil? Any particular church?"

"Oh. Catholic. Gate of Heaven off East Broadway. Every Sunday. We go every Sunday as a family. Small church. Not a lot of fanfare. You know. To tell you the truth I'm not surprised they didn't close it down when they were selling off all those churches to pay the bills. You know the bills I'm talking about."

Cyrene didn't know, but neither did Franky. The image on the screen was a solid red. They were at the 'Beanstalk'. It put out another question. "Do you look forward to having children?"

"Oh, ho!" Phil cried. "You found me out! That's the secret. My wife's having a baby!"

The people in the studio clapped and Betty jumped up and the camera tracked her striding across the stage to give Phil a hug.

"Wow!" she said. "Wow! That didn't take long!"

Then Cyrene stated in a loud enough voice to silence the hubbub in the studio, "And you're not happy about it because you swing both ways. And you have a boyfriend."

Phil went pale. Betty gasped and stepped back from him. "What?" he said. "What did you say? No, don't repeat that." His mouth was pumping open and shut like a fish out of water.

Betty said, "And with that, let's take a break. We'll be right back!"

One of the things about live TV is that you can never be quite sure what's going to happen, like the famous 'wardrobe malfunction' at the Super Bowl. No one knew quite what to say or what to do. It was clear that what Cyrene had said could not be erased. It was also clear that there wasn't a lot of time to recover and move on.

Cyrene said, "I just read what was on my screen. I didn't make that up."

"It's clearly a lie!" Phil shouted. "It's just not true. I need to call my wife. I'm very happy about her pregnancy. I'm thrilled that she's having a baby."

"Well, that's just the point, isn't it?" Cyrene said in her very precise voice. "You keep saying that 'she's' having the baby. You didn't say you were excited to be a father, did you?"

Pooch came out on the stage to restore order and tell Phil to take it lightly. The best thing to do was to move on and not make a big deal out of it. He told Betty to just quickly close out the segment and move on to the weather. He sent Betty and Phil to their seats behind the anchor desk. He had Gus and Cyrene escorted back to the dressing room.

"Jesus, it worked!" Gus exclaimed. "Wow! That was better than I could have hoped for. At least I think so. Great job."

"I just read what was there," Cyrene replied.

"Really? The guy's gay?"

"I didn't say he was gay."

"You said he had a boyfriend."

"Yah, but he also has a wife."

"This isn't going to go over so well with her." Gus paused for a moment. "Damn. I hope he doesn't sue us for slander."

"That would, of course, mean that he would have to prove that it wasn't true."

"True. That might be awkward for him. Maybe you shouldn't have said it."

Cyrene smiled. "I couldn't resist. He's such a pompous ass."

Chapter Eleven

September 2014

It had become quite clear to Gus that the truth did not help you make friends. The legal proceedings with IIDT had blossomed from sparring to the lawsuit, sliding merrily into the discovery phase where the lawyers continued to dance and where depositions were required, where you sat down across the table from an opposing attorney who was out for your blood and answered questions, providing information that was likely to come back at you. This minor drama was scheduled to take place in an expensive conference room in the offices of Tittle and Baines, a first visit for Gus but compelling Boyd to revisit his past. Despite the fact that over fourteen years had passed, the place still brought a sour taste to his mouth. When he and Gus walked into the building, it made the hair on the back of Boyd's neck tingle. He knew he shouldn't let it bother him. He knew that these old negatives were not productive and he should let them go. Most of the staff, most of the attorneys that he had worked with were long gone. Diamon Jakes had moved on to the court. He wondered if old Ronald Baines was still there or even still alive! But the negativity was deeply imbedded in Boyd's bones.

Gus and Boyd passed through security in the lobby, waited for the elevators, and then shot up through the building, exiting into the lobby of the law firm. The wine red carpet stretched out to the windows overlooking Boston Harbor. The impression made by all the glass and wood and chrome plated steel reeked of money and power. Not much had changed in fourteen years. The reception desk had switched sides. The paintings had been changed. There was a massive abstract featuring what looked like a six-foot high avenging angel behind the receptionist's desk. People bustled through the lobby carrying stacks of paper, talking to each other, talking to themselves (although they were probably on cell phones), and accumulating billable hours.

Boyd stepped up to the receptionist who glanced up from her computer screen and gave him a weak smile over the top of the counter across the face of which was emblazoned the Tittle & Baines brand. Boyd identified himself and was told that Mr. Lovitz, the attorney handling the case would be out momentarily would they care to wait in the reception chairs?

Gus wondered if the president of a major oil firm or car company would be asked to wait in the reception chairs, flipping through magazines like waiting to go into the dentist's office. This was a power shift dance, putting the visitors in their place. It at least momentarily forced the visitor to set aside all their personal mantel of power and exist in limbo, reduced to the level of office staff. The visitor remains in that condition, flipping mindlessly through old magazines until either another member of the office staff comes out to greet them with a shallow welcoming smile and guides them someplace, maintaining their diminished status, or a bustling attorney comes dashing toward them, hand outstretched, bubbling out reinforcing phrases. It was a common dance to manipulate the state of mind of the visitor to these lofty environments.

While they were waiting, Gus called Cyrene. Gus wondered if cell phone calls were permitted. He decided that he didn't really care. This whole legal exercise was a waste of his time, playing the lawyers' sandbox.

Cyrene was fond of using the camera capability of her phone and she smiled at him as he held his own phone away from his face.

"Hi," he said.

"Hi," she replied. "How's it going?"

"We're waiting." He held the phone up and gave her a panoramic sweep of the lobby.

"Very impressive," she said.

"Where are you?" he asked. He could see that there were people moving in the background but he didn't recognize the space behind her.

"Oh, just out. Doing some shopping. Are we on for tonight?"

Shopping seemed to be a pretty typical pastime although Cyrene was neither typical nor open about how she spent her time, and even with the camera images you couldn't be sure where people actually were. There were applications like *SceneSet* that created a fictitious background so they could seem like they were in an office or climbing the Rockies, for example, when they were actually sitting in their living room. He didn't believe she was lying, but she didn't move her phone around, keeping it focused on her face, which was certainly a pleasant sight. He was beginning to wonder, however, if he was losing his trusting nature.

Gus noticed an extremely well dressed elderly man crossing the lobby.

"Anyone you know?" he asked Boyd. "He seemed to recognize you."

"Christ. It's old Baines himself. I thought he would be dead by now. These guys never seem to let go. You'd think with all their money they would back out of this swamp."

"You worked here didn't you?"

"Long ago and a lot of water under the bridge."

Baines glanced at him, seemed to shake his head, and walked on disappearing around a corner. "I don't think the man knew me even when I did work for him," Boyd said.

Lovitz, IIDT's attorney, seemed to love the tactic of making people wait, to purposely get them agitated, to put them off balance. It is supposed to demonstrate how unimportant they are, to reduce them to a whiflet or a toady, that their time is not worth anything, and at the same time demonstrate the importance and value of Lovitz's time. Lovitz played it well, erupting from the hallway, stomping across the carpet, grin-

ning with hand outstretched, babbling how good it was of
them to come and meaning none of it.

Boyd stood to meet this onslaught while Gus continued to
appear to read the article in the magazine he had extracted
from the stack. "A moment," he said, waving his hand. Finally standing he dropped the magazine back onto the pile and
said, "Nice of you to supply these. I never get a chance to
read about the Red Sox in other places. Never get the time."

Lovitz flashed a weak smile. "Chris Lovitz," he said introducing himself.

"Yes, sure," Gus replied. "Is there a men's room before
we begin?"

Lovitz indicated a door on the left side of the hallway and
Gus left the two lawyers conversing.

"I was told you used to work here," Lovitz said to Boyd.

"A long time ago. Yes."

"With Judge Jakes? That is legendary."

"Yes. Of course she wasn't a Judge then."

Lovitz look a little surprised. But then he probably always
looked that way. He was overweight, balding with a round
face and ears that stuck out. His lack of height made him
seem shorter than he probably was. He had an annoying way
of 'huffing' at the beginning of his statements, as though he
permanently needed to clear his throat. He had strapped himself into his three-piece suit and Boyd wondered if he had to
suck in his breath to unbutton his vest.

"Must have been interesting," Lovitz flashed a smile.

"You could say that."

When Gus returned, drying his hands, they continued on
down the hall to the conference room. Seeing no trashcan,
Gus handed the damp towel to Lovitz, and shrugged. "Didn't
want to drop it on the floor. You guys don't produce any
trash?"

Lovitz took it tentatively with a weak smile and handed it
to a passing secretary. He pushed open the door to the conference room. One glass wall flooded the room with light and
looked out on the city and the harbor below. Most of the
room was filled with a wide, dark wood table, surrounded by
tilt back chairs. There was a stenographer and her machine

near one end of the table, and standing in front of the window looking down on the street and tiny people was Major Crum. When Gus had entered the room, he thought he recognized Crum's silhouette against the bright, natural light, but he wasn't sure until the man slowly turned to face him.

"You know each other?" Lovitz asked benignly.

"What are you doing here?" Gus asked Crum. "What is he doing here?" he asked Lovitz. "I thought this was a deposition. My deposition. What's he doing here?"

"Major Crum has an interest in these proceedings," Lovitz said, settling himself with his back to the window, indicating that Gus and Boyd should sit on the opposite side of the table.

"Sainte," Crum said, nodding his head slightly, a watery smile on his lips, bending his little black moustache, which Gus noticed, was turning grey.

"Always a pleasure, Captain," Gus said.

"Major," Crum corrected.

"Right," Gus acknowledged.

"Would anyone like coffee, tea, water, sparkling water . . . before we begin?" Lovitz asked.

He pushed a button on the phone on the table to summon a girl to fetch the required drinks and then adjusted the camera to point at Gus and aligned his file folders in front of him. Crum took a seat at the corner of the table.

"Not as good as water boarding, eh, Major?" Gus asked.

"Maybe we'll get some truth anyway," Crum replied, looking away toward the windows. "Lawyers are almost as good."

Boyd laid his hand on Gus's arm and shook his head. "Just answer what is asked," he murmured. "Keep it simple."

Gus didn't see the point in any of this, and he actually welcomed what he regarded as a chance to set the record straight, to tell his side of the story, whatever story they were interested in hearing about. IIDT was accusing Blaytent of patent infringement, that Gus had purposely spied on IIDT under false pretenses, and copied IIDT's layered voice stress analysis algorithms. On top of that they claimed that Blaytent's output infringed on IIDT's copyrights in the way that it presented the program's output.

Boyd had responded that there was no substance to the claims and the arguments were specious and that Blaytent should be granted Summary Judgment, ending the suit and throwing it all out of court. Apparently the judge was thinking about that, but in the meantime the preparatory steps such as these depositions and discovery activities needed to proceed.

The water and the tea arrived and was unceremoniously deposited on the table and a short "Thank you" from Lovitz and the questions began. Name. Address. Title and affiliation. How long have you lived there? Previous address.

Gus didn't see the relevance and said so.

"Just answer the question, please," Lovitz replied.

Educational background and confirmation of Gus's term in the Army. Stationed in Guantanamo? Army Intelligence?

Crum snorted. Lovitz held up his hand and glanced at him. Crum turned back to the windows.

Gus realized too late that they had been bush whacked in the seating arrangement. The light behind Lovitz and Crum was so bright that he had to squint at times to make out their faces. He scanned the windows to see if there were any blinds or shades that could be used to correct the situation, but saw nothing. It was the earth friendly version of the bright-light-in-the-eyes technique! "Where were you on the night of the twenty-third?"

Confirmation of Gus's role in starting Blaytent. "Who came up with the name, by the way? Like blatant liar, right? Very nice." Lovitz tried to smile with little success. Gus remembered what Arya had told him about liars' smiles or masking smiles, a "subtle contraction of the zygomatic major muscles". It was also the forced smile of group photos when the lip corners stretch upward as the risorius muscles contract, providing a small, upward curl. Easy to fake. It went along with the stereotype of the non-smiling Bostonian. Wandering down that thought path distracted him and disconnected his attention to Lovitz.

"What?" he asked when he realized that Lovitz had posed another question.

"I was asking what your relationship was to the Barnstable Police Department. That's on Cape Cod isn't it?"

Gus confirmed that it was.

Lovitz huffed and asked, "And what is your connection to them?"

"I know the Chief. I consider him a family friend."

"The Chief of the Barnstable Police Department?"

"Yes."

"And when you say 'friend' what do you mean?"

"Do you have friends, Mr. Lovitz?"

"Would you describe him as a family friend? A close friend? A drinking buddy? What kind of friend?"

"A friend *friend*, Mr. Lovitz. Someone I get along with."

"Would you describe him as someone who would do a favor for you?"

"Friends do that sort of thing. It's one of the reasons you can call them 'friend'."

Lovitz opened a folder on the table and followed his finger as he scanned down through the top page as though he was pursuing a loose bead of mercury. Then he looked up. Gus squinted at him.

"Did you visit the IIDT facility in Arkansas under the pretense of representing the Barnstable Police Department because your *friend* the chief deputized you?"

"*Deputized* me? No."

"So the rest of that statement is true? Did you visit the IIDT facility in Fayetteville, Arkansas under the pretense of representing the Barnstable Police Department?"

"No. It wasn't a pretense."

Lovitz huffed and asked, "What would you call it then?"

"Do you have trouble with the meaning of words, Mr. Lovitz?" Gus asked. He looked at Boyd and then back to Lovitz. "*You* actually used the word *pretense*. It wasn't me. A pretense is like a lie. It sort of seems like you are saying that I 'lied'. If IIDT's equipment worked, it would have known if I was lying. Isn't that what it's supposed to be able to do?"

Crum glared at Gus, his upper lip lifting slightly to expose his top teeth. Boyd laid his hand on Gus's forearm.

"Chief Allen of the Barnstable Police Department hired me to review various interrogation systems including the so-called FATE system promoted by IIDT."

"Hired you?"

"Yes, hired me."

"Out of the blue? He just called you up and asked you to do this?"

Gus paused. It was a real problem knowing about all this body language, lie detection stuff. It gave meaning to things that he would have overlooked before, and he found himself analyzing himself which caused even more difficulty because he got sidetracked and that gave the wrong meaning to what he did and how he responded. He could have given a snap, 'Yes', answer but that wouldn't have been true. He had proposed the idea to Chief Allen. But then, what difference did that make? It was amazing how the lawyers could tangle up a simple activity into something dastardly and nefarious. The problem was that no matter how he answered the question, the words could be twisted into something evil. Words. Words were a problem with interrogation. Words had different meanings to different people in different contexts. Charles Schulz's character, Snoopy, had said that once he had a dictionary he had all the words. All he had to do was put them in the right order to write a book!

It was said that the "Truth will set you free". How come it often seemed to be the other way around? The truth will tangle you up and throw you in the garbage! People only heard what they wanted to hear with the meaning they wanted it to have. You could only get close to the truth. You could never really get all the way there.

"A consultant," he said finally, "is a person who is knowledgeable in a specific area and can assist in making an educated decision. I was working as a consultant for Chief Allen."

"Did he express any interest in truth detection technology before you proposed your visit to IIDT?"

Questions like that are switches in a model railroad track. A 'yes' answer sends you along one track. A 'no' answer sends you along the other. It was like Yogi Berra's proverbial

'Fork in the Road'. "Take it." If Gus said 'yes', it would mean that he had proposed the visit to IIDT. If he said 'no', it would mean that the Chief had no interest in the technologies before Gus proposed the research. Gus created a third path.

"All police departments are interested in improving their interrogation techniques. Barnstable is no different."

Lovitz huffed again and asked, "But did Chief Allen know about IIDT before you mentioned it to him?"

"I don't know what Chief Allen knew or when he knew it. Let's get past this, Mr. Lovitz. I have productive work I would like to do. I did go to the so-called offices of IIDT in Fayetteville. I did have a friendly relationship with the Chief of the Barnstable police department. I did review various truth detection technologies for him. Does that answer your questions?"

Lovitz glanced up at Gus and then looked down at his folders and began flipping through the pages.

"Ah," he said. "Good."

Crum banged his fist on the table. "That does it. He was there spying on IIDT. He just used his daddy's relationship with the Chief as an excuse!"

Lovitz looked at him, but didn't reprimand him for his outburst.

"Where is this going?" Boyd asked. "Mr. Sainte has answered your questions."

"Crap!" said Crum.

"After your visit, did you produce a report of your findings for the Barnstable Police Department, Mr. Sainte?" Lovitz asked.

That was another poser for Gus. Lovitz wasn't as dumb as he seemed. If Gus were a legitimate consultant, a report would have been a logical work product. If the whole thing had been a scam, it wouldn't have been formalized. Blaytent had produced a report, but it was more of an in-house review of the technologies than it was a report specifically for Barnstable. Gus tried another tack.

"I delivered my report in person," he said. "I was not impressed with IIDT's techniques and told that to Chief Allen."

"So you didn't produce a written report," Lovitz said.

"It was a verbal report."

"So is it fair to say that you weren't really a consultant, a paid consultant, for the Barnstable Police Department?"

"Well, to tell you the truth, we never actually got paid." He laughed. "It's tough to ask friends for money!"

"Crap," retorted Crum. "All crap and hooey!"

"What other technologies did you review for Barnstable or any other police departments? Were there other police departments?"

"No," Gus replied. "Look. This stuff is not a secret. You can read about it all on the Internet. You don't have to be a police department to buy some of these lie detector things! You can order the software from your desk. As long as you can pay for it, you can have it. It's not a secret. Companies like IIDT make this sound like it is all for some secret society with a secret handshake and meeting in the basement. But it's not. It's not a secret."

"What about Blaytent's technologies?"

Gus looked at Lovitz. "What do you mean?"

"Can someone just order your technologies on the Internet?"

"No. Of course not."

"Why not?"

"Are we talking about Blaytent now? I thought we were discussing IIDT."

"This is a deposition, Mr. Sainte. It is part of the discovery process."

"Oh. No. We don't offer our technologies to the general public on the internet."

"Why is that, Sainte?" Crum asked. "Because you don't have a technology of your own? You're using IIDT's!" He paused for a moment. "Hey, you should ask your girl friend about her father. Maybe you should meet him. Great guy!"

Boyd said, "I'm going to have to ask you to remove Mr. . . . Major Crum from the room. He should not be participating in this deposition."

"You'd like that, wouldn't you, candy-ass!"

One thing about water boarding, Gus realized, was that all the pressure was focused on the person on the board. It didn't much matter how many people were in the room and yelling. At least that was the way it supposed to be. It turns out that there was pressure on everyone in the room, the pressure of anger and hatred and fear, fear of getting it wrong or not getting any information at all. The person on the board only had one job: staying alive. Gus was not afraid of losing his life. In fact, he was not afraid of anything that might result from the frenzy in this room with the lovely view of Boston and the harbor. He was just frustrated by the incredible waste of time.

Lovitz took Crum aside and hissed reprimands at him, then resumed his seat and resumed his questions. He probed further for a written report, demanding it as part of the documents of the discovery. He asked again about other technologies that Gus had reviewed during his research. He asked for the results of any comparisons Gus might have done between the technologies. He asked Gus if he considered himself an expert in truth detection technology.

Gus asked in return if there was some magic threshold that one had to cross to consider oneself an expert.

Crum snorted. Lovitz glared at him.

And so it went. On and on. Lovitz's neat stack of papers and files disintegrated into a tangled mess and Gus noted that he was beginning to sweat as the sun poured through the glass and onto Lovitz's back. Gus smiled to himself thinking that he had led the man on a merry and fruitless chase. He could see that Crum was particularly frustrated, although it was difficult to tell when he hadn't been frustrated. Gus knew that he had grown up on the streets of Queens, New York, and he still showed layers of a street-smart, gang kid wanna-be as well as the conflicts between the ethnicity of his Hispanic mother and Anglo father which never allowed him to fit easily into any group. Nothing ever satisfied him. For a fleeting moment, Gus wondered if Crum had ever been in love.

When the deposition finally ended, Gus and Boyd headed out to the elevators. "That went well," Gus said. "What the hell was that comment about Cyrene's father?"

Boyd was thinking about another time when he had stood in the same spot waiting for these same elevators. Once again they seemed to take forever. They didn't want to talk. Not there. Not yet. So they waited. And Crum appeared, walking slowly. They didn't acknowledge him.

Finally the elevator arrived, the doors slid open revealing an empty interior. Gus stepped in first followed by Boyd who pressed the button for the lobby. Crum stood there for a moment as though contemplating waiting for another elevator, and then stepped forward into the middle of the car. He pressed the button again.

Gus stared at the top of Crum's head. His hair was thinning, the black turning grey. Inside that skull there were nasty thoughts, squirming around like a bucket of worms. Gus looked away, up to the lights on the ceiling of the elevator and then down at his shoes. He could smell Crum's sweat. The man's chunky body was going gradually soft, sinking to the middle of his belly. He must have crossed the fifty-year line now. Probably got retirement benefits or would soon. What would a man like that do in retirement? Sit around on a beach sipping Mai Tai's and watching the sun set? Hardly likely. Maybe he would play golf. Jesus! Can you imagine playing golf with a guy like that? He'd get pissed off and throw his clubs in the lake and then sue the golf course for something or other. Not his fault that his balls don't fly straight. Gus smiled to himself.

The elevator stopped, the doors opened and a young lady stepped in. Gus backed up against the back wall and Crum stepped back so their shoes touched. Crum turned and glared at Gus as though he should evaporate out of the elevator all together. Gus flared him a smile. Crum snorted. The young lady clasped her handbag to her chest.

The elevator dropped five more floors, stopped, doors opened and two young men stepped in. Crum pushed back even farther until he slid into the space between Gus and Boyd. He stared pointedly up to the changing number display over the door.

One young man was on his cell phone. "Look," he said as though he were alone, "I'm not going there, Martha. I'm just not. I'm not even going to be around! If you want to go, fine! Go without me."

As the elevator dropped the occupants looked either up at the changing numbers over the door or down at their shoes.

"I honestly don't care. Honestly! It's your problem and you're going to have to deal with it. I'm not involved." Gus wondered why people on cell phones always seemed to need to talk louder. Maybe it was the old can-on-the-string mentality.

The air in the elevator car seemed to grow denser despite the fan in the ceiling and the fact that it was an object falling through a shaft at an exceptional rate of speed. But just not fast enough.

Finally it reached the lobby and began to purge its passengers and in the process Gus kicked Crum's heel causing his left foot to catch the back of his right resulting in Crum stumbling forward pushing the young lady in the back as she exited. "Hey!" she yelled as stepped forward catching herself. "Watch it, old man!"

Crum kept himself from falling and pointed behind him. "That idiot tripped me!" he hissed. He spun around and faced Gus. The people in the lobby who had been waiting for the arrival of the elevator, filtered around them and into the empty car. The doors closed leaving Boyd, Gus and Crum alone.

Gus couldn't leave without pushing Crum over so he remained where he was looking down.

"What the fuck's your problem, Sainte?" Crum demanded. "Forgotten how to walk now? Do I need to teach you?"

"You couldn't teach a gopher how to dig a hole," Gus replied.

"Get the fuck away from me, you faggot, you Taliban sympathizer!" Crum replied and pushed Gus back toward the elevator door.

Gus could feel the anger rising. This whole experience had been an exercise in idiocy. "Hey!" He stepped forward until he was directly in Crum's face, an inch from his chest. Crum was forced to look up into Gus's face. Gus pointed his right forefinger directly between Crum's eyes. "You are an insecure, officious, little piece of shit!" Gus said.

Crum grabbed the finger and twisted it down. Gus swung his left fist into Crum's stomach, causing him to exhale with a grunt and step back. But as he straightened, his fists came up.

It was clear to Boyd that this wasn't going to end well. Gus was bigger, stronger, and younger than Crum, but the outcome wasn't going to be beneficial to either man. "Whoa," he said stepping forward and holding up his arms.

Crum tried to push Boyd out of the way, but Boyd didn't move.

"He assaulted me!" Crum shouted. "I want him arrested!"

"Oh, shut up, Crum!" Gus demanded.

Boyd grabbed him by the arm and guided him away leaving Crum standing there fuming. "Did anyone see that? Oh, come on, you assholes! One of you must have seen that guy hit me!"

Gus and Boyd walked down the steps and out of the building. "Shit. What an ass! That guy really, really pisses me off!" Gus said.

"Next time, we should take a different elevator," Boyd replied.

+++++

So where was Cyrene when she had called earlier? Crum's comment about Cyrene's father was sticking in Gus's brain like a pebble in his shoe. He wanted to shake it out and make it go away. Crum was an idiot so everything he said, did or thought should be taken with a grain of salt and discounted. That, however, was much easier to say than to do. Wouldn't it be a wonderful thing if one could actually take one's own advice? Gus knew better than to dwell on it. Chances were extremely good that it was a lie and meant nothing, but then why the comment about Cyrene's father? To conjure that connection up out of the blue would have been pretty damn creative for an unimaginative idiot like Crum.

And what was Cyrene up to? Why had she just appeared out of nowhere after all these years? It crossed Gus's mind that he would like to get her in front of Franky and see where the truth was. Maybe there was something to the concept of a home version of the machine. There was definitely something going on.

No. He wouldn't let Crum take him there. He liked Cyrene. He really liked Cyrene. In fact, if he understood love, he loved her. So if he loved her, he needed to trust her. It was that simple. Bang. Done. Set it aside as a nasty poke by Crum and move on to all the other things that needed to be done.

It was a beautiful, early fall day. Boston was great at this time of year. The air was clear, the humidity was low, and there was a special energy in the atmosphere as thousands of students moved into their apartments and dorm rooms in the more than sixty universities and colleges in the area.

Gus made his way back to the garage where he had parked his car and worked his way out of downtown back to Waltham and his office. As he drove he struggled to shift his thinking from Cyrene to Blaytent, but he found himself thinking about his father and Chief Allen and Guantanamo and the screams and yelling and heat and sweat and the sun and Crum's red and sweaty face. Arabic words bubbled up in his mind, shifting his thoughts to sitting with Cyrene on the grass outside the high school when she was getting used to being in the U.S. and dealing with the issues of an American High School. She was so worldly! He was so plebeian. How could she deal with small American town mentality? It must have been severe culture shock. Maybe not as bad as some places. Woods Hole is part of Falmouth and Woods Hole is filled with international, oceanographic scientists. But it isn't a desert and it isn't a city and there is no obvious Islamic community.

She had experienced war. She was ten when Saddam Hussein invaded Kuwait, drove the leaders out, and took over Kuwait City. She lived through the bombing and burning and the smell of death. Eight years later she was attending high school in this prototypical, quiet New England town. She was beautiful. She was exotic. She was smart, and Gus had been in awe.

And then she was gone. Their communications had been sporadic. Facebook didn't exist yet. Social media was in its infancy. Immediately after she left Falmouth, they wrote the occasional letter. She moved around. The World Trade Center was destroyed and Gus joined the Army. Although he thought about her every now and then, Gus wasn't sure where she was or what she was doing. In the anti-Arab miasma that blurred clear thinking and overwhelmed logical thought particularly in the military world Gus was living in, he even occasionally had thoughts that they might be working on opposite sides.

And then she just reappeared! She seemed to be acting oddly. He shook that thought off. She was from a different culture. He loved the fact that she was different.

He had to pay attention to his driving. He reached for the radio and looked up just in time to see a Volvo cut off a U-Haul in front of him. Tires squealed and horns blared. He should have known better than to cut through Cambridge. He should have taken the Pike.

He pushed a button on his steering wheel and responded to a beep with, "Call Office!"

He watched the local drama unfold in front of him while he listened to the phone ring on the other end.

When the receptionist answered, Gus said, "Hey, Helen. Connect me to Allan would you?"

Allan asked how the deposition had gone. Gus told him it had been a waste of time. He briefly described his run-in with Crum.

"Very civilized," Allan replied.

Gus told him he was on his way back to the office but stuck in traffic in Cambridge. "Why didn't you take the Pike?" Allan asked.

"It's a beautiful afternoon," Gus said. "I needed to clear my head."

"I'm sure being stuck in traffic is helping!"

Gus asked him if there was anything going on at Blaytent that he should know about. Allan told him nothing that couldn't wait.

"Are you going to be around for a bit?" Gus asked. "I need to talk to you about Cyrene."

"Need some advice, lover boy?" Allan asked.

"Ha, ha, ha," Gus simulated a laugh. "No. Just some weird shit going on."

"I'll be here," Allan replied.

"Just going to grab a sandwich. Have you eaten?"

"I'm all set," Allan replied. "Thanks."

Gus stopped at Barney's Lunch and Deli near the Blaytent offices and ordered a pastrami sandwich to go. He watched while the crew pulled things together, working like a well-oiled machine. He had missed the bulk of the lunch crowd, but camaraderie of the staff was clear to see. They danced between the refrigerated chests and the paper dispensers and the coffee machine – concocting, wrapping, cleaning without ever getting in each other's way. It was obvious that they had been together for a long time. Gus considered that they came into this space every day, day in and day out, week after week, year after year. Once in a while something happened to one of them – a baby, an engagement, a death, a disease, a bad bet, a rotten tooth. They came together, absorbed the blow and went on. They would never find a cure for cancer or write a symphony or travel into outer space. They just made sandwiches and poured coffee. They were one of those infinite, small groups that made life work. Individually, each of them had their own story, their own family, and their own experiences. But here, in this Lunch and Deli they were safe from lawyers and depositions and venture capitalists and the Army and other craziness. Sometimes Gus wished he could just put down his computer and put on an apron and make pastrami sandwiches and pour coffee. But that wasn't to be. He was on a different road and he didn't know where his islands of safety were.

As he walked back to his car in the small parking lot he noticed a man with a shopping cart filled with his belongings – a street person, a bum, a vagrant, a homeless person – depending on what vocabulary you wanted to use. Gus didn't have a lot of time, and sometimes these people were dangerous, and they generally smelled, and you just didn't know what you were getting into when you engaged them in conversation. His internal safety mechanisms told him to ignore the man and assume that he didn't exist although he felt guilty doing that. What did he need? Money? But if Gus gave him money the man would probably just go buy alcohol and that wouldn't be good for him. He would be enabling him.

Food. The man probably needed food. Gus thought he should have bought two pastrami sandwiches. But he hadn't noticed the man before he went into the deli, and if he gave him this one, Gus would have to go back in and buy another one and when he came out, who knew what the man would want? And he really should get back to the office.

By that point Gus's hand was on the handle of his car door. He looked up, and the man was looking at him. Chances were good that the man was a veteran. Gus had read that about forty percent of the homeless men are veterans, guys that got out of the military and were regurgitated back into "normal" life and just couldn't deal with it, couldn't find a new path, couldn't get the sounds out of their heads. Gus could understand that.

By standing there at his car door for so long, Gus had committed himself to doing something. Not that anyone had noticed or cared or would have criticized him for just shrugging this all off, getting into this car, and driving away. But the ethics jury in Gus's mind wouldn't let him get away with that. So he walked over to the man. His hair and his beard were wild, long and turning grey. His skin was bronze and wrinkled. His eyes opened wider as he assessed Gus's approach. He pushed his cart around behind him. As Gus got closer he realized that the man was wearing an old tea cozy on his head for a hat.

Gus recognized that he considered the man an alien as though he was from a different planet, and he wasn't quite sure how to communicate with him. His reaction was to keep it simple. "Hungry?" he asked and then thought to himself, 'dumb question.' "Pastrami?" Another dumb question with no meaning. He held the wrapped sandwich out in front of himself.

The man stepped back a step, pushing his cart away from Gus and the pastrami sandwich.

Gus's reaction was to try to sell the concept. "It's good. Fresh. I just bought it. Actually I was going to eat it myself."

The man looked down at the sandwich and then up at Gus. Gus was beginning to feel a foolish standing there holding the sandwich in front of him. This offer of charity was becoming more complicated and taking too long and the longer it took the less likely it was to result in the sort of warm and cuddly, 'I did a good thing' feelings. Gus considered if he should set the sandwich down on the ground and step away or if he should just back up, step by step, to his car.

What was the problem? What was the guy's story? He must be hungry. Maybe he didn't like pastrami. Maybe he thought Gus had poisoned it.

"Thanks," the man croaked finally, and snatched the wrapped sandwich out of Gus's hands so quickly that it almost ripped apart.

"No problem," Gus replied, wiping his hands on his pants and stepping away. "No problem. Glad to do it."

Gus turned and walked back to his car. As he put his hand on the handle he heard the man yell, "Hey!"

Gus looked up.

"Get yourself another one," the man said. "On me! You can't miss lunch!"

Gus considered for a moment. He really needed to get back. What would the people in the Deli think if he went back in and asked for a second pastrami sandwich? Why did he always have to evaluate whether he was being judged for his every move?

"Yeah," he said finally. "You're right. I can't miss lunch." He shook his head and the man smiled and turned away. Gus went back into the deli where they asked him what he wanted as though he had never been there before. Gus thought he would need to explain why he needed a second sandwich or what had happened to the first one, but they never asked. When he got back out to his car, the man with the tea cozy on his head was gone.

+++++

Back at the Blaytent offices, Bob confronted Gus in the hallway before he could get to his office. "We've made a really bad mistake!" Bob said.

"And good afternoon to you too," Gus replied, striding down the hall. "Can the mistake wait until I've had my lunch?"

"No, I'm serious. I mean, yes. Sure. Lunch."

"What sort of mistake, Bob? Have you been waiting for me by the front door."

Allan heard them walking down the hall and came out of his office. "Yes," he said. "Bob's been waiting for you. He's concerned that we are doing bad science."

"Oh?" Gus looked at Allan to see if he was kidding. The three of them flowed down the hall to Gus's office. Gus dropped his pastrami sandwich on the meeting table and set his computer bag on the floor by his desk.

"Sit. Sit," Gus said. "What's this all about?"

"I can't get a consistent and true confirmation that what I am seeing is directly related to truth or lies."

"What do you mean, Bob?" Gus asked with a mouthful of pastrami.

"All right," Bob replied. "Look, there have been all these studies on using the voice stress for defining the truth, right? People have sold thousands of these things to law enforcement people and employers are using them and TV shows are using them, but there really isn't anything that proves that they are actually detecting anything."

"Okay," Gus replied, "but we've been over this before. Jesus, Bob, we've been at this for more than two years! It's a bit late in the game!"

"That's the point," Bob said and began to pace the office. "The proof of this is that it seems to work, that more people are confessing, and that sort of thing. But it may just be because of the *bogus pipeline effect*. People are more likely to confess because they think that some machine is going to actually be able to read the inside of their brain! The machine doesn't actually detect the lie at all!"

Gus and Allan looked at each other, and then turned to Bob.

"Don't you see? We could make a fancy black box with LEDs blinking all over it like a movie prop and the results would be the same! It has the scientific validity of a horo-scope or a fortune cookie!"

"Bob, Bob, Bob," Gus said. "Slow down, will you? Take a deep breath. We're way beyond the fortune cookie."

"No, really. The science is bogus. They based this on some studies where there was nervous twitch coordination in a subject bicep or the physical muscles in the larynx of one, just one subject that coordinated with something that disturbed him. I mean there really is nothing. The frequencies are all over the place! I mean, the responses are showing up in completely different ranges for different subjects."

"But they are showing up?" Gus asked.

"Yes, but . . . ."

"So we confirm those signals with the three other technologies, right?"

"They aren't really 'signals'."

"Whatever. They are showing up." Gus took another mouthful of pastrami. He turned to Allan, "Remind me to tell you about getting this sandwich."

"I'm serious!" Bob said. "It's not like we can test this thing against known lies."

"But we have, haven't we? We even got a guy who'd been in prison. We even got an accountant to confess as well as information from a potential terrorist. We've even proved it on TV!"

"How do we know that it's not just the *Pipeline* effect? You must have read the papers on that. How do we know it wasn't just people's fear that there actually is a machine that can read your thoughts or your lies? How do we know scientifically that it works?"

Gus didn't respond for a moment. He knew that Bob was sincere about his concerns, and he didn't want to diminish them in any way. Bob wanted to do good science. He was about as far from producing something bogus like some other Charlatans in the field, but in point of fact if people wanted to believe in something and that provided the desired results, did it really matter whether it was real or not? If the Vikings wanted to believe in Thor or Odin did it really matter if they actually existed or not? If the Aztecs really believed that life would be better if they sacrificed people to their Gods, people were going to die whether or not the Gods existed and whether or not they actually had feelings and whether or not the people would ever know if the Gods' feelings had been assuaged or not!

It came back to the water boarding. The subject believed that he was going to die. It was that belief, that understanding, that comprehension that caused him to reveal whatever the interrogators wanted him to reveal. If the Blaytent machine could cause that much fear without hurting the subject, then as far as Gus was concerned it worked. He didn't want to do bad science. He wanted to be able to defend their technology in court if necessary, but the bottom line was that it needed to be able to effectively and accurately extract the desired information.

But he couldn't tell Bob not to worry about it. Quietly he said, "Bob, do you believe in God?"

"What?" Bob looked up at Gus. "What does that have to do with anything?"

"Do you believe in Heaven or Hell?"

"What?"

"A lot of people do, and it causes them to change the way they live. If someone thinks they are going to spend eternity either in eternal bliss or to eternally have their livers torn out as they writhe in pain, they alter the way they live to meet those expectations."

Bob look at him as though he had lost his mind.

"The fact is that no one has scientifically proved that Heaven or Hell exist. No one has scientifically proved that God exists."

"You're not seriously comparing what we are doing to finding God?"

"No, of course not. But the point is that it is what is in the mind of the subject of the questions. If the subject believes that they can improve their future, or even extend their future by talking, by revealing information, by unburdening themselves, then that's is what they will do."

"That's bogus," Bob said.

Gus pulled a twenty-dollar bill out of his wallet and held it up. "What's this?"

Allan smiled.

Bob said, "It's a twenty. Money. It's money."

"It's a piece of paper with printing on it. Writing and pretty pictures. Scientifically that's all it is. It's what you and I believe it is that changes it. The government is willing to take these to pay my taxes. The bank is willing to take these to satisfy my mortgage. And those beliefs extend beyond that to clicks on a keyboard where we believe that some of these twenty-dollar bills will go from one place to another that we will never ever see! It's how we live. It's how the system works. People fight and die and steal for things that we can't scientifically prove."

Bob had stood looking at Gus and Allan. Gus realized that maybe he had gone too far. The Wizard of Oz had a lot going for him as long as he stayed behind the curtain.

"I'm not saying that we are producing something that is fake or some sort of a scam or somehow wrong. You know and I know that peoples' voices change when they are under stress, right?"

Bob didn't blink.

"For God's sake, Bob. You've spent the past two plus years working on this. Why now? Why are you doubting what you are doing now?"

Bob looked at the other two men and then walked over to the windows. None of them talked. Gus took another bite of his pastrami.

Very quietly finally Bob said, "Zack lied to me."

"Zack? Your son?"

"Yes. Zack lied to me, and I didn't figure it out."

Gus and Allan looked at each other. "I don't understand," Allan said. "What did he do?"

Bob turned and faced the two men. "It doesn't matter. I have been working with lies and liars for years now and I should have seen it. I should have heard it. I should have known."

"I hate to ask," Allan said, "but what does this have to do with the machine?"

"I took one home. All right? At least some of it. I was showing it off."

"Oh shit," Gus said.

"It's all right. It was just my family. I didn't show it to anyone else."

"You shouldn't have done that, Bob," Allan said.

"But that's the point! It didn't work. Zack lied, and it didn't tell me that. It didn't fucking work. In fact it lied to me! It told me Zack was telling the truth!" Bob flopped down into a chair.

"All right, Bob," Allan said. "Let's take this from the top."

Bob described how he had gotten excited about how the system had worked on TV, and he was frankly proud of what they had been doing, and Annabelle, his wife, had been giving him a hard time about the amount of time he was spending at work, that he wasn't home enough, that they needed to plan a vacation, and all that sort of thing. And so he had decided to show her what they had been working on, to prove to her that it was going to be great.

Obviously it wasn't all together yet or finished, but he didn't have to tell them that. But he thought that it worked well enough that he could show it to her. So he took it home. That wasn't such a big deal, right? After all they had been showing it off to millions of people on TV. They had been testing it. They wanted to test it. So he didn't think it would be such a big deal to show it to his family.

"Go on," Allan urged.

So he'd taken it home and set it up. It wasn't much more than setting up a video game. That's what they had wanted, right? That's what they were shooting for.

Gus and Allan looked at each other but didn't answer.

It wasn't like his family didn't know what he was doing. "I told them this was the Blaytent machine, what we've been calling 'Cranky Franky'. I don't really know why or what that's all about. But that's what the guys in the back are calling it."

"Okay," Allan prodded.

Bob told them that he had brought his wife in and asked his son to help him demonstrate Franky. Bob thought that would be good. He said his wife watched while he turned it on and fired it up and organized Zack so that the machine would recognize him. And that all worked great.

At this point in the telling of Bob's story, Cyrene tapped on Gus's office door. "Busy?" she asked. Bob swallowed his next words. Gus remembered that he had wanted to talk with Allan about what had happened during the deposition but hadn't had a chance yet. He wasn't ready to confront Cyrene yet.

"Yah," Gus said. "We've got a bit of a crisis here."

Cyrene stood at the door looking at the three men. None of them stood up. She smiled.

"Okay," Cyrene replied after what Gus thought was a significant pause. "You want me to wait?"

"Uh, sure," Gus said.

Cyrene turned and walked away from the door.

"We probably should have closed the door," Gus said.

Allan got up to do it, and Gus waved at him. "Wait," he said. "Wait until she's not in the hallway."

Gus tried to refocus. "So it worked great? What's the problem?"

"I just meant to ask him some basic questions. Didn't mean to go farther. You know, like 'What's your name?' and 'Where do you live?' Stuff that we all knew the answers to so that Franky could show that everything Zack said was the truth."

"And?" Gus prodded. He needed to get on with things. He had finished his sandwich and crushed the wrapping paper and attempted to toss it into his trashcan but had missed.

"Well, I asked Zack where he was which was in our house which was another obvious question, and the machine said to ask, 'Where are you going tonight?' I mean that night, the night we were talking."

"Which was when?" Allan asked.

At that point the monitor on Gus's desk flipped up a live image of Arya who asked, "Gus? Are you here?"

"I'm here," Gus called out. "But I'm kind of busy at the moment."

"We've got the Google Glass working," Arya said.

"Great. Love to see it. I'll get there as soon as I can."

"We'll keep it warm for you," Arya replied. He paused. "That wasn't meant literally. See you when you can." His image swooshed off the screen.

"You need to close that 'door' too," Allan suggested.

"It's set to open as soon as I come into my office. I can't decide if this stuff should be dumber or smarter."

"That's what I mean," Bob said. "I mean this stuff is supposed to be smarter than we are. It's supposed to know when someone is lying."

"So what makes you think Zack lied?" Allan asked.

"I asked him what he was going to do that night, you know, like visit friends or do his homework that sort of thing."

"Did you expect our machine to be able to predict the future too?" Gus asked.

Bob looked at him. "No. No. Of course not?"

"And the machine told you to ask this question?"

"Well, sure. I mean it should have been able to detect voice fluctuations that would indicate that he was going to tell us something that wasn't true."

Gus got up and walked over to the windows. His thoughts were twisting around all the stuff that was going on. Finally he said, "Look, Bob. Think about this. If the machine recognized something in what Zack was telling you and hadn't even said yet that caused it to suggest that you ask about an activity that hadn't even happened yet, don't you think that it was detecting something? Wouldn't you say that it was working pretty damn well?"

Bob looked at him. "Yeah, but, when Zack answered the machine said that he was telling the truth."

"The machine doesn't really do that, does it?"

"Well, no. I mean it indicates when you're close to the answer, the truth, reality, whatever you want to call it."

"And don't you think that some of that revelation happened because of your work with voice stress? I think what you're telling us is pretty remarkable, don't you?"

"But the voice stress stuff has been shown to be bogus! Scientifically there's no substance! It's the *bogus pipeline effect*."

"Is it? I think you've gone beyond that," Gus said. He thought to himself that it would useful if they could keep Bob from looking things up on the Internet. It was like being able to describe some pain and look up self-diagnosing a deadly disease! A little knowledge . . .. But Bob had much more than a little knowledge. He was a key member of their team. He had to be kept on track and enthusiastic.

"I should go," Bob said. "You're obviously busy and I've really said my bit."

"Bob, the *bogus pipeline effect* is a two step process as you know. You convince the subject that the machine is somehow all knowing. And since people want to believe that there is something or someone that knows it all, that isn't all that hard to do. That's why palm readers and horoscopes and fortune-tellers and soothsayers are all successful. Somewhere in each of us there is that mystical belief that there is much more going on in the universe than we can ever know. It helps to believe in Santa Claus and the Easter Bunny and fairies and even God.

"People want to believe that there <u>could</u> be a machine that could give them all the answers to life. So the only challenge is convincing them that *this* is the machine. So researchers built machines with wires and lights and had someone in the next room manipulate the output using answers to questions that the subject had already answered to prove that the machine worked. Then the subject answered new questions and magically they were the right answers! But we don't manipulate anything, do we?"

"No. Of course not," Bob answered.

"No. We don't. I don't doubt that IIDT's machine is a classic of the *pipeline* effect. But if there is any manipulating going on in our machine, it's by whatever little gremlins there are in the computer! We give it lots of information about lots of things, and it sorts them out and tells us if we are getting close to something useful. Isn't that right?"

"Yes, but . . . ."

"No, 'buts'. Maybe we don't have it fine-tuned to detect teenage variations! In fact there are a million subtleties that we need to work on: terrorists, paraplegics, menopausal women, pathological liars, people with Asperger Syndrome, and so on. We still have a lot of work to do, and you are a major part of it. Bob, I think it is critical that you look at the results of what happened with Zack. Allan and I are going to have to talk about the impact of you taking the machine home. You should have cleared that with us in the first place, but I think you have achieved some valuable insight."

Bob stood up. "Okay," he said. He looked at Gus. "You know, if a machine like ours could help to explain teenage behavior, maybe we'd really have something."

They all laughed.

When Bob had left, Gus closed the door behind him.

"You want me to get out of here so you can talk to Cyrene?" Allan asked.

"No. I want to talk to you about that first." Gus came back and flopped down in his chair. "Crum said something in my deposition that disturbed me. The deposition turned out to be a mess."

"Why?"

"Well, it wasn't the deposition itself that was the problem. It was what happened afterward. I actually hit him."

"What? You hit him?"

"Well, sort of. I mean I didn't hit him hard. He was in my face."

"Oh, shit! In public? You hit him in public?"

"Yah. It was in the lobby. He was being an ass in the elevator, and he got in the way as we were getting out. He got in my face, and I had to hit him. Not hard."

"What did Boyd think of all this?"

"Boyd was great. Stopped it from going any further. But that's not what I wanted to talk to you about. Crum implied that Cyrene's father was somehow involved."

"What did he say?" Allan asked.

"I don't remember exactly. It was more the way he said it, you know?"

Allan looked at him. "Don't just let it bug you! Just ask her."

"Ask her what? 'Where were you when you called me earlier?' 'What does your father have to do with IIDT?' 'What are you really doing here?' Maybe I don't want to know the answers to those questions."

"Can't help you with that, my friend," Allan said. "You're just going to find out from her."

Gus found Cyrene sitting in the waiting area at the front of the building. She looked great. She always gave him that little hitch in his throat. He devoutly wished that was all that he saw, that he didn't have this nagging gremlin in the back of his mind that something was off the rails, something wasn't quite what it should be, that something about Cyrene was unreal like the *SceneSet* background she put on her cell phone.

"Hi," he said in greeting. "Sorry about that. Minor crisis." He smiled and hugged her. "I have to see Arya. He's got the Google Glass working. Want to see?"

She returned his smile and his hug and walked beside him down the hall to Arya's production area. While they walked they didn't talk and that in itself was a sign that something stood between them.

Arya was leaning over one of the technicians and when they came into the room he straightened up, turned and faced them. It was extraordinary how much of a change wearing glasses made to his face. It made him look older and more serious, which was belied by the fact that he was grinning from ear to ear and the glasses certainly weren't ordinary. The right side of the frame was colorful and there was what appeared to be a solid block of glass in the upper corner.

"These are amazing!" he gushed.

"You've had them for awhile," Gus pointed out.

"Yes and they were amazing before, working with other people's stuff. But now . . . now they work with our stuff!"

"That's great," Gus said. "Do you want to show us?"

Arya looked at Cyrene for just the blink of an eye. "It's okay," Gus said.

"I know," Arya replied. "She's on my screen! It's not all smooth yet. But it's a Hell of a start!"

Arya pulled the glasses off and handed them to Gus and showed him how to work with them. "I don't know if I can work with these," Gus said. "Things look pretty blurry without my regular lenses." He took off his own glasses and handed them to Arya. In moments Arya had snapped the Google Glass components to the right side of his wire rimmed frames and handed them back to Gus.

Gus had been wearing his glasses for so long that they had become generally invisible to him. The new configuration felt somewhat lopsided and heavy but it took just a moment for Gus to notice the computer-generated image in the upper right corner of his vision. Arya showed him how to adjust the picture until it became clear. The computer generated image seemed to float but he could see through it. It definitely was a bit distracting, but then the image disappeared and there was just a small object at the edge of his peripheral vision.

Arya gave him a briefing on how to interact with the Glass and it quickly became intuitive. Gus found himself grinning despite all the issues of the day. He felt a bit foolish talking to his glasses, sort of like walking through an airport talking to yourself but really on a cell phone. It was becoming a world of people talking to invisible objects!

"Okay, Arya, show me how it works with our stuff, " Gus said.

Arya guided him to a spot in the lab. Cyrene followed them.

"Look at Cyrene," Arya said.

Gus did as he was told. Cyrene smiled. Letters on the Glass screen read "Cyrene Al-Masri".

"Whoa," said Gus. He turned to look at Arya.

The Glass screen read, "Arya Jain".

"Cool," said Gus. He looked back at Cyrene.

"Okay," Arya said, "ask a question. Something simple." Cyrene turned away.

"Are you Cyrene Al-Masri?" Gus asked.

"Yes," Cyrene said, turning back to face him.

The background in the Glass image turned a little pink.

"See the way the color changed?" Arya asked, looking up from his monitor. "We can see what you're seeing on these monitors. "The reddish color means the subject that you are talking to believes they are telling the truth."

"Whoa," said Gus. "That's amazing!" He asked Cyrene, "Were you born in Kuwait City?"

"Yes," Cyrene said.

The Glass image didn't change, but stayed slightly red or pink. "Brings a whole new meaning to your 'Rose Colored Glasses'!" Gus said.

"Ask her something that you know isn't true," Arya said.

That set off an array of issues in Gus's mind. There were all the 'yes' or 'no' questions and then there were all the questions that needed defining. He told himself to keep it simple for now. "Are you over a hundred years old?"

Cyrene looked at Arya as if to know whether she should tell the truth or lie without saying anything. "No," Arya answered the unspoken question. "No, lie so he can see how this works."

"Yes," she said. "I'm one hundred and ten years old! But you never ask a woman her age." She smiled.

The glass image changed to a slightly blue tint and displayed "Age 34.5."

"You're getting colder," Gus said. "And you're only thirty four and half? It's a bit hard to see that," he said to Arya. "I mean the room background has to be pretty white and bright to notice the change."

"True," Arya replied, "but it also depends on the intensity of the emotion behind the answer. If you accused her of killing her dog, for example, she might feel more emotionally committed to the answer and the color would be more intense. But it's working, isn't it?"

"And it shows the true answer? How does it know that?"

Cyrene leaned over the monitor. "Oh, my," she said.

"Of course it's connected to the Internet," Arya explained. "It looked her up. Anything that is public knowledge, anything that it can connect to it can provide on the screen."

"This could get out of hand," Cyrene said.

"And on top of that, of course, we have added all of Blaytent's capabilities for facial recognition, body language, voice stress and so on."

"All right," Gus said looking at Cyrene, "where were you when you called me earlier?"

Cyrene looked at him and paused. "When?" she asked.

"When you called me before the deposition? Were you using *SceneSet* to provide the background?"

"Yes," she said. The Glass screen glowed pink again.

"Why?" he asked. He was getting used to having the image in the corner of his eye so that he could talk with her directly with just a subtle awareness that there was something else going on. It was sort of like tuning out the background of a busy public place.

She hesitated. The pink on the screen began to fade. "I don't think that is important," she said. The screen turned pink again and the word 'uncomfortable' appeared.

Arya said, "Well, it's great isn't it?" in an attempt to redirect the drift.

"Yes," Gus said. "You're right." He took off his glasses and handed them to Arya who snapped off the Google Glass attachment.

There was a stretched out moment of silence surrounding the three of them. Finally Gus said, "Does that work anywhere or do you have to be near our equipment?"

"For right now," Arya replied, "you have to be near our stuff because of the acoustics. The mics in these things are pretty good, but they don't have the directional or range accuracy we need. The mics may be the biggest drawback to downsizing these things. Don't know yet. Things have gotten pretty small," he laughed.

"Yup," Gus said. "That's great. Thanks, Arya." He turned to Cyrene, "I guess we have some things to talk about without the machine."

Walking back to his office, Gus wondered if it wouldn't have been better to just keep going with the machine. It sure made it easier. In fact it seemed like they had accomplished what he had set out to do! He got a little lump in his throat and smiled to himself despite everything that was going on.

They really had done it! They really had created a machine that could indicate the truth. Wow! What would that do to conversations or life in general? People said they wanted to know the truth. Would a new way of lying emerge? "Does this dress make me look fat?" "Absolutely!"

It was like a whole new social order would emerge. Social media had opened up people's personal lives; this would go a step beyond that . . . or maybe not. Maybe people would just stop talking to each other all together. All communications would be electronic and at a distance. That wasn't what Gus had intended. Did you need to be able to lie or at least manipulate the truth to communicate face to face? Would there have to be new laws on when and where this stuff could be used? Would there have to be an Act of Congress to create some sort of licensing? What did this do to trust and taking something on faith? And where did his trust and faith in Cyrene stand at this point?

Back in his office he closed the door behind them, and as soon as they were alone, she hugged him and kissed him hard on the lips.

He felt himself pulling away and then losing resistance and giving in to the feelings and the moment. He felt her warm, small, hard body in his arms and he resisted the urge to just pick her up and carry her over to his sofa. She felt good. She felt like she was a part of him. He felt her hands on the back of his neck. His hands felt the small of her back, the sharpness of her shoulder blades, the curve of her ass in the tightness of her dress.

He stepped back. "That wasn't a lie," she said with a smile.

"I guess!" he replied with a gasp. He walked around and flopped down in his desk chair.

"I've missed you," she said perching herself on the edge of his desk and hiking up her skirt.

"So what was the background hiding thing when you called me? Where were you that you didn't want me to see?"

"Oh, I just forgot to shut that thing off, you know? It's just one of those apps on my phone. Really. I really was just doing some shopping. Nothing mysterious." She smiled.

"Oh," he replied. He didn't really believe her, but did it matter? He told his brain to stop wandering. "Something came up during the deposition this morning."

"Oh," she said.

"Yeah. Something about your father. Crum made some comment about your father. Captain . . . I mean Major Crum. That guy is such a piece of work."

"Really? Why?"

"Why is he a piece of work?"

"No. Why would he say something about my father?"

"I don't know. You tell me."

She slid off the desk and walked over to the windows. "What did he say?"

"Who? Crum? He said something about that I should ask you about him."

"What does that mean?"

"I don't know. You tell me."

Cyrene paused for a moment before turning back to face him. "To tell you the truth, I don't know what he meant by that. You said it yourself. The guy is a piece of work."

"Do you know him?"

"Who?"

"Crum. Do you know Crum?"

She hesitated for a split second. "No. I don't"

"Does your father know him?"

"I couldn't say. My father knows a lot of people. He had dealings with the U.S. government during the war."

"The Gulf War? 'Desert Storm'?"

"That's what you Americans call it."

It was another one of those moments where Gus would like to have had one of his own machines available, and yet he wished he didn't even know it existed. He wanted this to be a one on one natural conversation, but he couldn't help watching Cyrene's body language and her change of pronouns from *we* to *you*. Maybe she didn't think of herself as American. Was she? He hadn't even asked her. Was he really that blind? But why would he have asked her what passport she was carrying? He forced himself to focus.

"There's a lot I don't know about you," Gus said quietly.

She didn't answer.

"Speaking of which, I don't know why you came by here today. Did you want to talk about something?"

She turned and walked back to the desk and perched herself back on the corner close enough so that he could smell her perfume. He couldn't resist putting his hand on her knee and feeling the smooth surface of her stockings. She smiled. "Talk?" she asked.

He stood up. "Yes. Was there something you wanted to talk about? And I really need to know what Crum meant. What connection does he have with your father?"

She jumped down from the desk. "Look," she said, "what if your machine is wrong?"

He was taken aback. "What?"

"What if your machine is wrong? How do you know that what it has figured out is correct, that it is the right answer? If you rely on the machine, you could get things very wrong, make huge mistakes. Just because it 'says it on the Internet' doesn't make it true. What if it's all a fairy tale?"

"You've lost me." He looked at her, trying to understand what she was telling him by reading her body language, trying to extract more meaning than what was in her words.

"If I say, my name is Cyrene Al-Masri, you believe me. Why? Because you trust me. You trust me not to lie to you. If your machine, says that's true as well, it confirms what you think you already know. But what if I am able to convince your machine of something that is a lie? What if your machine says that I'm lying when I say that I am Cyrene Al-Masri? Are you going to believe yourself or your machine? Just because it is a machine doesn't mean that it doesn't make mistakes." She paused. "Or have you built the perfect machine? What does your machine do that Major Crum's machine doesn't do?"

"A lot," Gus said. "Our machine looks at more than just one element of communication."

"Yah, but ultimately it's a matter of perception, isn't it?"

"For some things, sure. But for others, it's black or white."

"Really? What's ever black or white?"

"Well, for example, do you know Major Crum?"

She looked at him, eyes flicking back and forth over his face. "Why is that black or white? Do I know of him, have I heard his name? Sure. Have I slept with him, known him in the Biblical sense? No." She shuddered in mock disgust.

"You know what I mean!"

"See. It's the meaning of the words. It's not black or white."

"Did you run over a cat when you drove over here? That's a black and white question. Either you did or you didn't. Black or white."

"I don't know. I could have without knowing it."

"You're impossible! And you're avoiding the subject. I want to know what Crum meant when he made that comment."

"Well, I'm not going to tell you. I don't know."

They stood looking at each other; too far apart to touch. The intimacy that was smoldering moments before had winked out and the coolness of something unspoken lay between them.

"I better go," she said finally. "You have a lot to do."

Chapter Twelve

December 2014

It was a tradition in the Medici family that they all get together and eat with some drinking involved as well. In some cases it was the other way around. And there were a lot of relatives. Sometimes Julia was surprised at how many relatives there were. Boyd wasn't actually surprised because he had been forewarned. The family gathered in Boston like flies to honey, around Tony Medici's restaurant in the North End. Of course the whole thing was amplified by the fact that the Medici's had lived in the North End all their lives and knew most of the people who lived there. Things had changed over the years, Tony would tell you, but still they stayed the same.

The Christmas season was the best time for a family reunion. There was always the issue of where people would stay when they came in from other parts of the country, even other parts of the world. Stepping over a bed in the living room to get to the bathroom was part of the experience.

The North End of Boston is where the Harbor meets the continent. It is an area that is ripe with history from Paul Revere and the Old North Church to Copps Hill Burying Ground to Parziale's Bakery where Former Governor Sarah Palin made her famous comments about Paul's ride to warn the British! Like many dynamic and historic neighborhoods, it has swung back and forth from boom to bust to boom, welcoming the wealthy, the immigrants, and back to the wealthy.

It is a quaint neighborhood close to downtown Boston and at this moment in time was filling up with young executives who raised both the property values and the cost of living by pouring more money into renovations while seeking to maintain the quaint neighborhood atmosphere, almost like recreating Downtown Disney where even if there were cockroaches they would dress properly.

On the Friday before Christmas the Medicis closed the restaurant to the public and opened it to the family. It happened every year. It was tradition! In 1959 Anthony's father opened La Cucina de'Medici. There were some tough years as the Central Artery cut off easy access to the area and shops and businesses closed, but the Friday prior to Christmas closing stuck. Some years only a few family members showed up, but most years, the place was bursting at the gills. Julia had always looked forward to the event more than Christmas itself.

This would be Boyd's second year. Over the years, when Julia had a boyfriend, she was never quite sure how the family reunion would impact their relationship and if they would be around for a second year. Boyd, on the other hand, came from such a small and quiet family, that he had a hard time wrapping his head around all the noise and the people and how they would tear themselves away from their own families and traditions. Weren't they missing the children's Christmas concerts and parades and Santa Claus at the mall? The Medici family had drifted out to other parts of the country – Columbus, Ohio and San Diego, California and Knoxville, Tennessee and other places. And yet they gathered here year after year to laugh and eat and argue and catch up on the events of the year. Boyd could not possibly keep all their names straight so he had adopted names that helped him to at least identify them and to some extent their relationship with other members of the family.

When Julia made the mistake of asking him, "Did you like the family reunion?" it was akin to asking, "Does this dress make me look fat?" He honestly wasn't sure. It wasn't the sort of thing that a stranger could easily categorize as something he or she did or didn't like. All these people had histories with each other, connections, stories, incidents; "Do you remember the time Cousin Bill got so drunk he couldn't get out of his car when he got home? He couldn't find the handle." Ha, ha, ha. Boyd didn't have any of those connections. He didn't know why Cousin Bill drank so much or what was going on in his marriage or job that caused him to dig into the whiskey at the end of the night. He could only stand there and smile and nod appropriately.

It was even worse when they talked about who did what to whom in a marriage of people who were not even there and may have died years ago. They had no experiential or family connections to Boyd's stories because they hadn't been there and didn't know or care what he was talking about, so he had to make his own tales somewhat generic. Years before, Boyd had read a book about living with the Eskimos or Inuit which said that when two Inuit men met on the ice while they were hunting, the first thing they did was to discuss all of their family connections, seeking out the links they had in common. Sharing wives was one way to make a solid connection, and it was better than killing each other because they were not related in any way.

Julia took the day of the reunion off in order to help her father cook. Boyd arrived at the restaurant about four and found the door locked with a sign that read "Closed for the evening for a Private Event. Please visit us again soon!" Boyd knocked and stood there waiting, smiling apologetically at the occasional passerby. He knocked a second time. Maybe they hadn't heard. It was probably crazy in there. It seemed like there should be a better door. And what about all the family that would show up later? They would have to situate one of the larger cousins near the door to act as a bouncer. Maybe they should have a Medici family ID card or a reunion T-shirt like other families did. Otherwise who knew who would be seeking a free dinner at a great Italian restaurant in the North End!

He knocked again and this time a face appeared at the edge of the door, a face Boyd didn't recognize and who obviously didn't recognize him.

"We're closed," the woman said.

"Yes, I know," Boyd replied. "I'm Boyd. Boyd Willis. I'm with Julia." If he had been really cool, he would have remembered the woman's name and swept her off her feet like a soldier returned from the war. He had fantasies like that, like something from the movies in black and white. Instead he stood outside the door shuffling his feet.

"Juli!" the woman yelled back into the restaurant. "Juli. Someone here for you!"

Julia came bustling to the door, wiping her hands on her apron. She had traces of flour on her face that was streaked with sweat and her hair stood out in a variety of directions. But she smiled at him, grabbed him by the arm and dragged him off the street into the restaurant. The other woman pushed the door closed behind him. "Mariella. This is Boyd. You remember him. He was here last year."

Boyd vaguely remembered her. It seemed as though her appearance had changed. Maybe she had lost weight? Maybe she was Julia's sister that he had identified as 'Curly'? But he wasn't going to say anything. "Hi," he said with a smile.

"Come on," Julia said, guiding Boyd out to the kitchen. "Let's put you to work."

The main body of the restaurant was quiet, but the kitchen was banging and bustling as usual, filled with about a dozen people. Boyd wasn't sure how he would find a corner to stand in to stay out of the way. He was used to busy kitchens. His mother had been a baker, after all. Her baking had kept the family going when his father's landscape business had struggled. It was a dance of coordinated chaos; pans clanking against pans. Oven doors squeaked open and thumped closed. Whisks whispered around the whirlpool of mixing bowls. Eggs cracked. Bags of flour thumped onto counter tops. Refrigerator doors scraped open and vaulted shut. People shouted and laughed and chastised and sang out instructions to each other.

And the aromas were overwhelming. The smells of fresh baked breads and pastries and frying onions and spices and savory, sensuous fruits filled the air and caressed Boyd's senses and his memories.

Boyd grinned. Maria Medici, Julia's mother, looked up from her cutting board, dropped her knife and pushed through the madness with open arms and a wide smile on her face. "Boyd!" she gushed, wrapping him in a bear hug. "Wonderful to see you! Tony!" she yelled. "Tony! Julia's young man's here. Come and say hello!"

Tony was back by the stoves in his T-shirt. His face was red and he wore a sweat band around his head that proclaimed "Merry Christmas!" He wove his way through the crowd of relatives to where Maria Medici was holding Boyd's arm as though he were a prize that might run away.

Tony wiped his hand on his apron and held it out for Boyd to shake. "Hey," he said. "How are ya?" His hand was large and strong and strangely soft.

"Fine. Thank you, sir," Boyd replied. "It smells wonderful in here."

Julia held onto his other arm. It would have been impossible for Boyd to miss the silent family communications going on at that moment. "Is he going to marry her? Is he right for her? But he's not Italian? When? If he doesn't marry her, what will she do? She's not getting any younger? Grandchildren would be nice?" At other points, those hints and allegations would not have been silent, but they passed in a moment and could have been a figment of Boyd's imagination.

"Give the boy an apron," Maria Medici told her daughter. "Put him to work. Introduce him around. You remember Mariella at the door, that's Julia's youngest sister. She's not married. That's Cecilia over there chopping vegetables. She is married. She lives in Providence. Her husband . . . (Boyd was starting to lose names already) . . . will be here later. He drives a truck. Long haul. He's a teamster. Never home. No children yet. And you're a lawyer?"

This last statement was a loud confirmation; stated to be overheard. Boyd had seen Julia's parents several times over the course of the past year so, of course, Maria knew he was a lawyer. The statement was to put a uniform on him with badges and ribbons and a hat. It silently said, "Look at what

278 · PAUL H. RAYMER

our Julia has found! Finally!" Then she bustled back to her spot.

Boyd recognized many of the faces, but some names still eluded him. He could put together Tony's brothers and their wives – Pietro and Rosa and Franco and Caterina. They came together in pairs that were easier to remember. The third brother, Giovanni (known as Gio), hadn't arrived yet. He was flying in from San Diego. Everyone suspected him of being gay but no one said anything. Tony was the oldest and would be approaching the social security age of sixty-five in the coming year. Not retirement. He would never retire. He would probably drop dead into a pot of Italian Wedding soup at the age of one hundred and ten! Julia was already formulating plans for a memorable birthday party.

When Julia started to define the relations who had not yet arrived – like her brother Stefano and his wife Kris who were arriving from Columbus, Ohio, and her uncle, Ermano and his wife, Rachel who were driving up from Knoxville, Tennessee with their three children, John, Celia, and Alan – Boyd just smiled and took refuge in his mental happy place.

Boyd removed his jacket and Julia set him up stirring a large pot, which was more like rowing a boat while he listened to the family chatter, punctuated by laughter and kitchen clanks and whooshes.

"He didn't know what he was doing when he did it. He couldn't have or he wouldn't have done it."

"Nah. I don't believe it. He's always done stuff like that. Their family should be on reality TV!"

"Are they getting married or are they just friends? I mean isn't there a baby involved? How old is she anyway?"

"Who?"

"I don't remember her name. I'm terrible with names. Seems to get worse every year."

"There's medication for that, you know!"

"There's medication for everything these days. Pretty soon you won't need to eat. You'll just take a pill and get on with things!"

"Keep that to yourself, Pietro. You never saw a table of food you didn't like!"

While he stirred and listened, Boyd heard the odd, repetitive, musical notes of a cell phone that got louder when it was pulled from a pocket.

"YAH? MANNO? WHERE ARE YOU?" Maybe it is because cell phone microphones are so small that people feel they need to yell into them.

"YAH. WE'RE HERE. WHERE ARE YOU?" Seems like personal conversations and cell phones are in separate worlds. For a brief moment in history cell phones were status symbols; not everybody had them. Not everybody could afford them, but they had become as ubiquitous as shoes. They were not only everywhere, they were also constantly in use and some people carried more than one. And when the call came up on the screen it identified who was calling before you even said 'Hello'. Or at least whose phone was calling. No surprise. No privacy. No unavailability.

"ALL THE KIDS? HOW THEY DOIN'? LONG RIDE? WHO PUKED? IN JERSEY? Oh, dear! NO. FONSIE'S NOT HERE YET."

Julia appeared at Boyd's elbow, looked in the pot and took the spoon from him. "Good," she said. "Turn off the burner. Let's set up some tables."

She guided him from the cacophony of the kitchen to the relative peace of the dining room. It was a surprisingly large room that would hold close to thirty tables. By pushing the tables out of the way, a long buffet table could be set up at one end of the room giving plenty of clear space for people to mill around. It was likely that many of them would never leave the kitchen and another group would never leave the bar. Boyd felt sorry for the kids because it seemed as though there was nothing very kid-like in this gathering.

"What do you think?" Julia asked him.

He looked at her, trying to read her face to get some clue as to what she was asking him about. "About what?"

"About the family?"

That was one of those questions that didn't lend itself to a complete answer because the real question was not the question that was being asked.

"They're nice," he said as he smoothed out the tablecloth.

"They can be loud," Julia said.

Boyd didn't reply.

"This is such an important event for dad. Every year. They've talked about moving it around. It's a long trip for some of the brothers. And it's a tough time of year."

"It is. People are pretty busy."

They straightened out the tables and put out candles and sprigs of pine, moved the chairs to the outside edges of the room and then stopped for a moment, looking at each other.

"I know I shouldn't talk about work, but there's something I wanted to talk to you about." She lowered her voice. "Before it all gets started here."

Boyd looked at her and saw the concern on her face. "What is it?" he asked.

"You remember that guy that worked for Gudmudgion at Avitas, the venture firm? Pinel. Chris Pinel?"

Boyd nodded. "He was siphoning off money, wasn't he?"

"Yes. He took rather a lot." She looked at him.

"I thought that was all over with. I mean that was over a year ago."

"It was. I mean I thought it was. It had to go through all the legal stuff, and you know how long that all takes. And I thought that when it was done, Avitas would put the money back into Blaytent. I mean Pinel worked for them after all. It would have been fair and reasonable."

"This stuff usually isn't either fair or reasonable."

"Well, they didn't put it back in. And I've been counting on those funds. I probably shouldn't have, but it seemed fair and reasonable."

"Why would it be on you?"

"Well, it isn't really, but the point is that the money isn't there and that Blaytent needs it. I mean Gudmudgion is still demanding that we meet our projections even without that money! And the fact is that the company is sucking down money like a runaway train."

Boyd nodded. "I assume Gus knows about this."

"He just doesn't want everyone to know how serious it is. They'll worry. And that is distracting."

"Yes, but shouldn't people be aware of what's going on?"

"That's at least part of the problem. What is going on? What is going to happen? How do we know when we're there?"

Boyd looked at her. She was flushed from her exertions. The Christmas lights changed the colors of her face from a red to a green to a blue tint. "I suppose when the company is self-sufficient, selling stuff, making a profit? Isn't that written into the business plan?"

"What it says is that the company 'has to demonstrate commercial viability'. I don't think we have the resources left to produce a tangible, marketable product and generate all the collateral materials that are required to push it into the marketplace."

"What's that?" Boyd asked.

"You know . . . the public relations, the advertising, the packaging and distribution. I mean we'd have to hire an army of sales people. We'd have to be able to go head to head with some of the other companies out there."

"But isn't that the point? Blaytent wasn't doing all this as a science experiment, as fundamental research, was it? I mean at some point the company has to stand on its own two feet."

Julia's mother bustled through from the kitchen. "What are you two gossiping about out here? Anything we should know?" She looked back and forth between the two of them with her hands on her hips.

"Nothing that can't wait," Julia smiled.

"Gio is on his way from the airport. Boyd, didn't you help us with the bar last year? I seem to remember something about that." She laughed.

As the afternoon rolled into evening, family began arriving. There were hugs and kisses and handshakes and pats on the back and laughter. The noise level built. Boyd rolled up his sleeves and worked behind the bar. Relatives came up and leaned over the bar to shake his hand. Some worked around behind to hug him and give him pecks on both cheeks.

"You're Julia's guy, aren't you? The latest! That's wonderful. Are you two getting married? We haven't had a good family wedding in awhile. Oh, if you haven't seen a Medici wedding, you haven't seen a wedding! This family loves to party. Doesn't it? You can see. You can see. We do this every year. Every year! Right smack in the middle of the holiday season. Between you and me, this could be somewhere else, you know? I mean this place is great, but it's a long way. And right in the middle of the holiday season. We should be at home. Kids miss all the holiday parties. All that good shit. But it's family, you know? Family. Nothing more important than family. And we have a lot of them!"

And the food flowed out of the kitchen and spread across the buffet table. The relatives were everywhere; all the corners of the kitchen and the dining room. Once Gio arrived he gathered and gossiped with Tony's other brothers' wives. There were small groups where the conversation hummed around the children. Rachel, Julia's brother Ermanno's wife, organized their three children at a table off to the side and brought them milk and lasagna. They sat in their chairs, swinging their legs and taking it all in.

Eventually Julia's oldest brother, Stefano, joined Boyd behind the bar. "Crazy, huh?" he said, nodding at the swirl of humanity that filled the room around them.

Boyd smiled. "It is," he replied.

"Every year. Something to look forward to." He looked at Boyd. "So you going to make an honest woman out of my sister?"

Boyd smiled. He was well aware of the family pressure, but he wasn't fond of getting pushed.

"How long have you two been an item? It's over a year now, right?"

They were interrupted by people asking for drinks. Boyd hoped that would be the end of it. Stefano or Steve as the younger generation called him, was okay. Boyd wasn't going to let him get under his skin.

"Hey, Boyd! Good to see you again," one of Julia's balding uncles leaned across the bar to shake his hand. "Boyd, right? I have that right? Welcome. Couldn't get enough of us? You were here last year, right? I remember. Old memory's fading a bit, but I've still got it, right, Stefano?"

"You still got it, Uncle Franco," Steve replied with a smile. "What're you drinking?"

Julia's mother stood beside the bar surveying the buffet table and wiping her hands on her apron. "Do you think there's enough food? These people eat like locusts! I would hate to run out of food."

"Never happen, mom," Steve said. "Never happen!"

In the middle of the tumult of the voices and the flow of food from the kitchen to the table to the plates to the stomachs, someone began tapping on the side of a glass; "Tink, tink, tink!" More glasses were tapped and the room gradually quieted and fell silent as Tony rose to his feet like the best man at a wedding.

He cleared his throat and raised his glass. "*Cento di questi giorni!*", he boomed out. "Thank you for coming!"

"Didn't have a choice!" someone called back. "You've got all the food!" General laughter and chuckles.

Boyd worked his way over to where Julia was sitting.

"The fact is that I recognize how hard it is for all of you to get here, and I'm grateful. Family is everything! The world is a crazy place. Crazy things happen. We all struggle with problems every day. Some big. Some small. But no matter what, there is family. We have each other. The big wigs have summit meetings. We have each other. This is the world. This, right here, right now, this is life!"

He lifted his glass and they all followed suit. "*Per la vita! A noi!* To life! To us!" They all stood, raised their glasses, and drank.

A few others stood to make toasts and announcements. There were a few glances in Boyd's direction, but although he continued drinking he wasn't about to bow to the pressure. It was odd how the unseen emotions from a crowd can push an agenda forward. Peer pressure was real. Even the pseudo-panic in a crowd of people running can be an unconscious, almost uncontrollable motivating force. The affirmation of a family like this to welcome him in was powerful and the more he drank the more powerful it seemed to become. These were great people, nice people, a wonderful family.

"You have a wonderful family," he said to Julia.

She smiled at him. "Did you get desert?"

The main course dishes had changed into a wonderland of Italian pastries, breads and cheeses.

"Your mother was worried about running out of food!"

"She's always worried about running out of food! It's in the blood."

"I'm totally stuffed. Really."

Julia's oldest brother Ermanno was sitting with them. "It's a central theme," he said. "Life centers around food. Pop made sure of that. Is Juli keeping you straight on this cast of characters? It's hard enough for those of us that have lived with it all our lives!" He laughed.

Boyd smiled. "Not too bad," he said. "How's Knoxville?"

"It's a haul from here, I'll tell you that. Especially this time of year. Never know what the weather's going to do."

"Why did you move down there?"

"Job. Finding work around here was getting pretty tough, you know. Construction kind of dried up."

"That's what you do? Construction?"

"Yeah. I'm a contractor. I'm sure Juli told you. Work and politics. The politics around here is pretty liberal. And Rachel's family is from there. Seemed like the right place to be at the right time."

Boyd asked Ermanno if he wanted a refill on his drink. When he got back to the table, Ermanno said, "I thought about getting into politics. No, really!"

Julia grinned.

"No, really," he repeated. "I think it's important. We need more people who know what they're doing to get elected. Most politicians haven't had a normal job in their lives! I don't know where they come from."

"You think there is a breeding ground for people who go into politics? A people factory for politicians?" Julia asked.

Ermanno ignored her and faced Boyd. He drummed his fingers on the table. "Tap, tap, tap." "The point is that we are not well represented. No taxation without representation!"

"That sounds like a Boston attitude, Manno," Julia said. "Seems to me I've heard it before. Bordering on the liberal!"

"The original guys were conservatives! They were against taxes and big government. Now we've got this liberal dick head giving the way the store. Who knows where we're going to end up! I mean take the Supreme Court! You can't tell what they're going to decide these days. The fundamental values of the country are likely to get shaken to their roots! There's bound to be a new judge before long. They're so freakin' old!"

Julia said, "You're the lawyer, Boyd. What do you think? You know any likely candidates?"

Another image of another evening in a different Boston bar came flooding back into Boyd's mind. "You know Judge Jakes? I worked with her. Years ago. Long time ago. Ages ago. I worked with her."

"You think she might be a potential Supreme Court judge?" Julia asked.

"I don't know. Maybe she's changed."

"How so?"

Boyd took a deep pull on his drink. It was so comfortable here. These people were so nice. "She harassed me. She sexually harassed me!"

Julia laughed, but when she saw Boyd's face and how serious he was, she said, "Sorry. Just seems strange."

"Why? You don't think I'm harassable? Not pretty enough for that?"

She put her arm around him. "You're perfectly harassable to me! I'll harass you until you scream for mercy!"

Ermanno turned away. "Get a room, you guys."

"No, seriously, she did. It's just as feasible for a woman to harass a man, but, boy, do men treat it differently! Big joke! Beautiful woman comes on to a guy, he should love it. He should. But it's not the moment that matters. Not just the moment that matters."

"How are you feeling, Boyd?" Julia asked. "You look a little . . . you know."

"It's all the moments after the event that matter. What do you do afterward? What do you do? As a man, you are completely exposed just because people don't expect it to happen. They expect you to want it."

"So what happened," Ermanno asked.

"We worked together. Jakes was my boss in fact. We had a big case that we were working on, and you know, sometimes when you're working on a project really hard for a really long time and it turns a corner it's sort of like making a touchdown."

"Ha, ha, ha. Touchdown!" Ermanno laughed.

"No seriously. You know what I mean. You get excited. Elated, I mean."

"And that's what happened? She got excited and you made a touchdown?"

"You see. When it's a guy, nobody can take it seriously! But the fact is that doubles the problem because the other guys in the office think you should like the attention. They're jealous, in fact. And you can lose your job. And I did."

"I thought you quit?" Julia asked.

"I did, but they made me go through sensitivity training, and all that. But it wasn't me! It was Jakes that should have been through that."

"Now she's a judge."

"She is. She is. Powerful too. Even more than before. Black too."

"And beautiful. Don't forget that," Ermanno said. "I've seen pictures."

"Like the wicked witch of the west," Boyd slurred a bit.

"Another drink?" Ermanno asked.

"Maybe you should slow down?" Julia suggested.

"I'm good," Boyd said. "Just brings back some unwelcome memories."

"Did you two ever . . . you know . . . actually get it on?" Ermanno asked.

Julia looked at him.

"What? Logical question."

"No. We didn't."

"Were you tempted?"

Boyd paused and looked at Julia. "Hey," he said, "I'm human! Tempted? Maybe for a moment. Maybe. But the consequences were pretty obvious."

"Sometimes," Ermanno said, "sometimes you just have to forge ahead despite the consequences. Maybe you guessed wrong. Maybe it would all have been okay and you could have cruised along to stardom with her. I mean, she is smart. Maybe she was just trying to look out for you. Give you a thrill. Get you to step up your game."

"Jesus, Ermanno!" Julia said. "Back off. You can be such a pig!"

"He brought it up!"

"I don't think that was what she had in mind," Boyd said. "Don't think so."

"So you think she might be on the short list for the Court?" Julia asked.

"Don't know. I mean there isn't a short list at this point. There are no vacancies. I mean maybe there is a short list, but I don't know what it is. I'm not privy to that sort of thing. Just the President. I don't have connections to the President."

Despite the old negative feelings, Boyd was feeling pretty mellow. Good food. Good company, and a bucket of alcohol can do that to you. The Christmas lights looked pretty. The room was fairly dark. It was warm. The family chatter had reached a level slur that hummed along in the back of his mind.

"We should talk about this some more at another time," he said. "This is a family thing, you know? We shouldn't be talking business. Work. That stuff." He smiled and leveraged himself into a standing position. "Think I'll get a breath of air."

Julia's mother called her into the kitchen while Boyd headed for the front door where he pushed out into the street to be bit by a blast of cold air. Mariella was standing just outside the door smoking.

"Hey," she said in greeting.

"Hey," Boyd replied.

"Didn't know you smoked," she said.

"I don't," he replied. "Just air. Just needed a bit of air."

She looked at him. He looked up at the buildings and sucked in a deep draft of Boston, winter air.

"It can be a bit much," Mariella said.

"Excuse me?" Boyd asked.

"Family. You know. They're great, but they can be a bit much; especially for someone like you, someone who's not used to them."

Boyd smiled.

"They have their dreams, their visions of what a family is, but the pieces don't always fit. You know?"

It was Christmas season in the North End of Boston, the Friday evening before Christmas. Colorful lights blinked and twinkled and flashed in the buildings and across the streets. The streets were busy. It was still early. A couple turned toward the entrance of La Cucina.

"We're closed," Mariella said.

"Closed?" the man asked.

"Closed. Family Christmas party."

"Seems like a stupid time to be closed," the man said.

"The restaurant is closed," Boyd reiterated. "Sorry about that."

"Who are you? Like the bouncer?" the man laughed and looked at the woman he was with grinning.

"No. Like family," Boyd said.

Chapter Thirteen

February 2015

When Allan saw Gus, he didn't need a machine to tell him what his friend's face and body were screaming. Gus was pissed off. Unfortunately Allan couldn't tell from his expressions the precise cause of his anger although he could make a good guess. The course of love can make life difficult.

"What?" Gus responded when Allan asked him what was bugging him. "I'm fine!"

When Allan pressed him, he admitted that he had had a fight with Cyrene. "There's something going on, Allan, and she won't tell me what it is. I think it's something to do with IIDT."

"Like what?" Allan asked.

"I don't know," Gus replied his voice rising. "But those people piss me off. I want to take those bastards down."

Allan looked at him and studied his friend's face.

"No, seriously. I want to take those bastards down. They have this lawsuit going on that's tying our hands and scaring away any potential investors. What can we do?"

"It's business. You can't blame business on your love affair," Allan replied.

"I'm sick of that shit! 'It's business!' No it's not! It's a whole lot more than that. It's my life. It's your life. It's everyone here's life! We've borrowed money. People believe in what we're doing. People believe in me!"

"It's still business," Allan said.

"I want to take them down."

"How? Why?"

"I don't know how," Gus replied. "How would you suggest?"

"I wouldn't. I would suggest we just keep focusing on what we're doing, what we're good at and not get distracted."

Gus looked at him, searching his face for a trace of emotion. "Tell you what," he said finally, "their technology is bullshit. Right? So we just have to prove that it is smoke and mirrors, the Wizard of Oz, slight of hand. Right? It's bullshit. If their customers know that, they'll stop buying their stuff. We'll get *Consumer Reports* to write an article on truth telling machines. We'll get some scientist to write an article in *Scientific American* about all the charlatans in the industry. Maybe we can get *60 Minutes* to do an expose. They still do that sort of thing, right? That would be a great story! All those creepy pseudo-science guys."

"That might spill over. Sweep us in."

"We've got nothing to hide! What we're doing is real. It's legit. It's based in scientific facts."

"I'm not sure we want to go there, Gus. As much fun as that might be."

Gus looked at him again. "Hey, lots of stuff seemed like smoke and mirrors when it started. I mean what about television? Who really though you could send pictures through the air? What about copier machines? You stick a document in and out slides a perfect copy! Magic. Fax machines. People used to wonder where the original went! It all seemed like magic."

"Can you hear yourself? You're arguing against yourself."

"I want to bring them down."

"I know. But let's not go running off because you had a fight with Cyrene and she won't tell you what you want to know. You're angry."

"You're right," Gus said. "I am."

They sat in silence for a few moments, their world spinning around them. Time ticking by.

Finally Gus said, "I think we have created something truly amazing. No. I know we've created something truly amazing, as amazing as television or copier machines. What we have put together could change the world."

"You've reached your goal?"

"No. It's not perfect yet, but it sure as hell is better than anything that has come before."

"So let's prove it. That's what Avitas wants. That is what will bring IIDT down."

"I feel like we have done all this work, put these amazing technologies together, and even proved that we know what we're doing, but it's like jumping out on the stage of an empty theater and going, Tah Dah!' All this work for nothing. So some idiot like Crum can take it all away?"

"We need to put it on the big stage. Something more than a reality show or a morning show."

"Yeah? Like what?" Gus asked.

"I don't know. Something that's in the news. Something that people will pay attention to. We need an event. Anything going on now?"

They thought for a moment. "Not much. Just the usual wars. Conflict in the Middle East, but that's always going on. We need a Bernie Madoff or something similar."

"Yeah. Where's a good Ponzi scheme when you need one?" Allan asked.

"Let's see. There are people killing each other and starving in Africa. Any good revolutions in South America? The Canadians are quiet as usual. There used to be some good sex and spying scandals in England, but they don't seem to do that sort of thing any more. What the hell is in the news these days? The weather? And Congress. They just keep fighting with each other. There's always politics. Elections and stuff."

"Yeah. Life seems pretty dull, doesn't it?"

"Wait a second! A supreme court Justice died, didn't he? And they're going to have to replace him, right? There's going to be hearings," Gus said with a smile.

"Yeah, but nobody really pays attention to those things. Not real people."

"Okay, but what if we could get involved? What if we could put this up front? Maybe the TV folks would like that. What have they got now? Weather? Fat politicians making stupid statements? Getting more stuff made in the U.S.? Human interest crap. Maybe we could make this interesting, dramatic, like a reality show! Prove that the candidate is lying!"

"Listen to yourself," Allan said. "We're talking about the Supreme Court. This is not some tribal wannabes on an island. This is our country. This is a person who is going to impact the lives of our grandchildren."

"I don't have any grandchildren," Gus replied. "In fact I don't have any children. I don't even have a wife!"

"Aw," Allan sympathized. "You might have. Some day if you stop feeling sorry for yourself. And what if the candidate doesn't lie? What if he or she really is a good candidate and tells the truth?"

"All right, but it could still be front page news if we helped to put it there. Truth. Lie. It doesn't make any difference to us. It would be more interesting than the other dull stuff. We could make this work. I think this is what we need. And I know . . . I KNOW that IIDT couldn't pull this off." Gus paused. "And this is exactly what Avitas wants. This will prove it!"

"If it works," Allan said.

Gus looked at him. "What? What do you mean if it works?"

"I'm just saying; it's a big risk. Big stage. Big risk. If it doesn't work, we're dead."

"If we don't do it, we're dead anyway."

They sat looking at each other. Gus was gasping for air. He pushed his glasses up his nose. "So there it is then. How long have we got?"

"I don't know," Allan replied. "Never really paid much attention to these things. A couple of months maybe. Could be more. Could be less."

Gus pulled the team together and told them what he intended to do. The object was to get the Blaytent system into the televised judicial hearings so that the audience could witness whether or not the candidate was telling the truth about their opinions and their experience.

Bob said, "It's not ready. Not for that. We'll get killed!"

"Why isn't it ready, Bob?" Gus asked. "We have to be ready. We told Avitas we would be ready about now. Does something not work? Let's fix it. Let's make this happen. Who knows how long this judicial process takes and how it works?"

No one responded.

"Well, we have to find out. We have to find out about the legal stuff – permits, licenses, anything like that that we need to get into the hearing rooms. Arya, you have any connection with those TV people we worked with on the morning show?"

"I'm not sure they are all that happy with us," Arya replied.

"Why? We did what they wanted us to do."

"Sometimes the truth isn't what you want to hear. I think your connection with them was better. Who was that talent agency person? Maybe she could help?"

"Perry," Gus said. "Yeah, Blythe Perry. I'll see what she thinks. We need a plan, people. And we need it fast. I'll talk to Boyd about the legal stuff. We need to know how much time we have. We need to know what the process is . . . I mean for the candidate or candidates as well as for the coverage, the TV coverage. We don't need to be in there for all the preliminary stuff. Just the ultimate result. The final hearing. That's where we want to be, right?"

Bob stood up. "Look, I know you want to have this big show, and I know that I worry more than I should, but what have we got that would stand up to that kind of national and international scrutiny?"

"What have we got?" Gus asked the group. "You guys still believe in this thing, right? What have we got?"

There was a general silence. Gus looked around the room at his team. Allan stood with his arms crossed – stoic and poker faced. Arya was squirming in his chair, eager to move on, his dark brown eyes flickering back and forth. Julia smiled at him reassuringly and looked down at her hands in her lap. Bob paced over to the windows and looked out, away from the group.

They'd been through a lot to get to this point, and undoubtedly they could accurately read each other. There was a general understanding that time was running out with their financial support. There was a rumor going around that their finances weren't what they should be. They were all worried about what would happen next. Although they all knew that Bob was the worrier, and they usually discounted his concerns as just a part of his personality, this time it was different. This time they were on the edge of the battlefield and what was coming would prove whether their cause lived or died, whether they lived or died. Gus had the vision of being the king in one of Shakespeare's plays the night before the ultimate conflict, the troops in their tents behind him, campfires crackling, banners snapping in the wind. When dawn came there would be a terrible rending of flesh and clashing of swords and shields, arms and legs chopped off, thundering of horses' hooves, and many would give their lives for him. Their king! Or maybe it was more like a football game?

"Beanstalk," said Julia.

They all looked at her. "What?" Gus asked. He was trying to formulate some deeply moving, motivational speech that would go down in history as one of the most important of all time. Something that Yogi Berra might say.

"Beanstalk," Julia said again. "Huckle, Buckle, Beanstalk! We're there. Remember, when Jack traded the family cow for those magic beans, his mother was so irritated that she threw the beans out into the back yard and sent him to bed without his supper. The next morning, Jack climbed up the beanstalk into the clouds and found the giant's castle and the giant's wife who was nice enough to give him breakfast. The story goes on about Jack finding the giant's gold and the goose that laid the golden eggs and finally the giant's singing harp. And he steals all that stuff and brings it home to his mother."

She looked around the room at her co-workers who were staring at her with open mouths. Allan said, "What?"

"Yeah. Well, so that's us. We're Jack! We grew this thing. We kept climbing up to prove that it worked, and we kept bringing it back to Avitas and they kept asking for more. Well it's time to do it one more time and get the signing harp and get them to either put up or shut up. We couldn't be facing a much bigger giant than the Supreme Court and the entire population of the country could we? I don't know why the kids say 'Huckle, buckle' before the Beanstalk when they find something, but I'm saying it now: Huckle, Buckle, Beanstalk! We're there. We've found it. Let's show it off! We've created the Beanstalk. That's what we should call it!"

Gus wasn't sure that it would go down as a speech that would compete with Yogi Berra for eternal fame, but it sounded good to him.

"Beans are good," Arya said.

+++++

"Yah. Good," Julia said to Gus after the others had left the room. "But we are going to have a problem with economics."

"How bad is it?" Gus asked.

"Not something we can cover by borrowing on our credit cards. If we really tighten our belts . . . we should be able to meet payroll for another two months. Can you talk to Avitas and see if they will stretch it out? After all, their guy caused much of the pain. I mean they are at risk here too. They've got a lot of money hanging out here. You'd think they'd want to make sure that we could take it all the way home."

"They're waiting to do the second round financing until we prove we've got a marketable product."

"Haven't we proved that it works? We've been on TV, for God's sake. Probably before we should have been."

"I offered them my first born child," Gus said with a smile. "Gudmudgion didn't think that was funny. She doesn't have much of a sense of humor. She's a grouch like Scrooge. Money is God."

Julia grunted.

Gus added, "But we can't slow down now. We can't. This is going to be the big one. We don't want everyone in duck-and-cover mode waiting to get laid-off. Like Bob. The only way we're going to climb this beanstalk of yours is to be positive. Bob is the best at what he does, but he can be a wet blanket at times. I don't know how we can cut back. We can't exactly start shutting off the lights or cutting off the phones. We don't do any advertising. I don't think we have much by way of unnecessary expenses."

"True, but I'll take a look." They sat looking at each other for a couple of moments of silence. "It's mainly payroll."

Gus looked at her and then at his computer screen and then at the windows. Like so many times in life there was no, one, big answer. Big answers were always made up of dozens of little answers. Sometimes there was the '*Deus Ex Machina*' – the God in the Machine that would come down at the end of a Greek play that would fix everything. The hand of God would straighten things out; the winning lottery ticket, the death of an unknown distant relative, the finding of a Rembrandt painting in the attic. Those things <u>did</u> happen just often enough to keep people buying lottery tickets and visiting Las Vegas. But the majority of big answers, big solutions are made up of lots of smaller answers and, unfortunately, those smaller answers don't happen all at the same time.

Personally Gus was doing all right financially so that he didn't have a hard time volunteering to have his own checks held, but there was something about getting paid regularly that confirmed his value, even if it was only to himself. It was more than just the flow of cash into his bank account, and even though he was an owner and ran the company, there was an emotional connection to remuneration for action and time given. That was why venture capital people didn't like to see business plans with the principals not getting paid. Without pay, there is a loss of value. It becomes something less than a complete engagement.

Gus recognized that, but he asked Julia if she would look into the impact that holding some payroll would make. He needed to know the scale of the problem. How big a hole was there and what it would take to fill it? And would it work to fill it partially?

"Part of that answer depends on what happens next," Julia said. "I mean we are essentially running full bore to develop this thing, but what are we running toward? I know there is a plan to license our technology, but maybe we should rethink that. The sooner we can turn this around from a research project to something producing income, the sooner the bleeding ends. Creating the 'take home' version would be great but we don't have the funds to finish it."

"How's the SA development going?" he asked.

"Great," she replied. "The databases are all set for English. We have some of the other languages worked out, but some are going to take more time. The nuances of sentence structure are a challenge. Arya has been wonderful at speeding the process up. We're very close to real time now. And Bob has been helping me with the frequency and tone of the statements that people make, the words they emphasize. There is a lot to how people say things not just what they are saying. And it varies from sentence to sentence. We are also working on the speed and rhythm of sentences and speeches. That is also culturally weighted. But in a nutshell, we've made a lot of progress. Your vision of adding all the technologies together has a lot of value."

Gus smiled. Coming from anyone else a statement like that might have been insincere. But not from Julia; he knew the praise was real. "Great," he said. "You'll have to show me."

Julia was absolutely right. Gus needed to clarify what they were running toward. He had been concentrating so heavily on proving the concept and the technology that he had lost sight of the fact that from a financial standpoint they had to have a tangible product that could produce an income stream. And that, it had seemed clear from the beginning, was licensing the technology that could be embedded in many products produced by others with Blaytent getting a steady royalty flow. What Gus needed was to be able to summarize and present the package so that he could convince Gudmudgion and Avitas that they had this bull by the balls. Televised, congressional hearings for a Supreme Court Justice would do that quite well.

Chapter Fourteen

Late February 2015

When it was announced that Judge Diamon Jakes
would be the President's candidate for Associate
Justice of the Supreme Court, Boyd nearly lost his
lunch. Was she smart? Absolutely. All the best of credentials: Graduate of Wellesley and Yale Law School, worked as
the General Counsel for the Massachusetts Department of Environmental Protection taking on big developers, and as an
African-American woman, battling for truth, justice, and the
American Way! She became a judge early in her career, writing opinions that made the textbooks. She was cream of the
crop, state of the art, except for one little flaw that Boyd knew
something about. Was it important? Did it have anything to
do with her future decisions? It would be easier, oh so much
easier, just to let it go.

"You can't let it go," Julia said when they got into the
conversation. "You can't. It's important. It speaks to her
character and that's what we all need to know. I mean what if
she gets cases involving sexual harassment, sexual rights . . .
will she condone and lean toward lenient treatment of abusive
husbands or wives or children?"

"You can't think that one little incident in a bar a million
years ago is really going to have any effect on the decisions
she makes now?"

"Yes, I do. I certainly do. How do we know that she
didn't do to a bunch of other people what she did to you?

How do we know that? She's been in a position of power for a very long time, and from the way you describe her, she certainly doesn't seem reluctant to wield that power for her own gain."

Boyd was silent for a minute. "No one else is stepping forward."

"You don't know that," Julia replied. "We certainly don't know what the FBI is looking into or who has said what. It's certainly not all revealed to the public."

"I shouldn't have told you."

"Why? So I wouldn't push you to do the right thing?"

"How do I know it's the right thing? It would be a mess. I don't know how . . . I mean, is it going to mess up our lives if I start telling tales? I mean she has powerful friends. How's it going to look if, as a man, I get up there and start talking about how this beautiful woman harassed me? And I didn't like it? I rejected it? Who's going to believe me? And with the work that I do with Blaytent, isn't that going to get in the way too? Aren't they going to think that this is just a publicity stunt?"

Julia looked at him. They were sitting at the kitchen table in their apartment. Their relationship had been flowering. Julia and most of her family thought Boyd would be asking her to marry him soon. They were just waiting although some of them wondered what he was waiting for. From his own thoughts, since the family Christmas get-together, Boyd felt like an integral part of the family and it pleased him. He enjoyed being drawn into the complexities of their inter-relationships. There were moments, of course, when he wondered what he was getting himself into. His own family was so much simpler and easier to understand, almost like a plain but elegant blanket as opposed to a complex tapestry. He knew what his family was thinking pretty much before they thought it. He would never have that understanding of Julia's family. And that caused him to pause and wonder if he would be adding or detracting from the Medici family, whether or not it would be best for him to step away and allow Julia to find someone more suited.

He didn't talk to her about those doubts. She would have poohed them, telling him he was thinking nonsense. But that wouldn't have diminished the doubts in his mind. He was nine years older than she was. That seemed a lot. He would age faster. Was there still time for children? He was almost too old at forty-two. If they had kids right away, by the time they were twenty he would be over sixty! Would he be able to keep up with them? Would he be able to get up for the late night feedings and diaper changes? But he would like children. He would. He would like to pass on the family name. That was one thing about family that was important to him. He envisioned the family tree on the genealogy pages with a dead branch. He thought that Julia would like children. They hadn't talked about it and they should probably do that. It seemed fundamental. And if he did what she was asking him to do now, to stand up in front of the whole country on television and accuse a candidate for the Supreme Court of sexual harassment that would be on the Internet forever. His kids would know what he had done. So maybe the way things stood at the moment, telling the FBI wouldn't be all that big a deal; not if it was just him and his own life to be considered. But it wasn't. It was their lives and their unborn children's lives.

"Have you thought about what this might do to us?" Boyd asked. "I mean it's going to be a feeding frenzy for the press . . . for a long time. I mean these things just don't go away. What about our kids?"

Julia looked at him. "Kids?"

"Yah. I mean what if we have kids? They'll see reports of this stuff on the Internet for years."

"Kids?" she asked again.

"Well, I know we haven't really talked about it or anything, but it's a possibility." He paused. "Isn't it?"

"Are you asking me to marry you?"

"Uhm. Well. No. Well. Sort of. I mean we were talking about kids, and we probably should. I mean we are living together now. Aren't we?"

Julia looked at him. There is this look that all men are aware of (or should be if they're not) that is impossible to describe. It is a combination of incredulity and accusation and a whole lot of other things rolled up in one. There are probably a million micro-expressions in "THE LOOK" as well as barrels of Non-Verbal Communications. And if the man continues to be blissfully unaware of being the subject of "THE LOOK", he is certainly in for spending some time sleeping on the sofa . . . or worse.

In this case it was a non-verbal expression of, "You-are-being-unbelievably-insensitive-and-stupid-and-you-better-come-up-with-a-great-answer-in-a-hurry. I'm waiting. I won't wait for long."

Boyd recognized "THE LOOK" instantaneously and had realized a millisecond after he had mentioned the word *kids* with the simple modifier *our*, that he was venturing into difficult territory. He was scrambled to come up with a positive path out of this hole. One solution was to confirm the fact that he was asking her to marry him although this was not the way he would have chosen to have done it and there were all those other doubts and questions about such an important decision.

He could attempt to make her feel sorry for him, pushing the mothering button by going to the impact on his manhood of revealing his conflict with Judge Jakes to the public. That would have the advantage of bringing the conversation back around to where they had been, but it would leave the marriage and children subject incomplete and that wouldn't last for long. It would be akin to his asking with a smile, "How about those Red Sox?" in an attempt to change the subject. This was too deep a hole for a light subject change to have any impact.

He could attempt the innocent lack of understanding response, "What?" That might force her to elaborate, giving him more time to shift the subject. The "What?" response has an accusatory level to it as well, implying that the subject doesn't have enough information to provide a clear and adequate answer, and it really isn't his fault that he isn't responding quickly. But it was unlikely that that would work either in this situation.

All of these thoughts flew through Boyd's brain while he squirmed under Julia's piercing gaze like an insect sample on a display board.

"Well?" she asked. He had run out of time.

"I do want to have kids. Do you want to have kids? I mean we've never talked about it. And if I go talking to the FBI this is going to have an impact on their lives as well as our lives and that's something we should think about before I do this. I mean with the Internet, just about every part of our lives becomes part of the public record. People tweet everything! I don't understand it. I wasn't brought up with it. Those were different times." He was babbling. He hardly ever babbled. But this was one of those rare occasions that babbling seemed appropriate to him.

Julia stepped around the table to him and leaned over and took his face between her two hands. "You're babbling," she said.

"I know," he replied.

"Do you want to marry me or not? I'm proposing to you."

He looked her in the eyes. They were such a rich, hazel color, like flowers, the black pupils centered on a flair of yellow, out to the hazel petals. There was such kindness, such understanding, such tenderness, that he lost all of himself there. With a flash he knew that there was no dancing, no swaggering, no individual concerns, and no doubts. They were one.

"Yes," he said, and then more strongly. "Yes, definitely. Without a doubt or hesitation! But I'm supposed to be asking you!" He was standing now, hugging her, and for a microsecond he wondered how this had happened. It was not what he had planned, but it was definitely right.

Later, after they had made love and they were back in the kitchen, he said, "Before we do anything else, though, I need to resolve this issue about Jakes. Am I going to talk to the FBI or not? We need to get that resolved before we do anything else because of the impact on our lives and everything."

"I don't think there is any question about it," Julia replied. "You have to. I said it before and I meant it. The Supreme Court makes decisions that impact all of our lives in one way or another for many, many years. The people who choose the judges for the Court have to know all about their characters. What if they were thieves or child molesters or blackmailers? You wouldn't want them making the ultimate decisions about our laws, would you?"

"But they're not. They are vetted before they get nominated. Jesus, the President wouldn't pick someone who was a child molester."

"Isn't sexual harassment as bad?"

"I don't know," Boyd said. "Seems like it's not one of those black and white things."

"Good one," Julia smiled.

"No, I don't mean just because she is black and I'm white. I mean it's one man's garbage is another man's treasure sort of thing."

"But isn't sexual harassment blackmail? 'Want to keep your job, then be my sex toy!'"

"I suppose," Boyd replied. "I never thought of it that way."

"You should!" Julia said. "You're the lawyer. It's a crime, and she should be punished for it and it doesn't sound like she ever was."

"No, she wasn't. But you do have to recognize what this will mean for us. The press is going to have a field day with this. This is usually a female problem. Sexual harassment of men is not familiar. Even today. It's an affront to the male psyche. It's not macho. And I'm likely to be the butt of a lot of jokes."

"I think you can take it. You seem pretty comfortable with your manhood." She laughed and winked at him.

"So you say," he replied, and smiled. "So you say. You probably don't remember Anita Hill. 1991. You were what nine? You probably weren't paying a whole lot of attention to the doings at the Supreme Court."

"I do remember something about that."

"It was a black woman charging a black man with sexual harassment and she was hammered. I mean people didn't believe her. They accused her of all sort of things. Making it all up for her own benefits. I remember watching the hearings and feeling somewhat the same way. Not that I particularly liked Judge Clarence Thomas. There was something about him that didn't sit well, but she didn't look all that believable – to me and to a lot of other people. And she was a professor and associated with Christian universities and stuff. How much better witness could you find?"

"Hmph," said Julia.

"I'm not a professor. I'm not female."

"That would be weird."

"And I don't have all the Christian and family value potential background good stuff that would make me totally believable. It will truly be my word against hers."

"Yah, but here's the thing, Boyd. Bottom line. Bottom of the pile. She harassed you, right? You've got to get your facts in order. You have to be clear, really clear about what happened and when. We have to go through this from top to bottom, completely so that we know what is likely to come out so we can be ready for it. They're going to try to tear you apart."

"Great! Tell me again why I should do this?"

"You did let her know her advances were unwelcome."

"Yes. I mean I don't have tapes or videos of the incidents, but I definitely let her know. And that wasn't easy. She was an intimidating character even then."

"When was this?" Julia asked.

"Oh, Jesus, a long time ago. Let me think. I was working for Tittle and Baines at the time and so was she. I was a couple of years out of law school. I guess it was 1999 or 2000."

"You need to be sure. You need to get dates. Actual dates. You can't guess. You know this stuff. You're the lawyer."

"That was about fifteen years ago. It's going to be difficult to put it together."

"Were there multiple incidents or just one?" Julia asked.

Boyd looked at her. "Multiple approaches. You know her touching me, comments, that sort of thing." Boyd outlined all of the events that he could remember and Julia urged him to get it down on paper.

"Wait," he said suddenly. "Wait! I did write it down. They sent me to sensitivity training. Remember? I told you."

"You? They sent you to sensitivity training? Why not her?"

"Who knows? Company politics. But the training was about what to look for and how to file a claim, and I recognized that I should make notes on what had happened. Oh shit! Where did I put them? Oh, that's going to make me sick until I figure out what I did with them. I mean that was fifteen years ago! There have been so many moves and papers and other crap in between. That's why I did that. It's not exactly hard evidence, but it is documented clarity on the events. You know that feeling? When you have the perfect answer to the question – the perfect response, the perfect quote – but you don't know where it is? "

"You'll find them. You're detail oriented. I'm sure you have them in an important documents file of some kind."

They spent time rummaging through boxes they hadn't unpacked from their move. Papers and files were not the first things to come out in the new space, in fact boxes of papers could lie around for years before they got sorted out. They could find their way into the attic or down to the basement to be addressed later when there was more time, which never seemed to happen. So many papers had enough importance to be packed at the time, and then the reason for their importance disappears. Some people say that if you haven't used or looked at something in the past three years, throw it away. Boxes of papers follow us through our lives until our children have the unpleasant job of getting rid of them when we're dead. They stand there and shake their heads, "What the hell did he keep this for?" And of course they don't know.

But some things are important and should be kept, and Boyd knew that those notes were important. There were times, even while he was writing them, that he wondered why he was doing it, that it was highly unlikely that there would ever come a time that he would need them. But here it was. The time had come. And he tried to figure out the last time he had ever seen that file.

He sat in the middle of the floor surrounded by papers and cardboard boxes. "How the hell did I ever accumulate all this stuff? And an even better question, why does it keep following me around?"

"Do you have a safe deposit box that you haven't told me about," Julia asked.

Boyd thought for a moment, trying to recall his safe deposit box and what was in it and why he had it and if he'd paid for it recently.

"Really?" Julia asked. "You really do? You really do have a safe deposit box? I hope it's full of the family jewels."

Boyd laughed. "No. No jewels. I can't even remember what's in there." He was puzzling it through. "I'd forgotten about it. I really had. I think it gets paid for automatically out of my account. I've had that account for years." He paused. "Maybe. Maybe it's in there. That would say something, wouldn't it? Just the fact that I can't remember what's in that box says something. I think I must be losing my mind. But that would make sense. If I put those notes in a safe deposit box, I must have thought that something like this would happen someday. Who puts notes in a safe deposit box? I mean family jewels make much more sense."

"It's clear then," Julia said sitting down beside Boyd on the floor. "It's clear that you have to do this thing. If what she did to you was so important that you put your notes about it in a safe deposit box and then put that box out of your mind, you expected to have this come up again. We have to do this thing."

He looked at her and smiled. "'We?' *We* have to do this thing? I guess it really will be we as long as you're willing."

She kissed him.

+++++

Gus's primary challenge was how to get Cranky Franky or Beanstalk or whatever they were calling it into the hearing room. This was the government and security was supposed to be tight with all the crazy people running around blowing things up and shooting people in schools and malls. Security was tight, but the press was going to be there. Television coverage was going to be there. He had to figure out a way to get the television coverage to include Beanstalk's input. He had to convince them that it would help to increase the public interest and that it was a serious tool for discerning and displaying the Truth of what was being said. And it certainly wouldn't hurt to have an ally in those conversations, someone who had an affiliation with Blaytent. Gus remembered that Robert Adams, who had a friendly investment in Blaytent, had broadcasting interests, and even if he didn't directly connect to the DC television stations, he probably knew someone who could make the connection for Gus.

Gus wondered as he dialed the number for the Adams's house whether the number was still good and whether or not they even had a land line, a real, hard-wired phone. It was hard to imagine any more, but it was more likely in the Adams's house. Time didn't change much there. And the phone did ring when he called and a woman did answer it, and she asked, "Gus? Is that you?"

Gus hesitated for a moment trying to place the voice. "Rebecca?" he asked.

"Yes," she said, drawing out the word. "Absolutely. It's me. Wow! I haven't talked to you in an age! How _are_ you?"

As pleasant as it was to chat with an old girl friend, Gus's mind was on other issues. But she was trained to control the conversation and her voice triggered memories of different times and how things might have been different if he had pursued her more vigorously or if they had lived different lives. Those had been good times. Rebecca had always been exciting and adventurous, daring him to do things that he wouldn't have otherwise done, flirting with the edge of trouble. He realized that he had probably pulled away from her in those days partially because he saw the risks as too high.

They were older now; over thirty and mature. His relationship with Cyrene seemed to be in trouble, and there was certainly risk there. He wondered if Rebecca was married. "What are you doing now?" he asked. "Married? Children? What are you doing at home? I really didn't expect you to answer the phone. It's a surprise."

"A good surprise, I hope," she replied.

"Yah. Sure. Always a pleasure."

"I'm not married. Not any more. Divorced. No children. Too short. The marriage not the husband." She laughed. "It was a mistake. I should have married you, Gus. We could have settled down to a cozy house somewhere."

"You would have hated it, Becca. You would have. You're a wild spirit!"

"Oh, well," she said with a laugh. "How about you?"

He told her that all his efforts were focused on developing the business that he didn't have much time for a social life. She asked if he had a steady girl friend. He told her that he had been going out with someone fairly regularly, but that it certainly wasn't steady. The drift of this conversation reminded him strongly of days gone by and days that might have been. He momentarily marveled at how small twists, incidents, and interactions could send life in an entirely different direction. There are those rare, life changing, and monumental decisions – Should I take this job or that job? Should I join the army? Should I move to England? - But the bulk of the road is made up of small bumps and unanticipated inflections. If he had somehow managed to marry Becca, this could be his family they were talking about. He could have spent his life as a dilettante with his debutante, flitting about the world, hanging out on beaches and yachts, tasting the best food, and drinking the best wine, and listening to those around him babbling about nothing – a wastrel on the wind.

He tore his attention away from the vision of that life and of her beauty and her youth and angled the conversation back around to her father. "I need to ask him about his TV connections."

She said she didn't know anything about his interests, but she gave him the office number and told him that if he called now, Gus should be able to catch him. "This is one of those days when daddy sits down with what he refers to as his 'staff' and catches up on things," she said. "I don't think he'll ever give that up. It makes him feel like he's doing something, something more substantial than puttering in his Chinese garden. You should call him. I'm sure he would love to talk to you. He always liked you, you know. Mother too."

Gus dutifully asked about Tanny, and ascertained that Rebecca's mother was just fine, off in their apartment in Palm Beach, doing her social thing.

When he hung up talking to her, he had a momentary feeling of loss, as though he had missed the train. At the same time, he felt like the chauffeur's son, tolerated but not quite up to the mark. She lived in a different world, one that he had eschewed long ago.

He called the number she gave him. Bob Adams's long time assistant, Rosemary McKenna who had a mind like a steel trap, answered his call. She recognized his voice immediately despite the fact that she hadn't seen her since before he had gone into the army, almost fifteen years previously. She told him to come in and that she would love to see him. "Mr. Adams isn't fully engaged at the moment, if you know what I mean," she said with a laugh. "He would love a project. I'll tell him you're coming."

Gus wasn't sure he wanted to be considered a 'project', but he welcomed the invitation.

Robert Adams's office wasn't grand. It wasn't the office of a titan of industry on the top of some skyscraper. It wasn't pretentious or ostentatious like those offices in the old movies that looked more like ballrooms than offices. It was, in fact, solid and subtle as behooved a member of an old Boston family. It was on the fourth floor of a four story, recently built office complex with a good view of the city in the distance and the parks and the fens or former wetlands that wandered through the neighborhoods. His office was properly furnished, comfortable but a place to work, with oriental rugs and dark oak and mahogany furniture, and a couple of large paintings of Adams ancestors on the walls. One entire wall was decorated with books with matching color, leather bindings. There was a large leather sofa with matching chairs and a low, glass topped table with one or two *Forbes* magazines and the day's edition of the *Wall Street Journal*, a Steuben glass ashtray and an empty silver, cigarette box.

Rosemary greeted him at the door and guided him into the inner office. Gus was surprised at how much older she looked. She was a fixture in his mind with a certain, timeless image that he had thought would never change. Certain people are not meant to look different. They are not meant to age. They are guideposts, navigation marks, and should be eternal. When she shook his hand, her's felt cold and boney, as though she was losing weight. Her eyes were still the sharp and piercing blue that he remembered. Her hair was all grey now, pulled back into her standard bun. He towered over her and felt awkward walking along behind her, no longer the boy.

Robert Adams heaved himself up to come around from behind his desk with his hand outstretched. "Gus!" he exclaimed. "Good to see you. Good to see you. You called at a good time. Between projects. How's your dad?"

"Fine, sir," Gus said. "He asks after you. You two should get together."

"We should. We should. Time, you know. Time. Slips on by. Next thing you know, another year gone. Under the bridge and down the drain."

Mr. Adams guided him to the leather chairs and asked Rosemary to bring them some coffee. "So how's the project? How's Avitas treating you?"

Gus started to bring him up to date, but Mr. Adams stopped him with a wave of his hand. "Been reading your reports. Nasty business that Pinel person siphoning off the funds. That doesn't help. That was first class that your device was able to ferret him out. First class."

"Thank you, sir," Gus replied.

"So what's the problem now?"

Gus felt as though a schoolmaster was pushing him along a hallway.

"Well, we need to demonstrate our technology to prove to Avitas that it works, in essence. And I would like to get it into the hearings for the Supreme Court, the televised hearings. They have all sorts of things on the TV screen now, it would be great if we could get our technology to be a part of that."

Gus was surprised when Mr. Adams emitted a low, breathy whistle.

"I wondered if you knew the right people to talk to to make that happen?"

Robert Adams leaned back in his chair and contemplated the idea. "Bold," he said finally. "Bold and gutsy. How well does it work? That's the first thing. You never want to be showing off a technology in front of a customer and have it fail. In this case, you would be showing it off in front of the whole country – the whole world!"

"We've already had it on TV and that was almost a year ago. We've improved it even more since then."

"I suppose it doesn't really need to work anyway. People will believe it."

"But it does work," Gus said defensively. "That's the point, Mr. Adams. It does work. It scientifically does work. If something really happened, it really happened. There is a real, rock solid, actual truth. As solid as this table." Gus tapped the table with his fingers. "This table is real and so is the truth."

Robert Adams looked at him. "It is a strange world," he said. "Strange world. When my father was born, there were no electric lights or airplanes or cars. Now we have television and computers and cell phones and, you're telling me, a tangible indication of the truth. Or lies!"

"Yes, sir," Gus replied.

"I mean you've been telling me this in your reports. I do read them, you know. I've been following along. But I hope you have thought about the consequences of something like this, have you?"

"I think so."

"You better do more than guess at something like that, Gus. More than that. This is life changing. It's a weapon. The military will be interested. It's a weapon. The police will be interested. But you know that. You've expressed that. But you are suggesting that when they question a nominee for the Supreme Court that his testimony will be scrutinized by an electronic system to determine whether or not he is telling the truth?"

"She," Gus said. "Judge Diamon Jakes has been nominated."

"What?" Mr. Adams asked.

"The nominee is female."

"Doesn't matter. The point is the Judiciary Committee would never allow a candidate to be scrutinized in public by a lie detector. It isn't seemingly. The Supreme Court judges are not even allowed to clap during the State of the Union Address! It wouldn't be impartial. They've got to be there, but they can't clap."

"Lie detector technology isn't real," Gus said. "And the machine has to be connected to the subject; ours doesn't. And we're not asking to provide the results or the feedback to the Senators or the members of the Committee. We're asking to be a part of the TV reporting. There was a time when TV cameras were not allowed in these hearings. Now people expect it. And TV coverage now has all sorts of notes and scrolling messages. We're only suggesting that they allow us to be a part of that."

Mr. Adams looked at him. "Interesting point."

"And, I hate to suggest this, but I think the TV folks would like this. It would enhance their ratings. I mean these hearings aren't exactly edge of the seat stuff."

"You are treading a thin line there, Gus," the older man said. "You say your technology is scientifically factual, but you are suggesting its appeal to popular culture. That's implying that professional wrestling is real! Will you gain or lose credibility for your technology with this stunt?"

"I don't look at it as a 'stunt', sir," Gus replied. "The reason they have these hearings is to determine if the candidate is telling the truth. That's the reason. So if we can assist in proving that what they are saying is the truth, we are doing the country a favor. We would be helping to bring the right person to the job."

"You're saying that you want your information to go out to the public but not to the people, the Senators, who are actually making the decision. That's a delicate line between facts and popularity."

"This time. This time, only because I don't think we could get a legal ruling in time for the Senators to use the technology. We could do it. We could give each Senator a connection to the Blaytent information so that they could follow the questioning through a logical path to the truth. But it would be too much to hope for permission to do that in so short a time."

"So you would be presenting Blaytent's information to the court of popular opinion, the electronic crowd watching the hanging!" Mr. Adams laughed.

Gus smiled. "It's not ideal, I know. But it's a start."

Robert Adams looked at the young man that he had watched growing up, who had dated his daughter, and was a son of a friend. He shook his head in wonder. "It's an amazing world," he said. "Don't know where it's going. Moves way too fast to keep track of it. You'd think they could find a cure for cancer or even a cure for the common cold. Seems like the more we know, the more we find out we don't know!

"This is quite a concept, Gus, quite a concept. Something pulls at my gut that you are messing around with something akin to proving the existence of God and that's pretty scary." He saw Gus's eyebrows go up.

"No. It doesn't come as a surprise. I have been reading your stuff, paying attention. I was intrigued by the comment about the 'bogus pipeline effect'. I don't know if what you're doing is real, as real and solid as this table, as you say, or not. I've been thinking about this. That's one thing, Gus. You've got me thinking about this. If you can prove the existence of truth, can you prove the existence of Love?"

Gus was indeed surprised. This kind of thinking was a little like hearing the Pope swear! People like Robert Adams didn't talk about love! It wasn't proper. It wasn't manly. The drift of the conversation was making Gus very uncomfortable.

"I don't know," Mr. Adams continued, "but I think this is a subject that needs to get out there. Some things need to get discussed by the public. They need airing, you know? That's how our democracy started, people airing ideas. Not that I'm comparing what you're doing to the founding fathers. Not that at all." He paused and looked at Gus.

Gus wondered if you reach a point in life when you realize that you are babbling, when your thinking goes off the rails,

you forget what it was you were talking about. Does some
little warning light go off in your brain telling you that you are
sounding foolish and you better get it together? He doubted
that Mr. Adams ever had such thoughts.

The man finished his thought by saying, "I'll make some
calls and see what I can do."

+++++

Gus stepped out of Mr. Adams's office and was smacked
in the face by the surprising warmth of the day. The weather
seemed shockingly unpredictable. It was probably always
shockingly unpredictable but it always came as a surprise.
Gus wondered if all the electronics and radar and satellites
made predictions of weather conditions more or less surprising. Maybe we're surprised because we think the
meteorologists have this weather thing under control and we
can stop thinking about it, he wondered. But it had been a
winter of wild fluctuations between heat and cold, ice and
rain, Arctic Clippers and Polar Vortex's. And then along
comes a February day like this where it was in the mid-sixties
here in the Northeast. The birds seemed to be getting confused!

He decided to walk and try to clear his head and get a handle on where things were going. Leverett Pond was across the
street, and although the trees knew it was still winter and the
grass was still brown, the air felt refreshing and the city was
all around, and Gus appreciated the out-of-sequence warmth
of the day. He had been brought up to feel as though everything he did had to have a purpose, that just taking a stroll in a
city park had to have meaning. He had to be exercising or
walking a dog or solving a complex problem. He couldn't
just walk. He couldn't just breathe in the air or listen to the
sounds of the city or smell the earth warming, spiced with the
occasional twist of fried food from the Chinese restaurant
somewhere in the neighborhood. He wrestled to not think, but
his mind kept drifting back to Truth and money and the Supreme Court and the lives of the people who worked for him .
. . with him. Allan and his parents. The wisdom of the Allan's mother's ancestors. The Kickapoo knew the truth when

they saw it. The truth was all around, in everything, especially in her Jewish, business school husband.

A young man wearing a bicycle helmet, backpack on his back sped by in the opposite direction. Gus noticed the Leg Shields he wore around his ankles. "Interesting product," Gus thought. "I wonder where the developer had those made? Is he growing that company organically? Probably didn't need venture capital."

Were they really moving toward finding the truth? Was what he had said about the truth being as real as a coffee table mean anything? Was interrogating a prisoner or suspect really seeking the truth or was it something else entirely? Maybe this whole thing was a serious waste of time and money and they would never find the answer and if they did find an answer, would it be the right one and was it even the right question? You could chase your tail endlessly. Perhaps it was simply true that life was the passage of time and there wasn't any point. People just added meaning and importance so there would be a point.

The vision of Maria Gudmudgion floated into his brain unsummoned as he strode down the path. She was being unreasonable as she had from the beginning. Blaytent was doing better than most. Avitas was going to make money. They were all going to make money. A pigeon dropped down onto the path in front of him, stopping him.

Pigeons in cities were so used to people that he wondered if he put his foot out to step on the bird if it would fly away. Are they trusting or are they stupid? Someone once claimed they were "dumber than shit". How dumb was shit? Did the government have data on that? Trusting or stupid? How close together were those two feelings? Thoughts? Emotions?

Gus looked around to try to break that chain of nonsense. The breeze rippled the surface of the pond. A sinking page of a newspaper drifted across the water. He looked up at the extraordinarily blue sky above him, seeking the whiteness of a cloud to shape the surface of the dome of heaven above him.

He started walking again, taking deep breaths. He didn't want someone to think he was hyperventilating and rush him a hospital. Hospitals were expensive. Blaytent did give their employees health insurance but he didn't want to test it. He wondered if Arya or Julia or Bob had had annual physicals or had doctors they could talk to. That would be important. They were the key people in Blaytent's success. Julia probably had. She was good at staying on top of things like that. Arya may be too distracted. He might think he could get all the health answers he needed via his computer. It was difficult to tell what Arya was thinking about. He was so deep into what he was doing that he was working with the fundamentals of his universe, manipulating the building blocks of the ones and the zeros that answered all the cosmic questions about why Gus's smart phone was smarter than he was. Someone had to do that stuff! But did he know how to get ketchup out of the bottle by tapping the label? Probably not. Did he use ketchup?

And what about Bob? If anyone needed health insurance, it was Bob. He had a family. Families always needed health insurance. Kids broke their arms falling out of trees or got sick or needed shots. And Bob really should give up smoking. And he should calm down. Jesus, the man worried all the time. About everything! It got really frustrating. Gus would have been happy to turn all the worrying over to Bob. It was pointless for both of them to do it. That was what they should work on next. Worrying. Now that they had this truth thing down, they should move on to worrying. Maybe they could figure out a way to bottle it up so it could be passed on. Wouldn't that be great if you really could, "Pack up your troubles in your old kit bag and smile, smile, smile" as the old song said?

Gus wondered if the young lady who was jogging along the other side of the pond, headphones in her ears, ponytail bobbing up and down was worrying about anything. Did the music flush the worrying out of her brain? Was it music or was she listening to lessons on quantum physics? Could you think about quantum physics while jogging?

Gus felt that perhaps he needed lessons on nothing, not thinking, hushing the monkey mind. But that seemed a bit like the "Department of Redundancy Department". He sat on a bench and rested his arms along the back and stretched out his long legs. He really should get back. He took a deep breath and looked up at the sky again where a plane was making an approach to Logan Airport. Traffic hissed in the distance punctuated by the occasional blare of a horn or siren. It was surprisingly quiet . . . like the minutes before a storm.

He leaned forward and rested his elbows on his knees and head in his hands and looked down at the asphalt between his feet and marveled for a moment at the roughness of the surface. Sky to earth, moment-to-moment, person to person. They were all connected, linked by time and the dark matter of the universe.

"Yes," he thought, looking up. "That's enough of that shit. Time to get on with things."

+++++

Boyd had been dealing with legal issues for a lot of years. During that time he had met a lot of people in a lot of different roles including people at the FBI. It seemed ironic that his first contact with them was when he had been working with Tittle and Baines on the environmental case with Diamon Jakes. There had been some questions about an organized crime connection with the developers. Connections grow cold as people move on and make changes in their lives, but the history gave him connections that allowed him to start conversing with them as more than just a kook out of the blue. Still, he was reluctant to call.

He had put his notes of the events in his safe deposit box, folded neatly into a manila envelope, sealed and dated. He probably should have mailed them to himself so that he could have gotten the official, post office date stamp on the envelope. But he hadn't and it wouldn't have proved much more anyway. He debated whether or not he should break the seal on the envelope. He couldn't remember exactly what he had written or how he had written it. He knew he had been pretty angry at the time, but editing the words would have weakened the historical veracity of the documents.

He sat in his office looking at his phone. Once he started this conversation, it would be official, and it couldn't be stopped before reaching some sort of conclusion. If he didn't start it, he could just move on. Get back to other things. No one besides him and Julia would ever know. Would she think less of him if he didn't pick up the phone and make the call? Would she think he was cowardly to back down from the confrontation? Being a lawyer was all about confrontation. He'd never backed away before. What would he think of himself? There was always that tribunal in his brain that judged what he was doing, how he did it, and whether or not they would throw him to the mental lions. They were much worse than a single, nagging conscience because they didn't always agree.

He looked at the phone and watched his hand reach out and grab the receiver, watched the fingers of his other hand punch in the numbers as though he was disconnected from the actions. And so it began.

He asked for the agent that he had worked with on the environmental case years before and was told that the man had retired. Boyd was asked what he wanted to talk with him about, and Boyd told the person on the other end of the phone that he had some information to report on a public figure. He was asked if this was a corruption issue.

Boyd hesitated. It wasn't exactly corruption, but maybe that was where it fit into the menu of issues the FBI was concerned with. Report on the background of a candidate for the Supreme Court was not one of the regular daily activities although Boyd might have been surprised at some of the things that the FBI heard on a daily basis. So he stated that his information really didn't have a particular category but that it was in regard to the background review of a candidate for the Supreme Court.

Boyd was put on hold listening to classical music. He looked out of his office windows at the city beyond and was tempted to hang up the phone and end this whole thing right now, but he knew that the call was already in the system, and he would have follow-up contact and visitors so he held on until a male voice came on the phone and asked him what this was all about.

He repeated his explanation that he had some information that he believed reflected on the character of a candidate for the Supreme Court.

He was asked for his identifying particulars and how he knew this information. Boyd explained that he had worked together with the person he was referring to.

"We treat information like this very seriously, sir," the man said. "We'll need you to fill out a report."

Boyd expressed the fact that if he hadn't thought it was serious he would not have wasted the time making the call.

The man asked whom Boyd was referring to.

Boyd said that maybe this wasn't something that should be done over the phone.

The man agreed and asked Boyd to come down to his office at his convenience. How would 10:30 do?

Boyd opened the envelope and unfolded his notes of the events of fifteen years before – a lifetime ago. As he read the words he wondered at how young he sounded . . . how young and how angry. He had been that person. He had written these words. His fingers had typed the computer keys. His mind had developed the images that he had put on the paper, and yet they seemed like a different person, as though he was reading evidence of a witness in a case he was developing. But it wasn't someone else. These were his words describing something he had experienced. A young Diamon Jakes developed in his mind. She was beautiful. She was in fact still beautiful, but she was more mature now, fifteen years later. It was hard to think of a judge, a candidate for the Supreme Court in terms of youth and beauty. She was a judge, a cut from a stone lawyer who held people's lives in her hands.

She had held his life in her hands. She had wanted to hold something else of his in her hands! He shuddered. Where would it have gone if he had allowed her to do what she wanted him to do? Even just her wanting that, had put them in this position, in this confrontational situation. Would it have been worse if he had agreed, if he had gone home with her, gone to bed with her, made love to her? Supreme Court judges are human too. They have needs. They must have desires. They must stand naked. They must lust and love and hate and regret. They have to be human in order to be able to reflect on and judge the human beings that come before them. Was it so bad that Diamon Jakes had found him attractive?

He didn't think of himself as attractive. He didn't have the blond crew cut any more. His hair had darkened and started turning grey. His eyes were still blue. He didn't think he had shrunk in height. His blood pressure was up. His belly had expanded although he had tried to keep himself fit. It was hard with the Medici food connection. He definitely didn't get enough exercise. His face seemed to have gotten rounder. The fact was that he was not going to look particularly attractive to the FBI and that was going to make his story a bit less believable.

On the other hand, his looks made him the perfect target for someone like Diamon Jakes. She would make a less than perfect looking man feel flattered by her attentions. If he had looked like a movie star, he wouldn't have needed her. The girls would have been falling all over him. She would have had to get in line!

As he read his notes, his anger rekindled recalling how Ronald Baines had shrugged him off, had doubted what he was saying, had completely diminished the issue to the point of sending him to sensitivity training! It should have been Baines at those sessions. It should have been Jakes.

Julia was right. He had to do this. A Supreme Court Judge had to be scrupulously honest, be one with the law of the land, but also had to have an understanding and compassion for the people. The law was supposed to be about the people and for the people. Sexual harassment was an abuse of power. Is that something you can get over? "I used to abuse my power, but I don't do that anymore. I'm more humble now. Can't you see? I'm a Supreme Court Judge!" Boyd didn't think so. The fact was it was part of Jakes's personality to elevate her position, to climb the ladder, to be on top.

It was unfair to say that was all of her personality. She was a good lawyer. Smart. Clever. Knowledgeable. Certainly. She was a good judge. Her rulings had consistently made the law journals. Her reasoning was intensely persuasive. She had gathered power to herself like a black hole, surrounding herself with powerful people, while throwing off just the right amount of favors, contacts, connections to keep growing, to keep respect and the gratitude accumulating. So was her focus on the careful dissemination of the fairness of the law or her place in history? As a Supreme Court Judge would she do more good or more harm?

That wasn't his responsibility to judge. He looked up. But that was exactly what he was doing. People thought she was pure. What he was revealing would besmirch that beautiful record. In the popular mind, Clarence Thomas was better known for his hearings with Anita Hill than for what he had actually done as a judge. Despite the fact that he had been appointed to the court, he would always have that cloud of doubt regarding his behavior.

It was clear to Boyd that Jakes would lie. She would deny this ever happened. She was unlikely to admit that she sexually harassed anyone. If she did admit it, would that disqualify her? She would lie because she didn't like that possibility in her future. She would try to totally eliminate him, to reverse the roles. He was the liar seeking his moment in the sun; seeking the substance for the book he would write.

Of course before any of that could happen, the FBI had to believe him. If they thought that he was a kook and a liar, his testimony would never see the light of day. There was little doubt in his mind that they wouldn't want to stir up this hornets' nest if they didn't think he was a reliable witness.

He shrugged. He folded up the pages of his notes and put them back in the envelope. The ball had been put in play.

+++++

What reaches the general public in terms of the information revealed during the senate judiciary committee hearings on a candidate for the Supreme Court is surface fluff. There were innuendoes that Diamon Jakes was too Liberal and the Conservatives on the committee were going to shoot her down. There were hints on the other side that she was too Conservative, that she was pro-life and would weigh the court down entirely on the Conservative side. All of the substance side of the debate was far too weighty to get into the press – her legal writings, opinions, testimony and speeches were not light reading.

There was all of the political posturing as well. The Conservatives on the committee had not made it easy for the

Liberal president to have his way. Adding another Liberal member to the court for life was not something they were going to allow to happen easily. The candidate's backers were going to have to prove that she her opinions would be solidly in the middle.

The process requires reviewing the candidate's questionnaire with all of the associated papers and reports that have been vetted by the FBI, going through the committee hearings with the candidate answering the committee members' questions, assembling more written questions, the candidate answering those questions, and finally reaching the level of the subcommittee vote to approve or reject or to send the nomination to the full Senate without a recommendation.

Once it reaches the full Senate, they have to have their own hearings and debates, and then the full Senate votes with a simple majority winning the day. Typically the entire process takes about two and half to three months.

The general consensus seemed to be that Judge Jakes wouldn't have much problem with any of it. There was always the possibility that something might come up to derail the process, but on the surface she looked like a sure thing. Because of that, the TV coverage would be light. The public liked conflict. No conflict, no interest, no ratings. The brass at the networks had moved on to other, more dramatic issues of the day – mass graves in Afghanistan, the pursuit of the international gun dealer who had made a fortune off the Olympics, mysterious animal migrations in the South Pacific that implied the end of the world. But with a little pushing from powerful connections, Gus was contacted by one of the more aggressive networks about Blaytent's technology, which might add an additional layer of interest in the process. The story might not be about the Supreme Court but about a scientific means for discerning the truth. They would be doubling their odds of getting the biggest audience. Gus knew that building the audience was the key in the network minds when Pooch Williams was the one to call him.

"Gus, baby!" Pooch said. "Small world! Small world! How long has it been? This is Pooch, Pooch Williams. Remember? You outed our anchor, Phil Gerber? Remember?"

"Pooch?" Gus was shocked. The network had moved Pooch Williams to the news? They had moved Pooch Williams from morning gossip to hard-core, national news? Gus tried to refocus the project, to find a way out of this. Was anyone going to take this seriously if Pooch Williams was directing it? He seriously doubted it.

"So you're still doing this thing!" Pooch exclaimed. "Still at it. Still finding the lawyers . . . I mean the liars. Ha, ha, ha!"

"They put you in charge of covering the confirmation hearings?"

"Yes, they did, Gus. Yes, they did. Little old me! You seem surprised. Are you surprised, Gus? Don't you think I can handle it?"

Gus paused for the briefest of seconds. "Sure. Sure, Pooch. If they think you can handle it, I'm sure you can handle it. Just seems a bit out of your field, your interests, if you know what I mean."

Silence on the other end of the line. "I recognize that this is serious business, Gus. I can be serious. I'm a professional."

"Oh, I didn't mean anything negative, Pooch. But hearings like this can be . . . you know . . . dull."

"That's why I'm talking to you, Gus, my friend. That's why I'm talking to you. You and I are going to spice this thing up. We're going to find the truth. That's what you do, right? That's what your machine does. And I am familiar with your machine. That's why they had me talk to you. Big move for me. Big opportunity. They're moving me to the national stage for this one! National! Right? The whole freakin' country! And it's because of you and that little event . . . what was it about a year ago? Revealing the truth behind our anchorman. Tried to kill himself after that. Did you know that? You probably hadn't heard. Wasn't successful, however. His wife left him though. Took their baby. Phil's off with his boyfriend somewhere else. Probably selling cars in Albuquerque! Ha, ha, ha." He choked down his giggles. "How's the machine?"

"It's good," Gus replied, trying to assimilate what had happened to Phil Gerber. Once again he was confronted with the impact that the revelation of the truth could have on people's lives. Pulling back the curtains on emotions that individuals hid in their private selves was not the purpose he had intended. But it wasn't possible to draw the line between revealing good truths and revealing bad truths. It wasn't the truth that was the issue. It was the revelation itself.

"No, the machine's good. We're calling it Beanstalk."

"Beanstalk? Sounds very hush, hush. You know like Operation Falcon, or something."

Gus explained what Julia had said about the children's game of Huckle, Buckle, Beanstalk that as they approached the truth, they got warmer. And there was the tale of Jack and his magic beans.

"Beanstalk. Hmm. And you're talking to me about being serious? Ha, ha, ha. Jesus! Magic beans! I'll see what I can do with that. Maybe we can come up with some sort of explanatory segment, you know, rather than just having you sit there and talk about it. You know, like 'Up close and personal with the Beanstalk!' Ha, ha, ha. People like those things. Jesus, they do enough of them in sports, don't they. I mean they get to find out that their hero was born a poor, little black boy, pulling himself out of the ghetto. They all seem to be like that even if they were born on the beaches of Malibu!

"But I guess we can't get that out of your machine." Pooch paused. "Wait a second. Brilliant thought! Brilliant thought! I'm full of those. Didn't you tell me that you were in Guantanamo? Didn't you tell me that last time? Didn't you tell me that was where the idea for this thing . . . this Beanstalk came from?"

"I was in the military police."

"Yah! Yah! Fantastic! So up close and personal: Beanstalk was born in the sweatboxes of Guantanamo. I love it! Don't you love it? Great idea! We'll work with that. We can't exactly interview the machine though. Ha, ha, ha. But we can talk to you. It's creator! It'll give us some background color. Explain what we're doing. It'll be great for you too, right? Almost like a free commercial on national news. Couldn't ask for better than that."

"Are you going to cover all of the hearings?" Gus asked trying to bring the conversation back to earth. It didn't surprise him that Pooch was trying to push the project into the sensationalism of the technology rather than emphasizing its fundamental and serious function or even the serious function of the congressional hearings themselves.

"No. Too dull. Too boring. Too dull. Look, nobody's going to want to sit there and listen to these dull old men asking questions that don't mean much to anyone. I mean anyone normal. Sure there are people who will sit around and watch the paint dry or graph the growth of their finger nails, but they're definitely not normal. Not our audience. No, we'll play it by ear. And your Beanstalk stuff might make it interesting. Maybe something will come out. Usually these people they talk to are so damn perfect. I suppose that's why they get chosen, you know? But that's not good television. It's not entertaining. Watching paint dry isn't entertaining!"

Pooch asked if the machine had changed.

Gus described the improvements they had made in integrating the technologies, that they had been able to focus on the frequencies in the voice stress analysis much more exactly and the analysis algorithms were much more accurate, although Bob Thatcher was still stuck on isolating the sounds generated by a particular subject in a multi-person room, particularly because the frequencies he was looking for were so low and people have a tendency to mumble when they are being questioned. He described the difficulties that they had run into with the non-verbal communications in actually seeing the movements of the body when the subject was sitting at a table or behind a desk. He explained that Allan had been able to note the subtle movements of the shoulders, neck, head and hands that reflect the positions of the feet and legs that couldn't be seen under the table. Even the stillest of subjects couldn't hide those subtleties. But those subtleties wouldn't mean much if they weren't integrated with other 'tells' like the micro-expressions and statement analysis. He explained that Julia had been able to greatly expand the statement analysis library and even integrate other languages and cultural nuances.

"Great," Pooch said, interrupting Gus's enthusiastic flow. "Very exciting. Okay. Well, we'll have to get together and work out the schedule and details."

+++++

"Time's up!" Gudmudgion said on the phone the next day. "Clock is coming down to its final ticks and tocks and I don't see a product on the market. I don't even see a plan for a product on the market. And that means, I don't see how Avitas is going to recoup our money!"

"Hello to you too, Ms Gudmudgion," Gus replied, trying to make some room for further discussion. What she was saying was partially true, he had to give her that. They didn't have a finished product that was ready to go to market, and it was difficult to forecast when there really would be one on the market, but they had come a long way and he said that to her.

"That's like the good intentions thing. We didn't put all this money up to invest in a science experiment. That doesn't generate income or cash flow or keep your company running. The facts are that we have very serious doubts that you will ever get beyond the R & D stage, and while that's laudable, it doesn't get us repaid. We need to know how you're going to do that, and we gave you four years to accomplish that. Tick tock, Mr. Sainte."

The phone felt slippery in Gus's hand and he felt his scrotum tightening as he pulled himself together to come up with answers. He explained the advances they had made as he had to Pooch Williams. He told her that they were going to get Beanstalk into the Congressional hearing room for the Supreme Court nomination hearings.

"What's Beanstalk?" she asked.

Gus laughed. "That's what we're calling it."

"You're calling this multi-million dollar project 'Beanstalk'?" she asked. "I'm sure there is story behind that but I don't want to hear it. I really don't care about stories. I know companies are successful with all sorts of weird and screwy names these days. It is the curse of the Internet, but there it is."

Gus adjusted his position in his chair and tried to relax the muscles in his body without much success. "It comes from the kid's game, you know, 'Huckle, Buckle, Beanstalk'. When you're getting closer and closer to an object."

"I don't know, but as I say, I don't really care either. If you have a name, you can have a product. I've also said this before, Mr. Sainte; you need to get serious about this. I agree you have made progress and had some successful demonstrations, and your project will probably get into some textbooks and research papers, but that does not pay the bills! You told us that you would have a marketable product in four years. Where is it? And how are you going to deal with this lawsuit? Did you do what they say? Are they going to win? This situation doesn't make me feel comfortable at all."

Gus realized that she was right. He had been pursuing the science, the concept of discerning the truth. If a subject had information that they didn't want to reveal, he had wanted to find a way to extract it without violence. Seemed pretty simple. It was the method that he had been chasing, but they hadn't clearly figured out how to monetize the method.

Those little junky, plastic products like moustache glasses that have movable eyebrows that go up and down in response to a clockwork motor in the fake nose always fascinated him. Someone had actually said, "I know, let's design moustache glasses that have movable eyebrows that go up and down in response to a clockwork motor in the fake nose." And the other people at the table said, "Yeah! That's a great idea. Let's do that. We'll sell a million of those." And then the engineers got out their computers and designed molds for the dozen or so parts in the moustache glasses that have movable eyebrows that go up and down in response to a clockwork motor in the fake nose. And then they molded all those parts and had people put them together and stick them on cardboard display cards that had a design of a kind of fake glasses and stuffed them in boxes, shipped them off to the U.S. where they were mounted on the end of the aisle where people could stop and go, "This is too funny! I have to get some of these!" They take them home, the kids play with them for a while, everyone takes pictures with their cell phones, the glasses snap when the kids wrestle with them, they get thrown in the trash, and that's the name of that tune!

Moustache glasses that have movable eyebrows that go up and down in response to a clockwork motor in the fake nose don't have much impact on the history of the world, but they are a product and they go through the entire product life cycle from concept to design to product to market to trash. Cash flows in and out at various points in the cycle and the designers come up with the next brilliant idea.

Blaytent had solved some amazing technical problems in pursuit of the method for discerning the truth. Oh wait, Gus thought, can't think of it that way. That's the other company's name: International Institute for Discerning the Truth, IIDT. That company had figured out how to monetize their method. The answer was simple: Blaytent just needed to package Beanstalk and price it, and come up with a sales and marketing plan.

He wasn't ready to tell Maria that she was right. "We've been telling you where we're going all along," he said. "We needed to develop the technology, and we're moving toward packaging it so it can be resold. The hearings will give us big time exposure and we'll get the marketing people to figure out the details."

"You have been saying that for awhile."

"What is it that you tell me, Maria? 'It always takes longer than you expect?'"

When he hung up the phone, he found that he was breathing more heavily. He leaned back in his chair and stared at his computer for a few moments. Then he popped his chair upright and banged his feet on the floor and wished he were making *moustache glasses that have movable eyebrows that go up and down in response to a clockwork motor in the fake nose.*

Chapter Fifteen

March 2015

Ore of the things about a fast food restaurant chain is that not only the food is the same, but also the layout of the restaurants is the same. There are variations to give the space some individual character and relate it to its surroundings, but for the most part a customer can be as comfortable and familiar with the layout as he is with the food. It is easy to find the bathrooms and the drink dispensers and the napkins from one MacDonald's® or Wendy's or Burger King® to another. For the most part, people don't linger in these places. One of the features of the design is that the seats are hard and most of them are bolted to the floor so that a large group of friends can't pull up extra seats and sit around and chat for hours. The majority of people who eat at fast food restaurants want to eat and run.

So it was unusual for the kid cleaning up the restaurant on this particular March afternoon to find a customer ostensibly asleep in the back corner of his booth. The kid was tall and skinny and suffered from a bout of adolescent acne. He had been assigned the task of sweeping up after the lunch rush, after the customers had thinned out. He pushed his broom around under the tables, pulling out the discarded wrappers and dropped French fries and the occasional crayon.

For some reason the guy asleep gave him the creeps. He nodded to the man in case his eyes were just closed, but he didn't get a reaction. The kid went on pushing his broom

down the aisle under the other tables. But he came wandering
back. He couldn't really finish the job without doing this table too, and he didn't want his boss to yell at him. He wasn't
afraid of his boss, exactly, but the guy could get irritable for
the dumbest things, and he had this issue with keeping everything in order.

The kid looked at the man in the booth. It was clear that
the man wasn't seeing him. His head was back and his eyes
were closed and his mouth was open. One hand lay on the
table holding a cell phone, face down. The kid couldn't see
his other hand as it was down beside the man's leg, on the
bench and under the table. The man was clearly asleep . . . or
something. There were those movies where spies are shot in
complete silence in public places. 'Thwump!' The kid
looked for a telltale bloody circle on the man's shirt but he
was wearing a black sweater so he couldn't see anything.
And he certainly didn't have a bullet hole in his head! And
there was no blood under the table or anything, just a couple
of old French fries. It would have been exciting if he'd been
shot or something! The kid shuddered a bit.

What the hell, the kid thought. "Excuse me, sir. Do you
mind if I sweep under your table? I won't touch your feet or
anything?"

There was no response. In fact the man didn't move. That
was creepy.

The kid said a little louder. "Excuse me! Sir!"

No response.

Another customer turned her head to see what was happening. The kid was kind of embarrassed to be making a scene,
so he shrugged and moved off. "Weirdo," he thought.
"Dumb place to sleep."

When he got back to the kitchen, he put his broom away
and went to find the manager to get his next assignment. The
manager appeared out from behind the ovens wiping his
hands. He pushed his glasses up his nose and cocked his head
back. "Yeah?" he asked.

"I've finished sweeping. What do you want me to do
next?" the kid asked.

"You swept all of it?"

"Yeah. Well, there was one guy at a table who wouldn't move his feet."

"You are not supposed to disturb the customers when they are eating," the manager reprimanded.

"He wasn't eating!" the kid responded.

"Well, what was he doing?"

"Sleeping. I think."

The manager looked as though he had eaten a bit too much of the company's products, his tie was loose and he was clearly sweating. He peered at the kid.

"Sleeping?" he asked. "Is he a street person or what?"

The kid shrugged. "I don't know. You know, he looked okay. He just looks like he's . . . you know . . . asleep." The kid paused. "So what do you want me to do next?"

"Is he still here?"

The kid shrugged. "I guess."

The manager let out a massive sigh. "Jesus!" he exclaimed. "It's a three ring circus in here. Never a dull moment. We're not running a damn dormitory for street people. I'll take care of this. Go help them in the back."

The kid shrugged again and shuffled off toward the back of the restaurant.

The manager pushed through the door out into what they called the dining room although it was about as far from an aristocratic dining room with a tablecloth and candelabras as it could get. He was strongly hoping that the man the kid had seen was gone. It wasn't that he didn't like confrontations. He'd had too many of those in his life which was why he was here, managing a fast food restaurant and not something more elevated that would have paid more and would have been more suited to his knowledge and his talents. The problem was keeping the confrontation under control. Control was the operative word. Anger management. What a great term! It was just that the street people smelled, and if he had to touch the guy to get him to move on, that would be pretty disgusting. And bringing the cops into the dining room was disruptive to the other diners, and he couldn't really afford to have an interruption in the afternoon trade. He needed to meet his numbers. It was lucky that it was such a beautiful day outside at least for this particular moment so that the restaurant was relatively quiet, quieter than it would have been had it been different weather. If the man was just not there, they could clean up and move on.

But the man was there. Seemingly asleep in the corner, his head back leaning against the corner with his eyes closed and his mouth open.

"Sir!" the manager said. "Sir, you can't sleep here. I'm going to have to ask you to move on."

The man's meal was in front of him on the table – paper bag, drink with the straw protruding out of the plastic cover, a crumpled napkin.

"Sir! You need to finish your meal and move on!" the manager said a little louder. The man didn't look like a street person. His black, sweater vest made him look kind of geeky. He looked a bit overweight. There were a million engineering firms in the area, so maybe he'd just had a long night or something. But he didn't move. He didn't close his mouth. He didn't blink his eyes.

The manager was starting to get creeped out. It is common for fast food restaurants to be anonymous like a big city where people don't notice each other or pay much attention to odd dress or behavior. But like a knot of traffic on a highway, other drivers want to know the cause; other viewers want to know why a reality show is attracting an audience. They are waiting to see someone get hurt, or better yet, die. It was becoming clear that something unusual was going on here, and other diners were turning their heads toward the table. They could feel it, and so could the manager.

He thought, "I don't need this right now." As opposed to other times when some body in the restaurant would have been a good thing! "He can't be dead. What the hell am I supposed to do now? This isn't in the manager's manual!"

Out loud he tried again, "Sir! Hello!"

"I think he's dead," one old lady said. "I've seen that look before."

"Who is he?" the manager asked the surrounding tables.

"No idea," said the old lady. "Didn't much notice him. I think there was a girl with him. But she left. You know that

happens in places like this. People don't notice each other.
That's why some people . . . ."

"Thank you," said the manager, cutting her off. He started
to lean over the table and reach out to touch the man. His intention was to gently shake him to wake him.

"Don't touch him!" a man said. "He's evidence! You're
not supposed to touch evidence. It might be a crime scene!"
There was a general gasp. Several people stood and
started to back away.

"Look," the manager said, "he's probably just asleep. I'm
going to see if he's asleep. That's all. So everybody take it
easy. People don't get enough sleep these days, you know?
I'm sure he's just asleep."

To the man in the corner he said again, "Sir! You need to
wake up!"

Just then the man's hand holding the cell phone began to
jump and buzz and light up. Startled, the manager jumped
back and then grinned sheepishly. But the man didn't move.
He didn't open his eyes. He didn't lift the cell phone to his
ear. He just remained leaning against the corner with his head
back and his mouth open. Either he was a very sound sleeper
and very tired or he was dead.

The manager stood there looking at him. He mentally
ruled out a street person, using the restaurant for shelter. No,
this guy didn't look like a street person. The manager mentally thumbed the pages of the management manual and
arrived at the section on emergencies, but he couldn't focus.
He had always thought of himself as being clear headed, of
calmly knowing what to do, one of those people who remembered to pull the alarm before leaving the burning building
and holding the door for everyone else before leaving himself.
One of those people they interview on the evening news.
"No, I don't think of myself as a hero. I just did what anyone
else would have done!" Then turning and walking away with
a small, self-deprecating shrug.

Instead, he found himself screaming internally. "What the
fuck DO I DO NOW!"? He took a deep breath and realized
that he needed to determine for sure that the man was dead.
He had to touch him. Jesus, maybe he needed CPR. Maybe

he had a piece of meat stuck in his throat, and he could be saved, and instead the manager was just standing there! The manager looked at the food bag. It didn't look like it had been opened, so hopefully if he had choked on a piece of meat it wasn't from this restaurant. Maybe there wouldn't have to be an inquiry. Jesus, he would have to make sure all his paperwork was in order and . . .. Tick, tock. Time to move.

He reached out and touched the man's hand. "Sir!" he said at the same time. When he touched it he was shocked at how cold the skin was. "Sir!" the manager said again, a bit more quietly. He wrapped his fingers around the man's wrist and gently shook him. "Sir!" There was no reaction. The man didn't move. He didn't open his eyes. He didn't close his mouth. He was no longer a functional human being. He was clearly dead. He would not get up and walk out of the restaurant after he had finished his lunch.

The manager stepped back. "Okay," he said to himself. He pulled out his own cell phone and dialed 911 and reported the situation. Then he turned to the surrounding diners who were now rising from their seats. "Could you folks please hang around for a bit? I'm sure the police will want to get statements from you. Shouldn't take long I'm sure. I'm sorry for the inconvenience."

"Can I get a refund for my meal?" one man asked. "I mean you shouldn't have to put up with people dying around you when you're eating! Know what I mean?"

"It is an inconvenience," said one old lady. "Damn right. People shouldn't go out to lunch if they're going to die. I know that I'm not going to do that when my time comes. It's like little kids. They're an inconvenience in places like this too. Yelling. Screaming. It's annoying, I tell you. "

The manager left them mumbling and murmuring and moving toward the counter. He realized that he would have to close the restaurant while all this was going on, so he got the staff to lock the doors and put signs on them that said 'Closed for Repairs'.

"What's being repaired?" asked one of the kids who had come out of the kitchen.

"Nothing," replied the manager.

"So why are we saying that?"

"Just do it!" the manager blurted.

After what seemed an interminable length of time, but was actually only a few minutes, the police and the emergency crews came. The remaining diners stood back like a herd of goats watching in awe. The manager was impressed at how efficient the emergency crews were. This is what they did every day: remove dead bodies from restaurants and rescue cats from trees! What a life! He could have done that. When he was a kid, he'd always wanted to be a policeman. He would have been good at it too, he thought. Instead he was running this damn restaurant, and now he would have to do all the paperwork and management would want to know every- thing that had happened and so would the insurance company. He would be tied up in red tape until the cows came home! And who knows when that would be? Who was the guy and why did he have to come HERE to die? This would probably be on the news and what would that do for the publicity of the restaurant? Customers wouldn't want to come here to eat. "Oh, don't go there. Don't you know? That's the place where the guy died."

"Was it the food?"

"I don't think so. But who knows. You know?"

The EMTs removed the body. The police talked to people and made notes, and gradually things began to settle back down. "Who was he?" the manager asked.

"We're notifying the family," the officer replied. "We'll let you know."

When all of the emergency personnel had left and the last of the customers had filtered out through the door, the man- ager stood there with his staff. He looked at them. He needed words of wisdom, a pep talk, time to get back in the game. Shrug it off. Move on. It's just a body. But they were so damn young! Most of them anyway.

He knew that none of them would move past that table without thinking about it. He clapped his hands to break the spell. "Okay!" he said. "We have a restaurant to run. Get the signs off the doors and get them unlocked. Let's move on. Good news is, we didn't kill him! He just died."

+++++

Diamon Jakes was in Washington preparing her responses to the Senate Judiciary Committee's questions. She was intensely aware that everything she was and everything she had done was likely to be revealed in these hearings. But she wanted it. She deserved it. Pride, she knew, was not a virtue, and therefore she didn't consider it pride. She considered it just a part of her exceptional character that she had risen so far. At forty-eight, she would be the youngest woman to be appointed to the Court. She just regretted that her father wasn't alive to see this day. His suicide would forever haunt her. His success in the ice and oil business in Washington had driven envious whites to consider him an uppity nigger and not worthy of their society. He had given Diamon everything he could, but he was haunted by the color of his skin.

She had inherited his *Dracaena Massangeana*, his corn plant. If she had been less argumentative and less driven, she fantasized that she could have become a gardener. Over the years, she had attempted to grow plants in her apartments with little success. She couldn't keep up a regular and disciplined watering and feeding schedule and most of them died. It annoyed her that they seemed to have different needs and didn't succumb to her efforts at regulating their lives.

She had felt the same way about relationships with men and particularly black men. She had little respect for most of them because she felt they lacked ambition. She was well aware of society's fear of a young, black man slouching down a dark street, with their trousers hanging down around their ass and a hoodie pulled up over their heads. Young men that behaved that way were doing nothing to enhance their image. They looked threatening, and they were threatening. Threat equaled fear, and fear resulted in consequences especially when so many people were walking around with guns. Old men , young men, mothers, and children, people in movie theaters, people on buses, kids in kindergarten were all carrying guns and addressing their fears with their guns. And when people behave that way, the government makes more laws. And the courts have to make more decisions.

Diamon was convinced that the rule of law in the country was breaking down. The government couldn't agree on much of anything. It required a firm hand, and it was her intension to provide that.

She wasn't concerned about the confirmation hearings. There was nothing in her life that she was ashamed of. It was the nature of being a lawyer or a judge that her decisions would be disagreed with by half the people. It was a very rare situation when both sides were happy with any decision. She had had her share of threatening letters and phone calls and text messages and emails. Although the law was a messy business, she felt that her slate was clean.

So she was surprised when the FBI asked her about Boyd Willis. "Who?" she asked.

They told her that he had filed a report that she had attempted to have sexual relations with her, which he rejected.

She laughed. "When was this?" She expected there would be termites like this crawling out of the woodwork to bring her down. This was the big time. Not everyone wanted another woman on the Court, and certainly not everyone wanted another black liberal. They would challenge her stand on everything from guns and hoodies to *Dracaena Massangeana* when they found out about it.

"You kill plants, don't you, Judge Jakes? How do you feel about Native Americans?"

So what was a challenge from a young lawyer whom she barely remembered? When the FBI asked if they should take his information seriously, in good judicial fashion she replied that they should take all such challenges seriously. They should look into his background. She might have worked with him many years before, but she had no memory of any personal encounters, and she put the question aside and went back to assembling her financial records and legal writings.

It was an interesting exercise searching the Internet for her quotes and thoughts and things that people had written about her over the years. The first page stuff was obvious. It was when she got into the back pages, the dark recesses that things got weird. There were citations of articles that she had forgotten she had written. She had grown through a period of controlled radicalism during her college years, enjoying the companionship of the women in Ethos at Wellesley. She struggled not to be sucked in by the feeling of security among peers that might have dulled her spirit to try and change the world. She organized protests in a time when Bobby McFerrin was singing "Don't Worry. Be Happy!"

She was grateful that the Internet hadn't existed when she was doing thing that she might now regret. She was surprised how much some people had dug up and reproduced and published. There were even some old pictures of her that must have come out of someone's scrapbook. "I knew her when she was little! Wasn't she cute?"

And there were the people who hated her for a million different reasons: the color of her skin, the shape of her nose, the money her family had made, her opinions on race, her opinions on the environment, the criminals she had put away. She hadn't kept all of the threatening letters, but she passed along what she had kept to the FBI who were looking into them. She had security now. Her life, her thoughts, her ideas were exposed. Her time was no longer her own. She tapped her fingernails on the table next to her computer as she read through the questions posed to her by the Judicial Committee. Tap, tap, tap.

+++++

Julia came into Gus's office to tell him that Boyd was going to Washington to testify in Judge Jakes's confirmation hearings and that Bob was late getting back from lunch.

"Why?" Gus asked. "I mean why is Boyd going to Washington?"

"Something happened a long time ago between Boyd and Judge Jakes, and he feels he has to let them know. Before she gets confirmed," Julia explained.

"They knew each other?"

"They worked together. At Tittle and Baines. She harassed him."

"What?" Gus asked, with the flicker of a smile on his face. "She harassed him? Sexually harassed him?"

"It's not a laughing matter, Gus. Men get sexually harassed too. Most of them are extremely reluctant to talk about it. I'm really proud of Boyd."

"He doesn't have to do this."

"I know which makes it even better."

"I mean there's not much point. She's going to get confirmed. How many candidates don't get confirmed? Hardly any, I'd say. And she's the perfect candidate. Both sides like her because she seems to be in the middle of most issues. There do seem to be a growing number of women on the court. That might be against her."

Julia nodded.

"Well, good for Boyd. I hope all the publicity doesn't hurt him. I'm sure he's thought about this pretty carefully. He's a careful kind of guy. We'll be there to get it all on tape, by the way. Pooch Williams is setting up our connections. We won't be on all the networks, but we'll be there. Pooch's pretty excited about it. The politics and back stabbing in that business makes Afghanistan look peaceful!"

"What can I do?"

"I wish Boyd wasn't going. I'm sure we will need his legal advice as things come up."

"I'm not going to try to talk him out of it. We've probably talked it to death! He's not going off to war for three years!" Julia said. "He'll be available."

"Good. We'll need to be absolutely sure that the system is working. I want it to be able to keep up with every word, every phrase, every nuance, and every twitch that Jakes or the other witnesses make. We have to get this right."

At that point, Gus's cell phone rang. He had set the *Lion Sleeps Tonight* ringtone for in-house connections, so he held up a finger to Julia, picked up the phone, and flipped his finger up across the screen to make the connection. He was smiling at Julia, but his smile disappeared. Julia saw the color go out of his face. Gus bent his head down to face the floor and dropped into his chair.

"What?" He paused to listen. "When?" He paused again. "How do they know it was him?" He paused again. "Thank you," he ended quietly, breaking the connection.

"What?" Julia asked. "What's happened?"

"Bob's dead."

"He's what? Our Bob? Bob Thatcher?"

"He died at lunch. They found him in his booth. They thought he was asleep."

"What about his family?" Julia asked. "How did he die? Did he choke on something? One of those lovely pieces of meat?"

"They aren't sure yet, but it doesn't appear to have been the food. Probably his heart or something."

"Are they sure? I mean sometimes, you know, these stories get exaggerated. We don't really know, do we? Not until we have all the information. Who was that? Who was that that called? Maybe he just collapsed and they hauled him off to the hospital."

"That was a friend of his family's. Over at his house. It was nice of them to call."

Julia said, "I knew he was late getting back from lunch. That's one of the reasons I came in here. I told you that didn't I? That he was late getting back from lunch."

"Well he's really late now!" Gus said.

"So, you mean he just . . . died?"

"I guess," Gus replied.

"We need more details. You can't just stop living. That's not the way it's supposed to happen."

"He didn't take very good care of himself. He was always stressed and anxious and he smoked. I wonder if he ever had his blood pressure checked. We should have known stuff like that. But he was really young, wasn't he? There were times when he didn't look young, but he was, wasn't he?"

Julia thought for a moment. "I think he was thirty-eight or not quite thirty-eight."

Gus looked at her. "Really? People die that young? I know, that's a stupid thing to say. But that's really young."

They sat in silence, trying to make sense of a nonsensical situation. There were a million clichés rolling through Gus's head, but he didn't want to say any of them. Bob had been part of the team from the beginning, from that meeting in the "Library" on Commonwealth Avenue. Bob was anxious even then. But they had been through a lot together. Was this really where it ended? Just like that? What about Beanstalk? What about the hearings? Was Bob's piece finished or was it hanging in the middle of something? Gus couldn't ask him! He just couldn't ask him any more. Gus was sure there would be dozens of questions that he would want to ask, but couldn't. Not any more. At that moment he couldn't even remember what he had said to Bob that morning. He was so used to having him around that it never occurred to him that he wouldn't be able to talk to him later. Time is a river that goes on and on. People don't. Another stupid cliché.

Lion Sleeps Tonight tinkled out again from Gus's phone. "What?" he answered. "Yes. It's true." He paused to listen. "I don't have all the details. He apparently died at lunch. They found him his booth. They thought he was asleep. But he was dead. Passed away." He paused to listen again. "Jesus! I can't believe it."

He broke the connection and looked at Julia. "Well, we have to do something."

"Do you know what restaurant he was in? I can contact the police and see if I can get any more details. I'll call the hospital too and see if they brought him there. Do you think it's too soon to talk with his wife, Annabelle? Maybe she needs help. Although she does have family in the area and it seems like people are there already. I wonder who told her? I can't just sit here. This doesn't make sense."

Julia was rushing for the door.

Gus stood up. "Wait," he said. "We need to take a breath here."

"I can't just sit!" Julia almost shouted.

"This is really sad, I know," Gus replied, trying to get his thoughts together. "It's really sad, but we have to think about what this means to Blaytent and the hearings. We have to. I know that's hard to do. I want to help Bob's family too. I mean how old's his son? Zack, isn't it? I want to help too, but we have to think about everyone else here."

Julia looked at him with her hand on the doorknob. "Priorities, Gus," she said. "That's your problem."

+++++

The raw, abrupt news of Bob's death stunned the staff at Blaytent forcing them to a stop. Day to day, mundane activities didn't seem important in comparison to life and death. Death was supposed to happen somewhere out there in the future. Not now. Not today. Not this moment. It was different. You could put it out of your mind if it happened to someone you didn't know or hadn't even met. It was like those reports of the dozens of people who die in revolutions or wars. You could just sit there, watching the news and forget it the next minute. The fact is that you have to. Even if you wanted to care about every human being on the planet, your brain can't handle it. It's part of life. Religions have tried to explain that for thousands of years. As the connection gets closer and closer . . . from an unknown person on the news to a family member . . . it necessarily becomes more difficult to ignore.

A company is a complex, familial network. On the one hand people working with each other side by side, day after day are moving down parallel life tracks. Employees get to know each other and their families. They make associations and friendships as well as dislikes and even hatreds. Companies, on the other hand, are business enterprises, a collection of people working as a machine to make money. If parts of the machine are not working properly, they get removed – fired, laid off, dismissed. That can't happen with a family. Family members might get ignored or shunned, but the blood connection is still there.

If a fellow employee dies, their death crosses the line and confuses the connections. Gus knew he had to address that. For the health of Blaytent, they had to succeed at the hearings. Beanstalk had to work without Bob. They wouldn't forget him, but they had to keep moving forward.

After Gus had brought the company together, and they had talked about what had happened and aired their thoughts, he urged them to keep going, telling them how important the success of the effort had been to Bob. While he was in the midst of this pep talk, his phone rang again, this time with the old fashioned jangling ringtone of a mechanical bell indicating an outside call. He cut it off with a push of a button sending the call to his voice-mail, apologized for the interruption, and turned back to the staff gathered in front of him. It was an impromptu combination of condolences and pep talk. "Let's do this for Bob! Remember him. Feel sad. But get your work done." It wasn't one of his better pep talks. He went back to his office feeling unsatisfied.

He brought Allan and Arya back with him to assess the status. After a few moments of mumbling and silence and recounted memories, he asked them what this would do to having Beanstalk ready for the hearings. "How critical is the voice stress stuff?" he asked. It was sort of like asking how important was Bob to the project. It wasn't that Bob hadn't done a lot, but they had three other, functional technologies working together.

"We've said this before," Arya said, "there's not much about truth that is black and white, yes? People have too many filters, and we don't know what they are for each person. We each have different filters generated by time, our life experiences, our cultures, and lots of things. I'm not even sure that when I see green, something that appears to be green to me, that I am seeing the same thing you are."

"Yes, I know," Gus replied. "We've been through that."

Allan added, "I think we're in good shape with the non-verbal communications. We've done a good job of blending 'fisherfaces' with the *AAM*, and that has allowed us to work at almost any angle in almost any light."

"Forgive me," Gus asked, "but I've forgotten what *AAM* stands for."

"*Active Appearance Model*. It decouples the face's shape from its texture. That helps us with the *ME*s, the micro expressions, bringing the two technologies closer together. This is stuff other companies are using very effectively now in facial recognition. But we have taken it beyond facial expressions into body positions, adding in all the research that the FBI has done as well as my own work in the studio here."

"Hard to test," Gus said.

"It is," Allan replied. "But we have successfully built up a fairly extensive positional reference library; like a dictionary of body positions what they are and what they mean. Feet, hands, shoulders, head position, body position and angle. We've been able to coordinate all of that information with the facial stuff, *Me*s, Julia's *Sa*s and Bob's voice stress. As Arya said, though, there are lots of filters. Body language in one culture is different than body language in another culture, and not only the culture but also the age and generation. An adult slouching down in a chair has a completely different meaning than a teenager! We have to try to remove the positions that are learned from the positions that are natural. A person testifying in front of a congressional committee for one of the most important jobs on earth is going to sit differently than a husband and wife sitting around the kitchen table drinking coffee! We have to filter some of that out without impacting the real message."

"Julia said she was making good progress universalizing her *SA*s, *Statement Analyses*. I hate these acronyms!" Gus said. "It's hard enough to know what people are talking about without trying to keep up with acronyms."

Arya replied, "You'll have to ask her, but she's given me a lot to work with. In a lot of languages, yes? It's very helpful when the subject is making lengthy statements, telling stories, you know? She likes to say that, 'it is possible because people mean exactly what they say. It's just how you hear it!' And we can hear it all. The computers can unravel the statement, word by word, as fast as the subject speaks it. She has also been trying to unravel the morphosyntactic alignment of other languages."

"So that gets us back to Bob and his voice stress," Gus said.

Arya and Allan looked at each other. "I think we're okay," Allan said finally. "There hasn't been any radical changes since our last review. You've heard all this. His *IVSA* . . . *Integrated Voice Stress Analysis* . . . has advanced well. Testing has been tedious. It's not hard to find people who are willing to lie. It's just difficult to get them to admit to it! And at the same time be lying truthfully. It has to be a real lie. Not a fake lie or an induced lie, and they have to be under stress. That's why this takes so long."

"I know," Gus sighed. "I know this. I wish Avitas did. Gudmudgion is driving me crazy."

"There have been some interesting articles in *The International Journal of Speech, Language and the Law* on this and I think Bob was working on something for the *IAFL* . . . *The International Association of Forensic Linguists*. I don't know if he finished those. I think he might have been waiting to run them by you."

"We should do that!" Gus said. "Stuff like that, peer reviewed, would go a long way to legitimizing what we're trying to do."

"I don't know if they're finished or how far along he was," Allan added.

"Yeah, but, we could get them published in his memory."

Allan looked at him. "Wouldn't that be taking advantage of his death?"

Gus replied, "No. I don't think so. It would kind of be his legacy, you know? Something that would go into his history."

All three of them were quiet for a couple of minutes. "We have to move on, as I said. It's sad. We'll miss him. But we have to move on. Beanstalk has come together well. Do you think Julia could finish those?"

"She's definitely our best writer," Allan said.

"I'm not sure you have to be a great writer for those journals," Gus smiled. "You just have to use a lot of technical words. Better yet a bunch of formulas!"

Arya smiled back. "'One man's trash is another man's treasure!' Yes?"

"On another subject," Gus said, looking at the two of them, "Gudmudgion wants us to have a marketable product . . . soon. She likes the press and stuff, but she wants us to get beyond the technical journal jargon and into what she thinks of as the real world. Arya, can you get me set up in here with something so when I am talking to people I can see if they are telling the truth?"

"It's not exactly an 'app'!" Arya said.

Gus looked at him. "That would be cool! But I'm not asking for that. Could you do it and how long do you think it will take? I mean if we've got the heart of this thing down, how hard can it be to package it?"

The natural light was fading in Gus's office as the day wound to a close. Most days slide by with little notice or memory making. The same thing happens with small variations day after day until one of the life changing days comes along. Some of them are planned like weddings or perhaps the birth of a child, but many of them are unplanned like a death, the removal of a person from the stream of life we are immersed in. Gus's thoughts kept going back to Bob like a tongue to a tooth. He didn't need a machine to interpret the body language of the other two men in his office despite the fact that they came from vastly different cultural backgrounds. He knew that all three of them were struggling to move beyond it. He also knew that when they stopped talking about the day-to-day elements of the life-stream, they would sink into the sadness and loss.

"I know you have a lot to do getting ready for Washington, and I know we'll all be struggling to fill the hole that losing Bob has made, but I want you to see what you can do to get something in here." Gus looked at Arya.

Arya hesitated. "Yah," he replied finally. "I'll see what I can do."

"I've got to go see Annabelle," Gus stated. "Annabelle and . . .. Jesus, I'm blanking on their kid's names. Do you remember?"

"Christa, Zack and Kirsten," Allan said.

"Jesus. I'd forgotten he had three kids. How old are they now?"

"I'm not sure," Allan said. "I think the oldest, Christa, must be close to eighteen."

"Wow. Tough age to lose a father. I'll call Julia. She should be over there now."

+++++

It was until much later that Gus checked the message that had been left on his phone while he was talking to the staff at Blaytent. He and Allan had driven over to Bob's house where there was general turmoil. Julia had gone with Annabelle to the hospital where they had taken Bob. Close relatives had poured in to be with the kids and be together. Christa, the eldest daughter, was trying her best to be the head of the household and keep things together. Although there was a great deal of murmuring and bustling about to get food and drink, there was a general holding-of-the-breath while they waited for Annabelle to return with a kind of distant hope that maybe it hadn't really happened, that he would be alright. It was serious, certainly, but he wasn't really dead. Things would get back to normal. They could chastise him for not taking better care of himself, but at least he would be there to chastise.

But he was dead. When Annabelle returned, she was as white as a sheet. Julia held her arm to keep her steady. Christa and Zack came to her and hugged her. Kirsten hung back, refusing to accept the reality, tears pouring down her face. The others in the room stood back not to intrude on this private moment.

Julia came over to Gus and Allan. She told them that they still didn't know exactly what had killed him. They would have to do an autopsy, but it was pretty clear that it was his heart. Gus asked if there was anything they could do. Julia said she would stay for a while, and Gus and Allan drifted away, feeling uncomfortable.

Back at home, Gus slung his coat over a chair and flopped onto the sofa in the living room. His house was quiet and empty. There was no wife and no family. For a moment he thought about who would come if he had died. Who would mourn? Who would come to his funeral? Was it the number of people who show up in the funeral parlor that indicates how important you are, how much of an impact you have made on life? Is it the number of cars in the funeral procession? What if no one shows up? Does that mean you might as well not have lived? Of course it wouldn't really make any difference to him at that point. He'd be dead. Bob was lucky. He had lots of family and friends to miss him. Well not exactly lucky. He was no longer around to enjoy his family or his friends. They had the hard part.

Gus shook it off and stood up and got a beer out of the fridge. Then he looked at his phone and remembered that someone had left him message.

The voice on the voice message was garbled and not one that Gus recognized immediately. " . . . ahny Flack . . . membr me . . .? need . . . talk . . ." Gus listened to it a second time and realized that it was Johnny Flack from IIDT and he wanted to talk. "Whoa," Gus said to himself. "That's interesting. Quite the coincidence." The whole IIDT organization led him to thinking about distrust, that there must be something underhanded going on. It was impossible that his call would have any connection to Bob's death. Bob had died from natural causes. Hadn't he? But IIDT was tied into military intelligence stuff. They had means to do things. Make things happen that shouldn't. Why Bob? The lawsuit was one thing, but killing people? That was something else entirely.

Gus took a deep pull on his beer. He stared at the wall across the room. Crum was a creep, but would he have someone killed? Was Bob working on something that he hadn't told Gus about but Crum had found out about? Was Cyrene involved? How about her father? What was going on? Why would Johnny Flack want to talk to him?

Gus realized he was tired and he was being paranoid. A friend had died . . . a good friend . . . a co-worker. Gus's reasoning was all over the block. This was not a time to make decisions or drive a car or figure out what moves a government agency might make. It was time for another beer and then perhaps some attempt at sleep. He would call Flack back in the morning.

Just as he was setting the phone down on the table, it rang. Gus jumped and dropped the phone. "What the hell?" he said, picking up the phone. He didn't recognize the number. He made the connection. "Yes?" he answered tenuously.

"Gus? This is Johnny Flack," the voice on the other end said. "Did you get my message?"

"Ah," Gus replied. "Yes, I did. I was just listening to it. Busy day."

"Yes, I know," Flack replied. "Sorry to bother you. But we need to talk."

"What about?" Gus asked. "And what do you mean 'I know'? What do you know? Are you watching me?"

"You shouldn't be so paranoid, Gus," Flack replied with a light chuckle. "We all have busy days. Can we meet?"

"Why?"

"There are some things that you should know. I'm in Boston."

"I know," Gus said even though he didn't. It caused the man to pause for a second.

"Someplace neutral."

Gus wondered what he meant by 'neutral'. Gus did not feel as though he was on top of his game. It had been a tough day. There were too many things going on. He wanted to believe that he had it under control and that Bob's death hadn't induced some level of shock. He looked at his hands. They seemed steady. He looked at his feet. Could you tell anything from your own feet? They seemed okay. He shrugged.

"I need to know what this is about," he said. "Is it something to do with the lawsuit? If it is, the lawyers should be involved. Is that what you mean by neutral?"

"It's not for the lawyers."

"Why are you in Boston?"

"Business," Johnny replied. "Just business if you want to know the truth."

"I'm sure that's what you're about. The truth. Always."

"Look do you want to meet me or what? It's kind of urgent."

"What's the point?" Gus asked. "If you won't tell me what it's about, what's the point? A friend of mine died today, and I'm kind of tied up."

"I'm sorry," Johnny replied. "I'm sorry about Dr. Thatcher. I heard he was a good man; good at what he did."

"How did you know that?" Gus asked.

"He had a reputation in the field, you know. Technical stuff."

"No! How do you know he was the one who died?"

"Oooh. Nothing too secretive about that. It was on the news. Guy who died in the fast food restaurant. Probably wasn't taking too good care of health. Probably shouldn't have been eating fast food. Guys like that should take better care of themselves."

By this time Gus's brain was doing all sorts of underworld gymnastics. These guys had killed Bob! He didn't know how. He didn't know why. Well the why probably came with his association with Blaytent. He hadn't liked this Johnny guy from the start, but he didn't believe he was capable of murder. No, there was no reason to think anything of the sort. No reason at all. Crum was a nasty person, but he wouldn't go around taking out hits on people! That stuff didn't happen in real life. Bob had died of natural causes and he should have taken better care of himself, but Gus didn't want this creep making statements like that. He didn't even want him talking about Bob.

"I don't want to talk to you," Gus said.

"Your loss."

"And you can tell that to your friend, Crum as well. I've had enough of these charades. So fuck off." And he broke the connection. He flung the phone down on the coffee table and flopped back against the back of the sofa. Now his hands were shaking. "What the hell?" he said to himself. "What the hell was that?"

Chapter 16

Late March 2015

"Innocent until proven guilty." Boyd wondered where that phrase had come from. On the surface it was simple. You couldn't just go around accusing people of doing things without being able to prove it. In many situations, however, just the accusation was enough to tar the accused with the obliterating brush of implication. He felt strongly that the FBI thought that he was guilty of making false accusations when he reported his issues with Judge Jakes. She was living at a higher level of innocence than he was, and it would take a lot to make his reported incidents pollute her purity.

It was difficult to prove. Sexual harassment was often evidenced by a handful of words said at the wrong time in the wrong place. The line was not clear between the occasional, joking remark and harmful implications. When the words are used as weapons to gain sexual favors, the line becomes clearer, but even then it is often difficult to know what the perpetrator has in mind as a reward for their advances. And how do you prove what happened fifteen years ago with a candidate for the supreme court who had such an exemplary record that she was able to rise rapidly to that position? Her years of success provided layers of armor that made it difficult to believe that she would do the things he was accusing her of.

This wasn't some trivial finger pointing either. There were significant consequences to what he was claiming. Now that he had said it, the ball was rolling and the FBI had to investigate. The incidents had to be defined in painful detail. As a man, Boyd had to admit that the attentions and the touching and the propositioning by a beautiful woman were undesirable and unwanted. The agents thought he should have been flattered!

"Jesus! I would have been," they chuckled to each other.

Boyd knew that they weren't supposed to be saying things like that. They weren't supposed to be implying that they thought a candidate for the Supreme Court was hot. He wondered if they were trying to push him to recant or admit that he was not interested in women or had some other motive for making these claims. Men didn't turn down the advances of beautiful women. The attention of a beautiful woman was an affirmation of manhood, of desirability, of power. A man could decline it only if he were already powerful. So if Boyd had declined it, it reduced his stature with the agents and their inclination to believe his story and care about his issues. It would have been much easier if this little man went away.

Reading through his notes of the incidents reignited his anger at the situation. The words seemed so foreign. His writing style had changed in fifteen years. The descriptions seemed crude although there were flashes of description that he surprised himself with his own writing skill. He regretted that he hadn't pursued it with the EEOC at the time. He would have had a more official backing for his claims.

He had wanted to put it behind him. He had wanted to get on with his life. He hadn't wanted Jakes to have that kind of continuing power over him. But she had and she still did have that power. This was another of those life-changing moments. Describing the events now, telling his story . . . which made it seem fictional . . . in this place at this time under these circumstances would put it in the history books and what now served as the history books: the Internet.

Over and over again he had asked himself why he was going through this. Jakes wasn't a bad lawyer. She certainly wasn't stupid. She wasn't evil . . . in the majority of ways. There certainly could have been worse choices for the court. The FBI had not been able to turn over any other rocks where she was hiding past indiscretions. Her record was apparently clean. It was all good until Boyd came along. Was a little office hanky-panky all that important?

Boyd wondered what Ronald P. Baines would say to the FBI. It was doubtful that he would even remember a minor incident with a minor associate in the office from fifteen years before. He would certainly remember Jakes. She would stand out in his memory like the North Star on a clear night! He would forget the cloud that had drifted momentarily across her celestial light. He certainly wouldn't support Boyd's story.

What about the other associates? The FBI would track them down even though they had probably all drifted off to other positions. At the time Boyd had felt the situation was embarrassing and hadn't opened himself up to any of them. There was a certain amount secretiveness that permeated the firm. You were expected to keep things to yourself to protect your clients and yourself.

The people who had taught the sexual sensitivity training were not likely to reveal anything about what he had said in those classes. They weren't supposed to remember, and he hadn't written down the trainer's name. He thought the FBI agents would probably dig out that information if they were thorough anyway, at least uncovering whom Tittle and Baines contracted with at the time.

So where did that leave him? It didn't look good. It was his word against hers. It was his power against her POWER. It was his innocence against her INNOCENCE. It was his truth against her version of the truth. It didn't seem like much of a contest. He would be sitting there in front of all those politicians and cameras and microphones on his own. Why should he pursue this?

He went through his notes again. He wouldn't be able to question Judge Jakes. That was up to the politicians. He wouldn't be able to ask her the questions that would reveal to him whether or not she believed that using a position of power to manipulate people's lives was fair and equal justice. Life wasn't fair. He knew that. But weren't laws supposed to be made to protect people's lives and to level the playing field?

It wasn't fair to steal your neighbor's cow just because you wanted it. The law says you can't do that. It wasn't fair to own people. Slavery was against the law. Wasn't controlling a person's life with sexual power the same thing as enslaving that person? Could a person who thought so little of an associate make good decisions in the interest of all the people of the country?

Maybe she'd changed. Maybe that was an aberration – a one-time incident, a mistake. But he couldn't ask her. The politicians could ask her, but they wouldn't because they wouldn't even think she was capable of such a thing unless he stood up.

He was surprised when the FBI asked him if this was all a publicity stunt for Blaytent. They asked him if he knew that Blaytent equipment was going to be in the hearing room with one of the TV stations. He told them that was the first he had heard about it. He was Blaytent's corporate counsel, but nothing more than that. They seemed skeptical. They repeated that they took accusations like his very seriously. This wasn't a game. They said they would have to look into his relationship with the company . . . in detail.

Julia immediately came to his mind. They had talked about this. She had urged him to present his story. She had told him that she was completely behind him and could take anything that was thrown at her. But he still had to be careful. An FBI probe into your life was not exactly a walk in the park. He wasn't afraid of anything in his own past. He felt that he had led a clean life. There were no skeletons that he could recall stuffing in a closet. Of course as time passes, things get forgotten.

But he didn't know what Julia might have hidden away . . . or her family. They weren't the quietest bunch. How deeply would the FBI dig? He didn't want to do anything to hurt her or their relationship. And what difference did that make to what he was saying about Diamon Jakes? What was really important was that he was telling the truth.

It was then that he realized that he wouldn't be alone. Besides his own legal counsel, the Blaytent Beanstalk system would be there. Beanstalk would confirm the truth of his statements. He thought of it like the Robin Williams Genie in the Disney *Aladdin* movie. "You've never had a friend like me!" That system would make things like this so much easier and quicker. It might even put the FBI out of business. That was the first time in days that Boyd had smiled.

+++++

Bob's casket was open during the viewing. Gus had never liked that process. He had gone to wakes for people he didn't know to support their families. A strange body lying there like a wax figure just seemed like a gruesome tradition to subject people to. It was a bit different when it had been a friend or a family member. There was something to be said for closure, for the confirmation that the person really was dead, really was in that coffin and that you would never see them again walking into the room or laughing or crying. That was it. The end, and you would just have to move on.

When he walked into the funeral parlor, the family was in a line near the foot of Bob's coffin. Gus glanced at Bob's body. He seemed peaceful. Gus had to wonder about people that worked with dead people every day, making them up, doing whatever it was they did with the bodily fluids, dressing them, making them look peaceful. Did they think about the person they were working on or did death just become routine? "Ho hum. Another day. Another five bodies. We have to get more bodies in here. The cash flow is slowing down. Where do we find more dead people?" Strange business, but someone had to do it. And it was certainly a stressful time for the family, a time when they weren't likely to make the best of decisions.

Gus told himself to concentrate. He turned to Annabelle with a weak smile. He didn't hug her. They weren't on hugging terms. He took her hand in both of his, tilted his head slightly to one side and said, "I'm so very sorry. Bob was a wonderful man."

"Thank you for coming," she replied looking down.

"If there's anything I can do, please don't hesitate to ask. We'll all miss him."

"Yes," she said.

Gus felt a twinge of guilt. Maybe they had worked Bob too hard. Maybe they hadn't given him enough of a break or told him how much they appreciated his work. Maybe there was more that they could have done to keep him healthy, to keep him alive. Maybe Annabelle blamed him for that. He was sure that she was angry; angry with Bob for dying, for not taking better care of himself, angry with Gus for making him stress. There wasn't really anything he could say about any of that and certainly not right then when she was standing there between her husband's body and her three, fatherless children.

"I think you know our children, Mr. Sainte," Annabelle said. Gus winced internally at the formal introduction.

At eighteen, Christa was growing into an attractive young lady. She held her head high and looked him in the eye and shook his hand firmly. Gus asked her if she was going off to college soon.

"I hope so," she replied. "Might not be that easy now."

Gus went through the scenarios in his head. There might be money issues. She might need to be around her mother. Life had changed for the whole family. It was a fork in the road.

"Let me know if there is anything I can do," he said. He turned to Zack.

Zack's handshake was weaker, and he looked down at Gus's feet. "I'm sorry for your loss, Zack. Your dad was a very smart guy. And a friend."

Zack gulped and huffed out a "Yes".

"And you are Kirsten?" Gus asked turning to Zack's left. Gus guessed that she must be about twelve now, but it was difficult for him to know. Girls seemed to mature really fast these days. They dressed to match their TV and movie idols.

Kirsten had her hair in braids. Her brown eyes blazed at him. Her arms were across her chest and she made no move to uncross them to shake his hand. "I know who you are," she said. "And there's nothing you can say that would make me feel any better."

"Kirsten!" her mother said. "Mind your manners. I'm sorry, Mr. Sainte. It's all been such a shock."

"No apology necessary," Gus replied with a smile. "I understand."

He moved along into the room. He had always wished that he could have come up with the classic words to say at times like this, words that would actually mean something, words that would make people feel better. Such words are elusive.

Not knowing Bob's family or friends, Gus was in a crowd of strangers. He moved through them with a sympathetic smile on his face, nodding to people here and there, working away from the coffin toward the back of the room, seeking a more isolated spot.

"Hey," Julia said, coming up behind him. "Sad day."

Gus turned to her. "It is," he said. "I'm glad you're here though. I always feel out of place at these things."

"I don't think anyone enjoys them! You never get *good* at them."

"I suppose," Gus replied. "I didn't know he had such a big family. That should be good for Annabelle and the kids, won't it?"

"I've met a lot of them in the past few days. They're nice."

"I'm sure."

They sat in the plastic chairs watching the people mill about, hug, and talk in clusters and all the while Bob lay there in his coffin. It was sort of like intruding on his bedroom when he was napping, napping in his suit! Gus wondered if people ever got buried in their Hawaiian shirt and Bermuda shorts! He supposed they did. People do all sorts of strange things. Bob would have been more natural with a cigarette in his hand and a worried look on his face.

"How's Boyd doing?" Gus asked.

"It's tough," Julia replied. "The FBI is not being gentle. They are probing way back into his past. And they don't seem too happy about his connection to me and my connection to Blaytent. They think it is some sort of publicity stunt."

Gus thought about that for a minute. "I don't think there's anything we can do at this point. We're sort of committed."

"I know," she said.

"Don't get me wrong, Julia, but I am surprised that Boyd wanted to put himself on the line like this."

"Then you don't know him very well."

"I'm starting to think I don't know anybody very well." For the past few years virtually all of Gus's attention had been focused on Blaytent and the development of Beanstalk. It was part of his mind, his every waking thought. In a sense it was good that they had chosen an awkward name like *Beanstalk*. If they had given it a more human name like Howard or Sylvester or stuck with Franky, it would have been even more difficult to get out of his mind. It had become part of his family. And one of Beanstalk's parents had just died.

"Boyd really believes in what he is doing."

They sat in silence for a while: people watching.

"So what's going on in your life? What's going on with Cyrene?" Julia asked.

Gus looked down at his hands. "I don't know," he replied quietly. "Is she lying?"

"How much did she tell you? And forgive me if I'm prying. It's none of my business. I mean you are my boss, and all. So I'll shut up if you tell me to. But this is the kind of event where people tell each other stuff . . . at least sometimes. I think it's the emotional intensity of the moment."

"Well, you know, there's something, something she isn't saying. I don't know."

"I think you take things that threaten your project, that threaten Beanstalk, too seriously and you might not listen as well as you should. Again, if I'm stepping out of line here, stop me. Let me know. You know I'm with you lock, stock, and barrel on this. I think everyone is. But maybe you should talk to her and get the rest of the rest of the story."

"You're probably right. But it's not easy." He stood up. "I gotta go. Are you staying?"

"Yeah. I'm helping with the food."

"Of course," Gus smiled. "Of course you are."

Back in the office, Pooch Williams called to tell Gus that the FBI was throwing up some roadblocks, and he wasn't sure he could pull it off. "They're making it difficult," he said. "They seem to be looking into everyone's background."

"Isn't that standard procedure for stuff in the capital?"

"That's what they saying, but I don't believe it," Pooch replied. "We have all our press credentials, and this is standard coverage stuff. They seem to be more aggressive than usual. And who is this Williams guy? Should I worry? Maybe he's a distant relation!"

"Oh. Willis. It's Willis not Williams. He's our attorney. You're Williams," Gus laughed. Then he added, "But he's down there on his own. Nothing to do with us."

"What's it all about?"

"Can't say," Gus replied quickly. "You'd have to ask him. But it's nothing to do with us. Something personal."

"They seem to think you're connected. They are making things unusually difficult."

"Oh, you can handle it, Pooch. Nothing keeps you from a story and besides adding the Beanstalk technology to your broadcast is going to give you an exclusive. We're not working with any other network. A little FBI whining shouldn't cause you any heartburn! Right?"

Pooch said it wasn't him. It was the network brass. It was one thing to be first to the mark, but this wasn't like defrocking the queen of England or pulling the mask off the Lone Ranger. They didn't expect a major audience so it wasn't a big enough deal to make waves and take risks.

"I think you'll find the audience is bigger than your brass anticipates. This is important, history making stuff."

"What's history making about it?" Pooch asked. "We've got women on the court. We've got minorities on the court. She's not the first anything. She's just another lawyer, just another judge. Where's the news?"

"Beanstalk is the news, Pooch. We're giving you a way to show your audience whether or not she is telling the truth!"

"Hocus, pocus," Pooch said. "It's a gimmick. A good gimmick, but a gimmick."

"This isn't a gimmick, Pooch. This is science. This is the future. Our technology is far from a gimmick. What about that in-depth and personal story on Beanstalk we talked about? Explain to people what it is and how it works. Explain to your audience all the science behind it. We're not a bunch of goof balls with black boxes and wires. This is real, science based technology!"

"Yeah. Sure. I know that's why I agreed to this in the first place. Don't think our audience is ready for in depth science stuff. But I'll think about it."

A message popped up on Gus's computer screen. "Man in lobby. Insists on seeing you. Flack."

"Oh, shit," Gus mumbled.

"What?" Pooch asked.

"Nothing. Look, I gotta go. Let me know if there is anything else I can do to move this along, okay? I'm confident you can pull it off. If anyone can, you can."

Flack hadn't taken 'no' for an answer. The events of the last few days had not put Gus in the most charitable frame of mind. He didn't care about what was bothering Johnny Flack. He didn't like the man. He hadn't liked him from the first moment he saw him, and he would have been perfectly happy never to see him again.

The only thing that was good about this visit was that Arya had set up Beanstalk on Gus's desk and this would give him a chance to check it out since he was confident that Flack was going to lie to him.

The primary component was the game transducer that looked a little like an elongated head of a robot that was motor driven to follow the subject and that Blaytent had modified to look less like a familiar toy and more like a scientific device. There were some additional computer connections to the main frame in Arya's lair, but in general Beanstalk did not look intimidating. It looked more like a curious child to Gus, tilting its 'head', eager for 'input'.

Arya had updated the recording features for both sound and images and the display screen as well. Gus could now see the four separate technologies in the big screen on his desk along with a fifth element that added the outputs of those screens together to give him the summary of the subject's truth as well as suggestions for paths of questioning to follow to increase the accuracy of the analysis. The questions were based on the subject's response to keywords that had evoked reactions in the four technology quadrants to previous questions.

Gus was eager to test Flack, but on the other hand he wasn't sure that he wanted to reveal the status of Beanstalk to the man. Gus got enthusiastic about things he was working on and had a tendency to say too much. But, he thought, we're going to put this on national television. He had just been telling Pooch Williams to produce a revealing tell all segment. Gudmudgion wanted a commercially viable product. They better be ready for prime time.

"This might be interesting," Gus said to himself. He activated Beanstalk and watched the display come to life.

"*READY,*" it said on the screen. And then, "How are you, Gus?"

Gus hadn't expected that. His eyebrows went up and his mouth dropped open. "Huh?" Arya had done more than update the screen. It was clear that Beanstalk now recognized and remembered people and collected data files that it could compare to previous behavior.

Beanstalk repeated the question. "How are you, Gus?"

Hesitantly Gus replied, "I'm fine. Thank you."

Beanstalk printed, "You look upset."

"Wow!" Gus said involuntarily.

Flack was escorted to his office. Gus would have liked to avoid shaking the man's hand, but he had to get up to close his office door, and stuck out his hand in response to the habits of years, pulling it back quickly when he realized what he was doing. Flack's round face seemed even redder than the last time Gus had seen him. His glasses needed cleaning and the strut in his stature had slumped. He was wearing a light tan trench coat that was unbuttoned, and he exuded a slight body odor stench.

"I told you I didn't want to see you," Gus said. "And that still stands." He returned to his desk and sat in his chair.

Flack stood in the middle of the room looking at him, then he shrugged and ambled over to a chair facing Gus's desk and flopped down into it. "Good to see you too," he replied with a watery smile.

Beanstalk's transducer head found Flack and tuned him in, inserting a small image of the man on Gus's screen, starting with a full body view then zooming in on his face, and then backing up to the full view again where it stopped. Gus knew that Beanstalk's numerous cameras were looking at multiple points on Flack's person, recording the data and analyzing it even before they had started talking. The non-verbal communications readout was forming a baseline of the man's hands and feet and the tilt of his shoulders. It was prompting Gus to ask baseline questions like *"Please state your name"* or *"What is today's date?"* But that would have made for extremely unnatural communications. Gus was tempted, but he stuck with saying what he felt

"What the fuck do you want?" he asked.

"Interesting," Beanstalk printed on the screen.

Flack slouched back in his seat. "I came here for your benefit. I didn't have to. There's stuff going on."

"Should I care?" Gus asked. Julia had told him that in order for the Statement Analysis to work, the subject needed to make a statement. He needed to get more than a one liner out of Flack. The more of a narrative that he could create, the more solid the patterns would be. So he broadened his question. "What is it that is so important?"

It would have been difficult for Flack not to notice that Gus was sitting stiffly and kept glancing over at his computer screen. "Ah," he said. "You're testing me."

"That's what we do, Mr. Flack."

"I'd love to see a demonstration. Want to turn your screen around?"

"Nope," said Gus. "Why are you in Boston?"

"I came to see my old aunt who lives in Dorchester. She's not well."

Beanstalk printed, "Lying!"

Gus didn't need Beanstalk to tell him that this was far from the truth. If Gus hadn't had so much distaste and distrust for the man he would have been tempted to continue down that path, forcing Flack to elaborate on his relationship with this fictitious relative: paternal aunt, maternal aunt, aunt by name only. In a casual conversation that might have been considered polite *small talk*. But Gus was not feeling polite.

"Bull shit," he said.

"Did your machine tell you that? What are you calling it now? I heard it is something like Beanstalk? Really? Not very technical. I would have expected something like X19 or Super Flagilator. Are you guys into fairy tales? Jack and his magic beans! Woo hoo!"

"Why are you in Boston, Mr. Flack."

Johnny looked at him for a moment and seemed to suck in his breath. "To tell you the truth," he said finally, "I came to see you."

Gus looked at his screen. The man was definitely nervous. Gus could smell it, and it wasn't pleasant. He thought that maybe down the road they should add an odor analyzer. Beanstalk could see that he was sweating and there were slight twitches at the corner of his eyes, and he had his feet tucked back behind the legs of his chair. What he was saying was at least partially true.

"What about?" Gus asked.

"What?"

"What did you come to see me about?"

"Well, we probably could have done this on the phone, but you wouldn't listen."

"If we could have done it on the phone, why did you come to Boston. You said you were already in Boston when you called me."

"I know," Flack replied.

Gus looked at him expectantly. "Well, you're wasting my time!"

"Look, this is a bit delicate. IIDT pays my salary; at least for now. But look, they know about what you've been doing. And Crum is crazy and getting crazier all the time."

"Well?"

"Well, I don't want to say anything bad about the dead. That's not nice. That's what makes this so awkward." Flack looked at him.

Gus didn't have a clue what the man was talking about. Beanstalk wasn't helping. He realized at that point that the result of questioning depended on the emotional engagement of the interrogator. It was like driving. Over the years with the development of the car, the driver has become more and more isolated from the actual functioning of the vehicle. Initially, full engagement was required to keep the car on the road and to keep it running. With automatic transmissions and power steering and power breaks and noise reducing bodies, the driver is divorced from the functioning of the vehicle and is free to talk on their cell phones or text or watch videos and listen to music. But the underlying fact is that full engagement still is required but few drivers feel compelled to do that.

If the operator of Beanstalk were emotionally involved with the subject of the questions, they would be less likely to pay attention to the mechanics of the questions. It was increasingly difficult to be analytical. There are times when multitasking splits into component parts and one task gets short changed.

"You got all kinds of holes in your product security," Flack said.

"Really?"

"Yeah. I mean there's your girlfriend; your Muslim girlfriend. That wasn't very smart. Loose lips sink ships as they say. Secrecy and a love life don't mix well."

"My private life is none of your business, Flack!" Gus spat.

"Yeah? Well, maybe you don't know everything about that."

"Get on with it."

Flack looked at him. "Did you know that Dr. Thatcher, your buddy Bob, took your gadget to his home! His son's a smart boy. Remembers everything. Proud of his father, God rest his soul. But Zack puts too much information on his Facebook page!"

Gus was up out of his chair and coming around the end of his desk. Flack jumped up. Gus towered over him.

"What are you saying, you piece of shit? You assholes didn't lay a hand on Zack Thatcher, did you?"

Flack stepped back. "Nah. We didn't touch him. He's just proud of his father. You know he was talking to his little friends about what he saw. Look, I don't want to cause any trouble here. I just think you need to know where you stand. Seems like you're running a nice personal business here – a kind of touchy-feely people kind of business –an Arabs and kids kind of business. And you should know that this isn't that kind of world. People can be mean and do cruel things! Crum thinks you're a terrorist!"

"You're a piece of work," Gus said. "Get the hell out of here. You needed to meet with me to tell me stuff like that?"

"No. No I wanted to warn you about Crum. I tell you: the man is losing it!"

"No news there either and why would you care?"

Flack looked at him and swallowed. "Look," he said, "I think your project is better than IIDT's, and I wanted to ask you to hire me! You could use me. Use what I know. Particularly now that Thatcher is dead. My expertise is in acoustics. I could finish what he was working on."

Gus was stunned. "What?"

"I could help you beat Crum! He's getting more unpredictable. You gotta be careful. I'm warning you. I'm just trying to help."

"Get the hell out of my office!" Gus thundered. "I don't want your help! Why would I ever trust you? I don't want to see you ever again!"

"You should consider it. I could tell you a lot about what goes on in IIDT. I know a lot that could be useful for you. Want to know what your girlfriend really does?"

"Get the hell out of my office!" Gus repeated. He was exercising all his restraint not to pick the man up and throw him bodily out the door. His emotions were stretched to the limit and his reason was slipping to the edge of control. Flack may have been lying, but he wasn't making statements that Beanstalk might have flagged. They were just hints and innuendos not outright, blatant lies. But he was throwing them directly on the fires that burned in Gus – the romance that may have become a betrayal and his loss of a co-worker and friend. If there had been logic in his mind, the most sensible thing for him to have done would have been to sit and listen to the man, extract his information, test him with Beanstalk, hear what he had to say and reveal. But Gus was not feeling sensible.

"You'll regret this," Flack said as he backed toward the door.

"I already do," Gus replied. "Eat shit and die! Hey!" he yelled down the hall. "Someone come and take this man out of the building! I'd show you out myself, but I'd probably kill you on the way!"

Allan burst out of his office, stopped, looked at Gus and Flack and then hustled Flack down the hall and out of the building. Flack was mumbling the whole time. When Allan returned to Gus's office, Gus had dropped back into his office chair and was staring at the ceiling.

"What was that all about?" Allan asked. "Who was that guy?"

Gus explained who Flack was and expressed his disbelief that the man wanted to work for Blaytent! And he had proposed this while threatening and offering to reveal IIDT secrets! "What the hell is going on with that company?" Gus asked rhetorically. "Seems like their plan for survival and success is to sue people!"

Gus was breathing heavily and his hands were shaking. Allan urged him to sit down and get himself together.

Beanstalk printed, "You are very stressed, Gus."

Gus said to Allan, "Have you seen what Arya has Beanstalk doing? It's analyzing me! I want this lawsuit to be over. I want to be done with those guys. It's pissing me off that Boyd is not available when we need him. What the hell is he doing down there anyway?"

Allan replied, "We don't really need him at the moment."

"I thought we were going to ask the judge for Summary Judgment because this suit is so frivolous. What happened with that?"

"Apparently the judge's still thinking about it."

"Well, Boyd should be pushing him. This legal shit is just hanging over my head."

"You can't go pushing a judge," Allan replied.

"You look impatient, Gus," printed Beanstalk.

"Innocent until proven guilty." Boyd wondered where that phrase had come from. On the surface it was simple. You couldn't just go around accusing people of doing things without being able to prove it. In many situations, however, just the accusation was enough to tar the accused with the obliterating brush of implication. He felt strongly that the FBI thought that he was guilty of making false accusations when he reported his issues with Judge Jakes. She was living at a higher level of innocence than he was, and it would take a lot to make his reported incidents pollute her purity.

It was difficult to prove. Sexual harassment was often evidenced by a handful of words said at the wrong time in the wrong place. The line was not clear between the occasional, joking remark and harmful implications. When the words are used as weapons to gain sexual favors, the line becomes clearer, but even then it is often difficult to know what the perpetrator has in mind as a reward for their advances. And how do you prove what happened fifteen years ago with a candidate for the supreme court who had such an exemplary record that she was able to rise rapidly to that position? Her years of success provided layers of armor that made it difficult to believe that she would do the things he was accusing her of.

This wasn't some trivial finger pointing either. There were significant consequences to what he was claiming. Now that he had said it, the ball was rolling and the FBI had to investigate. The incidents had to be defined in painful detail. As a man, Boyd had to admit that the attentions and the touching and the propositioning by a beautiful woman were undesirable and unwanted. The agents thought he should have been flattered!

"Jesus! I would have been," they chuckled to each other.

Boyd knew that they weren't supposed to be saying things like that. They weren't supposed to be implying that they thought a candidate for the Supreme Court was hot. He wondered if they were trying to push him to recant or admit that he was not interested in women or had some other motive for making these claims. Men didn't turn down the advances of beautiful women. The attention of a beautiful woman was an affirmation of manhood, of desirability, of power. A man could decline it only if he were already powerful. So if Boyd had declined it, it reduced his stature with the agents and their inclination to believe his story and care about his issues. It would have been much easier if this little man went away.

Reading through his notes of the incidents reignited his anger at the situation. The words seemed so foreign. His writing style had changed in fifteen years. The descriptions seemed crude although there were flashes of description that he surprised himself with his own writing skill. He regretted that he hadn't pursued it with the EEOC at the time. He would have had a more official backing for his claims.

He had wanted to put it behind him. He had wanted to get on with his life. He hadn't wanted Jakes to have that kind of continuing power over him. But she had and she still did have that power. This was another of those life-changing moments. Describing the events now, telling his story . . . which made it seem fictional . . . in this place at this time under these circumstances would put it in the history books and what now served as the history books: the Internet.

Over and over again he had asked himself why he was going through this. Jakes wasn't a bad lawyer. She certainly wasn't stupid. She wasn't evil . . . in the majority of ways. There certainly could have been worse choices for the court. The FBI had not been able to turn over any other rocks where she was hiding past indiscretions. Her record was apparently clean. It was all good until Boyd came along. Was a little office hanky-panky all that important?

Boyd wondered what Ronald P. Baines would say to the FBI. It was doubtful that he would even remember a minor incident with a minor associate in the office from fifteen years before. He would certainly remember Jakes. She would stand out in his memory like the North Star on a clear night! He would forget the cloud that had drifted momentarily across her celestial light. He certainly wouldn't support Boyd's story.

What about the other associates? The FBI would track them down even though they had probably all drifted off to other positions. At the time Boyd had felt the situation was embarrassing and hadn't opened himself up to any of them.

There was a certain amount secretiveness that permeated the firm. You were expected to keep things to yourself to protect your clients and yourself.

The people who had taught the sexual sensitivity training were not likely to reveal anything about what he had said in those classes. They weren't supposed to remember, and he hadn't written down the trainer's name. He thought the FBI agents would probably dig out that information if they were thorough anyway, at least uncovering whom Tittle and Baines contracted with at the time.

So where did that leave him? It didn't look good. It was his word against hers. It was his power against her POWER. It was his innocence against her INNOCENCE. It was his truth against her version of the truth. It didn't seem like much of a contest. He would be sitting there in front of all those politicians and cameras and microphones on his own. Why should he pursue this?

He went through his notes again. He wouldn't be able to question Judge Jakes. That was up to the politicians. He wouldn't be able to ask her the questions that would reveal to him whether or not she believed that using a position of power to manipulate people's lives was fair and equal justice. Life wasn't fair. He knew that. But weren't laws supposed to be made to protect people's lives and to level the playing field? It wasn't fair to steal your neighbor's cow just because you wanted it. The law says you can't do that. It wasn't fair to own people. Slavery was against the law. Wasn't controlling a person's life with sexual power the same thing as enslaving that person? Could a person who thought so little of an associate make good decisions in the interest of all the people of the country?

Maybe she'd changed. Maybe that was an aberration – a one-time incident, a mistake. But he couldn't ask her. The politicians could ask her, but they wouldn't because they wouldn't even think she was capable of such a thing unless he stood up.

He was surprised when the FBI asked him if this was all a publicity stunt for Blaytent. They asked him if he knew that Blaytent equipment was going to be in the hearing room with one of the TV stations. He told them that was the first he had heard about it. He was Blaytent's corporate counsel, but nothing more than that. They seemed skeptical. They repeated that they took accusations like his very seriously. This wasn't a game. They said they would have to look into his relationship with the company . . . in detail.

Julia immediately came to his mind. They had talked about this. She had urged him to present his story. She had told him that she was completely behind him and could take anything that was thrown at her. But he still had to be careful. An FBI probe into your life was not exactly a walk in the park. He wasn't afraid of anything in his own past. He felt that he had led a clean life. There were no skeletons that he could recall stuffing in a closet. Of course as time passes, things get forgotten.

But he didn't know what Julia might have hidden away . . . or her family. They weren't the quietest bunch. How deeply would the FBI dig? He didn't want to do anything to hurt her or their relationship. And what difference did that make to what he was saying about Diamon Jakes? What was really important was that he was telling the truth.

It was then that he realized that he wouldn't be alone. Besides his own legal counsel, the Blaytent Beanstalk system would be there. Beanstalk would confirm the truth of his statements. He thought of it like the Robin Williams Genie in the Disney *Aladdin* movie. "You've never had a friend like me!" That system would make things like this so much easier and quicker. It might even put the FBI out of business. That was the first time in days that Boyd had smiled.

+++++

Bob's casket was open during the viewing. Gus had never liked that process. He had gone to wakes for people he didn't know to support their families. A strange body lying there like a wax figure just seemed like a gruesome tradition to subject people to. It was a bit different when it had been a friend or a family member. There was something to be said for closure, for the confirmation that the person really was dead, really was in that coffin and that you would never see them again walking into the room or laughing or crying. That was it. The end, and you would just have to move on.

When he walked into the funeral parlor, the family was in a line near the foot of Bob's coffin. Gus glanced at Bob's body. He seemed peaceful. Gus had to wonder about people that worked with dead people every day, making them up, doing whatever it was they did with the bodily fluids, dressing them, making them look peaceful. Did they think about the person they were working on or did death just become routine? "Ho hum. Another day. Another five bodies. We have to get more bodies in here. The cash flow is slowing down. Where do we find more dead people?" Strange business, but someone had to do it. And it was certainly a stressful time for the family, a time when they weren't likely to make the best of decisions.

Gus told himself to concentrate. He turned to Annabelle with a weak smile. He didn't hug her. They weren't on hugging terms. He took her hand in both of his, tilted his head slightly to one side and said, "I'm so very sorry. Bob was a wonderful man."

"Thank you for coming," she replied looking down.

"If there's anything I can do, please don't hesitate to ask. We'll all miss him."

"Yes," she said.

Gus felt a twinge of guilt. Maybe they had worked Bob too hard. Maybe they hadn't given him enough of a break or told him how much they appreciated his work. Maybe there was more that they could have done to keep him healthy, to keep him alive. Maybe Annabelle blamed him for that. He was sure that she was angry; angry with Bob for dying, for not taking better care of himself, angry with Gus for making him stress. There wasn't really anything he could say about any of that and certainly not right then when she was standing there between her husband's body and her three, fatherless children.

"I think you know our children, Mr. Sainte," Annabelle said. Gus winced internally at the formal introduction.

At eighteen, Christa was growing into an attractive young lady. She held her head high and looked him in the eye and shook his hand firmly. Gus asked her if she was going off to college soon.

"I hope so," she replied. "Might not be that easy now."

Gus went through the scenarios in his head. There might be money issues. She might need to be around her mother. Life had changed for the whole family. It was a fork in the road.

"Let me know if there is anything I can do," he said. He turned to Zack.

Zack's handshake was weaker, and he looked down at Gus's feet. "I'm sorry for your loss, Zack. Your dad was a very smart guy. And a friend."

Zack gulped and huffed out a "Yes".

"And you are Kirsten?" Gus asked turning to Zack's left. Gus guessed that she must be about twelve now, but it was difficult for him to know. Girls seemed to mature really fast these days. They dressed to match their TV and movie idols.

Kirsten had her hair in braids. Her brown eyes blazed at him. Her arms were across her chest and she made no move to uncross them to shake his hand. "I know who you are," she said. "And there's nothing you can say that would make me feel any better."

"Kirsten!" her mother said. "Mind your manners. I'm sorry, Mr. Sainte. It's all been such a shock."

"No apology necessary," Gus replied with a smile. "I understand."

He moved along into the room. He had always wished that he could have come up with the classic words to say at times like this, words that would actually mean something, words that would make people feel better. Such words are elusive.

Not knowing Bob's family or friends, Gus was in a crowd of strangers. He moved through them with a sympathetic smile on his face, nodding to people here and there, working away from the coffin toward the back of the room, seeking a more isolated spot.

"Hey," Julia said, coming up behind him. "Sad day."

Gus turned to her. "It is," he said. "I'm glad you're here though. I always feel out of place at these things."

"I don't think anyone enjoys them! You never get *good* at them."

"I suppose," Gus replied. "I didn't know he had such a big family. That should be good for Annabelle and the kids, won't it?"

"I've met a lot of them in the past few days. They're nice."

"I'm sure."

They sat in the plastic chairs watching the people mill about, hug, and talk in clusters and all the while Bob lay there in his coffin. It was sort of like intruding on his bedroom when he was napping, napping in his suit! Gus wondered if people ever got buried in their Hawaiian shirt and Bermuda shorts! He supposed they did. People do all sorts of strange things. Bob would have been more natural with a cigarette in his hand and a worried look on his face.

"How's Boyd doing?" Gus asked.

"It's tough," Julia replied. "The FBI is not being gentle. They are probing way back into his past. And they don't seem too happy about his connection to me and my connection to Blaytent. They think it is some sort of publicity stunt."

Gus thought about that for a minute. "I don't think there's anything we can do at this point. We're sort of committed."

"I know," she said.

"Don't get me wrong, Julia, but I am surprised that Boyd wanted to put himself on the line like this."

"Then you don't know him very well."

"I'm starting to think I don't know anybody very well." For the past few years virtually all of Gus's attention had been focused on Blaytent and the development of Beanstalk. It was part of his mind, his every waking thought. In a sense it was good that they had chosen an awkward name like *Beanstalk*. If they had given it a more human name like Howard or Sylvester or stuck with Franky, it would have been even more difficult to get out of his mind. It had become part of his family. And one of Beanstalk's parents had just died.

"Boyd really believes in what he is doing."

They sat in silence for a while: people watching.

"So what's going on in your life? What's going on with Cyrene?" Julia asked.

Gus looked down at his hands. "I don't know," he replied quietly. "Is she lying?"

"How much did she tell you? And forgive me if I'm prying. It's none of my business. I mean you are my boss, and all. So I'll shut up if you tell me to. But this is the kind of event where people tell each other stuff . . . at least sometimes. I think it's the emotional intensity of the moment."

"Well, you know, there's something, something she isn't saying. I don't know."

"I think you take things that threaten your project, that threaten Beanstalk, too seriously and you might not listen as well as you should. Again, if I'm stepping out of line here, stop me. Let me know. You know I'm with you lock, stock, and barrel on this. I think everyone is. But maybe you should talk to her and get the rest of the rest of the story."

"You're probably right. But it's not easy." He stood up. "I gotta go. Are you staying?"

"Yeah. I'm helping with the food."

"Of course," Gus smiled. "Of course you are."

+++++

Back in the office, Pooch Williams called to tell Gus that the FBI was throwing up some roadblocks, and he wasn't sure he could pull it off. "They're making it difficult," he said. "They seem to be looking into everyone's background."

"Isn't that standard procedure for stuff in the capital?"

"That's what they saying, but I don't believe it," Pooch replied. "We have all our press credentials, and this is standard coverage stuff. They seem to be more aggressive than usual. And who is this Williams guy? Should I worry? Maybe he's a distant relation!"

"Oh. Willis. It's Willis not Williams. He's our attorney. You're Williams," Gus laughed. Then he added, "But he's down there on his own. Nothing to do with us."

"What's it all about?"

"Can't say," Gus replied quickly. "You'd have to ask him. But it's nothing to do with us. Something personal."

"They seem to think you're connected. They are making things unusually difficult."

"Oh, you can handle it, Pooch. Nothing keeps you from a story and besides adding the Beanstalk technology to your broadcast is going to give you an exclusive. We're not working with any other network. A little FBI whining shouldn't cause you any heartburn! Right?"

Pooch said it wasn't him. It was the network brass. It was one thing to be first to the mark, but this wasn't like defrocking the queen of England or pulling the mask off the Lone Ranger. They didn't expect a major audience so it wasn't a big enough deal to make waves and take risks.

"I think you'll find the audience is bigger than your brass anticipates. This is important, history making stuff."

"What's history making about it?" Pooch asked. "We've got women on the court. We've got minorities on the court. She's not the first anything. She's just another lawyer, just another judge. Where's the news?"

"Beanstalk is the news, Pooch. We're giving you a way to show your audience whether or not she is telling the truth!"

"Hocus, pocus," Pooch said. "It's a gimmick. A good gimmick, but a gimmick."

"This isn't a gimmick, Pooch. This is science. This is the future. Our technology is far from a gimmick. What about that in-depth and personal story on Beanstalk we talked about? Explain to people what it is and how it works. Explain to your audience all the science behind it. We're not a bunch of goof balls with black boxes and wires. This is real, science based technology!"

"Yeah. Sure. I know that's why I agreed to this in the first place. Don't think our audience is ready for in depth science stuff. But I'll think about it."

A message popped up on Gus's computer screen. "Man in lobby. Insists on seeing you. Flack."

"Oh, shit," Gus mumbled.

"What?" Pooch asked.

"Nothing. Look, I gotta go. Let me know if there is anything else I can do to move this along, okay? I'm confident you can pull it off. If anyone can, you can."

Flack hadn't taken 'no' for an answer. The events of the last few days had not put Gus in the most charitable frame of mind. He didn't care about what was bothering Johnny Flack. He didn't like the man. He hadn't liked him from the first moment he saw him, and he would have been perfectly happy never to see him again.

The only thing that was good about this visit was that Arya had set up Beanstalk on Gus's desk and this would give him a chance to check it out since he was confident that Flack was going to lie to him.

The primary component was the game transducer that looked a little like an elongated head of a robot that was motor driven to follow the subject and that Blaytent had modified to look less like a familiar toy and more like a scientific device. There were some additional computer connections to the main frame in Arya's lair, but in general Beanstalk did not look intimidating. It looked more like a curious child to Gus, tilting its 'head', eager for 'input'.

Arya had updated the recording features for both sound and images and the display screen as well. Gus could now see the four separate technologies in the big screen on his desk along with a fifth element that added the outputs of those screens together to give him the summary of the subject's truth as well as suggestions for paths of questioning to follow to increase the accuracy of the analysis. The questions were based on the subject's response to keywords that had evoked reactions in the four technology quadrants to previous questions.

Gus was eager to test Flack, but on the other hand he wasn't sure that he wanted to reveal the status of Beanstalk to the man. Gus got enthusiastic about things he was working on and had a tendency to say too much. But, he thought, we're going to put this on national television. He had just been telling Pooch Williams to produce a revealing tell all segment. Gudmudgion wanted a commercially viable product. They better be ready for prime time.

"This might be interesting," Gus said to himself. He activated Beanstalk and watched the display come to life.

"*READY*," it said on the screen. And then, "How are you, Gus?"

Gus hadn't expected that. His eyebrows went up and his mouth dropped open. "Huh?" Arya had done more than update the screen. It was clear that Beanstalk now recognized and remembered people and collected data files that it could compare to previous behavior.

Beanstalk repeated the question. "How are you, Gus?"

Hesitantly Gus replied, "I'm fine. Thank you."

Beanstalk printed, "You look upset."

"Wow!" Gus said involuntarily.

Flack was escorted to his office. Gus would have liked to avoid shaking the man's hand, but he had to get up to close his office door, and stuck out his hand in response to the habits of years, pulling it back quickly when he realized what he was doing. Flack's round face seemed even redder than the last time Gus had seen him. His glasses needed cleaning and the strut in his stature had slumped. He was wearing a light tan trench coat that was unbuttoned, and he exuded a slight body odor stench.

"I told you I didn't want to see you," Gus said. "And that still stands." He returned to his desk and sat in his chair.

Flack stood in the middle of the room looking at him, then he shrugged and ambled over to a chair facing Gus's desk and flopped down into it. "Good to see you too," he replied with a watery smile.

Beanstalk's transducer head found Flack and tuned him in, inserting a small image of the man on Gus's screen, starting with a full body view then zooming in on his face, and then backing up to the full view again where it stopped. Gus knew that Beanstalk's numerous cameras were looking at multiple points on Flack's person, recording the data and analyzing it even before they had started talking. The non-verbal communications readout was forming a baseline of the man's hands and feet and the tilt of his shoulders. It was prompting Gus to ask baseline questions like "*Please state your name*" or "*What is today's date?*" But that would have made for extremely unnatural communications. Gus was tempted, but he stuck with saying what he felt

"What the fuck do you want?" he asked.

"Interesting," Beanstalk printed on the screen.

Flack slouched back in his seat. "I came here for your benefit. I didn't have to. There's stuff going on."

"Should I care?" Gus asked. Julia had told him that in order for the Statement Analysis to work, the subject needed to make a statement. He needed to get more than a one liner out of Flack. The more of a narrative that he could create, the more solid the patterns would be. So he broadened his question. "What is it that is so important?"

It would have been difficult for Flack not to notice that Gus was sitting stiffly and kept glancing over at his computer screen. "Ah," he said. "You're testing me."

"That's what we do, Mr. Flack."

"I'd love to see a demonstration. Want to turn your screen around?"

"Nope," said Gus. "Why are you in Boston?"

"I came to see my old aunt who lives in Dorchester. She's not well."

Beanstalk printed, "Lying!"

Gus didn't need Beanstalk to tell him that this was far from the truth. If Gus hadn't had so much distaste and distrust for the man he would have been tempted to continue down that path, forcing Flack to elaborate on his relationship with this fictitious relative: paternal aunt, maternal aunt, aunt by name only. In a casual conversation that might have been considered polite *small talk*. But Gus was not feeling polite.

"Bull shit," he said.

"Did your machine tell you that? What are you calling it now? I heard it is something like Beanstalk? Really? Not very technical. I would have expected something like X19 or Super Flagilator. Are you guys into fairy tales? Jack and his magic beans! Woo hoo!"

"Why are you in Boston, Mr. Flack."

Johnny looked at him for a moment and seemed to suck in his breath. "To tell you the truth," he said finally, "I came to see you."

Gus looked at his screen. The man was definitely nervous. Gus could smell it, and it wasn't pleasant. He thought that

maybe down the road they should add an odor analyzer.
Beanstalk could see that he was sweating and there were
slight twitches at the corner of his eyes, and he had his feet
tucked back behind the legs of his chair. What he was saying
was at least partially true.

"What about?" Gus asked.

"What?"

"What did you come to see me about?"

"Well, we probably could have done this on the phone, but
you wouldn't listen."

"If we could have done it on the phone, why did you come
to Boston. You said you were already in Boston when you
called me."

"I know," Flack replied.

Gus looked at him expectantly. "Well, you're wasting my
time!"

"Look, this is a bit delicate. IIDT pays my salary; at least
for now. But look, they know about what you've been doing.
And Crum is crazy and getting crazier all the time."

"Well?"

"Well, I don't want to say anything bad about the dead.
That's not nice. That's what makes this so awkward." Flack
looked at him.

Gus didn't have a clue what the man was talking about.
Beanstalk wasn't helping. He realized at that point that the
result of questioning depended on the emotional engagement
of the interrogator. It was like driving. Over the years with
the development of the car, the driver has become more and
more isolated from the actual functioning of the vehicle. Initially, full engagement was required to keep the car on the
road and to keep it running. With automatic transmissions
and power steering and power breaks and noise reducing bodies, the driver is divorced from the functioning of the vehicle
and is free to talk on their cell phones or text or watch videos
and listen to music. But the underlying fact is that full engagement still is required but few drivers feel compelled to do
that.

If the operator of Beanstalk were emotionally involved
with the subject of the questions, they would be less likely to

pay attention to the mechanics of the questions. It was increasingly difficult to be analytical. There are times when multitasking splits into component parts and one task gets short changed.

"You got all kinds of holes in your product security," Flack said.

"Really?"

"Yeah. I mean there's your girlfriend; your Muslim girlfriend. That wasn't very smart. Loose lips sink ships as they say. Secrecy and a love life don't mix well."

"My private life is none of your business, Flack!" Gus spat.

"Yeah? Well, maybe you don't know everything about that."

"Get on with it."

Flack looked at him. "Did you know that Dr. Thatcher, your buddy Bob, took your gadget to his home! His son's a smart boy. Remembers everything. Proud of his father, God rest his soul. But Zack puts too much information on his Facebook page!"

Gus was up out of his chair and coming around the end of his desk. Flack jumped up. Gus towered over him.

"What are you saying, you piece of shit? You assholes didn't lay a hand on Zack Thatcher, did you?"

Flack stepped back. "Nah. We didn't touch him. He's just proud of his father. You know he was talking to his little friends about what he saw. Look, I don't want to cause any trouble here. I just think you need to know where you stand. Seems like you're running a nice personal business here – a kind of touchy-feely people kind of business –an Arabs and kids kind of business. And you should know that this isn't that kind of world. People can be mean and do cruel things! Crum thinks you're a terrorist!"

"You're a piece of work," Gus said. "Get the hell out of here. You needed to meet with me to tell me stuff like that?"

"No. No I wanted to warn you about Crum. I tell you: the man is losing it!"

"No news there either and why would you care?"

Flack looked at him and swallowed. "Look," he said, "I think your project is better than IIDT's, and I wanted to ask you to hire me! You could use me. Use what I know. Particularly now that Thatcher is dead. My expertise is in acoustics. I could finish what he was working on."

Gus was stunned. "What?"

"I could help you beat Crum! He's getting more unpredictable. You gotta be careful. I'm warning you. I'm just trying to help."

"Get the hell out of my office!" Gus thundered. "I don't want your help! Why would I ever trust you? I don't want to see you ever again!"

"You should consider it. I could tell you a lot about what goes on in IIDT. I know a lot that could be useful for you. Want to know what your girlfriend really does?"

"Get the hell out of my office!" Gus repeated. He was exercising all his restraint not to pick the man up and throw him bodily out the door. His emotions were stretched to the limit and his reason was slipping to the edge of control. Flack may have been lying, but he wasn't making statements that Beanstalk might have flagged. They were just hints and innuendos not outright, blatant lies. But he was throwing them directly on the fires that burned in Gus – the romance that may have become a betrayal and his loss of a co-worker and friend. If there had been logic in his mind, the most sensible thing for him to have done would have been to sit and listen to the man, extract his information, test him with Beanstalk, hear what he had to say and reveal. But Gus was not feeling sensible.

"You'll regret this," Flack said as he backed toward the door.

"I already do," Gus replied. "Eat shit and die! Hey!" he yelled down the hall. "Someone come and take this man out of the building! I'd show you out myself, but I'd probably kill you on the way!"

Allan burst out of his office, stopped, looked at Gus and Flack and then hustled Flack down the hall and out of the building. Flack was mumbling the whole time. When Allan returned to Gus's office, Gus had dropped back into his office chair and was staring at the ceiling.

"What was that all about?" Allan asked. "Who was that guy?"

Gus explained who Flack was and expressed his disbelief that the man wanted to work for Blaytent! And he had proposed this while threatening and offering to reveal IIDT secrets! "What the hell is going on with that company?" Gus asked rhetorically. "Seems like their plan for survival and success is to sue people!"

Gus was breathing heavily and his hands were shaking. Allan urged him to sit down and get himself together.

Beanstalk printed, "You are very stressed, Gus."

Gus said to Allan, "Have you seen what Arya has Beanstalk doing? It's analyzing me! I want this lawsuit to be over. I want to be done with those guys. It's pissing me off that Boyd is not available when we need him. What the hell is he doing down there anyway?"

Allan replied, "We don't really need him at the moment."

"I thought we were going to ask the judge for Summary Judgment because this suit is so frivolous. What happened with that?"

"Apparently the judge's still thinking about it."

"Well, Boyd should be pushing him. This legal shit is just hanging over my head."

"You can't go pushing a judge," Allan replied.

"You look impatient, Gus," printed Beanstalk.

Chapter Seventeen

April 2015

There wasn't much interest in the Senate Judiciary Committee hearings regarding the confirmation of Judge Diamon Jakes to the highest court in the land, at least not enough to pre-empt the other reality shows and talking head programs to gain a reasonable audience share. It wasn't that the hearings were peaceful. Politics being what they are, there was the usual sparring and jibing among the different Senators as to what Judge Jakes's position was on the issues. She was too liberal on guns and too conservative on housing and taxes. She had been a bit too radical when she was a member of Ethos at Wellesley where she had written an article that promoted cultural and political awareness that gave some of the Senators heartburn. She had been outspoken on fighting racism and sexism and led a rally that tied the campus up for a couple of days, supporting the rights of campus workers to get better pay. On top of all that, if they agreed to put her on the court, almost half the justices would be female! And there would be a lot of minorities on the court, and if they were minorities, could they fairly represent the majority of the population of the country?

Of course they didn't ask the questions that way. That would have been biased. They asked her about her role as the General Counsel for the Massachusetts Department of Environmental Protection. They wanted to know how she felt about urban growth, how she felt about the recovery of cities like Detroit. Was enough being invested in public transportation?

Some of the Senators thought that she was too young and hadn't had enough experience and wouldn't be able to imbue her decisions with enough wisdom. At forty-eight she wouldn't be the youngest judge to join the court. Clarence Thomas had only been forty-three when he joined the court, so her age didn't pose a barrier. They were having a hard time finding reasons to reject her. But they had gone through her writings and her decisions searching for flaws. It would have been better if she had grown up in the ghetto and worked her way out of it delivering papers and mowing lawns instead of having an economically solid family life, but that gave her a different perspective that moderated her background, apparently pushing her toward economic conservatism.

And besides that, she was quite attractive. They never would have said that to each other – certainly not in public. But there was a certain amount of haughty beauty that had some appeal. She exuded an aura of power that appealed to them as a challenge to their own power.

She had been through three days of Judiciary Committee hearings. They sent her follow-up questions to be answered, and then it was on to the full Senate hearings. She was used to paperwork, and although she mentally challenged the thinking behind some of the questions, she didn't let it lead her off in anger or sarcasm. She was smart enough to know that there were times to challenge people and there were times to give them what they wanted, even if they didn't know what it was that they wanted. So she sat there, day after day, reading, typing on the computer, rewriting, editing, going back over her own notes, and creating a picture of a thorough, responsible and fair jurist. She was careful not to come across as pure and perfect. She carefully selected her words so that there would be elements that they could challenge her on, elements that she would have direct and thorough answers to, carefully placed openings in her responses that guided the Senators to the questions she wanted to answer.

They had given her ten days to write her responses to this second round of written questioning, and then she spent three more days face to face in the hearing room facing the full troop of Senators.

The press had been all over the story outside, poking microphones and cameras in any direction where they might extract a shocking revelation, some newsworthy tidbit. Many of the press's questions related back to the president and had little or nothing to do with the Judge at all. They wanted to know if she was married and if she had children and if her parents would be attending the hearing. Was she an athlete? Did she drive fast cars? Had she ever been a model? They dug into her background, posted any old pictures they could find, reposted pictures that her friends had posted. Once again she was grateful that she had been born and grown up before the social media craze. She had never posted crazy pictures of drunken festivities of herself or her friends. She had never posted absurd and hurtful comments about anyone or any event. She might have done things and had regrets as she was growing up, but they were just her memories and her regrets. They weren't public documents that would haunt her for the rest of her life.

And even those momentary lapses were few and far between. She had worked too hard and been too driven to succeed to have had time for debauchery. It had, in fact, never occurred to her. She didn't have many friends and she hadn't been under significant peer pressure to do something she didn't want to do. Except for her looks, the press found her to be boring.

There were several of her cases that popped to the top of the news. The Brand case was notable because of its association with the Brand family as well as Desert Storm. Other than that it was a pretty standard accusation-of-rape case. Jakes's defense of young Mr. Brand had been based on what he saw in Kuwait, implying that after what he had been through, it should be forgivable. After all, things like that happen in war, and Francis Brand had just not gotten over the conflict when he returned home. The Brand family was a pillar of the community, philanthropists, associated with the great history and conservative values of Boston and Massachusetts and the United States of America. And it wasn't clear that an actual rape had occurred. Because of the family connections, it seemed as though there might have been a bit of gold digging going on, one side trying to get into the deep pockets while the other side was trying to get into the pants. It was notable from the fact that Jakes had not settled the case out of court to protect the family, but had taken it all the way to judgment believing that an example had to be made to protect the family name and reputation so that others would think twice before taking on war heroes. Not everyone felt that Jakes had been right but there was a general feeling of admiration for her legal skills for pulling it off as a young attorney.

The other case was a landmark decision in environmental law, known as the Fuller Case, that occurred in the late 1990s at the confluence of a weakening land development investor market, changing environmental regulations, and the risks of remediating polluted properties. A well-established community development non-profit and a real estate management company were attempting to develop a former industrial site that had been vacant for over ten years. It was an eyesore and a magnet for crime, and close to growing communities. The proposed green development offered housing and jobs and recreational areas that were sorely needed. Superfund money was available to clean up the site and the interest in "Green" development was a relatively new buzzword for environmentalists, but reminded the blue-collar neighborhood of hippies and flower children. Functional and workable regulations did not exist. Nonsensical and impractical roadblock after roadblock had to be navigated and in the process new environmental regulations were developed and implemented by the Massachusetts Department of Environmental Protection.

Jakes had shown her skills at staying true to the spirit of the project and the participants while finding consensus among politicians and actually helping to create regulations that were practical, understandable, and workable. It was not surprising that after such success, that she was offered a position at the DEP.

While the hearings went on, the politician interviews probed for controversy. The press wanted to know if the Re-

publicans were trying to shake her. Standing at the entrance
of the hearing room, the chairman replied that as a trial attorney, there had been many opportunities for Judge Jakes to be
shaken. Standing outside at three AM in the rain at a crime
scene was an experience where Jakes might have been shaken,
but it would take a lot more to shake her after her life experiences. "Someone who has tried murder cases as she has
doesn't shake easily. This should not be a case of trying to
play 'gotcha'. This should be a time for the American people
to get to know what kind of a Supreme Court Justice Judge
Jakes will be. If the Senate does its job, the American people
will get the best view of her background and character that
they could ever get." He went on to say how impressed he
was with her, that she was a mainstream judge, and how she
followed the facts and followed the law.

The reporters wanted to know why the president had chosen another woman as the candidate. "I'm sure," the
chairman replied, "that he simply chose the best candidate
regardless of gender or ethnicity. But again, your questions
seem to keep returning to what the president is thinking or
doing. These hearings are about Judge Jakes and her qualifications. Now if you'll excuse me, I'd like to get started."

No matter how hard the press pushed they weren't able to
stir up anything that would improve viewer interest. There
were too many other stories in the news and the audience had
been indoctrinated by what was considered reality on TV.
Unless people were physically hurting each other, it wasn't
interesting. A public execution might have been interesting!

The hearing room was full of photographers who poked
their cameras into Judge Jakes's face, trying to catch just the
right angle, just the right look, grimace, or smile. They took
pictures of her standing up, sitting down, shaking hands, writing notes, leaning back to speak with her council. And
indeed, they didn't shake her.

The Senators did their best to ask questions that would
compel the candidate to make sound bite worthy statements,
revealing inner biases based on legal decisions she had made.
These decisions mainly regarded the workings of the law, and

although they certainly involved the rights and actions of people, they blended into the background of blah, blah, blah.

The output from Beanstalk was flat. Beanstalk indicated that Jakes's comments were bland, non-committal and true. Her body language spoke of confidence. Statement Analysis indicated consistency and lack of prevaricating words. Voice Stress did not even register. There were some occasional twitches at the corners of her eyes and lips that indicated frustration or annoyance at some of the questions and their repetitive nature, but nothing that would indicate that she was hiding something. If there was anything there, she was keeping it out of site and under cover. Just a couple more days to go before the full Senate would vote on the confirmation.

Pooch was getting frustrated, and it occurred to him that if people knew about Boyd's accusations, that the audience might perk up a bit. So at a bar called the *Café Crafty* that evening among his fellow journalists, he quietly let it slip that he had an exclusive, but he was afraid that it might never happen unless other people knew about it. He had heard, he said, that the FBI was looking into the accusations of a witness who hadn't yet testified. The main network journalists took this with a grain of salt since they didn't have a great deal of respect for Pooch's network, but because they were bored, some of them climbed out of the bar and up to the street, and got on their cell phones to their research departments to at least look into it.

The FBI received enough phone calls and emails to revisit their decision not to have Boyd testify. Having looked carefully into his background, they didn't doubt that he was a competent and honest lawyer, but they did doubt that his story had enough substance in it to be of concern to the confirmation hearings. It just didn't seem that important, and it was certainly inconclusive. After all, witness after witness had testified how stellar a character Judge Jakes was. Not a blemish could be found, and now they were going to present what appeared to be a wart.

Boyd was notified that he was to testify.

The hearing room was packed. The stories had been circulated by the press that Judge Jakes was being accused of sexual harassment! She was human after all! Those who felt that she was wrong for the job, that she would swing the court radically to one side or the other, drooled at the thought that maybe, just maybe she wasn't a sure thing after all. They knew she was evil. Had known it from the beginning and now they would be justified.

So they tuned in, many of them to Pooch's network where they tolerated this new "truth indicator" gadget. They'd learned to put up with the scrolling information across the bottom of the screen. They could put up with one more distraction. It was what was said that really mattered anyway.

As Boyd approached the room with his lawyer all the cameras were pointed in his direction. The flashbulb pops and the motor drive whirs and shutter clicks were gone. It was all electronic which meant that there was no limit on the number of images they could take one right after the other after the other. It was blinding. The photographers jockeyed for position, pushing each other out of the way. It was like slogging through a swamp of mud up to the thigh, each step extracted from the morass before the next one could be taken.

They were able to reach a security detail that guided them through a phalanx of security police and senate staff and wound their way to the front of the room and Boyd took his seat at the table, microphone pointed at his nose, water glass at his right hand. The room was stuffed and overheated and murmuring like a pot on the boil. The Chairman of the committee greeted him and then asked him to stand and swear to tell the truth.

Boyd had written out the statement he was going to deliver. He went through the details of his early life, painting the picture of a child of a hard working family in upstate New York, the struggles of his father in his landscaping business, the courage of his mother, baking celebratory cakes for wealthy clients. He described working his way into Vassar, graduating Cum Laude in 1995 and successfully graduating from Harvard Law in 1998.

While he was providing all this background information, the "truth" indicator was no more excited than it had been during the early hearings with Judge Jakes. It did indicate that

what Boyd was saying was true, but nobody doubted that. All
of that information could be checked and verified and vetted.
The indicator wobbled a bit on some of the descriptive words,
particularly when Boyd talked about religion. His mother
went to church regularly, but his father only went to keep his
wife company, and Boyd didn't have strong feelings one way
or the other. However, he had felt that it would be important
to shade his background at least into the fringes of what was
considered as mainstream family values, and Beanstalk confirmed a lack of substance there.

He went on to describe getting hired at Tittle and Baines in
Boston, one of the city's top ranked law firms. "I believe you
were employed there at one time, Senator Jeffries," he pointed
out to one of the Senators who nodded his head in confirmation.

Boyd described the tasks that he had been given as a first
year associate up until the point where he was assigned to
work with Ms Jakes who was a rising star in the firm. He was
flattered by the trust the firm had put in him and honored by
the prestige. And he recognized that associating with Ms
Jakes, Judge Jakes, would teach him a great deal.

"I want you to understand that coming here today has not
been easy for me. I have lost a great deal of sleep over the
decision to discuss these matters publicly and certainly get no
pleasure from doing so. I have great respect for Judge Jakes
and all that she has accomplished. However, I think it is important that the committee be aware of these facts."

Beanstalk was indicating that the subject was under a great
deal of stress. There were certainly many in the viewing
audience, which had grown substantially since Boyd's testimony had begun, that thought this was a publicity stunt, that
Boyd was seeking his moment in the sun, that everything he
was saying was bull shit. But the "truth monitor" window
was indicating the opposite.

"At first the incidents were minor and just friendly. But
even that was out of her character, and so when she was
friendly, it was surprising. She made comments about liking
the way I dressed, and one day I turned to find her staring at
me, at . . . forgive me . . . at my ass as I was bending over the

vending machine. She was smiling in what I found to be a lascivious manner."

The "truth monitor" was glowing red, getting hotter.

"The pivotal moment came when we were working late on the Fuller Case. We were alone in the office and we were looking at information on Judge Jakes's computer. She put her hands on me and touched me in a way that I found unprofessional. I was relieved when she suggested that because it was late that we leave the office and then she suggested that we go to a local bar and have a drink together. I didn't know that she did drink, so I felt that this was out of character, but she was my superior and I wanted to please her."

Boyd continued describing the events of the evening right up through the moment that Judge Jakes asked him to sleep with her. Without missing a beat he continued on to describe how he had turned her down knowing that there would be consequences, but that he knew having a sexual relationship with his boss would not have a positive result. He described taking the incident to Mr. Baines and the brush off he got and the fact that he had submitted himself to sexual sensitivity training despite the fact that it should have been Ms. Jakes who should have received the training. And finally he described how Ms Jakes had humiliated him at every turn after that evening until it drove him to leave the firm.

Julia had built into her statement analysis algorithms the fact that when witnesses describe events that aren't true, they tend to spend a great deal of time on the details of the event itself because they feel that is what the interrogator wants to know about. They leave out details of what happened before and what happen after because all of that adds to the lie and adds to what the liar has to remember. Boyd's description had covered the entire event in equal detail, and Beanstalk defined it as true.

After Boyd presented his opening statement, the Senators began to question him, challenging the substance and motive of his accusation. They couldn't believe that after all the positive things they had heard about the judge that there was this single, solitary voice making horrible, negative claims about her behavior! Nobody else had ever seen this side of her?

Nobody else had ever had a bad experience with what she said or did? How was that possible?

The Senators who didn't want her confirmed were sympathetic. They tried to ask Boyd questions that were framed in such a way that it supported his claims. They challenged some of the wording of the FBI reports that implied that Boyd had exaggerated what had happened that evening in Boston.

The Senators who wanted her confirmed did their best to demolish Boyd's credibility. "She didn't ask you to have sex with her did she?" one Senator asked.

"Yes," Boyd replied. "She did ask me to have sex with her."

"She said that? She said 'have sex with me'?"

"Well, she asked me if I wanted to sleep with her."

"Is that the same thing, then, sex and sleep?"

It was a stupid remark. Boyd struggled to keep himself under control and Beanstalk was indicating his stress.

"She never used intimate words or asked you to watch pornographic videos with her or mentioned pubic hair or touched you sexually, did she?"

Boyd reiterated what he had told the FBI and what was in their report.

"Were you dating anyone else at that time?"

"No, Senator."

"Ah," the Senator replied knowingly. "So you were a horny, twenty-something, working late with a beautiful African American woman and thought you might get lucky and she shot you down. Was that how it happened?"

Beanstalk was locked in on Boyd so it was only reading his reaction to this statement. Beanstalk's interpretation, however, wasn't necessary to know that Boyd was about to explode. He managed to keep his face calm and controlled, but his lips were dancing in little tremors as he suppressed all the things that he wanted to say.

The Chairman of the committee banged his gavel down. "You are out of order, Senator! "

"Would it surprise you to know that Judge Jakes's response to your allegations describes the scene quite differently?" the Senator continued. "Obviously she will be back in that seat to refute your claims in person."

That evening the court of public opinion was having a water cooler party on the social networks about what had happened and who was right and who was lying and if Jakes would actually be confirmed. Most of the discussion was around Boyd's accusations and whether he was doing this for personal gain and whether or not the whole thing was a publicity stunt and numerous thoughts about his manhood and how he could turn down a woman who looked like that! But there was also a great deal of discussion as to the accuracy of the truth telling gadget that had been on the screen. It had certainly indicated that Boyd was telling the truth, many people agreed. Others thought that it was a gimmick and wasn't real and was just invented by the media and didn't actually do anything.

"I guess we'll see tomorrow," was the general buzz, "when she takes the stand again. One of them must be lying!"

+++++

Gus watched the hearings in his office. He was impressed with how well Boyd had kept his cool. Julia was sitting behind Boyd in many of the TV shots. It occurred to Gus that her being there might reinforce the concept that this was all a promotional stunt for Blaytent, but on a personal note, it was important for Boyd to know that she was behind him.

Gus was also impressed with how well Beanstalk did. It was too bad that Boyd couldn't see how his statements were quickly verified. It was also too bad that they had not been allowed to show Beanstalk's questions and results to the Senators. It would have made the Senators' job easier, but they couldn't see where the testimony was leading.

Like a proud father, he felt his chest expand as he thought about everything that had gone into creating what millions of people were now seeing on their television screens. Something that started out in his head as just a twitch, an inclination, was now reality all over the country. It was a reality that been grown and nurtured by the crew at Blaytent, piece by piece, challenge by challenge, until now, there it was. Bob had given his life for what was now on the screen.

At that moment, Beanstalk printed on the screen, "You look concerned, Gus. What's wrong?"

Gus had still not gotten used to these little messages from the mind of a machine, interpreting the expression on his face. "Nothing," he replied out loud. Julia had programmed Beanstalk with a huge vocabulary so that Gus could have said the same thing in a variety of languages and Beanstalk would have understood.

"Lying," Beanstalk replied. Good manners were not something they had taught it. "Something is bothering you."

"I was just thinking about . . . you. Your development. I'm proud of the people who put you together."

"There's something else, Gus."

"What?" Gus asked. They really needed to put a face or something on the monitor for conversations like this. It was very odd talking to a strange looking box even through it was tilting and moving to get the best angles on his face. "No, honestly. That's what I was thinking about."

"That's not all, Gus."

"I don't know what you're talking about. I don't know why you're talking at all. I don't know why I'm talking to you."

"You're in love, Gus."

Gus's eyes popped open along with his mouth. "What? What the hell are you talking about? What do you know about love? I've got to get Arya in here to find out what's wrong with you. You're supposed to be determining the truth." And then it struck him: if the machine could read body language and micro expressions and voice stress and analyze statements to determine the truth, weren't those manifestations related to emotions as well? Beanstalk could read how people were feeling! He let that sink in for a moment, trying to fathom the bottom. Could lying be defined as an emotion?

"This is the truth, Gus."

"So who am I supposed to be in love with?"

"Call her, Gus. She's about to leave the country. Call her."

Beanstalk was not only a transducer to convert what it saw and heard into an interpretation of a person's feelings it was also connected to the almost infinite resources of the Internet and all of the wonders of the social networks and what people said about themselves.

"Oh my God!" Gus said even though there was no one in the room. He stared at his computer screen. "Seriously?" He looked around the room and out through windows at the fading light of an early spring evening. He was filled with a disturbing mixture of awe at what they had created and fear at what venturing into this new world would mean. Where would it take them?

Beanstalk printed, "Call her" on the computer screen.

Gus was about to pick up the phone when it rang. The voice of Maria Gudmudgion rattled his thoughts.

"Good evening, Gus," she said. "Very interesting."

"Excuse me?" Gus replied, trying to get a focus on what Gudmudgion thought was interesting.

"The hearings. Well, not only the hearings, but also your system. I'm not sure what to call it. I can't call it a product, can I because it's not really a product is it? It's just a . . . system."

Gus tried to get himself back into the business frame of thinking. "It is a system," he agreed.

"That's just the problem, Gus. Is it a product? Is it a marketable product? I'm not saying that what you have done isn't interesting or clever. We're considering looking for a buyer for our interest. It's promising but still too risky."

For the second time that evening, Gus was speechless. "Did you watch what Beanstalk did today? Have you heard what the press is saying . . . what people are saying? Are you listening?"

"Yes," Gudmudgion replied. "It's too much of a gimmick. If we find someone, we'll let you know the details." She broke the connection.

"You look upset, Gus," Beanstalk printed on the screen.

"Oh, shut up, and stop looking at me."

+++++

The next day Diamon Jakes was back at the table in front of the Committee to answer their questions and refute Boyd's accusations. It was clear that the Senators that supported her thought that what Boyd has accused her of was evil and they apologized for having to put her through this. Senators who had been convinced from the beginning were even more resolved to block her confirmation. They had all been hearing from their constituents in phone calls and emails and tweets.

The press smelled a story. People wanted to know what government agency funded the development of the 'truth indicator'. How real was it? How accurate was it? The morning talk shows tucked in what little they knew between the sports and the weather even though it promoted a competitive network.

"Did you see that thing on the bottom of the screen?" one beautifully coiffured anchor with perfect makeup and sparkling eyes asked. "Where did that come from?" Ha, ha, ha.

"Does anyone know anything about that?" another responded. "I thought it was just another stock ticker!" Ha, ha, ha.

"They want you to invest in the truth? Is that what's going on here?"

"A machine can't really tell the truth."

"Everyone believes in these machines. They have faith in them, but faith in itself is evidence of falseness and faith is not a road to truth but instead a road to falseness."

"What are you saying?" Ha, ha, ha. "Let's go to commercial! This is too deep for this time of day." Ha, ha!

By now the social networks had drawn in a much bigger audience for the hearings. People hashed over what Boyd had said the day before. Besides the discussions about the machine itself, there were arguments about what a machine could know or not know and whether or not we should even talk about such subjects. The bulk of the chatter weighed in on whether Boyd was telling the truth and whether or not Jakes should be confirmed. After Boyd's moment in front of the cameras, the polls were reading 'undecided'.

Pooch was feeling great about this. His network's ratings for the hearing were through the roof. He called Gus to tell him how pleased he was and how well the system was working and to propose that they discuss an extended license. He was surprised that Gus's response was muted, but he didn't probe it. Things were going too well. The TV audience loved to hear about sex and scandals at the highest levels. Always had and always would. This was sex, lies, and high definition, digital video. It didn't get any better! Now there was controversy and public interest and a beautiful and elegant woman in front of a panel of old, white men talking about sex and seduction.

Boyd was able to tune in in his hotel room. He was going to see how Jakes responded and if Beanstalk would be his giant, genie friend.

"We've read your statement, your honor, refuting Mr. Willis's allegation," the chairman said. "We'd like you to make a brief statement in your own words, then we'll ask a few questions, and move this on. You have been subjected to enough turmoil." He smiled and looked at his colleagues to his left and his right who nodded benignly in agreement.

Jakes pulled the microphone toward herself, leaned toward it and said, "Thank you, Mr. Chairman. This has become a circus!" She paused and glared at the expectant and powerful faces. "This has become a circus, a media circus! That man's allegations are false!"

Beanstalk's indication on the TV screen glowed blue, far away from the truth. Boyd smiled.

"We were colleagues. Yes. He worked for me as an associate at Tittle and Baines. Yes."

Beanstalk's indication started moving back toward true, getting warmer.

"But I never harassed him."

Beanstalk indicated glowed blue again.

"I know what sexual harassment means. I am a Judge!"

Beanstalk indicated true.

Jakes went through Boyd's statement agreeing that they had worked together and that required some late night work, particularly on major cases such as the Fuller Case. They worked late and they worked hard. She agreed that Willis had been a hard worker and did a good job when he paid attention to the details. They did not socialize. "I never socialize with my associates," she said.

Beanstalk disagreed. Boyd slammed his hand down on the table in his hotel room. "Right! Damn right! Bull shit!"

She admitted that it was remotely possible that they had broken that rule once after a particularly trying day, and had a drink together. But that was it. It went no farther than one, simple drink.

When she finished her opening statement, one Senator asked her to address what Boyd had said about her behavior to him after that one, simple drink. What had changed her attitude toward him?

"My attitude didn't change, Senator."

Beanstalk disagreed. "It certainly did," Boyd commented.

"My attitude didn't change. His attitude changed. As you can see, he must have assumed that there was more to that one deviation from my no socializing rule. He must have leapt to that conclusion. He rewarded my trust and respect for his good work by accusing me of sexual harassment! My attitude never changed. But his did. His work deteriorated. He avoided me. I had to continually reprimand him for his poor performance and that reflected his performance with the rest of the firm as well."

Beanstalk confirmed her reprimand comment. "Liar!" Boyd yelled. "Liar!"

When Judge Jakes's testimony ended that day, the polls leaned heavily in Boyd's favor. The woman was a bitch that was easy to see. Not that being a bitch as a judge was such a bad thing. It would help her to make the tough decisions. But she was clearly lying. He was telling the truth. The machine said so. Even though he was probably a pansy for turning her down and going to that all girls' college. What was that all about? The Odds Makers had her getting confirmed despite the lies.

Besides the issue with Judge Jakes and her confirmation was the discussion of Beanstalk itself: was it real or was it a lie? Could a machine really know if people were lying? That required in-depth discussions on the evening news and interviewing the creator.

Chapter Eighteen

May 2015

In his hotel room in DC, when Boyd heard that the Senate had confirmed Jakes, he gasped and sat down. What had he done to his life revealing intimate details to a national audience? His face had been all over the newspapers and evening news, and it felt as though every single person in the world would know the details of that incredibly difficult and awkward evening all those years ago. People would point fingers at him on the street and in restaurants. His anonymity was gone, and not because he had done something wonderful or was a movie star, but because he had claimed that a Supreme Court Judge had sinned.

He walked over to the windows and stood looking down at the street watching people get on with their lives, get on with their shopping or their business meetings or their intimacy. That could have been him if he'd just let this go. What had he accomplished? He felt dirty and defeated. Maybe his mother hadn't been right about things *coming around*. And how much had it hurt Julia and their life together? She hadn't talked about it. She was concentrating on him.

While he was standing there, wallowing in the depths of his self-deprecation, Julia popped in, banging open the hotel room door bearing bags of Chinese food and a couple of bottles of wine.

"Let's celebrate!" she said.

402 · PAUL H. RAYMER

He turned and faced her grinning face. "Celebrate? She won. She will be confirmed."

"And . . .?" Julia replied.

"And . . . what?" Boyd asked. "And I lose."

"What did you lose? You don't think that what you did is not going to have an impact on the discussion of sexual harassment? You don't think that when Jakes has to make a decision in the Supreme Court that involves the misuse of power that she won't think about what has just happened? Boyd, she may have shoved what happened between you under her mental rug, but she sure as hell remembers it now! Did you really expect her not to be confirmed because of her peccadillo with you? All those years, all those decisions, all those learned documents she wrote could not be swept away."

He turned back to the windows. "If it was so unimportant, why did you let me do this? It wasn't unimportant to me! I put my life . . . our lives . . . on the line."

Julia came up behind him and wrapped her arms around his waist and laid her head on his shoulder. "It's not unimportant. And I never meant to imply that it was. It's not unimportant to me or to her or to history. Boyd, what you did took exceptional courage, and I couldn't be prouder of you."

He turned around to face her.

"Think about what you just put her through. She had to deny doing what you said she did. She was forced to replay those events in front of a huge audience. Maybe she lies to herself and tells herself that she never did those things. But just for a short period of time, she had to think about them. And I guarantee you that she won't stop thinking about them for a long time."

Julia unscrewed the top of one of the bottles of wine, filled two plastic glasses, and handed one to Boyd. "To us!" she said, raising her glass to his.

"And besides, Beanstalk was there to witness it all. You saw her testimony! It worked like a champ! It clearly called her a liar when she said it hadn't happened."

"Yeah. It did!" Boyd smiled at last.

"And that is all over the Internet by now. Huckle, Buckle, Beanstalk! She was lying. You were telling the truth. Beanstalk said so! Did it extract the truth from her? Did it force her to say things that she wouldn't have said otherwise? Absolutely. I think," she continued, "that a senate hearing is torture without the physical element or the threat of death. Mental death? Maybe. Reputational death? Possibly. But not physical death. Beanstalk accurately drew the line between lying and the truth, but the confirmation of Judge Jakes was the result of more than just a single element of her character. This was one of those times when a single truth was not the whole answer."

+++++

Major Crum stood in the shadows of the Blaytent building, his face glowing periodically from the light of his cigarette. "The predator has to be patient," he kept telling himself. "Waiting. Never losing focus. Concentrating. Muscles loose but adrenalin pumping. Waiting." He took a deep drag and peered into the darkness. His nerves were cranked tight. He was a warrior. He knew the mind of his enemy, the minds of his enemies. He knew. That's why they had put him into Intelligence. They knew he knew. He nodded his head in agreement with himself and took another deep pull on the cigarette.

His job wasn't fun. It wasn't meant to be fun. He had to deal with scum. All day. Every day. He had to. It was a dirty job, but he was proud of the work that he did for his country. Sainte was a terrorist. He was absolutely convinced of that. Sainte was put here to test him. He wasn't living up to his name, was he? Crum smiled a weak smile. He was no saint. He was the devil. But that was okay. That was okay. Crum knew how to deal with devils. He'd been doing it all his life - from his days on the streets of the Bronx. It had never been easy. He didn't want it to be easy. It was good for it to be hard. It made you stronger. Stronger!

It had been going well. The Institute had been developing well. Their technology was good. It allowed them to keep revealing the truth, uncovering the evil. But then Sainte came along with something different. Something they thought was snazzier.

Crum threw the cigarette down on the ground and crushed it under his boot. "Snazzier," he said the word out loud and smiled that watery smile again. He ran his hand along the smooth, cool metal barrel of his gun. "We'll just see what Mr. Snazzier Sainte has to say for himself."

It was night. It was dark. It was late. The building was empty. The parking lot was empty. People had gone home to their real lives, their safe lives. Crum knew their lives were safe because of him and because of people like him, giving up their own happiness to make other lives safer.

What the hell had Johnny been thinking coming up here? Boston! What did he expect to get from a terrorist like Sainte? Did he really think he could find something better? He was delusional! Delusional! Might have to kill him too. Crum spat on the ground to emphasize the thought in his head. He looked around at the modern glass and metal buildings that surrounded him. "This," he thought, "is exactly why our country is going to hell! Weak! We spend our money on weak shit! Snazzy places like this. Soft and comfortable. Weak!"

A car pulled into the lot. Crum stepped back deeper into the shadows. The car stopped. Its lights went out. For a moment or two nothing happened, then the driver's door opened and a man extracted himself. "Ding, ding, ding." The driver reached back in and pulled out the keys and slammed the door shut and walked toward the entrance of the building.

Crum recognized Sainte's bulk. He squeezed his gun more tightly and stood very still. He waited until Sainte was right at the door, using his key to unlock it and pull it open, then he stepped out of the shadows and shoved his gun into Sainte's ribs.

"Good evening, Mr. Sainte," he said with his watery smile. "Leave your key in the lock and let's step inside, shall we."

"Leave it!" he hissed as Gus started to pull the key out. "I would hate to blow a hole in that nice suit. Been talking to the press, have we? Building up your pile of fame and for-tune? Step inside. Now!"

Gus had been deep in his own thoughts. The interest in Beanstalk had been startling. The national evening news programs wanted to talk to him, and he had just finished taping an interview for the 20/20 program. He had not gotten used to the bright lights and famous people, and he had to admit that he was impressed. He was trying to process it all. What was the future going to bring? Would Avitas want to come back in . . . maybe do the second round of financing? And what about Cyrene? He hadn't called her yet. She had a lot of explaining to do.

So when Crum stepped up and put the gun into his ribs, he initially thought the man was kidding. He did recognize Crum. He could smell him moments before he saw him. He knew the man was dangerous and possibly crazy, but did things like this really happen? Everybody had guns these days, and if anyone would have one, Crum would!

"Seriously?" Gus asked.

Crum shoved the gun harder into his ribs. "Move! I don't want to kill you here."

Gus pushed open the door and stepped inside. Crum had one hand on his back and the other on the gun in Gus's ribs. "Your office," he commanded.

"Look . . .," Gus started attempting to turn.

"Oh, no," Crum said, shoving Gus forward. "No talking now. Not yet. Take me to your *snazzy* office."

Gus used his phone app on the inner door, and they pushed through and walked silently down the hall. In Gus's office, Crum stopped him and made him stand in the middle of the room with his hands laced behind his head.

Crum looked around. "Very nice," he said. "You've done well with the terrorist money."

"What? What terrorists?" Gus asked, dumfounded. "You need to come back to earth, Major. Why don't you put the gun down, and we can sit down and talk and you can tell me what's on your mind. Okay?"

"Not a chance, ass hole. Not a chance!"

They stood there in silence. Crum was breathing heavily like he'd run some distance and just arrived. Time clicked by.

"So, what do you want, Crum? Do you want me to confess to something? Do you want me to show you where the water bucket is? What do you want?"

Crum walked up to Gus, peered into his face, and shoved his gun into Gus's stomach. "One twitch, one quiver and this gun might just go off! Oh, dear. It was an accident! Two old friends just horsing around! BANG. Oops. Sorry about that." Crum smiled. "Shouldn't play with guns. They're dangerous. Should be a law!" Ha, ha, ha. He stepped back. "Get down on your knees, maggot!" he shouted. "Get down on your knees and start praying to whatever God you believe in because the fact is you are going to die. Do you know why people being water boarded confess? Do you know why?"

Gus was now down on his knees in the middle of the room with his fingers laced behind his head. He was still trying to sort this out. No doubt that Crum was crazy – always had been. But he had been under control. Now he was off the rails, off the reservation, down the rabbit hole.

"Do you know why? Answer me, you maggot!"

"No, Major. Tell me."

"They confess because they have hope, you idiot. We give them a choice. Part of that choice is hope. Hope that the pain will stop. Hope that we'll stop. Hope that we'll go away. They don't go beyond that. They don't know what would happen if we did stop. Maybe they hope that we'll pat them on the back and tell them to have a nice life. But that would be pretty stupid! They never did have a nice life!"

Crum was panting now.

"But at least those towel heads are honest about the fact that they are terrorists. You know just by looking at them. But you! You look like a normal all-American boy from an all-American New England town. Your parents must be so fucking proud of you! Where are they from? Russia? Libya?"

"Can I get you some water?" Gus asked.

"Trying to be nice?" Crum strode over to Gus and slammed him on the side of his head with the butt of the gun. The blow wasn't hard enough to knock Gus over but he did see stars for a moment.

"Jesus!" Gus exclaimed. "What the hell is wrong with you?"

"You know what your problem is?" Crum asked. "Your problem is that you have no hope. None at all! Your problem is me! And I'm going to kill you."

It was beginning to sink into Gus's mind that Crum wasn't kidding. "So what do you want from me?"

"That's just exactly the point, ass hole. I DON'T WANT ANYTHING from you! Nothing! That's the point. You have no hope of getting out of this at all! This is the end of the story. You're not coming back next season. This is not a dream. YOU ARE GOING to DIE. That's what I want. I want you to know that. You are to be terminated!"

Gus's knees were beginning to hurt. He shifted his weight. "You're just going to shoot me? Why? This is not a very clever set up. This just doesn't make any sense!"

Crum glared at him. "You're the fucking clever one. Not me. Oh no. I just get the job done. You, on the other hand, always had to be so clever. Twisting up the languages. Making a hit on TV. Playing with electronics. Trying to come up with soft and gentle and cuddly interrogation techniques. Clever. Snazzy! What do you call this thing; *Beanstalk*? That's a really stupid name, you know. I suppose you know the old story of the kid, Jack, stealing shit from the giant? Not only does he steal the giant's stuff, he kills him and gets away with it! He kills the giant and wins. What kind of a story is that? And the giant's wife lets the kid do that! What kind of kid's story is that? And you want to name your magic product after that story? Well, I'll tell you something. You can think of me as the giant and this time Jack's going to die. Not the giant! This time the giant wins and gets his stuff back!"

"Look," said Gus. "This is stupid." He started to get up.

Crum shot into the floor beside him. The noise was deafening. Gus winced and ducked and dropped back onto his knees.

Crum shot again, this time at Gus's desk taking out his computer monitor. "Was that your fancy little Beanstalk gadget, the one that everyone is gaga over? Was that it?" BANG he shot again.

"You're CRAZY!" Gus yelled.

"Yeah, I am. And proud of it! I'm eliminating a terrorist. It's my job. That's what I get paid to do. One more terrorist down the drain."

"Stop!" Gus yelled. "Stop. What's this terrorist stuff? What the hell makes you think I'm a terrorist?"

"The FBI dragged that sorry terrorist guy in here who was going to blow up Fenway Park on opening day, right? And you blew that interrogation! Snuffed it just when they were getting the heart of it."

"How the hell do you know about that?"

"Friends," Crum said with a grimace. "I got friends. And then there is that woman you've been hanging out with. What do you really know about her anyway? And what's your deal with Flack?"

"Nothing," Gus yelled. "Look let's talk this out. Johnny Flack came to me. I don't know why. He wanted a job. He knew that Bob Thatcher had died and thought that maybe he could fill in for us. There wasn't a chance in hell that I would have hired him! I never knew what you saw in him."

"What happened to Thatcher, anyway? Heart attack? You sure?" Crum asked.

It suddenly flashed through Gus's somewhat paranoid mind that maybe Crum had had something to do with Bob's death. Up until then he had assumed that it was just the fact that Bob didn't take care of himself that he smoked too much, that he didn't get enough exercise. "You didn't have anything to do with that, did you?" Gus demanded.

Crum smiled again. "Ooh. That's a delicious thought, isn't it? Clever. That would have been clever wouldn't it? Would have pulled the rug out from under you at a tough time, just when you were rushing to get your *Beanstalk* finished for that spectacular event in DC. That would have been clever."

"But you didn't, did you?" Gus asked, anger boiling up inside him.

"Oh, no. Not me. Would I do something like that?" Crum laughed

Gus started to stand up again.

"Stay down!" Crum order and fired another shot into the wall. "We're not done yet!"

"What else do you want from me? Why don't you just do it? If you're going to shoot me, shoot me."

"It's the anticipation, ass hole. Haven't you figured that out yet? It's the anticipation. Anticipation is the fun part. It's no fun when you're actually dead. Then you'll just be . . . dead. We won't be able to have these enlightening conversations! No fun when you're dead. I'm not into that sort of thing! It's the anticipation." He tapped the hot barrel of the gun against the side of Gus's skull. Tap, tap, tap.

Gus was starting to accept the fact that Crum was crazy enough to actually kill him. He scanned through options. He remembered seeing pictures of firing squads and wondering why people just stood there and accepted being shot. If they were going to die anyway, why not try to rush the shooters and attempt to overpower them? You couldn't be deader than dead! The only reason to stay there on his knees was if there was a chance that he could change Crum's mind, and that was beginning to seem unlikely. Although there was a limit to how many bullets he had in his gun. Then again, he probably had an extra clip or two in his pocket.

Watching Crum move around the room, he was about to leap to his feet and rush the self-proclaimed giant when he heard the reception room door open and footsteps coming down the hall.

Crum stopped pacing and turned toward Gus's office door. "Keep quiet!" Crum hissed in a hoarse whisper. "Don't make a sound!" Crum backed up, away from the open door. Gus's corner office had windows along both outside walls. The door to the office was in a corner, and where Gus was kneeling in the middle of the room he was facing the front windows with his back to the room door. He could just see Crum behind him out of the corner of his right eye. If he turned his head to the left, he could see Crum's ghostly reflection in night black glass of the office windows.

What happened next seemed to take forever yet be over in a moment. There was no way that Gus was going to allow Crum to ambush whoever was coming down the hall.

Chances were good that it was Allan, coming to see how the 20/20 taping had gone.

The footsteps were getting closer.

Gus was desperate to alert him. "In here!" he yelled, "But I'm not alone! Crum's here! He has a gun. Say's he's going to kill me."

The footsteps stopped.

Crum hadn't met Allan so he didn't know how big he was. Crum's plan of a secret, private assassination was now blown. He was exposed. He had been shooting stuff up in Gus's office so he couldn't just shove the gun in his pocket, say excuse me, nice to meet you, and scuttle out of the building. Besides that if he were crazy enough to think he could still get away with this, he would just have to kill both men. How hard could it be? The die was cast. He was ready to shoot whomever stepped through the doorway.

Instead of Allan walking into the room, however, Crum was stunned into immobility seeing Cyrene step in holding a gun. "Good evening, Major," Cyrene said. "Good to see you again."

For a moment, Gus thought that Crum was crazy enough to just start shooting. Crum looked at Cyrene. His hand was shaking. His mouth was open. It was impossible to know what was going on in his mind. Moments ticked by in the standoff. Gun to gun, face to face.

Cyrene was silent. There was a look on her face and in her eyes that Gus had never seen before. All of the humanity was gone.

"I was going to do it," Crum said.

"You're weak, Crum. You're all bluster. You have no spine. You have no cause. Nothing worth dying for. Nothing worth killing for. That's why you and people like you will always lose. You can be led around by your nose. You follow anyone that you think thinks like you and has a louder voice. You want to be guided. You bluster and blabber, but you're a baby."

"What the hell are you talking about, Cyrene?" Gus said, starting to stand up. "He's crazy!"

Crum was looking at Cyrene in surprise. His hand holding his gun had drooped down at his side. Now Gus could see his hand was starting to rise and lift his gun, but before he could aim it, Cyrene shot him in the middle of his forehead. One quick shot. Crum fell to the floor with most of the back of head missing.

Gus had only partly risen and the explosion of the shot caused him to jump backwards, stumble and sprawl on the floor. "What the hell? Cyrene, what are you doing? You just killed him! In my office!"

"I know," she replied calmly, lowering her gun. "He was supposed to kill you first. It would have been better."

Gus looked up at her from his position on the floor. His ears were ringing. He couldn't process what was happening. He suddenly thought that his hands felt dirty. He smelled sweat. He stared at Cyrene and wondered who she was and why she was there. He started to push himself up.

"No," she said, pointing the gun at him, "you might as well stay there."

He dropped back on his elbows and stared up at her. "What the hell are you doing?" he asked again.

"It was easy to convince Crum that you were one of his hated terrorists. The man was a bigot who was off in his lala land! He couldn't see what was really in front of him, which was ironic, don't you think, when he was possessed by this lie detecting technology. He couldn't stand it that you had a better system. That's why we had to have it."

"We?" Gus asked.

"He was so blinded by his hatred of you that he couldn't see his real enemies! He was so tangled up in his conspiracies that he thought we were just really clever government agents on his side!" She actually chortled. "He chose to ignore what his own technology was telling him!"

Gus looked at her. The sudden shift of realties and direction changes was fracturing his mind. It was as though this person that he thought he had loved and made love to was not that person. It was as though she was one of those shape shifters from science fiction movies. How was it possible to so thoroughly not know someone?

"He screwed up right down to the end," she said. "This is really awkward. I'll have to do it myself." Her face softened for a moment. For a moment he saw the person that he had loved and laughed with. It was only there for a flash and then it was gone.

Maybe, he thought, if I keep her talking, maybe someone will show up, and if I keep her talking, I'll still be alive!

. "How did you get in here?" he asked.

"At least he did that right. He got you to leave your key in the lock."

"Oh, yeah the key. That was weird. I thought that was weird. But what about the inner door?"

"It was easy to copy the app from your phone. You're too trusting."

Gus tried to piece it together. He realized that there were other moments, other clues in their relationship that should have tipped him off. They had, in fact, but he had chosen to ignore them. All this time, all this effort to find a machine, a device that would separate the truth from the lie, and the lie was here – standing in front of him, pointing a gun at him, and committed to killing him.

" . . . And Kadah? Why did you stop him?"

"Who? Oh that idiot. He shouldn't have gotten caught. He was too busy bragging about his cause and his purpose. He would have revealed other, more valuable assets. I had to stop him. Your system is too good. That's why we want it."

"What do you mean?" Gus asked.

"Get up!" she ordered. He got to his feet, not looking at the body of Crum and the pool of blood in the middle of his carpet.

"We want it because it's a weapon. It's a weapon that we want to take away from you and yours. We can buy the company, but I knew you wouldn't want to come with it regardless of our relationship. You might not want to think it, Gus, ..."

He cringed at her use of his name.

"You might not want to think it, but you are an idealist. You have this superman syndrome of 'truth, justice, and the American way'. Now kneel down where Crum had you."

"What about Allan? He's not going to go with you either."

"We need him to sign the papers. This is how this plays out. Crum killed you. I killed Crum. Allan signs the deal for patriotism, money, whatever. He gets a bunch of money. And life goes on. At least for some of us."

He looked at her. "Just one more thing I have to know: you didn't have anything to do with Bob Thatcher's death did you?"

"Enough talking. Tick, tock. Time's running out."

"No, seriously. Did you?"

"Seriously? This isn't serious enough for you? You want to know something seriously? Yah. I did. He wouldn't have come with us either, and we wanted to slow you down. But he had gotten too far already so it didn't do us any good. He was obviously over the hill already. He trusted me as a friend of yours. Sit down together at lunch. It nauseated me to smell that place. But he thought it was a nice surprise. Didn't take much to add a little to his fast food – his last supper."

She laughed.

It might have been that laugh or it might have been her betrayal or it might have been the absolute, carefree unfeeling murder of his friend or it might have been that he didn't think he had anything left to lose that pushed Gus through any barrier of fear or self-preservation, and he exploded. As they had been talking he had started to lower himself down on his knees in the middle of the room, but he surged upward and hurled himself at the much smaller woman, head first into her stomach, driving her back against the wall. The gun exploded once, a shot going up into the ceiling. He wrapped his arms around her, nearly snapping her in half. He threw his leg out and pulled her legs out from under her, dropping her to the floor. She screamed as he broke her arm and ripped the gun out of her hand.

As he got to his feet with her gun in his hand, Allan ran into the office. "What happened?" he shouted.

Gus pointed at Cyrene with the gun. "She did," he said. "She's the lie."

"I heard shooting! I heard screaming!" Allan said, and then he looked at Crum in the pool of blood on the floor. "Jesus!" he gasped. "Who's that?"

"You better call the police," Gus replied. "That's Crum. She shot him."

"Already have. I thought there might be something wrong when I was notified that your *Keypass* app was activated a second time. I tuned into the security cameras."

Gus's evening had gone from one unbelievable unreality to the next – the TV studio and television stars, Crum and his gun and death sentence, and now Cyrene. He handed Allan the gun as he felt his body deflating and he sank into a chair.

Allan ordered Cyrene to sit in the desk chair and secured her with some of the destroyed computer cables. She glared at Gus. "I should have just shot you," she said, spitting out the words. "All that explaining is pointless! It would have taken less than a second to pull the trigger. You made me soft! You don't really care what happens in my world! You weren't there when my mother was hauled out on the street and raped. They made me watch! And you expect me to respect 'Christian' culture? You're a bunch of animals."

Gus and Allan stared at her. Finally Gus asked, "Is that true, Cyrene? Is that true or are you just making it up? Is it just another lie? Do you know the difference any more?"

"There is no difference!" she said.

They were silent. At that moment it all seemed pointless to Gus. The spark of life that had animated Crum was gone. There was a clear line between being alive and being dead. That was simple. Everything else was a tangled web created by human minds.

His friendship with Allan was simple and something he could believe in and be sure of. He had thought his love for Cyrene had been simple. Even Beanstalk had thought that was true, but Beanstalk was only reading his face and his body. The machine could only read surface manifestations of lies, truths, and emotions. No machine, no technology could read all the way down to the center of a human, all the way down to the heart.

And where had he been in Cyrene's heart? If he had been nothing but a face in the crowd to her, she wouldn't have hesitated to end his life as she had ended Crum's or even Bob Thatcher's. What right did she have to take those lives away?

Eventually the police came and hauled Cyrene away. An officer took down Gus's description of the events that had taken place in his office. They took pictures of everything, doing their best to reconstruct the reality of what had just happened.

"This place is a disaster," Allan said. "Let's go to my office. I've got some Scotch, and I think we could use a drink." Once there, he poured Gus a glass and said, "Here. Drink this. So what happened? Did she tell you anything?"

Gus explained what Cyrene had told him, what her plan had been.

"Why us?" Allan asked. "Why Blaytent?"

"Truth is a weapon," Gus replied.

"I didn't think they cared about the truth. I didn't think they cared at all about torture, particularly the torture of someone who doesn't believe in God the way they believe in God."

"I don't know," Gus said in frustration. "If knowing something is the same as understanding it, then I don't know much anymore. All this work we have been doing . . ." and he waved his hand around the room . . . "all the work we have been doing to reveal the truth . . . whose truth? What truth? We don't even know what we're looking for!"

"Have some more Scotch," Allan replied. He sat back down at his desk.

"I can't believe that Crum actually hated me that much that he believed her lie that I was the terrorist! That man was sick. Johnny Flack was right to worry. It's really true that people believe what they want to believe. Is believing the truth?" He gulped down the Scotch. "And you know the irony of this is that if she had shot me, you could have used Beanstalk to prove that she was lying, to prove that Crum didn't shoot me! That she was guilty!" He laughed a dry and mirthless chuckle.

"No, the irony was that you had known her in high school! What are the odds that you would have developed a device that she felt she needed to steal for her cause? She must have been shocked when she found out it was you!"

"Or was she watching me all along?"

"Now you're getting paranoid!" Allan laughed. "No, but all the great press has been working in our favor. Funding shouldn't be a problem anymore. We do have a great product . . . a product worth killing for."

"I can't think about that right now," Gus replied. "I don't even know what's real any more."

The room dropped into silence.

"Recalculating," Beanstalk printed on Allan's screen.

CPSIA information can be obtained at www.ICGtesting.com
Printed in the USA
BVOW03s1417140914

366577BV00006B/10/P